THE PYRAMID
WALTZ

Visit us at www.boldstrokesbooks.com

THE PYRAMID WALTZ

by

Barbara Ann Wright

2012

THE PYRAMID WALTZ

ISBN 13: 978-1-60282-741-7

This Trade Paperback Original Is Published By
Bold Strokes Books, Inc.
P.O. Box 249
Valley Falls, NY 12185

First Edition: September 2012

Credits
Editors: Cindy Cresap and Stacia Seaman
Production Design: Stacia Seaman
Cover Art by Sam Hooker
Cover Design by Sheri (graphicartist2020@hotmail.com)

Acknowledgments

I owe thanks to so many people, namely my husband Ross and my mom Linda Dunn. I never would have succeeded without your faith and support. To my intrepid writing group, Nia George, Erin Kennemer, Janet Mallard, Trakena Prevost, and Sarah Warburton: Without you, this book would be a shambles. Special thanks go to Pattie Lawler for being not only an outstanding reader but also a champ at talking me off the ledge. Thank you, Faye Hignight, for always checking up on me, and thank you, Kansas crew, for prodding me on Facebook.

Thanks to Radclyffe and Bold Strokes for taking a chance on me, and thanks to Cindy Cresap for her wonderful editing work. And thank you to every teacher and professor I've ever had. None of this would have been possible without you.

One last special thanks to my supportive pets. If I coated this book in peanut butter, you'd totally eat it.

To Mom and Ross, for always believing in me.

CHAPTER ONE: KATYA

The afternoon air tasted of wood smoke, a sign of autumn Katya would have enjoyed if she hadn't been hunting a traitor. She crouched among the ferns dotting the forest floor and took slow, deep breaths, the better to hear the slightest movement.

Birds chirped to her left, and she turned to the right where the sounds of the forest had gone quiet. She saw a flash of white, Pennynail's Laughing Jack mask. Smeared as it was with dirt, a bit of brightness still shone through. The mask, with its ever-present grin, long nose, and rosy cheeks, seemed far too amused for the situation, as it did for every situation. He pointed to the eyeholes of his mask and shook his head. When Katya nodded, he moved back through the undergrowth as silently as any predator.

Katya took a slow step forward, her muscles threatening to cramp as she slinked. A twig snapped ahead of her, and she froze. Pennynail would never make such a noise, but it could be the other members of her team closing in. She tensed. Up ahead, a fern rustled, and she saw another flash of white, cloth this time. None of her team would be stupid enough to wear white clothing in the forest. Katya gripped her rapier. Soon, there'd be one less traitor to threaten her family.

The fern moved again, and Katya saw the traitor's face. His eyes locked with hers, and then he was off. Katya sprang up and after him, drawing her rapier as she ran. She closed quickly, and the fleeing man spun and aimed his short sword at her ribs. Katya blocked. The traitor turned and fled, and it took Katya a moment to switch from dueling to running again.

An arrow whizzed past the fleeing man. It clipped his arm and drew a thin line of blood across his white sleeve. With a yelp, he veered to the side. Maia emerged from the bushes, her pale blond hair floating loose from its braid as she nocked another arrow. The traitor tried to turn a different direction, but a brown blur tackled him. The two forms wrestled, leaves and twigs flying from the forest floor, before they became the fleeing man face-down on the ground and Pennynail astride him. Pennynail held the traitor's wrists together and put two gloved fingers to his forehead in salute.

Katya returned the gesture and took a few deep breaths. Now the hard work could begin. "I knew you'd be the one to nab him."

Pennynail touched his heart and then his mask's cheek as if he were blushing. The man beneath him squirmed.

"Bind him nice and tight," Katya said. "Brutal and Crowe should catch up any moment."

She kept her rapier at the traitor's throat as Pennynail tied his wrists and ankles with a leather cord. Even bound and kneeling at her feet, the traitor snarled. "You can't stop us." His tongue darted out to lick a cut on his lip. "You have no idea how high up we go, how many of us there are."

Katya slid her rapier home in its scabbard. "Educate me, Mr....what was it you called yourself? The Shadow? That's a fabulous name."

He spat a wad of blood at her feet.

"Brother Brutal will be here soon. Would you rather talk to me or to a member of a strength chapterhouse?"

The Shadow swallowed and glared at her, hate burning in his eyes.

"They claim that they can read a man's soul just by fighting him, that combat is the only path to enlightenment, that you can't learn the universe without pain." Katya leaned forward and fixed the man with her gaze. Weakness and fear shone in his shifting eyes and twitching muscles, but she didn't pity him. Anyone who wanted to hurt her family didn't deserve pity.

The sound of crunching leaves made the Shadow look to the side where red-robed Brother Brutal emerged from the trees like a bloody wall. "Ah, Brutal," Katya said, "at last. Persuade our friend, if you please."

The Shadow squirmed as Brutal put a hand the size of a dinner plate on top of his head. The huge monk's fingers tightened, tilting the traitor's head up. "If you wish a duel, I'll give it, brother." Brutal's deep voice matched his massively muscled frame but contradicted the reddish cheeks of his baby face.

The Shadow's neck muscles twitched as he tried to free himself. "Never...tell."

Katya shrugged. "Well, it would be easier, but you don't actually need to say a thing."

Brutal moved to stand at his back. "Shame."

"You'll get the next one," Katya said. "All we need now is Crowe."

She looked over her shoulder in time to see the Order of Vestra's oldest member come huffing and puffing out of the trees to join them. "Are there any others? Or is our Shadow the last one?"

Crowe shook his head, leaned on his knees, and breathed hard. He straightened after a moment and ran a hand over his thinning white hair. "Give me a minute!" When his breathing slowed, he took a clear pyramid about the size of a child's fist from the satchel at his side. "My sources indicated that this is the ringleader, and none of his toadies are about. We'd better hurry back to the city before we're missed."

"Do what you need to do. We'll keep watch."

"Hold him," Crowe said. Brutal grasped the Shadow's head again, and Crowe pressed the base of the pyramid to the Shadow's forehead. The Shadow's eyes rolled back and his mouth slackened at the touch of smooth crystal.

Katya couldn't fight a grimace. He looked like a dead carp. "What do you see?"

"This cannot be rushed, no matter how many times you ask that it be."

"You said it yourself; we've been gone too long. Hunting stags shouldn't take all day."

"Then you'll have to make up an incredible story about the one that almost got away. This man's mind is a jumble."

"Not surprising," Brutal said. "These people are smart. They'd teach their own how to resist a mind pyramid."

Crowe moved his head back and forth as if searching for something. "Lucky for us, he's not so good at it. I'm getting that one of his friends is influential, maybe nobility."

Katya sucked in a breath. "I knew it, a traitor in the palace. That's how his group has evaded us so long."

"That's all," Crowe said. He took the pyramid away, and the Shadow went limp against Brutal's legs. "He won't be coming around for a long while. There was a lot to sift through, and most of it I couldn't make heads or tails of. There was something about your father, Katya."

"Wait, King Einrich couldn't know who the conspirators are, right?" Maia seemed to realize what she said as soon as the words left her mouth. Blushing, she picked at her braid.

Crowe gave her a wry look. "Don't you think he'd tell us, hmm?"

"Yeah," Maia said. "You're right. That was a silly thing to say."

"Don't worry, coz." Katya clapped her on the shoulder. "We can't be right all the time."

"Wrong. You can just declare yourself right, *Highness*."

"And don't forget it." Katya pointed a finger in mock warning. "Crowe, you and Pennynail know what to do."

"Yes, one complimentary ride to the dungeons for our Shadow." His smile didn't diminish the dark circles under his eyes. "I wonder how many of the guards think it's funny that an old pyradisté like me still goes out hunting villains."

"Ah, but you're the king's pyradisté. Your duties are many and varied."

"I notice you didn't argue with the 'old' part."

"I wouldn't want to disappoint."

Brutal heaved the Shadow's unconscious body over one shoulder. "Lucky this one's light. C'mon, it's almost dinnertime."

"Trust you to notice," Katya said.

Brutal patted his large frame, but the muscled flesh didn't wobble. "I'm a growing boy, growing outward, anyway."

"I think your figure is very nice," Maia said. When they all looked at her, she went scarlet to her ears and moved ahead to take the lead.

Crowe fell into step with Katya. "Ready to turn back into a numbskull?"

"Don't remind me. It's bad enough to do it. I don't want to have to anticipate it, too."

Ahead of them, Pennynail poked Maia in the arm before pointing off into the trees and sprinting out of sight, lost in the undergrowth.

"I'll spot you," Maia called.

"Need any help?" Katya asked.

"I can find him."

"You shouldn't encourage them," Crowe whispered in Katya's ear.

"Let them play."

Crowe snorted. "And here I was thinking that the business of the Order deserved our complete attention."

"I'll be damned before I let my team stop having fun."

"There he is." Maia pointed into the trees and nocked an arrow. "I'll just get close enough to scare him." She took careful aim, oblivious as Pennynail loomed from the bushes behind her. He bounced his open palms off her shoulders, and she jumped with a cry, her arrow wobbling off into the brush. "Sneak!"

Pennynail covered the mouth of his mask as if stifling laughter and then swaggered ahead, his long red ponytail swaying from just above where the mask laced up the back of his head.

"You'll get him next time," Brutal said. Maia beamed at him before she ran to catch up with Pennynail. She tugged at one of the numerous buckles that secured his outfit and made his slender figure difficult to examine.

At the edge of the wood, the party turned toward the smoke of a campfire, this one carrying the odd scent of berries mixed with wood. They broke into the arranged clearing, and Averie stood beside a smoldering fire near their picket of horses. Her simple leather clothing was green and brown to match the forest, and the camouflage seemed to have aided her, as the stag hanging from a nearby tree could testify. "Seems we both got prizes today, Highness," Averie said.

Katya peered at the downed animal and tsked. "One shot through the neck, nice and clean. I'm getting better and better."

"Ready to trade one set of hunting gear for another?"

"I'd rather hunt traitors all day. Question is, are you ready to play the self-sacrificing, put-upon lady-in-waiting?"

Averie heaved an exaggerated sigh. "I never stopped."

"Jewel of my heart!" Katya cried in mock longing. She fell to one knee. "What would I do without you?"

Averie pulled a change of clothes from her pack and tossed them over. "You'd go about naked, that's what you'd do."

Katya put on her best leer, but Averie laughed it off and helped her out of her black tabard and leather breastplate. Katya tucked her pyramid necklace next to her skin before she donned a leather-accented hunting shirt and buckled her rapier back on. She tucked a clean tabard into her belt, this one stiff with embroidery and bearing the hawk and rose of the Princess of Farraday. Averie smoothed her hair, forcing any stray strands into the loose bun at the base of her neck.

"There, much more regal," Averie said.

Katya only muttered and mounted her horse.

"Your kill, Highness." Brutal laid the stag behind Katya's saddle. "The Shadow is similarly positioned on Crowe's horse."

Katya shifted away from the large dead animal. "Ugh. I'd rather have him."

"We'll meet you later for debriefing." Crowe and Pennynail started down the road.

"Be careful not to be noticed!" Katya called after him.

He gave her a dark look over one shoulder. "Go and teach the wind to whistle while you're giving out free advice."

"You tease too much," Averie said.

"It keeps him from descending into a sea of self-righteous grumpiness."

"Or it hastens his descent."

Katya shook her head, and they began the ride back to the city of Marienne, Farraday's capital, past the fields and the homesteads, and along the main thoroughfare. Katya cast off her true self, becoming Princess Katyarianna Nar Umbriel once again, moderately fond of the people, inordinately fond of hunting and weapon-craft. She waved disinterestedly or imperiously at most of the gawkers and winked or leered at any young women. She thanked the spirits she didn't have to play a pampered, simpering, garters-and-gowns princess. As a dark-haired peasant girl blew her a kiss, Katya also thanked her mother for deciding her persona should be a bit of a rake.

Katya caught the kiss and pressed it to her lips, but she didn't stop. Cutting a swath through the women of Marienne had been fun for a while. No chance of children, just a trail of broken hearts. All her affairs had ended the same way, though; she could almost hear the entreaties in her head. "Princess, could you help me with... Could you convince your father to...? My brother has been trying to get into the Pyradisté Academy, and..." It went on and on. She'd trusted some of them, not with her sacred duty as leader of the Order of Vestra, but with her person, with her heart. Now, at nineteen, she simply played the part, a fact she reminded herself of as the peasant girl waved farewell.

The gate guards bowed as she rode into the sprawling palace proper, a series of long rectangles with the occasional turret or tower rising out of the jumble. Her party passed the statues of the ten spirits that lined the wide passage into the courtyard. Brutal saluted Best and Berth, twins of strength and courage, the patron spirits of his brotherhood. Katya saluted Matter and Marla, needing their sharp intellects and wisdom if she was going to find her family's enemies.

Maia gave a half-hidden salute to Ellias and Elody, twins of love and beauty, as she passed. Katya hid a grin. The twin patrons of lovers couldn't help Maia unless she learned how to speak to Brutal without blushing. If he'd been there, Pennynail would have made a great flourish to Jack and Jan, twins of skill and deftness. Katya made the gesture for him. All of them saluted Fah and Fay, spirits of luck, the twin statues perched precariously atop a stone egg.

They rode to the rear of the palace, to the royal stable, and Katya left Brutal, Averie, and Maia with the gear and the grooms. The princess couldn't be seen tending her horse or her weapons or her kill. Getting out of brushing horses and handling dead animals were two perks she could deal with.

Still in her leather hunting gear, she passed through the halls of the palace to its interior and the winter apartments of the royal family. Pyramids set in the walls glittered as she passed, and she wondered for the hundredth time what they would do to an unauthorized visitor. She resisted the urge to touch her pyramid necklace as she always did when she thought of magic.

The guards at the entryway to her parents' rooms saluted with a snap as Katya passed. She heard her father's deep voice echoing down the hall and headed for the sitting room. Even after hearing him, she paused to knock at the door, recalling a time she'd slipped her nursemaid and seen her parents in a situation that was then confusing, but now unthinkably embarrassing.

"Come," her father boomed.

King Einrich Nar Umbriel stood upon a wooden block while a tailor fussed with the robes that draped him. Katya's father paid him no mind, leaving the fussing to Queen Catirin Van Umbriel, who supervised all aspects of the draping. Even while going about such mundane tasks, the two exuded an air of royalty that Katya strived to live up to. In her heart, though, they'd always be Ma and Da.

"Ah, Katya," Da said. After a nod in her direction, he continued dictating to a clerk at his side who wrote hurriedly upon an untidy sheaf of papers.

"Too much velvet," Ma said to the tailor. Though her mother only stood as high as the tailor's shoulder, her bearing gave her a commanding presence.

The tailor cocked his head to and fro. "Purple is very regal."

"There's regal and then there's looking like a window dressing."

The tailor re-draped the velvet into a shorter, knee-length cape and folded it back from Da's shoulders so that it wouldn't meet in front, showing off the tacked-together fabric that would be a new suit for the Courtiers Ball.

Ma tapped her chin. "A credit to your art." She smiled, and the tailor bowed nearly to the floor.

Katya ducked her head to cover a grin. One minute Ma was calling the tailor's creation a window dressing, and the next she was calling it art, but the smile made the tailor forget about the former. She couldn't stop politicking, even with tradesmen.

She turned to Katya with arched brows, a signal Katya knew of old. Anytime in front of witnesses was a perfect time for a "fight." "Why do you even bother coming in here dressed like that, Katyarianna?"

Katya sagged against the woodwork and shrugged. She could do disapproving mother and disinterested daughter in her sleep. "I'll dress up when there's something worth dressing up for."

"The Courtiers Ball is worth dressing up for. Your brother's impending visit is *worth* dressing up for."

"The ball's not for another few nights. The visit not for half a month or so."

"Still—" Ma started. Da cleared his throat and inclined his head to the clerk and tailor. The first was still writing, his tongue protruding from the side of his mouth. The latter was doing a poor job feigning ignorance. His eyes darted at them while he gathered up loose fabric. Da's cough and look guaranteed the story would get out. "And then the king had to silence them!" the tailor would say. It was like living inside a complex ballet.

"That'll do for now, Maxwell," Ma said. The tailor picked up his kit and stowed everything in a rolling basket before he exited in a rush. Da finished what he was saying to the clerk and then excused the man, waiting until the clerk picked up all the papers and vanished out the doors.

As he stepped down from the block, Da kissed Ma on the cheek. "Thank you, my love, for saving me from looking like a window dressing."

"The duties of a queen are many and varied."

"And you." Da gave Katya a squeeze. "You have made boredom into an art form."

"I was just thinking that," Katya said. Her mother squeezed her hand. For all their fake arguing, Ma really cared about her clothing, and Katya's leather outfit was dusty. Katya knew she'd get a hug when she was clean.

Ma looked her up and down. "You're all right?"

"Fit and hale."

"Well, then." Da sat on the tailor's block. "Pull up a chair and let's hear it."

Katya pulled her stiff tabard out of her belt and over her head and laid it to the side. "We caught the Shadow, although he's quite ordinary-looking for someone with such a nefarious name."

"What did he tell you?"

"The usual, that there are more of his kind and that I have no idea how high his group has penetrated, but this time, I believe it."

"The bastard has to have connections to have eluded you this long," Da said.

"Language." Ma stared off into space, and Katya knew what she was thinking. The second child of the monarchy had always headed the Order of Vestra, protecting the king, queen, and firstborn heir. If she fell in combat or had to assume her brother's duties, the Order would go to Maia. That knowledge, that the Order would live on, never seemed to stop Ma's worries.

"I'm fine," Katya said quietly.

"Of course you are," Ma said, but she didn't seem convinced.

Da patted Katya's knee, three quick smacks. "Yes, of course you are, my girl. Crowe is bringing the Shadow in?"

"With Pennynail."

Ma made a face, her mouth turning down.

"I know you don't approve of his fashion sense, Ma."

"I don't trust people who hide behind masks."

Da lifted a hand. "Let's not start that again. The girl has a right to choose her comrades."

Ma shook her head but didn't say anything else about it. "You'll be at the Courtiers Ball."

"Of course."

"Any idea what you'll be wearing?"

"My usual." As her mother frowned, Katya hurried on with, "Suitably embroidered and outstanding. I'm not a complete novice to this game, you know."

Da prodded her arm. "Lady Hilda still chasing you?"

"Yes, and my excuses for putting her off are getting pretty feeble."

"A good-looking woman."

Ma gave him a harsh look. "And ten years too old for you, Katya, as well as being what they'd call well used."

"Court gossip," Da said.

Ma gave him a harder look, and Katya had to wonder how her father had lived this long. "Oh, she's had lovers," Katya said, "but that should add to her appeal. Beautiful, experienced, and willing."

"And a backstabbing snake who only wants you for the influence it will give her," Da said.

They both stared at him.

"What? I'm not a moron, you know."

"I knew there was a reason you survived so long," Katya said. "Everyone knows Hilda's intentions. If I gave in, I would be acknowledging that it's only a string of pretty lovers that I'm after. That would add to the persona I've created, but…" She shook her head.

"You can still have your integrity," Ma said.

"Why do I get the feeling this isn't a normal conversation for a nineteen-year-old girl to have with her parents?"

Da shrugged. "To a nineteen-year-old princess in charge of a secret order tasked to protect the monarchy with magic and brawn, a secret which she can only share with a trusted few, normal conversations are coveted and often unfulfilled dreams."

"Speaking of," Katya said, "I'd better go. I've got to get cleaned up, laze around the halls for a bit, and then put together a plan of action."

"Do you think Crowe will learn more from this Shadow?" Da asked.

"He's the best pyradisté we have," Ma said. "If he can't learn anything more…"

"Then we'll have to do it the really old-fashioned way," Katya said.

Da rubbed his hands together. "Ears to the ground, eh? And once you find a source of information, you pound him into jelly until he tells you what you want to know!"

Ma grimaced. "Really, Einrich."

"Sometimes, I envy you, my girl, truly I do."

Katya had no intention of pounding anyone into anything, but her father's exuberance was catching. "I won't let you down, Da."

"'Course you won't. If you can evade Lady Hilda's poisonous tentacles, you can do anything. I have all the faith in the world."

CHAPTER TWO: STARBRIDE

Starbride wished for the hundredth time that she was anything but a courtier. The other young women clustered together with the young men, comparing fashion, talking of how exciting events at the palace would be, of the connections they could make, of the attachments court could bring. The palace at Marienne provided a host of future spouses, to say nothing of future lovers.

The thought of using another person for her own gain turned Starbride's stomach as much as the current fashion—layers of petal-like, pastel, gossamer fabric, a trend credited to the current Farradain queen. Petite, thin women carried it off. Tall, slender women could wear it well. Even tall and curvy could manage, but the layers turned short curvy women like Starbride into special-occasion cakes. She fought not to cross her arms over one of her mother's custom-designed dresses. At least there wasn't a mirror handy; she didn't have to see how much like a cupcake she looked. She blamed her mother's sweet tooth as much as her mother's fashion sense.

Starbride rolled her head from side to side, stretching muscles cramped from her long carriage ride as she waited for the tour of the palace to start. At least her dress was a soft cream color that complemented her reddish brown skin and black hair. If it had been one of the oranges or pinks that went with pale Farradain skin and hair, Starbride wouldn't have gotten out of her carriage.

A middle-aged man and woman eventually emerged from the palace doors. "This way, young charges." The woman gave them a smile that seemed a little wicked to Starbride's eyes. "I am Adele Van Nereem, and this is my husband Claude."

Together, the couple bowed and curtsied, and the answering greeting from the new courtiers was a gentle swish of skirts and fabric. "My wife and I are lifetime courtiers." The wink of mischief in Claude's eye matched his wife's smile. "Like some of the nobles here in Marienne, we stayed in court instead of departing after our connections were made.

We've dedicated our lives to instructing new courtiers in how the palace operates."

Starbride heard a few sniggers around her. "If they're not nobility and they haven't left," a nearby woman said, "they obviously haven't gotten *anywhere* in the world."

"Perhaps they're *provincial*," a man in the same group suggested. Those surrounding him tittered, and Starbride got a few snide glances herself.

Whether they heard or not, the Nereems didn't lose their smiles, and it soon became clear that they knew what they were doing. The palace was a maze, and the Nereems seemed to take pleasure in confusing their young charges with a lightning tour. Perhaps their real job was to teach humility. Starbride wished she could tell them she understood, but she was having a hard enough time keeping track of their directions.

Here was the main hall with its many staircases and hallways; this way to the courtiers' new rooms; this way to the dining halls or music halls or dancing halls; somewhere in that direction was the royal apartments; there the stables; there the kitchens; servants' quarters scattered here and there.

Starbride didn't catch most of what they said, and by the confused faces surrounding her, she wasn't alone. The Nereems encouraged the new arrivals to mingle with established courtiers whenever they could, but Starbride dismissed that idea immediately. There was one other woman from Allusia in this batch of courtiers, and if the frosty reception they both received was any indication, their chances of political alliances were slim to none. Ah well, it meant more time to devote to the law books. Starbride hadn't traveled so many miles into a foreign country just to meet people.

She ignored the Nereems' words on courtly life and studied the architecture and tapestries, the small statues, and the representations of the ten spirits that were everywhere. She knew them already, though she hadn't grown up with them. Like all aspects of Farradain culture, they had seeped into her homeland like a creeping tide of marmalade.

Allusia allowed Farraday into their land over one hundred years ago, to the mountains where the pale-skinned outlanders harvested the crystal to make pyramids. Some of the Allusian warlords had traded with them; others who attempted to drive them out were crushed by their army. The remaining Allusians organized to meet the Farradains on equal footing, learning more about these people, about their laws, but there was always more to learn. One hundred years hadn't solved all their problems.

Starbride raised her chin and set her shoulders back. As the descendent of the founder of Newhope, Allusia's trading capital, Starbride had every right to be at court. She lagged behind the tour, hoping to spot the famous Farradain library, but if it lurked behind any of the numerous doors, it didn't make itself known.

Once the Nereems assigned their rooms, Starbride ducked into hers without a word to anyone. Dawnmother stood at the small wardrobe, unpacking the traveling valise. She'd tied her hair in a simple horse's tail at her nape, not a black strand out of place. She pointed to a light snack that waited on the room's one table.

"How do you do that, Dawn?" Starbride gestured at the snacks. "How do you always know where to find the food?"

Dawnmother shrugged. "The fruit is excellent. You don't want to continue the tour?"

"Ha! They won't include the library. Why should I bother?" She popped a berry into her mouth, and the sweet juice rushed over her tongue.

"How will you catch a spouse if you don't deploy the nets?" Dawnmother asked. Her falsetto matched Starbride's mother to perfection.

Starbride plucked at her layered dress. "I hadn't thought of using this as an actual net. It would be more effective than as a dress."

Dawnmother shrugged again.

"Don't tell me you're partial to this style! When the luggage gets here, you can have all of Mother's cupcakes."

"I think they look more like meringues."

Starbride had to laugh, but when the luggage did arrive, Dawnmother started to unpack and then stopped. "Oh," she said, and the one word hung in the air.

Starbride's stomach curdled. "She didn't."

"She did. All the clothes you chose are gone, just like in your valise." She pulled out another frothy dress, this one a light mint. "There's nothing but these dresses."

"No trousers?"

Dawnmother rummaged through the trunk. "No shirts, no bodices, and definitely no trousers."

"That is *wonderful*! Now I'll look ridiculous every hour of the day." She eyed Dawnmother's comfortable traveling suit, loose-fitting trousers and a high-necked coat. "What about your clothes?"

"I have a servant's figure."

"But you're tall and thin; you'd look much better in these layers of spun sugar than I do!"

"We could have them taken in for me, but we have no material to let out the hips and bust of mine for you. Besides, you can't be seen in something as poor as this."

"I don't care what—"

Dawnmother interrupted with an upraised hand. "My life for you and also the truth. You must appear as a Farradain to gain their respect, and as much as you hate your mother's clothes, the dresses make you closer to them. You wish to do what's best for our people?" She held up the mint dress again. "This is one of the ways in which to do it."

Starbride bit her lip but nodded. "You speak sense, as always."

"Thank Horsestrong you see it that way."

"If I were Darkstrong instead, I would have staked you out in the sun for speaking the truth."

"But you listened to the old tales and picked the correct brother to emulate. Now." She cracked her knuckles. "Let's repair your hair, and then we can split up to look for the library."

Starbride shrugged in resignation, and gave herself over to Dawnmother's fingers.

Chalk would have come in handy, or charcoal, anything to mark her way through the palace maze. Even if she had marked it, Starbride was certain one of the many people in livery would have scrubbed it off. Where in the world could all the rushing uniforms be going in such a hurry? How many of them simply endeavored to look busy? On her next exploration, she vowed to bring pen and paper and make a map.

Starbride turned another corridor and recited in her head the way back to her room: two rights, three lefts, second right. When she noticed that the carpeted runner in the passageway had changed, she moved to the edge of the hall, out of the way. It was such a little thing, but after the sameness of the hallways, it had to mean something. Perhaps she'd entered another wing. Servants hurried through the new area with the same single-minded purpose, but now there were leather uniforms mixed with the livery, and down the corridor, she smelled the stink of horses. Ah, she'd found the wing closest to the stables, the *last* place the library would be.

"Excuse me," she said to a leather-clad man.

"Sorry, miss, can't stop." He turned as he spoke, never breaking stride, even while backward.

Starbride just refrained from one of her uncle's favorite swears. She'd hoped the leather-wearing servants, guardsmen perhaps, would be in less of a hurry than the liveried servants who had given the same answer. She'd also tried one of the many housekeepers, the men and women in stern black who carried rings of keys at their hips, but all she'd gotten from them was "If it's not my section, I can't help."

She wandered back the way she'd come and spotted a few courtiers gathered in the hallways, usually near large windows or perched on cushioned benches. They were always in little groups, little tittering clusters. One group parted to reveal the other Allusian girl alone in their midst. Starbride approached her with a smile, glad to see another person who looked lost, but the woman gasped when she met Starbride's gaze.

"Sorry," Starbride said, "I didn't mean to startle you. I just wanted to introduce myself." She laid a hand on her chest. "Starbride."

"Jewelnoble." She glanced to and fro as if afraid someone would overhear. "You didn't startle…I mean, I'm just…I'm just waiting for someone I know."

"Oh, I thought you might be alone."

"No, I already know someone here." She cast another furtive glance down the hall and then at a nearby gaggle of courtiers, male and female, who watched them with amused glances and many giggles.

Starbride couldn't resist shaking her head. "I can't believe these people. You'd think they'd never seen—"

"Look," Jewelnoble said. "I have a friend coming, I told you, and she's introducing me around." She leaned forward. "The last thing I need is for the others to think I'm part of a…a…an *ethnic* consortium."

"What?" Hurt stabbed through Starbride, surprising her, and the shock seemed to double the pain.

"Just leave me alone." She turned away.

Starbride sneered at the presented back and lifted her chin before she walked away. Ethnic consortium, indeed! She pressed her wounded feelings down. Even her mother, who wanted her to fit in very badly, never wanted Starbride to forget she was Allusian.

She hurried past other courtiers, her spine stiff. Distance, disdain, discomfort, mocking, she saw it all in their eyes. Some of them offered interested, amorous glances, but she equated their interest to that of a zookeeper with a new specimen, looking to add a little exoticness to their love lives. She'd heard a whispered comment calling her spicy, no doubt a reference to the dishes her people preferred. Well, they could forget it. She wasn't on anyone's menu.

By the time she'd walked off some of her anger and took a look around, Starbride realized she stood in an unfamiliar corridor with no idea of the way back. She bit off another curse, this one aimed at herself for being so busy worrying about other people that she'd become thoroughly lost. She grabbed her ridiculous skirt and turned back the way she'd come, hoping to see something familiar.

Two hours later, she sank onto a stone staircase in defeat, certain that the palace was a trap for unsuspecting courtiers. Any minute now she'd stumble upon a skeleton in a ridiculous dress. She'd seen nothing to direct a lost person; there were no guides, not that anyone would have answered her anyway, not the busy servants or the imperious housekeepers or the stuck-up courtiers who wouldn't talk to anyone provincial, ethnic, and possibly spicy.

Tears were only for times when they could be put to good use, or so her mother taught her; no use crying when no one was around to see it. After years of hearing that lesson, it was just easier not to weep. It never did any good anyway. Starbride plucked idly at her hair and retraced her steps in her head. Where had she gone wrong? Why did all the staircases look the *same*?

When she glanced down, she saw a small mountain of hair pins. "Damn." She patted her head to discover she'd picked out nearly all of Dawnmother's creation. The courtiers would add eccentric to her list of adjectives if she walked around with half a hairdo. Maybe she could tell them she'd run into a strong gust of wind or random coiffure thieves. They'd upgrade her from eccentric to odd.

From behind her, someone asked, "Are you lost?"

Starbride stood and whirled at the same time, almost losing her footing. A hand reached out and captured her flailing arm. "Steady."

Starbride focused on the dusty face, a young woman's. Her blond hair was pinned back, and her cobalt-blue eyes were smiling. She'd left a smudge on Starbride's frothy white sleeve, courtesy of her dirty leather clothing. A guardswoman or something, judging by the rapier at her hip. Why would anyone else go about armed indoors?

"I am." Starbride tucked a loose strand of hair behind her ear. "Steady and lost, that is."

"Where is it you want to be?"

Starbride almost said, "Anywhere but here," but that would have been not only childish but an invitation to scorn. "The library." The guardswoman looked her up and down, very rude like everyone else, but this was a *guardswoman*, not a lady of court. "Do you mind?"

The guardswoman's lips quirked up. "Not to worry, miss, I was just wondering if you always dressed so elegantly for the library."

Starbride felt the blood rushing to her cheeks, but she held her skirt out to the sides. "This was my mother's idea. She took every scrap of useful clothing from my luggage and gave me gowns like this instead."

"Why?"

"She loves desserts. I think she wants me to look like a meringue as often as possible."

The guardswoman crossed her arms, a considering look on her face. "No one can say no to dessert."

Starbride's laughter echoed through the stone hallway. A friendly person at last. "What's your name?"

The guardswoman stared for a moment. Starbride squirmed under her gaze. Had she forgotten another rule? Was she not supposed to ask? Was the identity of the guardswoman supposed to be evident by her dress? "Katya."

Starbride didn't dare ask about the hesitation. "I'm glad to meet you."

"And you, Miss…?"

"Starbride." She heard the dull acceptance in her voice, the same as whenever she had to introduce herself to a Farradain.

"Ah, I thought you might be Allusian."

Starbride gestured to her face, the Allusian features she couldn't hide. "Yes."

"So, if I understand it correctly, Star is the name those closest to you use, and Bride is your parents' fondest hope for your future?"

"Nearly that, yes."

"Bride?"

Starbride crossed her arms and rolled her eyes. "Yes."

"Mother again?"

"How did you guess?"

"The dessert look makes more and more sense all the time."

"Do you know the way to the library, or are we going to talk about my mother all night?"

Katya gave a wink that said she wouldn't mind, and swept her hand out in front of her. They strode down several winding corridors, and as the first servant bowed, Starbride assumed it was for her status as a courtier. By the second or third, she thought she'd arrived at a section of the palace where the manners were much improved. When the section housekeeper bowed, his ring of keys jingling, Starbride eyed Katya with rising horror. "You're not a guardswoman at all."

"No."

"I just assumed…"

"I know. Forgive me for going along with it as long as I could. You're not going to start bowing and scraping, are you? I enjoyed our conversation on the stairs."

"You're the king's…cousin."

"No."

Starbride's stomach hit her shoes. Katya. Katyarianna Nar Umbriel. She'd heard the name, but had never seen a portrait. "You're the princess."

"Yes."

"I rolled my eyes at you." She could feel her mother being horrified from hundreds of miles away.

Katya coughed to hide her smile, but Starbride could see it from the side. "It was refreshing." She stopped suddenly, and Starbride did the same. When Katya turned to face her, she began a curtsy.

"Finish that move, and I'll have your head lopped off," Katya said.

Starbride halted, but when she glanced up, Katya's cheeks quivered with a suppressed grin. She pointed to a pair of enormous double doors. "The library."

"Thank you."

"Quite welcome, Miss Meringue. See you at the Courtiers Ball." With that, she departed.

Starbride turned to the doors of the library, thinking at the last second that she should have asked for directions back to her room. With a deep breath, she tried to put the fact out of her mind that she'd treated the Princess of Farraday like a regular person and walked into the library to search for what she needed.

Every so often, she thought of Katya. Katyarianna Nar Umbriel, she reminded herself. The princess had laughed with her; more importantly, the princess hadn't laughed *at* her, but someone so important wouldn't have time for friends. Still, while researching Farradain law, Starbride also researched the royal family, just to see what the history books had to say. She couldn't find much, given that Katya (Katyarianna Nar Umbriel, her inner voice corrected), was nineteen, just one year older than Starbride.

Why would a princess not admit her identity right away? Starbride could think of one reason to hide it: to have an amusing story to tell about the provincial, ethnic, possibly spicy courtier with the odd hair, ridiculous dress, and absurd name. No, she reminded herself, the princess had laughed *with* her. She was certain of it. Or was she? In that last moment, Princess Katyarianna did seem to be having a good time at Starbride's expense.

Starbride shook her head. Those were all questions for later; now, she had work to do. She dove into her law books, losing herself in research.

Dawnmother found her sometime after midnight. "I was beginning to worry," she whispered in the cavernous room.

Starbride yawned as she stretched. "So was I. I thought I might have to sleep here."

"Better here than lost in the halls. I remember the way back. Come, it's late."

"How did you find the library?"

"Servants know how to get knowledge from other servants."

"You must teach me one day."

"Servants must have secrets, too. Now, to bed. The library will be there in the morning."

Starbride should have returned to her studies the next morning, but she spent the time making a map and lingering in the halls. Gossip about Princess Katyarianna wasn't hard to find at court, even to a person with no friends. All she had to do was be at the right time and place to listen.

Katyarianna Nar Umbriel was more than a princess. She was a legend, especially where courtiers were concerned—female courtiers, in point of fact.

A light went on in Starbride's head. The princess *had* been flirting with her. A flattered feeling tingled over her scalp, but she tried to wave it away. With her reputation, Princess Katyarianna probably flirted with everyone, and the use of the familiar name Katya was a ploy, probably a well-used one.

But there had been something in the princess's eyes when she'd apologized for not owning up to her identity, as if she enjoyed being anonymous for just a little while. Suddenly, the lothario princess cut a lonely figure, and Starbride was tempted to pity, but she warned herself not to fall for that. By the time of the Courtiers Ball, Katyarianna Nar Umbriel would have forgotten all about the new Allusian courtier.

CHAPTER THREE: KATYA

Katya had dreamt of rich brown eyes and dusky skin and a smile like a starry night. As she finished dressing in the morning, she had to shake her head to clear it. She had traitors to unearth and a court to fool. Even so, Starbride's pure laugh lingered at the edge of her thoughts.

After grabbing a lantern, Katya toggled the latch at the top of her long mirror, and as it swung silently outward, she stepped into the secret passageway behind. She ignored the symbols carved at the junctions, so used to the dark, cramped tunnels hidden between the palace walls that she didn't need directions.

The rest of the Order waited in her vacant summer apartment, and she nodded to them as she emerged from the secret passageway to take her place around their small table. "I hope you haven't been waiting long."

Brutal leaned back in his chair, long legs crossed at the ankles under his red robe. "Can we make it quick? I have seven duels this afternoon."

"Only seven?" Katya asked.

"When the weather turns cool, fewer people seek combat as the path to enlightenment. They turn to Ellias and Elody."

"Ah, love as enlightenment." Crowe scratched his chin. Katya noted the white whiskers and wondered if he'd been up all night. "It's a nice thought. Had a slow start this morning, did you, Katya? Late night with the new courtiers in town?"

Katya gave him a level stare before glancing at the others. Maia's head rested on her arms, her eyes shut; she could sleep with her hair on fire. Pennynail balanced one of his long knives on a gloved finger. Katya nodded toward Maia, and Pennynail sheathed the knife and flicked Maia's ear.

Maia jerked upright in her seat. "I'm awake."

"Of course," Katya said. "Let's begin. Averie won't be joining us."

"Not with the new courtiers here," Brutal said. "She needs to stay near your rooms to ward off the overeager hopefuls."

Maia shook her head and yawned. "She needn't worry. The guards and the pyramids will stop them all, and any they miss will get jumped by Lady Hilda defending her territory."

"I'm no one's territory!" Katya said.

"And here we thought the traitors were the biggest threat," Brutal said.

"Which brings us to the problem," Crowe said loudly. He smoothed the front of his cassock. "The Shadow."

"Did you learn anything new?" Katya asked.

Crowe shook his head. "I'm hoping a few days in the dark with no visitors will loosen his mind a bit. His control is better than we thought."

Brutal cracked his knuckles. "Maybe he'd like to go a few rounds."

"The Order of Vestra has never tortured anyone, Brother Brutal." Crowe gave Brutal a steely look with his slate gray eyes.

"Never?" Maia asked.

Crowe turned his hard stare on her, and she dropped her gaze to the table. She had the nerve to ask questions, but her follow-through needed help.

"Regardless of what others have done, we're not going to torture anyone," Katya said. "Torture only gets you what you want to hear, whether it's true or not. But we do need a next step."

For a moment, they were all as silent as Pennynail. Crowe finally shrugged. "Ask around with the usual contacts. We need to figure something out before the crown prince and princess's visit, before the Waltz."

Katya resisted the urge to reach under her tunic and fidget with her pyramid necklace. "This will be Brom's first time. You'll have to craft a necklace for her, Crowe."

He cleared his throat. "Already done." After a moment, she felt a light touch and looked up to meet his softened gaze. "Your sister-in-law knew what she was getting into before her marriage, Katya."

"I know, but the Waltz is…" Katya trailed off, pressing her lips together. They couldn't understand. *She* didn't fully understand, and she'd done it once, a year before her brother had married. She'd had to keep the Fiend Yanchasa the Mighty at bay, and she barely remembered it. "The people have mostly forgotten Yanchasa. It's…difficult to prepare someone."

Brutal shrugged. "People have lost their sense of fear. You said it yourself, some things can't be explained. From what you've told us, Brom won't even remember the Waltz after it's over."

Across the table, Maia rubbed her arms as if chilled. "But those watching won't forget. Too bad we can't let Yanchasa loose. One look at it and no one would claim our family uses the legend to keep the throne."

"That would only work if we wanted everyone in the kingdom to die," Crowe said. "Summoning Yanchasa killed the first king of Farraday and nearly destroyed his entire army."

"I know," Maia said "That's why I said we can't."

"Peace." Katya rubbed the bridge of her nose. "The people know there's a ritual, and that's all they need to know. The last thing we need is for traitors to find out the details of the Waltz." She touched the fabric covering her necklace. "Or the Aspect. Now, ideas on how to get more information on this particular group?"

"I'll check the other chapterhouses," Brutal said.

"Good," Katya said. "Pennynail, have your contacts turned up anything?"

He pointed to Crowe, who shook his head. "Whoever's leading this group is buried too deeply for our contacts. The best we can hope for is rumor or gossip to help us understand what they want."

"We don't want to understand them," Katya said. "We want to eradicate them."

Crowe shook his head. "If we know what they want, Highness, we can more easily find them."

"They want to kill my family."

"Mine, too," Maia said. Katya nodded to her.

"When you are working as the leader of the Order of Vestra, they are not *your* family," Crowe said, "they are the *royal* family."

"I know," Katya and Maia said at the same time.

"Then remember, anger is dangerous," Crowe said. Katya resisted the urge to grasp her necklace again. Anger could lead to rage, which would bring on the Aspect, and that could kill them all.

Katya licked her lips. "Maia, you asking questions of the courtiers will be less noticeable than me asking. Eavesdropping on hallway gossip while pretending to be an idle idiot suits me best."

"Pennynail and I will call in some old favors," Crowe said.

"Let's get to it." They all stood to go to their respective tasks. Her curiosity piqued, Katya lingered until everyone had left but Crowe. "What are these favors you and Pennynail did that you can now call in?"

"Ask and ask and ask again, but I shall never tell."

"I'm not asking about his identity. I'm just asking what you two do together."

"You've worked with him long enough to trust him, correct?"

"He's saved my life many times."

"Then continue to trust him. And me."

"Always. Even though you aren't blood, you feel like family. When I was little, I thought you and Roland were both my uncles instead of just him."

"Thank you." He stared at the table, his face like stone.

With a sigh, Katya wished she could take back the forbidden word: Roland. Her stomach burned with resentment. She was old enough to protect her family, to maintain a secret identity, but not to know what had happened to the former leader of the Order, her uncle—Maia's father—a man Katya had loved as a second father. "He's been dead seven years."

Crowe shook his head and didn't speak. He'd headed the Order until Katya turned sixteen; he knew the pressure, the terrible weight of secrets, and still he didn't share.

Katya gave up. Crowe could be as tight-lipped as a corpse when he wanted to be. "See you tomorrow." He nodded, and she took the secret passageway back to her room.

Averie greeted her with an impish grin. Dressed in a high-necked blue dress with Katya's hawk and rose on the hip, Averie still had the grace of a hunter as she moved about the room. "Don't worry. The guards drove the eager hopefuls off before they even got close to the pyramid traps."

"How many?"

"Three. Four if you count Lady Hilda. Our gorgeous redhead hasn't given up; it seems she likes the chase."

"I suppose that's flattering," Katya said; a fleeting recollection of Starbride played in her memory. "What did the others look like?"

"Oho, do you care all of a sudden?"

"It's only ego."

Averie described the suitors based on what she'd heard; there was no hint of an Allusian. Katya shrugged, but Averie nodded slowly, a knowing gleam in her eyes. "Not who you were hoping for? Do tell."

"Won't." Katya grinned as her lady-in-waiting set a plate of cheese and cutlets on the table beside her. "I take back every bad thing I've ever said about you, jewel of my heart." She bit into a slice of roast beef and closed her eyes in bliss. "I just realized I skipped breakfast."

"I'll fetch you a glass of wine."

"I might abdicate to you if you keep this up."

"Keep the crown. I'm holding the cake in reserve until you promise to give me your jewelry."

"Take what you like. I saw the coat you had made for the Courtiers Ball, by the way. It's genius."

"And the sapphires I found will go lovely with your eyes."

"When *are* we getting married?"

"I don't marry titles. You're going to have to try a lot harder than that."

Katya attacked the rest of her lunch as Averie brought her wine; her thoughts wandered to the task in front of her. She ruled out everyone in the Order as the palace traitor; she couldn't point fingers at her team. Crowe would have censured her, but Katya couldn't work with them if she didn't trust them. Was that how Uncle Roland had died, betrayed by someone he should have been able to trust?

As Katya sipped her wine, the encounter with Starbride flitted past her mind's eye. It'd been nice to be a face in the crowd, a guardswoman who could flirt with impunity, free to give directions to a lost courtier. Of course, Starbride would be at the Courtiers Ball—all of the courtiers and nobles would. They all wanted something, and a ball was the perfect place to continue their petitions. But what did Starbride want? When she'd found out who Katya was, she hadn't taken the opportunity to turn on the charm or plead her case. And out of all the years new courtiers had been coming to the palace, Katya never heard of one wanting the library before anything else.

Starbride could be a wallflower, she supposed. Courtiers could be shy, but a shy girl would've hidden in her room; she would've clammed up when meeting a stranger. A shy girl would have keeled over when Katya threatened to lop off her head. Starbride had even seemed a little offended.

The idea was…intriguing. It reminded her of her brother Reinholt, who'd chosen the courtier no one expected as his future queen. Brom's background was impeccable; it was an excellent match but still unexpected. Brom was plump and cute; she had a laugh that could cheer anyone. All the courtiers liked her because none of them thought of her as a threat. They didn't know that Reinholt valued her sweet disposition more than anything, or that he wooed her in private. Brom could keep secrets, and if Katya's unassuming sister-in-law could remain a mystery, anyone could.

Katya stood and pulled her arms over her head until her shoulders popped. She hadn't recognized the Shadow, but she didn't know everyone at court. Either he hadn't recognized her or his brain couldn't wrap itself around the princess chasing traitors through the woods. He might not live in the palace, but he knew one of his fellow conspirators had palace connections. Katya paced over her sitting room rug. All she could do now was keep the eyes of court on her while her team did its job and then run the traitor to ground once they sniffed him out.

With that in mind, Katya wandered. Through the halls of the palace, she languished, boredom as moving art. Whenever she found a group of hall-lingerers, she complained about not being able to go out hunting because she had to be presentable at the Courtiers Ball that evening.

The courtiers and nobles put on sympathetic expressions. Some of the ladies leaned close, their wispy, layered dresses whispering across the backs of Katya's hands. It made her recall Starbride's dress, more layered than all of them, and led to thoughts of Starbride's mother. Katya hid her smiles behind yawns.

When Lady Hilda turned the corner down the hall, Katya almost groaned. The courtiers gave way like sand before the tide at Lady Hilda's green-eyed glance. Their pinched expressions said they didn't want to yield, but something in Lady Hilda's sensuous walk spoke of danger as well as sex.

"Lady Hilda."

"Good afternoon, Highness." She curtsied low enough to display a great deal of cleavage. After a quick glance, Katya told her eyes to behave. "I've come to reserve my dance."

"Reserve your dance?"

"This evening at the Courtiers Ball. I assumed that was what you were doing." She cast a glance at the men and women who'd given them a bit of space. "Arranging dances."

"I've never bothered to make reservations before."

"Well, allow me to introduce you to the concept. It's sure to be the new trend. Dance the evening away with me, and I'll promise you a wonderful time."

In the past, it would have been tempting, but Starbride's self-mocking sense of humor kept surfacing in Katya's mind. Besides that, Lady Hilda's shamelessness made her edgy. It might have turned her on years ago, but now she could see that Lady Hilda's entire posture spoke of need, lust mixed with desire for power. Katya put on a crooked grin and cursed the fact that she had a part to play.

She took Lady Hilda's quite close hand and raised it to her lips. "I never make promises, and so I never expect them to be kept. All I can say is if I see you there, I see you there."

Lady Hilda chuckled, a low, smoky sound in the back of her throat.

"Oh, you'll see me. And I always keep my promises." She backed away, gave another one of those eye-towing curtsies, and then slinked back the way she'd come, leaving Katya's other admirers to crash back together in her wake. They didn't dare laugh behind Lady Hilda's back, not yet, not until they knew how Katya felt. She didn't give them any indication, as usual. She put her bored face on and wandered, letting all the talk wash over her and waiting for anything interesting to surface.

A small gathering of people congregated in the middle of one hallway. They talked excitedly, and not for her, though she caused the babble to swell for a moment. Her hangers-on were only too happy to inform her that the king was soon to be passing that way. He usually went from the function of the moment through the secret passageways to his apartment, but Katya knew an appearance now and again in the hallways helped spread goodwill amongst the nobles and courtiers.

Katya mingled with the knot of people and surveyed the crowd, hoping to pick out any grumbling about the Umbriels. She fixed on one man who didn't chatter but watched the hallway with a hard look, an intense anticipation that turned Katya's stomach to ice.

She passed behind the rest of the waiting crowd and glanced at him now and again, keeping her bored face on tight. She put off any who tried to speak to her with a wave. Down the hall, her father turned the corner. Cassock-clad pyradistés, Crowe included, surrounded him. Da spoke with various nobles as he strolled. He received their bows with a nod and clapped Earl Lamont on the shoulder, laughing loudly at something the old man said.

Katya's glance darted to the cold-eyed courtier. A pyramid glimmered in his fist. The sides were uneven and cloudy, not well made, but well enough to perform one task. The courtier grasped it and stared at Katya's father without blinking.

Anger brewed in Katya's chest, and she almost dropped her mask. This man dared to attack her father in his own hall? Her pyramid necklace flared as her anger grew, and down the hall, Crowe's head lifted. His eyes found Katya's, and she nodded toward the pyramid-wielding courtier. Crowe's right hand dropped to the split in his cassock, and Katya knew he was pulling a pyramid from his trouser pocket. He pushed toward her through the chattering crowd that pressed her father.

Katya continued toward the courtier. She stopped just behind him and forced herself to calm down. "Lovely day for it, don't you think?" she said in his ear.

He jumped and nearly whirled, but she caught his arm, keeping him still. "What…what?"

Katya dug into the flesh of his upper arm until he gasped. "Keep still, and you might get out of here alive."

He shivered. "I knew it might mean my life, but people have to know."

"What?" Katya's free hand inched toward the pyramid. "What do they have to know?"

"The Aspect. They're not human. The Umbriels are *monsters!*" He said the last part in a strangled whisper as he turned to look at Katya. "You…"

She reached the pyramid, but he jerked away. Crowe arrived and grabbed for him, but he leaned far to the left and rammed his pyramid into his own belly.

The king had nearly reached them. Someone bumped into Crowe, and he dropped the suddenly limp courtier to the ground. Katya stepped forward, over the downed man, shielding him from the view of the crowd as Crowe bent over him. "Fetch this man some help!" she commanded.

The courtiers and nobles turned. "What's wrong with the poor devil?" Da asked.

"He needs a physician!" Crowe said. The courtier was at his feet, unmoving, doubled over with one arm shielding his face. "He's overcome. Where have all the damned servants gone?"

"Never around when you need them," Katya drawled. A few people chuckled with her. No servants were a blessing. If the courtier was dead, any regular servant might panic.

Crowe gestured to two of his fellow pyradistés. "Let's take him to my study." The selected two stooped beside the downed man and lifted him.

"Perhaps it's the excitement," Earl Lamont said. The pyradistés bore the man away, Crowe right behind them.

"Yes." Da glanced at Katya out of the corner of his eye. "That must be it."

Katya shrugged and put her bored face back on through force of will. The downed courtier knew about the Aspect. He knew Katya's family shared something with Yanchasa, if not why. To control a monster, each Umbriel had to become one. But how did he know? She wanted to run to Crowe's office.

Da caught her shoulder. "Remember the ball," he whispered. "You have many duties. Leave Crowe to his."

Katya could only nod. The Order would have to wait, it seemed. After all, she had a very important *dance* to attend first.

CHAPTER FOUR: STARBRIDE

Dawnmother stood back and fluffed the voluminous gown. "This is one of the best."

Starbride made a face as she studied the dress, this one a mixture of smoky browns. "I look like milky tea."

"It goes with your skin."

"Red goes with my skin. This goes with a cake."

Dawnmother's eyes twinkled. "I think cinnamon coffee is a better fit."

Starbride put on her best withering look. "I'm glad you're having a good time."

"Don't be so gloomy. You might get a chance to speak with the royal family...again."

"Oh yes, I'm sure Princess Katyarianna will have a lot of fun at my expense."

"You told me she *wasn't* laughing at you."

"I don't know, do I?" But she could guess, and what she guessed hurt more than the chance of ridicule. Katyarianna Nar Umbriel would ignore her, or worse yet, not remember her.

"Cling to the wall," Dawnmother said. "There's bound to be more than one person who doesn't fit in. Maybe you can form an alliance of the unallied."

"Unless the other misfits are dying to prove they *aren't* misfits by standing at the edges of conversations and trying to look as if they're part of them. I'll probably retreat to a quiet corner until I can leave." Maybe one of the leering courtiers would make a pass at her, and as much as she hated it, she could talk to him or her for a little while. "All right, do the hair."

"I thought you'd never ask."

When Dawnmother finished curling and pinning Starbride's long hair on top of her head, she took a small, flat box from the chest of drawers. "I dare any of the other ladies to match this."

Starbride gazed at the diamond and crystal necklace, a set of interlocking geometric shapes that resembled snowflakes from one direction and stylized dancers from another. It was a fascinating, eye-bending creation, and she loved it, but at the moment, she didn't have much faith in it. "These are the richest people in the world, Dawn."

"Rich they may be, Star, but their fathers are not jewelers, and even if those fathers *were* jewelers, they wouldn't have the skill of yours." She fastened the necklace around Starbride's neck and then secured the matching diamond earrings.

Starbride touched the necklace and picked up a mirror so she could admire the glittering pinpoints of light. "You're right. They don't have his skill, but people from Marienne have commissioned pieces from him in the past."

"He wouldn't give them the same quality he'd give his daughter. Remember that when they're panting over it, and be smug."

Starbride had pictured a horde, but the sheer number of people swarming the Courtiers Ball exceeded her imagination. She'd glimpsed the ballroom on one of her forays and remembered it as cavernous. The glittering throng made it seem like a closet.

She heard multiple strains of music but couldn't spot the players. The people nearest to the doors stood and talked to one another, and beyond them was a hint of movement that suggested pockets of dancing. Giant chandeliers sparkled overhead, and four sets of doors on the other side of the room were thrown open to let the heat onto the balcony beyond. It was a huge palette of color, the women in the muted tones the queen favored, and the men in the bolder, grander jewel tones that put Starbride in mind of an enormous flock of birds.

With a deep breath, she melted into the crowd. She couldn't help but be jostled, and those responsible would glance at her with apologies on their lips that turned into varying expressions of surprise as they focused on her. Whether their surveys were polite, curious, or rude, she quickly grew tired of it, even the covetous glances at her jewelry.

A quiet corner presented itself, though it wasn't where she expected. A few people strolled on the outdoor balcony that ran the length of the ballroom, making long shadows in the light pouring from the room. Starbride moved away from the doors to watch the dim lights winking from Marienne below.

"You look familiar." The voice behind her eased her loneliness before she even turned.

In the light of the doorway, Katya's cobalt blue coat made her blue eyes shine. Silver buttons began at her right shoulder and curved nearly to the center of her chest before continuing to her waist. The coat fit tightly to her trim upper body and then hung loose and open to mid-thigh. Silver embroidery wound around her standing collar and then wandered to the buttons, descending in a vine-like pattern, with echoes of the same pattern at the hem and cuffs. Her tight white trousers gleamed between the blue coat and the black boots, and as she stepped closer, her sapphire earrings winked in the softened light, as did the slender sapphire and silver diadem that encircled her forehead, the ends of it lost in her loosely pinned-up hair. Starbride was tempted to ask her if she was a dream.

Katya tapped her chin. "Yes, very familiar. Are you a new meringue at this court?"

"You're much mistaken, Highness." Starbride held her arms out. "According to my mother, I am a frothy cup of cinnamon tea, heavy on the cream."

"Well, in your mother's defense, that would be a good cup of tea."

Starbride fought to hide a smile. The dusty girl in the hallway seemed miles away from this dazzling creature. "Thank you, Highness. I'll write her and tell her Your Highness said so." She turned back to the night.

Katya leaned on the parapet beside her and looked toward the lights of the city and the blackness of the countryside beyond. "You're not going to forgive me for not admitting who I am right away, are you?"

"I thought I'd found a friend." The words were out before she could stop them, and she had to face Katya's stare.

"What makes you think you haven't?"

Starbride's irritation vanished. "Thank you," she waited a heartbeat, "Highness."

The moment stretched, the music from the ball echoing behind them. Starbride's neck itched under the gaze of who knew how many watching eyeballs. With Katya on the balcony, there had to be quite a crowd.

"What's keeping your hair up?" Katya asked.

"A million pins and my maid's willpower."

"Not those little butterfly clips?"

"Those are just decorations."

"The sugar for your tea? I must meet your mother someday."

"She'd dress you like a blueberry pie."

Katya sputtered a laugh and turned it into a loud cough.

So, they *were* being watched. "How many guards will attack me if I thump you on the back?"

"About a half dozen." Her eyes widened as she glanced at Starbride again. "Oh, look there."

"What? Where?"

Katya reached toward Starbride's face with all the speed of a tortoise, and she had a sudden thought about Katya's reputation, but she couldn't move away. The slowness of the movement, as if Katya sought to creep up on a hare, caught her. It said, "I'm giving you a million chances to flee." At last, Katya's fingers brushed Starbride's jaw and slipped past to tug lightly at her hair.

"You have an escapee." A butterfly clip lay in Katya's palm.

"My hair doesn't like being restrained." Starbride felt her cheeks warm as she stared at the clip. She closed Katya's fingers over it, noticing for the first time the signet ring on Katya's left forefinger, a hawk clutching a rose. "Keep it. A few butterflies would look wonderful in your hair."

"I almost never wear anything in it, except when forced by my mother."

"We have something in common."

"Probably more than you think." She glanced over her shoulder. "I'm supposed to be boring you with stories about hunting."

"Is that what everyone expects?"

"Yes."

"Don't you enjoy hunting?"

"I must." It was almost a whisper. "Shall we dance?"

"Oh, um." Starbride thought of Katya's arms around her and was glad of the shadows that could hide a blush. "We could, but it's so crowded in there."

"We could dance out here."

"I can barely hear the music."

"Don't know how to dance?"

Starbride nearly stomped her foot. "Of course I do! I'm pretty good at it."

"I didn't mean to suggest otherwise. I'm excellent at it, if it's your toes you're worried about."

"I suppose you had to learn from an early age."

"It's the law."

Starbride tsked. "It's not."

"You're right. I don't want to go back into that crowd, either." Katya stared into the night but didn't appear to see it, seeming lost all of a sudden. Or trapped.

"Are you all right?"

"I'm just a little worried. I have a, um, sick friend."

"Oh." Starbride curled her fingers under to keep from patting Katya's arm. "I'm sorry. Can't you leave early and go see him? Her?"

"No, no, he doesn't want people to know he's sick. Someone might try to take…advantage of the situation. Politically."

"Ah. And if someone saw you leaving before the ball is over…?"

"They'd talk about it, or worse yet, follow me."

Starbride's heart went out to Katya even as the suspicious part of her nature warned her to be careful of tricks. Katya radiated sincerity, but Starbride could tell from the slight pauses that she was leaving something out. Still, if the sick friend was a secret, Katya would have to be careful what she told anyone, Starbride included. "I'm very sorry. That's terrible, to know something and yet be unable to do anything about it. I could distract everyone, and you could slip away."

Katya turned, pleased surprise lighting her face. "How?"

"I could…light a tapestry on fire!"

Katya gave another of those bursts of laughter that she turned into a cough, and Starbride had to wonder who she was hiding her mirth from.

"Or I could accept your offer to dance and help you waste some time."

"That would be wonderful, but I have to warn you about—"

"Highness?" a voice behind them asked.

Katya's face smoothed to blankness so quickly it sent a trill of alarm along Starbride's spine. They both turned toward the doors. "Yes, Lady Hilda?" Katya said.

Lady Hilda's red hair was so artfully arranged on top of her head that Starbride's mother would have wept in envy. She wore the same sort of frothy creation as all the women, but it floated around her, hugging her curves here, draping there, highlighting the good, and hiding the not-so-good. She didn't look at all like a cupcake. The neck of her gown plunged to the point of indecency, pointing past her breasts and showing off what had to be half of them. Starbride wondered how she kept them from tumbling out.

Lady Hilda didn't spare Starbride a glance. She played with the flounces of her dress, a blue that matched Katya's coat, and her eyes held a promise of lust that would have been a joke had she not been so good-looking. Her stance and expression said she had the experience to back up any offer her eyes made.

Starbride sneaked a look at Katya and saw only bored resignation, an expression that caused satisfaction to well in her, almost to the point where she beamed. Princess Katyarianna Nar Umbriel had come to the balcony to speak with Starbride, despite the hideous dress and without even a whisper of promised sex. This woman bored Katya, even for all her obvious physical charms.

"Why don't you come back inside?" Lady Hilda said. "Your father is looking for you."

Katya glanced at Starbride, but her face held little emotion. With a sigh that seemed to come from her soul, she followed Lady Hilda inside, and the crowd swallowed them both.

Starbride watched them go, her confusion rising. Why didn't Katya tell Lady Hilda to go away? Why the expression change, and what about that comment about boring her with hunting stories? Was it all to hide the sick friend?

Starbride watched the night again and tried to figure out this woman who claimed to be her friend, but she needed more information in order to form conclusions. She turned back to the ball, looking for but not seeing Katya as she waded toward the exit. On a raised dais at one end of the hall, she spotted two crowned figures: a broad-shouldered, dark-haired man and a petite blond woman, both over forty. It had to be the king and queen, and it struck Starbride after a moment that these were Katya's parents. Several people stood with them, including a younger woman with a circlet sitting in her startlingly pale hair. So many fair-haired people packed into one place. Starbride wondered if they ever confused one another but then reprimanded herself for the mean thought. There was no need to blame the blonds for a horrid end to the evening. Lady Hilda was a redhead, after all.

Starbride lost sight of the royals as the crowd engulfed her again. She sidestepped the grab of a red-eyed young man, his cheeks bright with drink. "Come, dance!" he yelled, not quite focusing on her.

"Sorry." Starbride twisted out of the way. He moved on, clutching at every woman he met.

When she gained the hallway, Starbride paused. It was still early, and she didn't feel tired; the library would be nice and free at that hour. She ducked into an alcove and pulled a folded map from the front of her dress. When she made it to the huge library doors without losing her way, she nearly crowed in victory.

Inside the shadowy room, time seemed to speed past. Before she knew it, she had to reread a paragraph about trading statutes several times before she realized she couldn't absorb any more knowledge. She glanced at the stub of a candle that had been much taller when she'd begun. It had to be near dawn. A jaw-cracking yawn overtook her. She stacked her books and stepped outside the doors.

Map ready, she began the shortcut near the stables that led to her room. Footsteps echoed down the hallway, and Starbride froze in fear at being caught out so early in the morning, though she couldn't say why.

Perhaps it was because she didn't exactly have permission to use the library, though Katya's presence the first time made it seem like she did. She didn't even know if a person *needed* permission. She ducked down another hallway and hid behind a statue.

Katya passed by a few moments later, wearing hunting leather and a rapier again. A slightly older woman with a bow slung over one shoulder followed her, and an enormous man in a red robe walked beside her, a large mace swinging from his belt. Behind them and also armed with a bow was the same pale-haired young woman Starbride had seen speaking with the king and queen.

It *had* to be dawn if Katya was going hunting. She didn't look happy, though. Her expression mirrored neither the gentle jokester Starbride had seen nor the bored royal she'd turned on Lady Hilda. She looked grim, as if forced to hunt, an activity she was reputed to love. Maybe she was using the hunting as a disguise to sneak off and see her sick friend.

Starbride realized how hard it must be, how much of a façade someone would have to adopt when everyone wanted a piece of her. Even without the sick friend, maybe Katya always used her huntress reputation to get away from court. Maybe she went into the forest with these few friends to escape so many grasping hands, like Lady Hilda's.

Her heart full of pity for Katya and anger at the court, Starbride followed them, only stopping when she'd nearly reached the stables. She wasn't dressed for riding, didn't even own anything for it at the moment. She supposed she could grab a saddle blanket, hike up her skirt, and follow without a saddle. Tempting, but she hadn't ridden bareback for years. She started for her room instead, wanting to talk it over with Dawnmother, wanting to do something nice for Katya, something without strings attached.

Dawnmother slumped in a chair, an embroidery hoop in her lap, with her eyes closed, and her mouth hanging open in a soft snore. Starbride touched her shoulder.

With a little jump, she sat up, blinking rapidly. "What time is it?"

"Dawn or thereabouts."

"Well, you must have had a good time."

Starbride took the embroidery hoop and glanced at the fabric inside. "What's this you're making?"

"A little pillow for you to sit on. A lot of the other courtiers and nobles have them. I tried to make the pattern a little like your necklace. It'll look better once I sew some beads on."

"Where did you get this material?"

"Out of a closet."

"You stole a pillowcase?"

"And a pillow. They have many. They won't miss one."

"You hope. What happens if one of those tyrannical housekeepers beats down our door?"

"Then I will throw myself in his or her path while you make your escape." She yawned, making Starbride yawn in turn. "Let's go to bed. We can talk later."

Starbride nodded, too tired to argue, and after Dawnmother helped her undress, she slipped under the covers of her narrow bed. Dawnmother lay down on her pallet.

"Have you learned anything about the rest of the town?" Starbride asked after Dawnmother put out the candle.

"A little. Why?"

"I need to purchase something, a gift."

"I see." Starbride heard the curiosity in the words, but she didn't elaborate, not yet. Instead, she drifted to sleep.

CHAPTER FIVE: KATYA

When they reached the first crossroads, Katya's party met Crowe and Pennynail, both men astride their horses. Crowe's wrinkled face was a study in impatience. Katya saluted them and pointed to Pennynail's Laughing Jack mask with its perpetual grin. "Why don't you take a lesson from him, Crowe? He's always happy to see us." Crowe rolled his eyes, and Katya had to admit the joke was rather flat. She'd only said it to try to cheer herself up.

Averie reined in her horse. "Meet you at the regular rendezvous?"

"Before nightfall." Katya winked in another attempt at lightness she didn't feel. "Catch us something nice." At least Averie had the decency to smile.

"Where is it we're going, Crowe?" Katya asked when they were on the move again.

He gave her a long glance. "It's the best I could get from the Shadow, Katya."

"I understand that."

"The courtier from the hallway was dead before we reached my study."

"I know."

"It's a tavern in Longside. It could be where the Shadow meets his contacts."

Katya wanted to say, "It could be where he meets his doxy, or where he likes to drink, or where his father is from," but she kept her mouth shut. This trip was a dead end; she felt it in her bones, but she took a deep breath and tried a more diplomatic route. "The courtier's pyramid proves that his group has a pyradisté, someone who knows we can pry their secrets from them. If the Shadow is part of that group, they won't use the same place to meet after one of them has been caught." When Crowe opened his mouth again, she raised a hand. "I know. It's all we have, which is why we're going."

Crowe turned to Maia. "What did the other courtiers have to say about our dead mystery man?"

"I couldn't find anyone who knew him. Everyone was gossiping about him, but no one knew who he was."

"People do not just *appear* in the palace!" Crowe snapped.

"Sure they do," Brutal said. "Someone stashes a courtier's clothes for him; he comes in wearing servant's livery and then changes. Instant courtier. He bides his time, waits for the king, and then *bam!*" He punched the air, and the enormous draft horse underneath him nickered and tossed its head.

Katya shook her head. "It's not like my father is some weakling. He could have disarmed that man."

Crowe gave her an incredulous look.

Katya rolled her eyes. "I'm not just saying that because I love him. I'm not playing my-father-could-defeat-your-father. It's the truth."

"And your father was escorted by pyradistés," Brutal said.

Maia nodded eagerly. "Right! Plus, the king is always surrounded by nobles; the courtiers complain that they can't get a word in edgewise."

Pennynail clapped his gloved hands. When they turned to look, he took a long, thin knife from his belt and wiggled it. He stabbed the air and then sheathed the knife in one quick, blurred motion.

"Yes," Crowe said, "just the point I was about to make. If the assailant is quick enough, all the strength in the world won't matter. The courtier could have waited until the king passed and then darted in behind him."

"One of the pyradistés would have sensed the pyramid. *You* would have sensed it, Crowe," Katya said. "It was active, after all."

"But we would *not* have known which person wielded it. We would've had to surround the king and whisk him away, calling for the guards. Someone would have been hurt. It was all too close."

Katya could still feel the courtier's arm in her grasp. If she had been quicker, she could have grabbed the pyramid, and they'd have a living man to question. She felt a touch on her shoulder and looked up into Crowe's gray eyes.

"Stop feeling guilty," he whispered. "I demand to keep all the self-recrimination for myself."

"Let's see what your tavern holds."

"The courtier recognized you, coz," Maia said. "Didn't you say that?"

"So?"

"Well, maybe you shouldn't come to the tavern, then. You can wait outside with Pennynail."

"He recognized me in the palace, in palace clothing. A little dirt, a lack of insignia, and they won't see a princess because they don't expect to see one."

"You can't know that, coz, even after this long."

"All right, then. I'm in charge, and I don't want to wait outside. If anyone asks, I'll say you're the princess."

"I could play princess." Maia scrunched her face as if confronted with a horrible smell. "Crowe, Brutal, kill that man, he's in my way."

"Rubbish!" Katya said. "If a man was in my way, I'd kill him myself."

"Thank the spirits we raised you right," Crowe mumbled.

They fell to good-natured bickering, and in the wake of it, Katya relaxed a fraction. She allowed herself to think of Starbride standing in the soft light of the ballroom balcony. Alone, Starbride still hadn't pleaded her case, whatever her case might be. She had expressed sadness for Katya's *sick friend*, and her feelings had seemed so genuine, so without guile. Katya had wanted to tell her the truth, and that desire was more perilous than any machination of Lady Hilda's.

Still, she smiled as she touched the spot on her clothes under which her pyramid necklace rested. It had a companion today, a butterfly hairclip threaded through the chain. She'd have to think of something better to do with it.

They reached Longside at midday, and it proved even smaller than Katya suspected. It was only a few acres of fields with a cluster of buildings in the center. Pennynail left them early, staying inside the forest, and Katya brought her horse into line with Brutal and Maia. Crowe took the rear so no one could be sure who led the small group. The largest building bore a sign of a foaming mug, and eight horses had been hitched out front. Judging by the noise inside, it was a busy afternoon in the small community. "Good place to start," Katya said.

Brutal took a deep breath. "There's a sense of chaos to it."

"Good for a fight?" Maia asked.

"Without a doubt." Katya dismounted and stretched. "No one as large as Brutal can walk into a small town without stepping on someone's toes."

Crowe snorted from behind them. "Local bullies, young bravos, someone *always* has to test his luck."

Brutal opened the door. "Suits me fine. Everyone involved gets closer to enlightenment."

Wooden poles held open long horizontal shutters along the sides of the tavern. Specks of sawdust, stirred up from the floor by so many feet, floated through the bright sunshine. The tables were small and square and sat scattered inside with no discernible order. Katya waved in front of her face, but it didn't do much to dispel the smell of wood and beer.

Dusty farmers in homespun occupied most of the seats, spending the hottest hours of the day out of the sun. Among them Katya noticed the hardier leather of a blacksmith and a few more well-dressed patrons, tradespeople or travelers. Longside was a busy little crossroads, even if the only people who lived there were farmers and their families, plus the few who sold to them. Katya's party took one of two unoccupied tables, a rickety square near the short bar at the back that seemed only for keg storage. Barmaids and servers hustled in and out of the doorway next to it, their pounding steps just audible above the drone of conversation and the occasional burst of raucous laughter.

Some of the burlier farmers nudged their companions, grinned, and gave Brutal challenging looks. "Won't be long now." Katya gestured at the burly farmers with her chin. "Watch for anyone familiar."

Crowe ordered a round of the local brew, nothing fancy that would give away expensive tastes. A few of the patrons glanced at Katya's party out of the corners of their eyes. These Katya made note of along with those who didn't look at all, especially the travelers.

Ten minutes after they sat down, a big farmer stood from an entire *table* of big farmers. He sauntered to Katya's table, his eyes filled with the prospect of a good-natured fight.

"Here we go," Katya mumbled.

Brutal wiped his mouth on the sleeve of his robe, set his mug down, and turned.

The farmer cracked his knuckles. "You're a big man," he said, as if that explained everything that was about to happen. "Been in many fights?"

They always underestimated his age. Even at nineteen, the baby face took off a few years. "Some, brother. It is only through combat that one may understand the universe."

"Ah," the farmer said, "a fightin' monk!"

Brutal stood, his face calm if a bit expectant. This was his meat and milk, after all. Katya scooted her chair back, the better to get out of the way in a hurry. Across from her, Maia and Crowe did the same.

The farmer started to say something else, and Brutal frowned. "The posturing that comes before a fight interrupts the purity of the fight itself, brother."

"Is that so?"

Brutal punched him, one hard smack. He didn't put his shoulder into it, but a man his size didn't need to give it all he had. The bar erupted in cheers as the farmer staggered and dropped to one knee. To his credit, he rushed up with a vengeance and wrapped his arms around Brutal. The farmer launched Brutal backward to crash into the table. Katya jumped, dumping her chair over. The farmer's buddies shouted and hit the air, and it was a short step before they were hitting each other. As the bar dissolved into total chaos, Katya circled around toward Crowe and Maia.

"Not so fast!" someone shouted behind her. Katya turned just as one of the female farmers punched her in the gut.

The air left Katya's lungs in a rush as pain blossomed in her stomach. She stared up into the woman's gleeful face.

"You can't just *leave* in the middle of a punch-up!" the woman cried.

Katya coughed and straightened. "Very well." Katya hit her square in the mouth, and when she reeled, Katya grabbed the back of her homespun shirt and launched her into the crowd. She landed on several patrons and started another pocket of fighting. More vigilant this time, Katya started through the rumble again.

A barmaid had Maia around the waist and swung her around. Maia, never a great one for brawling, fumbled for her belt knife. Katya crouched and waited for Maia's legs to pass overhead before she kicked the barmaid in the back of the knees. She crumpled and dumped Maia on the floor. Katya shoved the woman into another fight.

A bleary-eyed man stumbled out of the press. He launched haymaker swings at random. Katya ducked and then rolled out of the way as he tumbled forward, the remains of a chair clinging to his shoulders. Crowe threw the rest of the chair away and signaled for Katya to follow him. They picked up Maia and headed for the door.

When they reached the bright afternoon sunshine, Katya studied the other patrons who'd made a run for it. None of them wore farmers' homespun. They talked in small groups and gestured at the fight raging inside the tavern. A few of them shook their heads and pointed to their disheveled clothing, complaining. One traveler stood apart, and as Katya looked him over, he glanced up, and their eyes met. His widened; he recognized her, and as he took off running, Katya could only think that Maia had been right.

Maia took a step in pursuit, but Katya grabbed her arm. "No," she whispered. "Right now, he's the suspicious one, not us."

One of the other watchers pointed at the fleeing man. "What do you suppose he's so frightened of?"

"Must've had a big tab," Katya drawled.

Crowe clapped her on the shoulder. "Or maybe he took a few liberties with a barmaid on his way out!"

The watchers catcalled to the fleeing man as he cleared the line of buildings in the small town square. "Pennynail will nab him," Katya said in Maia's ear.

Maia nodded and rubbed her side. "That barmaid hurt my ribs."

Crowe snorted. "You'll live."

Maia gave him an angry glance and then stared down at her boots. Katya patted her shoulder. "Always the spirit of tactfulness, Crowe. If it still hurts in an hour, Maia, let me know."

One of the tradeswomen wandered close to Katya's group. "Your big friend is having a time of it."

"Watch yourself," Katya answered, "he'll probably be thrown from the door any minute now!"

They laughed, and true to Katya's prophecy, Brutal was ejected from the door by a great many people. They cheered each other, cheered Brutal, and then went back into the tavern as if nothing had happened. All the travelers and a few of the tradespeople headed inside; the rest wandered toward the other buildings.

Brutal pushed to his feet, his eye blackened and his nose bloody. He grinned from ear to ear. "Glorious."

"Lucky for you," Katya said, "it bore fruit."

She nodded toward the end of the square. They hesitated a moment longer and engaged in a mock debate about whether or not to go back into the tavern.

"I've had enough fun for the day," Crowe declared at last. Brutal put up a protest, half-fake, Katya decided, before he relented, and they rode for the trees.

Maia handed him a handkerchief. "Are you sure you're all right, Brutal?"

"I saw a bit more of the universe, a small sampling of... everything."

"What was it like?"

Katya watched him for the answer, equally curious.

Brutal stared at nothing for a moment. "We're all objects, constantly colliding. In the fight, our souls come closer to perfect understanding of one another. I am the farmer, and he is me. I know what it is to plant his crops, till his fields, and love his family."

"His family?" Maia asked. A blush darkened her fair cheeks, but she kept her head up.

"Yes."

"If we fought, would you understand me better?"

He looked away with a frown. "If you want to seek enlightenment via my chapterhouse, someone else will have to put you on the path."

Maia stared down at her saddle. When she smiled and blushed again, Katya knew they'd both come to the same conclusion. Brutal couldn't help Maia to enlightenment because he couldn't bear to strike her.

They collected a riderless horse in the middle of a field, and just inside the tree line, they found the man who'd fled the tavern. Pennynail had tied his arms and legs with leather cords and tied a handkerchief around his mouth. He touched the eyeholes of his mask and then tapped his temple.

"Good catch." Katya knelt and stared into the bound man's eyes. "Should we try the old-fashioned way first or go straight to the pyramid?"

"Look at his face," Crowe said. "Take that handkerchief from his mouth and he'll scream to the heavens."

"Pyramid it is."

"But what if he's not involved?" Maia said.

Crowe gave her a black look. "There is no risk of my damaging him, young lady. I've been using pyramids for quite some time." He drew one from his coat; the clear sides of it glinted in the light that penetrated the forest canopy.

The bound man shook his head rapidly as Pennynail hauled him to his knees. Crowe pressed the base of the pyramid to his forehead, and his eyes rolled back just as Crowe's slipped shut. Katya studied the captive's clothing. His dark green shirt and black coat were simple but finely made; his coat even had a hint of embroidery around the neck. A bit of lace poked from his shirt cuffs, and his black trousers were a little tight for a farmer or traveler. They were city clothes, too good for traveling a great distance unless he rode with a carriage, and she'd seen no carriages in Longside. Besides, his clothes were not quite good enough for someone who rode *inside* a carriage, unless he was a servant or footman.

"Pennynail," Katya said, "watch the town. If he's a servant, his master or mistress might be searching for him or making a run for it." She pointed at Maia. "You, too. If anyone runs, he pursues, and you come tell us."

Maia took off after Pennynail. After a few minutes of silence, Crowe straightened. "Smuggling."

Katya blinked. "What?"

"He did recognize you. He's a footman for Baron Sumpter, but he's a smuggler, not a traitor. He was in Longside to buy Bronian wine, but his contact never arrived."

"Bronian wine?" Brutal asked. "The stuff that eats holes in your brain?"

"Hence the need to smuggle," Crowe said.

"Does the baron know?" Katya asked.

"Not from what I gathered. This man smuggles the wine in order to line his own pockets."

"Hardly worth our time."

"But a crime nonetheless. I'll turn him over to the baron. It's likely that Sumpter will be so embarrassed he'll uncover the entire operation for me."

"And when the baron asks how you caught his footman?"

"Having a reputation as the king's personal sneak is not always a liability. No one questions how I know things anymore, and I don't bother to explain. It furthers the notion that I know everything."

"Might as well paint a target on your back," Brutal said.

"I've had one for years."

"Well." Katya rubbed her hands together and fought disappointment. "Let's collect the others. We're done here."

On the way back to Marienne, Katya mourned the day's trip. At least Brutal got a good fight out of it, but they were no closer to finding their conspirators. She moved her horse close to Crowe's. "Are you certain the dead courtier's pyramid would have killed my father?"

"It killed the courtier, didn't it?"

"It seems so strange. That courtier said we were monsters. He knew something about the Aspect. Wouldn't he want to expose us rather than kill us?"

"Perhaps he didn't care about exposure, just about ridding the world of King Einrich and the rest of your family."

"Assassinate us rather than overthrow us?"

"Maybe he thought killing would be easier than exposing. To bring on the Aspect, a pyramid would've had to overcome the power of Einrich's necklace. That would have been difficult to make."

"I know. It's just so *frustrating* trying to stay ahead of these people."

"Tell me about it."

"How can they make better pyramids than you? You're the best pyradisté there is."

"But not the best there ever was. You should have seen…"

"Who?" But she knew who he meant, the same person he always meant: Roland. "The traitor's pyramid was shoddy work, beneath you."

"An ugly tool for an ugly deed."

Katya thought on that and rode in silence.

They rendezvoused with Averie late in the afternoon. She had a brace of geese and a small pig waiting for them. Katya made a face as Averie slung both across her horse, the birds in front of the saddle, the pig behind.

"Lovely," Katya said.

Averie tsked. "My skills are unappreciated in my time."

"Forgive me, jewel of my heart. What I meant to say was that poets will sing your praises until the flame of time has burned to an ember."

"I'd settle for a thank-you."

"I'm royalty. We don't thank anyone."

Along with Maia, Averie, and Brutal, Katya bade Crowe and Pennynail farewell. The two started along their secret path through the city, and Katya and her party wound through Marienne to the royal stables.

It was close to sundown when Katya and Averie reached their apartment. Katya stretched behind closed doors, looking forward to a hot bath and then a long think. The usual stack of flowers and gifts from admirers awaited her, but a single box caught her attention. Deep red, with Allusian letters painted on the lid, it stood out like a beacon. Katya dug it out of the pile. There was no card or note, just a box of meringues when she opened the lid.

"Anything interesting?" Averie asked.

"Perhaps."

"Oh yes? I'll see to your bath. Do you want an early night?"

"No," Katya bit into one of the meringues and let the sugary confection dissolve on her tongue. "I'm in the mood for a bit of reading. After the bath, I think I'll visit the library."

CHAPTER SIX: STARBRIDE

Starbride was well into her second stack of books; her mother would have been appalled. Dawnmother had heard of at least two picnics, three riding parties, countless tea room visits, and who knew how many card and lawn games going on that day, but Starbride hadn't budged from the library. Three blue-robed knowledge monks were her only company, and they didn't talk much. Throughout the day, Starbride had learned to ignore their quiet movements, the swish of their robes, the thump of a book being set on a table, or a quiet cough.

She made note of a river trade law on her scroll, a law that could help keep the Farradain merchant families in Newhope from price-fixing. She had a contact she could send such things to, a friend of the family who tried to practice Farradain law but didn't have all the tools. Well, she'd put a stop to that.

She closed one book, shifted it to the side, and searched the pile of texts beside her. She pulled out another and scanned the first few pages. The smell of ink and paper was so familiar to her, but the language of the Farradains reminded her that she was far from home.

Without thinking, she touched her necklace and ran her fingers over the seven starbursts in yellow enamel and the delicate golden wire that ran between them. Her father had shaped the wire to form the character "bride" if she wore it one way and "lucky" if she wore it the other way around, which she did constantly. It was her favorite, made in her childhood with links added as she grew. The pages in front of her grew hazy as she thought of it.

"Why 'lucky,' Papa?" she'd asked.

Seated at his worktable with her in his lap, he'd bent the sparkling gold wire with ease. "It's my fondest hope for you, little Star, what *I* would have named you." He'd chuckled. "But your mother's will is as strong as an ox."

Starbride had frowned with childish stubbornness. "I hate my name. I'll never get married!"

His lips had smacked against her temple in a noisy kiss. "You'll fall in love and change your mind one day." He'd picked up one of the starburst links and held it beside the twisted wire. "This necklace will be there to remind you that you are both mine and your mother's child. And that Papa loves you, my lucky Star."

In the library in Farraday, Starbride shook her head. The creation of her necklace had taken place several hundred miles away and over ten years in the past. There was no time to be homesick. She had a job to do.

She barely noticed when someone took a seat beside her. It made sense. The huge library was nearly empty, but she'd chosen a spot near two wall sconces and a candelabrum, so the light was good. A blue sleeve entered her vision near her book, and five slender fingers drummed softly. Starbride glanced at the signet ring on the forefinger, a hawk clutching a rose. She didn't look up, smiling to herself instead.

"Trade law," Katya said. "Riveting." She plucked the sleeve of Starbride's gown. "Hmm, would your mother be thinking mint or limes with this?"

Starbride put down her pencil. "Mint. She's not a big fan of fruit." Katya wore the same loose bun that let her hair frame her face and the same dark blue coat she seemed to prefer, paired with dark trousers, except this coat had far less embroidery than her ball coat. When she glanced near Katya's collar, though, Starbride couldn't contain a laugh. Her butterfly hairclip perched on the fabric with the aid of a straight pin.

"You like my new jewelry?" Katya asked.

"It doesn't seem your style."

"Being royalty carries the luxury of choice when it comes to style."

"Of course it does, Highness." Starbride picked up her pencil again and twirled it in her fingers.

"Ah, we're back to that."

"What did your…admirers think of your pin?"

"It's going to be all the rage." Katya stuck her long legs out and crossed her knee-high boots at the ankle. "I expect to see several of the courtiers in full butterfly costumes by the next ball."

Starbride chuckled, and across the room, one of the monks gave her a dirty look that he hadn't bothered, or dared, to give Katya. "I'd enjoy seeing that, especially on Lady Hilda."

Katya prodded Starbride's slipper with her boot. "Jealous?"

Starbride sniffed and turned back to her book. "Absolutely not."

"Of course. I didn't really think so."

"So glad to hear it."

"Anyway, Lady Hilda is not a courtier."

"What is she?"

"A pain in the ass."

Starbride had to clap a hand over her mouth. This time, all three monks gave her dirty looks. She shifted her chair and leaned close. "Isn't everyone a pain in the ass sometimes?"

"Of course, but courtiers are pains in the ass who are at least paying to be here."

"Nobles don't have to pay?" Starbride's jaw dropped as she thought of the exorbitant price her family paid to keep her at Marienne.

"Not directly. Nobles are landowners. Their 'rent' is taken out of the taxes they collect."

"Then why do the nobles stay here? If they're landowners, don't they have homes elsewhere?"

"Undoubtedly, but court is the place to be. It's so *boring* in the provinces." Her head lolled to the side as if the mere act of talking about living outside Marienne put her to sleep.

Starbride grinned. "A place without courtiers and nobles? Sounds delightful."

"Would you like to get out of here?"

"What? Out of the palace?"

"Too late in the day for that, I'm afraid. No, out of *here*." She nodded toward the pack of monks, who still gave Starbride the occasional angry glance.

"My concentration *is* broken."

Katya put a hand over her heart. "My apologies, Miss Meringue."

Starbride secured her scroll and pencil inside one of her voluminous sleeves and narrowed her eyes as they stood. "You're not going to try to seduce me, are you?"

Katya's mouth slipped open before she blinked several times, and Starbride fancied she saw a slight blush in the royal cheeks. Katya gestured at the mint-colored dress. "In all that, I wouldn't know where to start."

"Where are we going?" Starbride asked. "One of the many activities for aspiring social climbers?"

"Funny you should mention climbing."

"I don't understand."

"Follow me."

Starbride followed, spurred on by Katya's infectious grin. Katya led her to the upper levels of the palace, through long winding hallways and narrow stairways. They passed many bowing servants, but every time they heard chatter from down the hall, Katya guided her into another passage. "Are you trying to avoid someone in particular?" Starbride asked.

"Any group of courtiers would stick to us like leeches."

"Ugh. How do you know who the voices belong to?"

"Well, servants don't linger in the halls to stand around or gossip. They do that behind closed doors so they won't be caught, same with guardsmen. That leaves courtiers. Nobles don't linger in the hallways unless they're searching for royalty."

"Like Lady Hilda might be looking for you." Starbride sniffed as she said it, but inside, she wanted Katya to call Lady Hilda another foul name.

"Come on. We're nearly there."

They ascended to a short hallway with no rooms leading off it and only a tapestry to mark the end. No servants rushed through the area; no courtiers loitered in the hall. "Where are we?"

"Near the royal summer apartments. Very few people here at this time of year, thank the spirits."

Starbride gestured to the hanging six-foot tapestry, wondering if that was what she was supposed to be looking at. "Seventh century, if I remember my art history."

Katya scanned the hallway behind them. Starbride did the same and saw no one. When she turned back, Katya was disappearing behind the tapestry. With a wink, she let go of the heavy wall hanging, and it fell as flat as if she'd walked through the wall.

Starbride let her mouth hang open for a moment. At first, she thought of pyramid magic, but she'd never heard of anyone using it to disappear. She waved to dispel the cloud of disturbed dust and touched the rough fabric of the tapestry. The wall was solid behind it. "What in Darkstrong's name?"

And then it hit her. Secret passageways! One of her childhood fantasies come to life! She heaved on the weighty tapestry, but revealed only blank stone behind it.

"Well." She pushed on the cold bricks and tried to turn them. Seconds had passed between when she'd looked away and when Katya had slid behind the tapestry. The mechanism couldn't be that complicated. She slipped behind the tapestry and let it shroud her in darkness; soundlessly, a door in front of her swung open.

On the other side, Katya waited, holding a lantern. "I knew you were smart."

Starbride couldn't help it; she stuck out her tongue. From miles away, she felt her mother die a little. Katya threw her head back and laughed. Like schoolgirls, they ran down the passageway, hand in hand, until they reached a narrow staircase only wide enough for one person at a time.

Katya held the lantern high and started up the stairway. "My brother and I discovered this one while we were playing, years and years ago."

"How many are there?" All thoughts of learning Farradain trade law blew from Starbride's mind as she thought of the enormous palace and all the secrets it could hold.

"Who knows? I've found quite a few."

"Was this one your first?"

"For me, not for my brother."

"How many hours did you spend looking for more after this one?"

"Too many! And quite a few that should have been spent sleeping."

Wan light filtered down the staircase. The top of the passage was guarded by a rusty old gate, not very secret from that side. Unlike the stone door, the gate creaked in the stillness of the evening as they emerged onto an old balcony. The view of the countryside around Marienne made Starbride stop in wonder. The palace lay on the west side, and she'd only seen the view of the east, that of the city. Rolling hills spread to the west, covered with a checkerboard of fields, dotted with the occasional tree. Past the fields wound the Lavine River, and the setting sun turned the waterway into a ribbon of gold. "It's gorgeous."

Katya set her lantern down and leaned on the worn stone railing. "My childhood tutor called it Hanna's Retreat, seventh century, as you pointed out. One of my ancestors used to climb up here to clear her head after dull meetings. It drove her staff mad the way she could walk down a hallway and disappear."

"Your tutor knew about the secret passageways?"

"Only that they exist. He didn't know where, and I didn't tell him the actual location of this one."

"Wise. Your brother may want to use it someday. Does your father ever come up here?"

"No, he retreats to his rooms and hides behind my mother."

"I saw your parents at the Courtiers Ball. Your father didn't seem like a fading flower, and your mother didn't look particularly threatening."

"Well, you have one correct observation and one incorrect. I won't tell you which is which. Thank you for the meringues, by the way. What did the letters on the box say?"

"Dawnmother—she's my maid—painted the words. They say, 'please accept this gift,' more or less. It's traditional for a gift in my homeland. And you're welcome." She laid her chin on one fist and studied the countryside. If she squinted, she imagined she could see far-off Allusia. She shouldn't have left the library. She had so much to do.

"Why were you reading about trade law?"

"How did you know I was thinking about that?"

"You were frowning. Law books always make me frown."

Starbride grinned wryly. "I'm learning trade law to better help my people."

Something in Katya's eyes froze. Her face didn't twitch, but her posture turned to ice. "Is that why you came to the palace?"

Starbride tried to shrug, but something in Katya's gaze stopped her. "It's not why I was sent, but it is why I came."

"Star*bride*. Your mother sent you to marry, or to find a lover, an *influential* lover."

Starbride stiffened, realizing the reason for Katya's frostiness. Katya thought she wanted something from her, just like those vulture courtiers! Part of her bristled at the implication, but she told herself to be calm, forced herself to soften…slightly. With all the grasping courtiers in the palace, Katya couldn't help but be suspicious. "That's what my *mother* wanted," Starbride said slowly, "but it's not the way I think. I came to study law on my own. I sent you the meringues as a friend."

Katya hesitated before she smiled. "I'm sorry. Sometimes…" She let the word hang in the air.

"It's all right. Let's not talk about it."

"That's not fair. I can't get to know you and then ignore what's important to you."

"If I tell you about the problems my people are having and it's in your power to fix them, won't one or both of us feel you have an obligation?"

Katya hung her head. "You're right."

"Then let me study my law books, and we'll talk about different things."

"Now who's seducing whom?"

Starbride waved at the countryside. "Thank you for showing me this. Do you use it often?"

"Court can be tiresome."

"That's why you hunt, isn't it? Speaking of what's important to us."

Katya hesitated a moment before she nodded.

"I saw you this morning, going toward the stables."

Katya blinked and then stared. "You're full of surprises."

"I wasn't spying! I was coming back from the library, and I just happened to see you, but you didn't look happy. Did you see your sick friend?"

Katya nodded, but her face turned guarded again.

Curiosity burned in Starbride, but she kept it in check. After all, perhaps the friend had gotten worse or died, and it was too painful to speak about. "I wish I had a fast horse sometimes."

"You like to ride?"

Starbride tsked and wished she had her long hair loose so she could throw it over one shoulder. "My people are born in the saddle."

"I hope that's not literal."

Starbride ignored that. "I love to ride. Unfortunately, these clothes weren't built for it. Now, my old clothes..." She trailed away, shaking her head.

"Traditional?"

"Traditional background but trendy."

"I wouldn't believe otherwise."

"Does flirting come natural to you?"

"Not with everyone."

Starbride decided to try another prod. "Lady Hilda?"

Katya's mouth twisted to the side. "She just keeps coming up in the conversation."

"Has she ever been up here?"

"No, and you must admit that your questions are starting to sound a lot like those of a jealous woman."

"Mere curiosity."

"I tolerate Lady Hilda because people expect me to."

"Like how people expect you to like hunting."

"You sound like you're trying to unravel a mystery. I never said I didn't like hunting."

"You never said you did."

"And?"

Starbride shrugged. "It sounds like neither of us can ever be completely honest about what we want to anyone but ourselves." She stared into the distance as the sun disappeared over the horizon, leaving a residue of light at the edge of the world. With another sigh, she shook off the melancholy that threatened to settle on her shoulders. "How much do you have in common with Lady Hilda?"

"I should introduce you," Katya said in her drawl. "You're more interested in her than I am."

Starbride wanted to continue the light chatter, but homesickness wouldn't be banished by the wave of a hand. "I'm just trying to understand this place. It's so different from where I grew up, and I haven't exactly… fit in."

She felt Katya shift. "Has someone been inappropriate with you?"

If she moved a little to her left, Starbride could lean her head against Katya's shoulder. As much as she wanted the comfort, she shook her head. "If you're asking if anyone's been mean to me, not really. No one's been anything to me."

Katya turned her with a gentle pressure. "I'm sorry. Even if you didn't come for a good time, it's terrible to be alone."

"You're here."

The bells from the chapterhouses in Marienne tolled with the setting sun. Katya's head hung again, and it seemed as if all the life went out of her.

"What's wrong?" Starbride asked.

"I have to go. I haven't seen my parents today."

Starbride nodded even as disappointment made her smile slip. "Ah, well. Maybe someday you'll introduce me, and we can compare mothers."

Katya cocked her head, and Starbride realized how intimate a relationship they'd have to have in order for Katya to introduce Queen Catirin as her *mother* instead of as the queen. Of course, friends could be as intimate as lovers. Katya's face softened as if Starbride had bestowed a great compliment upon her. "Maybe someday I will."

As she descended the stairs, Starbride tried to sort her feelings into an orderly row. The library waited, but all of a sudden, the books seemed deadly dull, and she wished all the harder for a fast horse and someone to ride with. Starbride nearly laughed out loud at the thought of asking Lady Hilda to come and then pushing her into the first deep pit that presented itself.

They walked toward the library in silence, as if they'd already said good evening. Starbride couldn't bring herself to ask when they'd see one another again. With Katya's schedule, it seemed wise to assume that she'd turn up when she could. Starbride told herself it didn't matter. She had *work* to do.

"You know your way from here?" Katya asked.

"Dawnmother and I made a map."

"Smarter and smarter. I hope you know how much I don't want to go."

A blush burned in Starbride's cheeks, but she kept her expression amused. "Even a princess must answer to a king and queen."

"True, and it *will* take some time."

"Well, when you want to find me again, I'll be in one of two places."

Katya stepped forward. Starbride froze, certain Katya was going to kiss her. She held her breath, her heart speeding. Katya smelled faintly of lavender and rosehips, with just a hint of leather, and at such a short distance, her eyes seemed to take up the entire world.

She lifted Starbride's right hand and held it between their two faces as her soft lips grazed the hollow between Starbride's first and second knuckle. "I will see you again," she said, and the touch of her breath turned Starbride's limbs to gooseflesh. She knew her mouth was open, but she couldn't close it.

Katya winked before she let go and started down the hallway. Starbride shook her head, the spell broken, and chastised herself for ever falling under Katya's sway. She almost shouted, "Scoundrel!" at the departing back, but the servants who'd faded into the background when Katya had kissed her had reappeared. Starbride rubbed her knuckles as she turned toward the library, but then she thought better of it and went to her room instead.

"I was just about to come and get you," Dawnmother said. "I've fetched some dinner."

"Thank you." Starbride dropped her scroll and pencil on the bed before she sat in the chair and stared at nothing.

"Did you hurt yourself?"

"What?"

"You keep rubbing your hand."

"No, no." Starbride stared down at her knuckles, seeing Katya's lips there again. "Katya kissed me there."

"Oh?"

"We're friends, Dawn."

Dawnmother snorted and took the lid off a covered dish, revealing a small roasted chicken on a bed of greens. "There are friends, and then there are *friends*, and then there are people you sneak into a hayloft with."

"How many haylofts have you snuck into?"

"Enough to know when someone else is thinking of doing it."

"I am not."

"If the princess sent you a note asking you to meet her in the barn, would you go?"

Starbride paused.

Dawnmother snapped her fingers. "A pause means yes." She carved the chicken with a few quick strokes.

"You don't know what you're talking about."

"My life for you and also the truth. You are smitten."

"I *should* have you staked in the sun for insubordination."

"That wouldn't change the truth, and I would go to my grave a much-maligned but honest woman."

"A woman who's been in quite a few haylofts, by the sound of things!"

"Did you ask her to help you with the problems in Newhope?"

"Absolutely not. That wouldn't be fair to her."

Dawnmother snorted. "If she wants to help, you should let her help."

Starbride frowned and thought about it. Katya had protested, but she hadn't exactly *insisted* on helping. That *did* hurt just a little. She shook her head violently. "No, Allusia has to fight its own battles. We can't expect Farraday to solve all the problems it creates. If we lean on them to do everything for us, we won't know how to do anything for ourselves. We won't even know when we're being taken advantage of!"

"All right. I see the wisdom in what you say, for now, but if you and the princess become…better friends, the issue will surface again." She gestured to the chicken. "Eat before it gets cold."

Starbride nodded, ate her dinner, and thought too hard about the task in front of her and Dawnmother's words. She also couldn't help glancing now and again at the area between the first two knuckles of her right hand.

CHAPTER SEVEN: KATYA

Katya put Starbride out of her mind as she entered the royal apartments. It would be hard enough to tell her parents about the Order of Vestra's wasted trip to Longside without her mother asking if she was distracted.

When she entered her parents' sitting room, though, she stopped in pleasant surprise. Ma sat on one divan, and Crowe occupied the chair opposite, no doubt already reporting. Katya thanked the spirits that he'd beaten her there.

Ma nodded at Katya before saying, "Please continue, Cimerion."

"Majesty, only my wife called me Cimerion and then only if she was upset with me."

"Crowe, then."

"As I was saying, the man we captured is a smuggler. I need to interrogate the Shadow again to get more information."

"My son arrives in two weeks."

"I know."

"This is the first Waltz that will involve his wife, and nothing can go wrong."

"I know, Majesty. I know." He rubbed the bridge of his nose, looking more tired than Katya had ever seen him.

Noting the tightening around her mother's eyes, the signs of strain, Katya frowned. They had to make some progress soon. An idea flashed through her head, a way to combine business and pleasure. "In two days, I'll ride into the city," she said, "as myself. The rest of the Order can be waiting nearby to nab anyone who pays me undue attention."

"A lure, eh?" Crowe said.

Ma's face grew more pinched. "Katya, I don't think—"

"I'm known for being able to take care of myself and for going out on my own. If I'm attacked, I can defend myself without raising anyone's suspicions. I'll find the traitors before Reinholt gets here. I'm doing this, Ma."

Her mother straightened, becoming the queen and nothing else; even sitting, Ma seemed about ten feet tall. Katya fought not to shrink from the royal presence. She was royalty, too, and taller than her mother. Katya matched her posture and threw a lifted eyebrow into the mix.

Ma smiled, there then gone. "No harm must come to her, Crowe."

"Of course," Crowe said before Katya got the chance. "A discreet escort. Brutal and Maia will stroll nearby. I can be shopping in the same vicinity, and Pennynail can watch from a hidden location. We'll stop anyone who comes near her."

"Shopping?" Ma's mouth twitched. "You?"

"Even curmudgeonly old pyradistés need goods once in a while," Crowe said. "And what will be your reason for venturing into Marienne, Katya? You never do your own shopping."

Katya tapped her chin, pretending to think it over. Now came the pleasure to mix with the business. "There *is* someone I'd like to show around the city."

"Not Lady Hilda?" Ma asked.

"Definitely not."

"Rascal."

"I also need a tailor who works quickly."

"I'll get you some names."

"I'll let you know how it goes, Ma…Mother." One slip of a baby name in front of the pyradisté could be forgiven, but not two.

"Might I have a word on your way out?" Crowe asked.

Katya nodded and stood, and as she was clean, hugged her mother good-bye.

"Majesty." Crowe bowed.

Ma inclined her head. "Take care," she said to Katya.

"Always."

In the hall, Crowe tugged on Katya's arm. "You've made a *new* friend?" he asked.

Katya rolled her eyes. "She's not a spy."

"And you know this because…?"

"Woman's intuition."

He snorted and crossed his arms.

She crossed hers back. "I like this woman, Crowe."

"You liked them all, Katya." He took a breath and seemed to realize the callousness of his words as soon as they left his mouth. "I'm sorry. That didn't come out as I intended."

"You…" Anger tightened the skin at her temples, and her pyramid necklace flared next to her breast.

"Calm yourself. I am sorry."

"I know about my past. I lived it."

"I didn't mean—"

"I *like* this woman, Crowe. I mean it. She makes me feel...free." She hated the word. It sounded whiny and ungrateful, but she couldn't deny it was the truth.

To her surprise, he nodded. "I understand. I...my wife...with her, I could forget..." He waved at the grandeur surrounding them.

Katya didn't know what to say. Crowe spoke of his dead wife rarely, and then only to make a joke. He did understand, perhaps better than anyone. Katya's mother would have lectured her about duty; her father wouldn't have known what she was talking about. Court was their lives, and they never wished for anything else. She supposed that if court was *all* she had to worry about, she could find some contentment, but living two lives, as Crowe also did, added so much strain. "She's a good person. You'll like her."

"I get to meet her?"

"Hopefully not in two days' time when we ride out, not unless something goes wrong."

"I agree. But eventually?" He seemed so hopeful, and she realized he was touched that she wanted him to meet someone she was interested in. She'd never introduced him to a lover before.

"Definitely. Her name is Starbride."

"Ah, an Allusian." His gaze went far away. As Katya began to ask what he was thinking of, he shook his head and patted her shoulder. "I look forward to meeting her." He left her then, and back in her apartment, she found Averie laying out a dinner of roasted chicken.

Averie nodded as Katya related the plan. "She has nothing for riding? Were you thinking a coat and trousers?"

"I saw the wistful look in her eyes when she spoke of the clothes she'd left in Allusia. We'll need to give the tailor special instructions on what to make. But first, we need someone who knows Allusian fashion."

"Her maid?"

Katya winked over her wineglass. "You're worth your weight in gold."

"Perhaps now *is* a good time to discuss my wages, but I'll put that off for the moment. If Starbride goes to the library every day, I'll ambush her maid after she's gone."

"Make sure she knows it's a surprise."

"Are you certain this trip into the city will be safe?"

"The Order will be there, and these traitors can't have a grudge against Starbride. If anything happens, I'll tell her to ride away at full speed."

"Are you sure she'd go? If she's as interested in you as you seem to be in her…"

"All right then, I'll tell Pennynail to carry her off at full speed."

"A better plan altogether."

Averie had the instructions for a modern Allusian outfit by midmorning the next day, and one of the recommended tailors claimed he could have the garments finished in the day and a half remaining. When he proved as good as his word and the garments arrived and passed Averie's inspection, Katya tipped him enormously. He bobbed like a buoy and grinned like an idiot as he thanked her over and over.

Averie had to shoo him from the room at last. "Don't you want to see these?"

"Since they passed your scrutiny, I want my first look at them to be on Starbride."

"She won't be able to resist you, you know."

"Are you saying clothes are the way to a woman's heart?"

"I'm saying that charm is, and you have it in plenty."

Katya sprawled in her chair. "You're lucky that men are your cup of tea, then."

"Oh, very." Averie wrapped the outfit in the cloth it arrived in and tied it with a ribbon. "Protective as I am with my virtue, I would've had my skirt over my head long ago in your charming presence."

Katya laughed until she had to wipe away tears. With giddy anticipation, she dug a small card out of her desk and wrote, *Dearest Meringue, please accept this gift in spite of your mother's wishes. Also, please join me on a tour of Marienne in the morning, when I will flirt with you mercilessly.* She left it unsigned and pinned it to the parcel's ribbon. "There, take this to her room, Averie. I only wish I could see her face when she opens it."

"When and where will you meet?"

"Three hours after dawn at the royal stables. Tell the grooms to expect her."

When Katya reached the stables the next morning, Starbride met her with a two-foot-wide smile in place. She turned full circle, showing off. A tight bodice, ruby red with gold accents, covered a loose shirt in darker red that hung to mid-thigh. Flared sleeves started under the bodice's straps, and the shirt collar followed the line of the bodice, making a wide neck that stopped just above her breasts, revealing nothing. The design flattered her curves, and the color made her skin glow. The fitted trousers were a dark wine, perfect for riding, or so Dawnmother had assured them. Half her hair had been pulled loosely behind her head, letting most of it flow over her shoulders. As comfortable as she seemed, she looked ten times as beautiful.

After her turn, she rushed forward and clasped Katya's hands. "I love it! Where did you find it?"

"I'm royalty. We have ways."

Starbride hugged herself and beamed. "I love it! Thank you."

Katya smiled so hard her cheeks ached. "You're welcome." She gestured to the horses, more than a little surprised at the heat in her face. "Whenever you're ready, the city awaits. Do you need the mounting block?"

"Ha!" Starbride slipped one foot in her stirrup and swung into her saddle without a second's hesitation.

"You weren't kidding about knowing your way around horses."

Starbride tossed her hair over one shoulder. "Of course not, though you should have heard Dawnmother teasing me about the princess inviting me to a stable."

Katya thought about that as they guided their horses into the city. "A roll in the hay?"

"We call it sneaking into a hayloft, but it's the same thing."

"It's the same the world over, I imagine." She leaned close. "And I have to warn you that, since I had that garment made, I know exactly where to start with it if I do decide to seduce you."

"Dawnmother snuck in some extra pins, just in case, so watch yourself."

As they rode, Katya pointed out several of the chapterhouses with carved façades of their patron spirits. She took Starbride past the outdoor market and Fountain Square, its two fountains bubbling away, one decorated with the five male spirits, the other with the five females. "It used to be Carnival Square," Katya said, "before the fountains were built."

"A place for celebrations?"

"No, they, um, they had the gallows here. I think the name was a dark joke."

"Ah." Starbride frowned. "I see."

Katya cleared her throat. What a wonderful conversation she'd started, sure to keep the day light and carefree. "How about some shopping?"

"Won't you get mobbed in the market?"

"We won't go there. I know some better places." As she turned her horse, she spied a white banner down the street. It flapped gently in the breeze, and Katya paused to stare as the large red symbol in its center. "Is that Allusian?"

"I don't recognize it. Do you?"

Katya frowned. The symbol seemed so familiar, but she could put no meaning to it. It was just a collection of lines and curves, but it almost spoke to her, telling her to go another way, away from the major thoroughfare it hung over. "No."

"We could find out," Starbride said. "Go ask the people in the building, if you're that curious."

Katya shook her head rapidly. "No, sorry. Shopping, right? Let's take this street instead."

Keeping up the light chatter, she led the way down several alleys to a wealthier district with less foot traffic. They hitched their horses at a small hostelry, the better to walk and window-shop. Katya started down one street and spied another symbol, this one hanging in a shop window. She paused, her breath catching. A different symbol, it still gave her the same feeling of knowing and not knowing it.

"Katya?" Starbride asked. "What's wrong?"

"I was…just trying to remember where we are." She backed away from the symbol. "I don't think we want this street." Uneasiness spread across her shoulders, a feeling of being watched, and she rested her hand close to her rapier.

Two more symbols turned them in different directions, and Katya's heart began to pound. Starbride was talking, but she couldn't pay attention. She tried to calm herself, to watch for danger, but there was nothing to see. Careful to keep her face calm, Katya guided them toward their horses through another shop-lined square.

Across the square, Crowe wandered in the opposite direction as he pretended to window-shop. Down an alleyway, Brutal and Maia strolled together, his larger form bending slightly as if to better hear her. Katya knew she wouldn't see Pennynail until she needed him. She made her shoulders relax. The Order was there, and everything would be fine.

Starbride pointed at a shop window. "Who would wear those shoes?"

Katya took a slow look around and realized that the square was empty of everyone except herself, Starbride, and Crowe. Overhead, the sun approached midday. Were all the shoppers resting? Gathering ingredients for the evening meal? Or had she and Starbride wandered farther from the city center than she'd thought?

"Why don't we...?" Another window caught her attention. She stepped forward, drawn by a series of intricately patterned scarves just inside the glass. An odd pattern of embroidered symbols seemed to dance across the green silk scarf in the center. Pretty from a distance, up close, the pattern seemed almost sinister. Like the symbols she'd been seeing all day, these had an allure to them, but they didn't put her off like before. They beckoned.

Starbride leaned around her shoulder and took her hand. "What are you looking at? Oh! My mother would like that one. How expensive do you think they are?"

The feel of Starbride's body pressed close chased Katya's anxiety away. "Well, you know what they say, if you have to ask..."

"...then you don't know?"

"...then you can't afford it."

"That doesn't make sense." She shrugged. "I guess I don't know what they say."

"Don't worry. They say it so often that you'll learn."

"Shall we go in?"

Katya almost said no, but what could a shop full of scarves do to them? Crowe would be hovering at the window, and Brutal and Maia were close. Katya wouldn't have been surprised to find Pennynail inside the store's walls.

The doorbell jingled as they entered, and the smell of leather washed over them. The place was filled not only with scarves, but also purses, pouches, hats, and gloves. Katya noticed the same patterns again and again, familiar and yet not, making her uneasy one moment and comforted the next. She wanted badly to scratch between her shoulder blades, as if her discomfort had settled as an itch.

A man stepped out from a curtained room at the back and gave Katya and Starbride a wide smile that didn't reach his eyes. Katya reached for Starbride's arm, about to drag them both from the shop when something shone in the man's hand, and she couldn't move.

"Can I help?" he asked.

Starbride studied a scarf without looking up. "We'd like some prices, please. Katya, what do you think of this one?" She turned and stared for a moment. "Katya?"

Katya could only watch, mute and motionless, lost in the shopkeeper's pyramid. Starbride stepped closer, and Katya wanted to scream as a larger man emerged from the curtain and picked up a scarf. She cursed the body that wouldn't obey her as the large man lifted the scarf and wrapped it around Starbride's mouth from behind.

Starbride cried out, but the large man jerked the scarf tight, cutting off her voice. He wrapped his other arm around her waist and lifted her, kicking and flailing, off the floor. He carried her behind the curtain.

Katya strained to move, but her body refused again. She heard several thumps from behind the curtain, and then the big man reemerged, alone.

"Bar the door," the shopkeeper said.

The large man moved behind Katya, and she heard him grunt, followed by another thump, this one the unmistakable sound of wood against wood. He walked back around, smirking, before he disappeared behind the curtain again.

The shopkeeper held the pyramid high. "Follow me," he commanded.

Katya stumbled toward him, her limbs like lead that nonetheless worked without her permission. The pyramid was perfect and glittering, the sides faceted, and the points set in gold. Rage blurred Katya's eyes, but her pyramid necklace lay dormant against her chest. The shopkeeper held the curtain open, and Katya lurched after him. Starbride's muted cries came from behind her. The shopkeeper relieved Katya of her rapier and knife and made her walk into a cage a little taller than her and twice as wide. He locked her inside and put the pyramid behind his back.

Katya hurled herself at the bars. "Release me!"

"I knew you'd see the symbols," the shopkeeper said, "but you wouldn't know what they meant. Well, I know what they mean. I know what you are, and I'm going to prove it."

He moved to the side. Four other people had gathered in the background, all masked and wearing nondescript clothing. The large man had bound Starbride to a short wooden table. At some point, they'd stuffed a rag in her mouth.

"Bastards!" Katya yelled. "You have me. Let her go!"

"Oh, we have you," the shopkeeper said. "And yet not you." He turned to the masked people. "You see?"

"We see nothing," one of them said, a man's voice. "The princess in a cage."

"You don't see, but you will." He lifted the pyramid over Starbride's face. She glanced at it and then strained against the bonds and tried to scream around the rag.

The shopkeeper frowned. Katya banged against the bars. Whatever he was trying on Starbride, it wasn't working. Katya didn't know if that was a mercy or a cruelty. It all depended on what they wanted.

The shopkeeper shrugged. "I had hoped to make this easier for you, but…" He gestured to the large man. "Do it."

Licking his lips, the large man gave Katya a languid look and drew a small knife from a sheath at his belt. He moved to Starbride's right hand and pried it open. She squealed and bucked. "Shh, shh," he whispered as he laid the knife between two of her fingers. "There's a good girl."

Horror tightened Katya's chest and spread up her neck to her head. "Don't." Rage tipped over into an eerie calm that left her face hot and her body shivering with cold. Her necklace pulsed against her chest. Back inside the shop, she heard someone pounding on the door.

On the table, Starbride tried to pull away from the large man, but she was bound too tightly. She whipped her head back and forth as the large man rested the blade against her index finger. "How many should I take?" he asked.

"That's up to her." The shopkeeper gestured at Katya with his chin. "If the fingers don't work, cut out the tongue."

"Don't do this," Katya said. She felt a tickle on the back of her eyeballs, and her necklace burned her skin. It awoke half a memory. She wanted to tear her necklace out of her coat, but she couldn't take her hands from the bars.

The large man bent Starbride's finger back and drew the blade across the joint, drawing a thin line of blood. Starbride gave a muted scream.

"Shh, shh, sweetheart," the large man said. "This your first time?"

There was a tiny sound, almost undetectable, and Katya knew without knowing that her pyramid necklace had shattered. Something inside her shattered with it. Tingles ran along her head, her limbs went numb, and then pain fractured her mind. She closed her eyes and heaved, and the bars parted like blades of grass. She stepped through, and all the unbound people stepped back, but they couldn't get away. She would have their blood, though she couldn't recall why. All that mattered was that they were there, fragile hearts waiting to be crushed, and she wanted to oblige them. The large man first.

CHAPTER EIGHT: STARBRIDE

Katya changed. Starbride felt it in the air the way she felt a warm summer breeze turn cool before a storm. It almost made her forget the man who was going to maim her. When he stepped away, she watched Katya's transformation.

Horns sprouted from Katya's brow, long and smooth. They curved over the crown of her head before pointing up at the sky. Her face had moved from pained to beautiful and inhuman, her eyes blue within blue. Unnatural cold rolled from her in waves, prickling Starbride's skin. Her face was calm, almost serene as her clawed hands lifted. Katya crossed the room in a blur and appeared in front of the would-be torturer in a blink. She reached between his legs and clawed him from groin to chin, cutting through him as if he were warm pie.

He barely made a sound as his insides became his outsides, and he dropped. The shopkeeper held his pyramid high, but the glittering shape had gone dark in the center. He stared at it in wonder until Katya relieved him of his head. The other people screamed and ran. Distantly, Starbride heard wood splintering from inside the shop.

Katya darted for the masked people, one after another, killing and killing in the space of a heartbeat, her movements too fast to follow. She murdered them all without losing the calm look upon her face, and blood dotted her fair skin like motes of flour.

At last, Katya turned a dark gaze on Starbride, and she feared that look almost as much as she had the idea of the torture.

An old man stepped through the curtained door. "Katya, no!" He held a pyramid aloft, and Katya shrank from it, hissing.

The large, red-robed man and young blond woman Starbride had seen in the palace hallway stepped around the old man, followed by another clothed and masked in leather. "Hold her down!" the old man cried.

Starbride tried to cry out, fearful that these people were like the others, but she could do nothing. The big man and the young woman leapt on Katya and pinned her to the ground. It must've been the pyramid that allowed them to do so with her strength. Even though the large man was twice Katya's size, he grunted as he struggled with her.

The masked man began cutting Starbride's bonds, and she yanked the gag from her mouth. "Who are you?" He finished cutting her loose without answering. She pushed off the table and wrapped the rag that had been in her mouth over her bleeding finger. The masked man ran back through the curtained door into the shop.

On the floor, the old man opened Katya's coat and shirt enough to press the pyramid to her chest, just above her heart. "Hold on, Katya."

Veins stood out in the large man's neck as he strained to hold Katya down. She screamed nonsense as her horns receded into her forehead, where there couldn't be room for them, and her features returned to normal. She breathed hard and sweated, her eyes rolling wildly. Two bloody drops rolled down her forehead where her horns used to be, and she wept tears of blood that smeared her cheeks with red.

At last, her eyes rolled back one more time, and she lay still. Her chest moved steadily up and down. The old man jammed the pyramid back in his pocket and took a deep breath. He wiped his sweaty forehead, slicked his thin white hair back, and said to Starbride, "You'd better come with us, miss. You must have questions."

He was wrong. At the moment, she didn't even have speech. The large man lifted Katya's unconscious body and started for the curtain. When he waved for Starbride to join his party, she hesitated, not feeling very trusting as things were.

Katya's body was going out the door, though, and she had to make a decision. Katya had transformed into something—Starbride's mind whispered, *Fiend*—but she had done it to save Starbride, and now she looked so helpless. These people seemed to care about Katya, but Starbride couldn't be certain of their intentions, not unless she watched them. "Yes...yes."

The old man inclined his head deeply, an expression that spoke of respect. Outside, the masked man drove up to the front of the shop in a horse-drawn cart. The others bundled Katya's body in cloaks and loaded her inside.

"Clean up," the old man said. "Don't forget their horses." The other two men walked back into the shop, and the old man helped Starbride into the cart while the young woman took the reins. They drove through the city streets for a few moments without speaking.

"Cimerion Crowe is my name," he said at last. "Everyone calls me Crowe." He gestured to the young woman's back. "She is Maia."

Starbride shut her mouth on the questions he had just answered. "Starbride."

"Yes, I know."

"From Katya?" Starbride swallowed. "From Princess Katyarianna Nar Umbriel?"

"I am King Einrich's pyradisté, and sometimes, I am hers."

"A bodyguard?"

"Unofficially."

Starbride nodded, but anger burned in her. She welcomed it. It chased away the terror that wanted her to run for Dawnmother's embrace. "Why did you take so long to come?" She tied the rag tighter around her finger. How much of her flesh would this man and his friends have allowed her to lose? Enough so that she could never write again? Never feed herself? Never speak?

"We didn't know anything was wrong until Katya's necklace..." He trailed away. "Never mind about that now."

"Thank you for rescuing...us." She'd nearly said, "Thank you for rescuing me," but Katya had done that. Or had she also been rescued *from* Katya?

"You're welcome." He said no more until they entered the royal stables. When the doors of a barn closed behind the wagon, Crowe and Maia surprised her again by lifting Katya's body between them and then moving to the back of the barn, to a wall that abutted the palace. A touch here, a pull there, and the wall slid open. "This way," he said.

Starbride gasped, about to exclaim about another secret passage, but then she remembered that Hanna's Retreat had been Katya's secret. She helped them carry Katya through long passages and stairways, past intersections, all of it sealed within the walls of the palace. Small symbols marked the way, but Starbride was more lost than she had been in the regular hallways with their carpets and pieces of art. When they emerged into a large, opulently furnished room, she had no idea where she was.

The other woman Starbride had seen going hunting with Katya rushed toward them. "Spirits above! What—?"

"Not yet, Averie," Crowe said. "Katya will be fine. Let's put her down on the settee." They did so, and Averie and Maia unwrapped her. "Let's have a chat in the other room, Miss Starbride."

Starbride glanced at Katya as Averie unbuttoned her coat and Maia brought a bowl of water to the settee's side.

"We're in her apartment," Crowe said. "This is her private sitting room. You couldn't have gotten past the pyramids that guard it if you hadn't been in our company, and it will be equally hard to leave. I protect the royal family, and I must ask, for their sakes, that we talk before you go."

Starbride focused on the possibility of explanation. "Then speak."

Crowe gestured for her to follow him. In the formal sitting room, the furniture looked incredibly uncomfortable, all straight backs and hard seats with a table big enough for six people. Crowe gestured for Starbride to take a seat on one side and then sank into a chair across from her.

He took a pyramid from his pocket and placed it on the table between them. Starbride eyed it with caution and didn't speak.

Crowe cleared his throat. "She's told me...a little about you, and what she said is the reason we're sitting here. I could have blanked your mind and left you anywhere."

Starbride eyed the pyramid again, remembering the way the shopkeeper's pyramid had gleamed, though it had done nothing to her. "And? What do you have to say?"

"What did she look like to you?"

Starbride didn't have to think about her answer. "Even the Allusians have stories of Fiends, creatures from before humanity."

"They're quite real. Have you heard about Yanchasa?"

"Are you saying that Katya—?"

"Tell me what you know."

"I've studied Farradain history. Yanchasa is supposed to be a terrible Fiend that once threatened this land, but surely this is legend, parable."

"Even Allusia has stories of Fiends, that's what you said."

Starbride put a hand to her forehead and tried to stop the world from spinning so quickly. "We have many stories, and that is all they are."

Crowe gave her a long stare. "Yanchasa is very real. It rests, but it was once awake. Long ago, the first king summoned it to help him conquer Farraday, but it was too much for him. To keep it from destroying the land and everyone in it, the king's sister Vestra and her husband took some of Yanchasa's essence into themselves, weakening it enough to trap it. The husband went mad, but Vestra passed this essence on, just as all Umbriels pass it, both to spouses and children, in the form of the Aspect."

Starbride's belly went cold. Laughing, joking Katya had a Fiend inside her? "That can't be true. The king and queen?"

Crowe gazed at her steadily.

"But...why?"

"They can pacify Yanchasa, keep it asleep, because they carry its essence."

"But Fiends are...evil, aren't they?"

"I've never met a true one, but that's the rumor. The Aspect in the

Umbriels is muted, buried beneath the surface of their minds. When the Aspect takes hold, the Fiend possesses their body and mind, and they can't remember what happened afterward. The Aspect emerges when they're enraged or during a ritual called the Waltz, which they perform to pacify Yanchasa every five years." He scrubbed his hands through his hair. "Though they all carry the Aspect, it can only present *after* they've participated in the Waltz."

"They can't be a Fiend until after they've Waltzed?"

"Correct. Katya Waltzed the first time five years ago, when she was fourteen."

"Those men, the ones that tried to..." She couldn't say it out loud. "They acted like they had something to prove to the masked people, something to show."

"They probably wanted to reveal Katya's Aspect, perhaps to prove why the Umbriel line shouldn't be allowed to rule."

"But if only those with the Aspect can appease Yanchasa...?"

"Some are convinced that Yanchasa no longer exists, that it's a child's tale to keep the populace in line and the Umbriels on the throne. Now it seems that some people think a monster shouldn't rule, even if he keeps a worse monster at bay."

Starbride rubbed her temples and tried to put her thoughts in a row. "Katya's always been so kind to me."

Crowe leaned across the table and patted her hand, a gesture that surprised her. "She's a kind person. The Aspect emerged because she cares about you."

"Would she have hurt me?"

He held her eyes for a moment. "Though Katya's worry for you brought it out, the Fiend cares about little but slaughter."

"Yes, I saw it in her eyes."

"But she didn't attack you first, did she?"

"True. I was the easiest target."

"A part of her remains, even through the Aspect. It looks so painful. It's a blessing that they don't remember it. The name 'Waltz' is a macabre joke, the sort the Farradains seem to love."

"The Farradains?" She studied him; his skin *was* duskier than other Farradains she'd seen. "Are you servant caste?"

His gaze bore into her. "My life for them."

"And also the truth."

"My father was Farradain, but my mother was a servant of Allusia. She named me Cinnamoncrow."

Starbride nearly laughed, even with everything. The name was worse than hers! "Your mother wished you to be a crow?"

"We lived in the hills above the northern salt flats, and the crow was a useful bird. You could follow it to water or food, and my mother had a poetic touch to her soul. She wanted me to be useful more than anything, as she was useful to her mistress." He rubbed his chin and smiled. "My father visited us in the winter. He was a pyradisté under Katya's grandfather, and when my mother died, I came to live with him and entered the Umbriels' service."

"Your life for theirs."

He nodded. "Though at times, I have to hide the truth for their protection."

"Do the Umbriels understand an Allusian servant's bond?"

"Their servants are hired. They can understand a pledge, but they still need proof. I've proved myself time and again."

Starbride pressed the cool surface of the table and took a deep breath. "It's a lot…all of this, but thank you for telling me about yourself."

"Now you know a secret of mine to go along with Katya's. She doesn't know about, or barely recollects, my heritage. I've been Cimerion Crowe for a long time. It was easier to adapt to them."

Starbride understood. She wouldn't change her name, as much as she hated it, but she wanted to adapt to Farradain law. To deal with them, it seemed the best way. "How long will she sleep?"

"A few hours. I can escort you back to your room. Or if it's all too much for you, I can arrange for you to go back to Allusia."

Tempting, for half a heartbeat, until she looked at the clothing Katya had given her, a gift from the heart. "My mother wouldn't like that." She couldn't abandon Katya, not even after what had happened or nearly happened. They were forming a bond she couldn't deny.

"Starbride, you don't need reminding, but I'm going to do it anyway. The Aspect is a secret. I don't know how those people in the shop found out, but that problem is being dealt with."

"And if I tell, I will be similarly dealt with?"

His kind eyes were steady. "It would pain me, but yes."

He would protect the family, his life for theirs, his life for their secrets. "And Katya?"

"I would suffer her hatred."

"Hatred?" Feelings swarmed Starbride's chest, too many to name. Katya would hate someone she trusted on Starbride's behalf? "How do you know?"

"I made the pyramid that she wears around her neck, the one that is supposed to keep her Fiend from emerging, even with her anger. If she changed to save you, she broke it using emotion alone."

Starbride matched him stare for stare. "I'll send a note to my servant about where I am, and then I'll stay until she wakes."

"I can still make you forget." He tapped the pyramid. "It will be hard for her, but she can pretend she never met you, and this day will seem like a bad dream."

Starbride touched the pyramid's smooth side with one finger. She wasn't so sure Crowe's pyramid could touch her, not if the shopkeeper's couldn't. "She cares for me, and she would pretend not to know me?"

"If it would protect or comfort you, yes. I know her very well. Memory erasure works in threads. I couldn't take just this day. I would have to take every encounter involving the princess from your mind."

The burden of responsibility would be gone, but so would all the little moments, the bright eyes, the easy smile. "No, thank you."

He retrieved his pyramid and went into the other room. Starbride breathed deep as the day's events roiled within her, free to coil around her mind now that she was alone. Crying by oneself was useless, she knew that. Her mother had drilled it into her. What good were tears with no one to see them? What good...?

When the first drop landed on the leg of her trousers, darkening the fabric, it shocked her. And then there were more, pouring down her face, unstoppable. She covered her mouth and wept, keeping her voice down to a moan when it wanted to howl, and crying until her eyes and throat ached, until her face turned hot and puffy.

That man, his touch on her skin, the knife slicing her finger, then Katya's Fiend, fear upon fear, that terrible cold, and then Katya's collapse. And all the knowledge? She'd wished to know the secrets, and now part of her wished she'd never asked, had never been in a position to ask.

Katya had become a Fiend to protect her. It had to mean something, maybe everything. If Katya had hurt Starbride, whether she remembered it or not, would she ever forgive herself? Would she blame herself for even being in a *position* to hurt Starbride?

Katya would pretend to forget her if Starbride decided that course was best. Katya could keep herself away when she clearly didn't want to, could ignore their flirty conversations, and could forget kissing Starbride's hand. It spoke of great affection but also of tremendous acting skill. Could she fool anyone? Even Crowe?

Starbride shook her head and told herself that *she* wouldn't be so easily deceived. Katya couldn't fake the transformation into a Fiend, something Starbride had seen with her own eyes. Katya cared for her, more than a little, and Starbride realized that she felt the same.

"Ah, Mother," she said as she dried her eyes on her sleeves, "you got your wish, though it wasn't exactly what you would have chosen. Would you be of two minds, I wonder?"

The door cracked open, and Maia peeked through. "Hello?"

"Hello."

"I'm...my name is Maia."

"I know." She smiled to put her at ease. "How is Katya?"

"She just needs rest. Crowe said you might be thirsty."

With a swallow, Starbride realized she was. "Yes, thank you."

Maia crossed to a cabinet and pulled out a decanter of dark amber liquid and two glasses. As she poured two fingers of liquid into each glass and set them on the table, she shook her head. "Please don't tell them I did this. They wouldn't approve of my drinking liquor, but I think we deserve it, don't you?"

"We certainly do." She tipped hers back in one swift swallow. Lights danced in front of her eyes as the strong stuff burned down her throat. She slapped the table and grimaced.

Maia's surprised face dissolved into a grin. She followed Starbride's example and then stuck her tongue out and coughed, doubling over in her seat.

"Are you all right?"

Maia nodded, still coughing, her face red. "How's your finger?"

"Blood hasn't soaked through the rag. I think it stopped." She didn't unwind the makeshift bandage, though, not yet. "How long have you known Katya?"

"Since I was born. We're cousins."

Starbride paused before she burst out laughing. "I'm meeting royalty left and right, and I still haven't learned how to greet them. Shall I bow?"

"Please, don't. Any more sudden moves today and I might collapse."

"Do you often serve as Katya's bodyguard?"

"Yeah, though sometimes, I don't feel up to the job." She pushed her glass around on the table. "I have the Aspect, but I've never done the Waltz. After seeing...that, I never want to. I don't want to become that."

Starbride cocked her head to the side. Maia might have been the king's niece, but she looked like any other scared girl at the moment. "This isn't the cure for fear, you know," she said, tapping the decanter.

"One more and we'll call it good enough."

"Agreed." After they both knocked back another glass and coughed around the strength of the liquid, Starbride asked, "How does the Aspect get passed to spouses? The children I understand."

"It's a ritual. While the person with the Aspect and their partner are, um, being intimate, a pyradisté uses a special kind of pyramid on them. Right as they…you know, finish, the pyramid shares the Aspect between them. I've never done it."

"I see." Starbride frowned and tried to fight the pictures her mind conjured.

"I suspect the pyradisté hides behind a curtain or something. It's so the non-Umbriel person can produce children that will have the Aspect, though it won't present until—"

"Until the Waltz," Starbride finished. "So, your children will have it?"

Maia shook her head. "I'm the cut-off, two removed from the throne."

Starbride leaned back in her seat, her mind more at ease. Even though Katya could turn her into a Fiend, she wouldn't bother. Starbride could never bear their children. She held her cool palms against her warm cheeks. "Do you know where I can find pen and paper? I need to write my maid."

"I can get it for you. Crowe said not to tell her about the Aspect."

"I know. I won't."

Maia fetched the writing materials after she put the decanter away. She didn't leave as Starbride wrote a quick note about having dinner in Katya's apartment. She didn't know quite what she would say later. Her finger protested being bent, and tears threatened again at the thought of what she'd almost lost. "Waiting to read it?"

"I was just keeping you company."

"I'm sorry. I'm just a bit…rattled."

"I know what you mean."

Starbride folded the note. "Could you show it to Crowe, please?"

"He didn't ask for that."

"I have to prove myself worthy of your family's trust. Right now, this is all I know how to do."

Maia took the note into the private sitting room and then emerged a few moments later. "I'll take it to your maid myself, since Averie's busy. Crowe says to please come in whenever you're ready."

Starbride smoothed her hair from her face and stood. She unwound the rag from her finger. The cut had gone from bleeding to oozing. With one pull, she tore a small strip from the rag and tied it tight around the cut. She was alive, and she was whole.

She paused at the door. There was still time to call for Crowe and his pyramid instead of going in, to back out of Katya's life. It might work.

With her chin lifted, she stepped through the door.

Chapter Nine: Katya

*S*ix-year-old Katya played with little Maia on the sitting room rug. Three-year-old Maia focused on her wooden horse, oblivious to the events in the next room, but Katya couldn't ignore the sound of their family arguing.

"How can one woman be so hard to find?" Da yelled.

"Untie my hands!" Uncle Roland yelled back. "If you want this done faster, give me leave to do what I need to do. Set me loose! You and all your damned rules, Einrich, I—"

Crowe spoke then, and even though Katya couldn't make out his words, she knew he was telling everyone to calm down. It was important to be calm; bad things happened if you weren't.

From the corner of the room, someone horrid whispered. Maia didn't seem to notice, but Katya saw the short table in the dark with the shadowy figure bound to it.

No.

Uncle Roland came in from the other room and scrubbed his fingers through his hair. Maia ran to him, and he scooped her up. She played with his bearded chin, so like Katya's father's beard, but lighter brown. He sat at the dining table, Maia in his lap.

"Where's your brother?" he asked.

"With his tutor." Katya sat across from him. "He can't play until later."

"You'll have your own tutor soon enough."

Katya rolled her eyes. "Boring."

With a chuckle, he pulled a pyramid from his pocket. Maia squealed and reached for it, and he deftly moved it away from her grasping fingers. "I made this for you, little K. Reinholt's too old for it, I suppose. Can you guess what it does?"

Katya eyed the glinting sides of the pyramid, and icy fear seized her until she almost shrank away. The pyramid would hold her mind; it *would keep her still while the horrid, whispering person approached the table-bound figure in the corner.*

No.

Roland touched the pyramid's apex, and it rotated on its own, painting the room with twinkling pinpoints of light. Maia giggled and clapped. "It's perfect," Katya said.

Roland chucked her under the chin. "Do you know what else I can do with it, little K?"

She shook her head, returning his grin with one of her own.

"I can cut up your friend."

Katya fell back from the table, down and down, over and over, the horrid whisperer coming for Starbride, saying "Shh, shh," as he did so.

"No!"

"Katya!" Starbride cried.

Katya opened her eyes to her sitting room ceiling, the entirety of it painted like rose-tinted dawn. Starbride leaned over her. She wore the same clothes as when…

Katya bolted upright, her head swimming. "Star!"

Starbride laid a steadying hand on her shoulder. "I'm all right."

"Are you? What happened?" The knife had been cutting into her finger, so close to ripping it off. Katya swallowed to stop the rising bile.

"I'm fine," Starbride said, though her sad smile hinted at a lie. She had a bandage at the base of her index finger. "*Completely* fine. Your friends rescued us."

Katya touched Starbride's chin, sliding her thumb over the smooth skin. She couldn't remember anything but the bars and the unfolding horror in front of the cage. "Did I pass out? Oh! I called you Star. I'm sorry."

"It's all right."

"What happened?"

Starbride stared for a moment without speaking, reminding Katya of Crowe. She picked up a necklace from the side table; the broken remains of a glass ornament dangled from the chain. Katya felt her shirt and the lack of necklace underneath. A pyramid rested on a nearby table, and she could feel the calming waves flowing from it. "Oh, spirits, what did I do?"

"You saved me."

Katya couldn't look her in the eye. She didn't know what her Fiend looked like, but she remembered her parents' and Reinholt's: the horns, the aura of menace, the burning cold, the claws, and the certainty of death. Katya covered her face as shame overwhelmed her.

Starbride's arms went around her, and Katya leaned into the embrace as tears dribbled down her cheeks. Starbride rocked her for a few moments and hummed tunelessly into her hair. "I'm so sorry," Katya said.

"Hush." Starbride brushed the hair from Katya's face. "This is wavier than I thought."

"What?"

"All this pretty hair."

"How can you even look at me, Star…Starbride?"

"Star is fine." She glanced down at the settee, a light blush making her cheeks darker. "You're the same as before."

"A monster?"

"The same sense of humor." She laid her cool palm along Katya's cheek, the smoothness of it only slightly marred by the rough bandage. "You *saved* me. You did. Not the Fiend."

"The Fiend would've hurt you."

"And you didn't let it."

Katya snorted and nearly recoiled from the bitter sound. "Or my friends stopped me."

"I don't think your friends could have subdued you if you didn't want them to, at least in part."

"You don't have any proof of that."

"I'm studying law. I can argue until I turn blue."

"What did Crowe tell you?"

"Enough."

Katya didn't want to press. Crowe had obviously filled in some gaps about the Aspect, and yet there Starbride sat, so close, as if she had nothing to fear. "Thank you for staying."

When Starbride touched her hand, Katya turned hers over to clasp them together. There was one secret out from between them. Starbride sat so close, and the moment was so fragile, her eyes so warm and inviting. The flickering candlelight brought out the high cheekbones in her honest, beautiful face, and Katya leaned forward until their foreheads touched.

Katya ached to kiss her, drawn by the curve of her softly smiling lips, but it was too soon after the events of the day. They leaned against each other until someone cleared her throat from the doorway.

"I've had dinner brought in," Averie said. "It's in the formal sitting room." She shut the door softly as she withdrew.

"Was that a disapproving cough?" Starbride asked.

"She just doesn't like food getting cold." Katya swung her legs over the settee and stood, reaching downward.

Starbride took her hand and followed. "My princess is always genteel."

Katya's heart warmed at the "my." Tears threatened her again, but they were relieved tears. Starbride had seen Katya's darkest side, and she hadn't bolted. If she had any doubts, they were well hidden. "My parents made sure I had the best upbringing, including never leaving a beautiful woman unescorted to the dinner table."

"A very important part of any education."

Katya ate dinner in near silence and drank in Starbride's presence. She wouldn't try to convince Starbride to stay the night; their current relationship was too sweet to leave behind so soon. Even with Crowe present and Averie serving, they shared many a glance, but Katya didn't try her usual tricks. No winks, no "accidental" meeting of the fingers over the saltcellar, no playfully long sips from the wineglass, just shy little smiles, and gestures that made her almost giddy.

In the past, when a lover had gotten too close, the threat of the Aspect had always ended things. She'd never found the courage to ask Reinholt or her father how they'd broken the news to Brom and her mother. She didn't know how anyone could admit such a secret. Well, her cat had been let out of the bag in the worst way, and Starbride still sat with her, had held her and leaned against her. She'd made no demands; she'd offered only comfort and warmth.

Crowe decided it would be better if *he* escorted Starbride back to her room, and Katya had to agree. Starbride needed someone who could protect her without distractions. They said good night with just a quick glance, a soft laugh, and then Starbride was gone with Crowe. Katya sank down in her chair and sighed.

Averie's hands settled on her shoulders. "I was worried you might have some repercussions from the transformation, but now I see you're just lovesick."

"Don't tease me, Averie. Let me bask."

"I'll draw your bath. Bask in there." She squeezed once before letting go. "I was worried about you." She dashed from the room.

Left alone, Katya remembered everything unpleasant about the day: the cool of the bars, the smell of the man's sweat, the knife against Starbride's skin. Katya pressed her palms over her eyes and tried to shut the images out.

Left to its own devices, the Fiend would have torn Starbride apart.

It wouldn't have stopped until it ran out of targets, Katya was certain of that. The royal family was chained to the great pyramid during the Waltz for that very reason.

The traitors had known how to bring the Fiend out. Katya only hoped they had no idea she preferred Starbride to other women, that Starbride's presence was *convenient* more than anything else. Katya prayed to Matter and Marla, spirits of perception, to hide their wisdom from the traitors' eyes.

Would she have to see Starbride less just as she wanted more? Did the gift of clothing make her a target, or was it the invitation to tour the city? However the traitors found out about Katya's actions, it was time to crack down. She'd given up almost everything for the Order of Vestra, but she wouldn't give up Starbride, not yet.

She tapped her chin and supposed she *could* ask Starbride to move into the royal wing for safety, but that would set too many bells ringing through court. Besides, neither of them was ready for that. What they had was still too fragile, too newly born.

After her bath, she donned her large robe and emerged into her private sitting room to find both her parents waiting. Her mother's expression seemed carved from marble, but her father waved in Katya's direction. "See?" he asked. "Just as Crowe said, not a scratch on her. Isn't that so, my girl?"

Katya nodded, smiling, but her mother's expression didn't change. "You were right, Ma. It was a bad idea."

"Is that what you think I want to hear?" Her eyes narrowed, and the skin of her face seemed to tighten. "Did I come here to say I told you so, or did I come here to ascertain whether or not my daughter was injured after she became a Fiend and killed several people?"

A flush crept up Katya's neck. Her mother had left out the part where she'd nearly let her friend be tortured, or maybe Crowe hadn't mentioned that. Da drew a pyramid necklace from his coat pocket. "Crowe gave us this to give to you. It's one of the spares. Saves you the trouble of carting around a larger pyramid."

Katya nodded gratefully, but she couldn't ignore her mother's anger forever. She had the sense to realize her mother was as much frightened as furious. Swallowing her own temper, Katya said, "I'm sorry, Ma. It's all I can say."

Her mother's face softened, but still she shook her head.

"My life will always be in danger."

Da rested his hand on her shoulder. "We know that, my girl. My brother didn't die so long ago that we've forgotten."

Ma covered her mouth and turned away. Katya swallowed hard, knowing her mother had just pictured her dead. "I'm so sorry I scared you."

Ma squeezed Katya's arm hard, her eyes misty but her cheeks dry. "Be more careful."

"I will, I promise."

Da clapped her on the shoulder and wrapped her in a bear-hug until she wheezed. "Crowe is gathering the Order in the summer apartments."

"I'll go right after I dress."

"Come on, Cat. Let's leave our girl to her duties."

When Katya reached her summer apartments, the rest of the Order was waiting. Maia's face was pinched and expectant; Crowe frowned at the tabletop, and Brutal seemed sleepy with his drooping eyelids. Pennynail's Laughing Jack mask had the same maniacal grin, and Katya had to restrain herself from ordering him to face the wall. It looked to be a long night.

"They were all dead," Brutal reported as she sat down.

Katya didn't need to ask who he meant. She wouldn't mourn the deaths, just the circumstances. "How is Starbride?"

"I wedged a little pyramid above her door when no one was looking," Crowe said. "It will alert me if anyone approaches her room with ill intent, unless of course that person is a pyradisté, and then it won't be able to read his or her thoughts."

"Can't you use one of the defensive pyramids like in the royal quarters?" Maia asked.

"Oh yes," Crowe said, "an exploding pyramid in the halls where everyone can pass is an *extremely* good idea."

"Peace," Katya said. "What happened to the bodies?"

"Being slowly digested at a pig farm." Brutal jerked his thumb at Pennynail. "The people he knows."

Pennynail tapped the temple of his mask and then laid the backs of his hands under his jaw, tilting his head coyly. "You're not just a pretty face," Maia said. He tipped her a salute, though no one laughed at the joke.

With a loud thump, Brutal dumped a bag on the table. "This was everything of significance that they had."

Crowe leaned forward to sift through the coins and handkerchiefs, one belt knife, three masks, and a blood-spattered bag of sweets. Katya's stomach rolled to the left. "The pyramid?" she asked.

"Darkened. We broke it just in case."

Crowe nodded, finishing his sift. "And the shop?"

"Supposed to be empty. The owner was an elderly man, deceased. Most of the stock was his, but the traitors added a few things."

"Articles embroidered with Fiendish script," Crowe said.

Katya started in her chair. "Is that why...?"

"You felt compelled? Yes. I should have seen it! But it's so hard to spot if you're not looking for it or if you're not..."

"A Fiend," Katya finished. "Someone whose Aspect can present. I didn't know what it was."

"You cannot blame yourself," Crowe said.

"Yes, I can!" She banged the table, making Maia jump. Her mother's worried face streaked through her memory. "I was a fool! I made myself a target. I put Starbride in danger. I have underestimated these people time and again."

No one responded. Katya forced herself to calm down. A headache began to pound through her temples, and her replacement necklace tingled against her chest.

"Isn't that the best trap?" Maia asked at last. "The kind that fits in with everything else? The kind you can't see, no matter how hard you look?"

"One thing is certain," Katya said. "We need to get ahead of these people."

Crowe glanced up, his expression grim. "You have something in mind?"

"Who knew I was going out into the city with Starbride?"

"Us," Brutal said.

"Your parents," Maia added.

Pennynail knocked on the table. When they looked at him, he made a shadow puppet of a horse on the wall. "The grooms," Crowe said.

Katya pointed at him. "Right. And how could the grooms have known where we were going?"

"Well." Maia rubbed her chin. "They knew you weren't leaving Marienne. If you were going to the forest, you would've had water skins at the very least, maybe even a picnic hamper."

"The royal grooms are supposed to have tight lips." Crowe frowned. "They had to know you were riding out in the morning on the night before, so they could have your horses ready. The Fiend speech, however, could have been in the city for a long time, or someone could have put it up in a hurry. I have to wonder what these people were hoping to accomplish. Were they going to parade you through the streets once the Aspect had presented?"

Maia looked sidelong at Pennynail. "The masks made them feel safe." He turned up his nose at her and crossed his arms.

"They expected to survive." Brutal waved at the pile of goods on the table. "Not a decent weapon among them."

Crowe's eyes darted around the room as if searching for the answer. "So, they knew about the Aspect, but had no idea as to the capabilities of the Fiend."

"They don't care about the means," Katya said softly. "If torturing Starbride hadn't worked, they would have killed her, but look where they started. They didn't even try hitting her; they went straight to maiming."

Maia shifted in her seat, and Brutal's serious face turned even more so. Pennynail was unreadable, but Crowe stared at her with sympathy. "You'll stop them, and we'll help."

"You'll interrogate the grooms by pyramid."

Crowe sat back. "Are you certain?"

Katya kept her gaze steady. "Look for anyone the grooms spoke with about me as well as any gaps in their memories made by someone who used a pyramid on them before."

"Do you recall the pyramid in the shop? Someone with that much skill will have covered his tracks. I'll have to dig deep into the minds of the grooms if the pyradisté has hidden his presence. The danger to them is—"

Katya thumped the table. "This is where we start. Interrogate them one at a time, with or without their permission. Do it, Crowe."

He shut his mouth with a snap. "Yes, Highness. Tomorrow morning?"

"Tonight."

Maia cleared her throat. "If we just start using pyramids on palace staff, people are going to find out, Katya."

"I need to know for certain," Katya said. "Crowe never hurt anyone with a pyramid."

Maia sat up straighter. "You shouldn't pry into the privacy of random people. You know it's not right. If you force them and one complains to the city Watch, they could start asking questions."

Katya rubbed her temples. Calm. She had to be calm. She was so tired of being at sea with this problem, but Maia's stubborn face reminded her that she would have other family breathing down her neck if she screwed up, not to mention troubles with the populace of Marienne. "Fine. Fine!

We ask for volunteers; we say it's in preparation for my brother's visit, that we've had a little trouble. We ask the senior grooms to go first, to set an example for the newer ones. Peer pressure should talk them into it. Pennynail, hide and watch; see if any of them try to sneak away. All right?"

Brutal cleared his throat in the still room. "Starting in the morning would look less suspicious."

Under the table, Katya pinched her leg, her need to do *something* grasping at her, but she forced it down. "You're right." She pointed to Pennynail. "But you go tonight, and make sure they're all accounted for."

Heads nodded all around, though Maia still seemed skeptical. Katya couldn't care about their feelings for the moment. They had a lead, and she was going to use it. And if any of the grooms refused to cooperate, she'd deal with them herself.

Chapter Ten: Starbride

Safe in Dawnmother's arms, it would've been easy to cry again, but Starbride didn't feel the need. She accepted solace with eyes closed and spoke of nearly everything that had happened. She left out Katya's Aspect, saying instead that they'd been rescued by friends.

"Those men are dead?" Dawnmother asked. She'd already inspected Starbride's finger and washed it before she wound it in a clean bandage.

"Killed in the fight." Starbride didn't relish the lie, but the truth bond didn't have to flow both ways.

"Good."

Starbride took a deep breath and offered a truth to pay for the lie. "I held her. We held each other. It was…I think she almost kissed me."

"The princess?"

"Yes."

"Right after?"

"No! Much later. She was blaming herself, and I wanted to comfort her. She didn't try to take advantage. She really is…the sweetest person." Starbride thought of their clasped hands, Katya's luminous hair, the depth of her sadness, of her worry. Before her memory could slip further back, Starbride shook her head to stop it. "She felt awful, Dawn."

"A girl who took you into such a bad part of town deserves to feel awful."

"What happened wasn't her fault."

"Well, if she feels so terrible, she will definitely help with the trading disputes in Newhope now."

"I'm not going to use her that way, Dawn."

The set of Dawnmother's face said she wasn't going to give up that easily. "If she cares for you, Star, she'll want to help."

"I won't ask."

"Star, my life for you and also the truth."

"Say what you need to."

"Are you sure her interest in you is genuine? That you're not simply an exotic flavor, another conquest?"

"Unless my ability to read a person's intentions has abandoned me, I'm certain."

"You'll forgive me if I keep my eyes open?"

Starbride hugged her once more. "Always."

"Rest now."

Dawnmother dragged her pallet to the bed's side before lying down. Once Starbride's head hit the pillow, she slept like the dead.

When Starbride awoke the next morning, Dawnmother was already up. Starbride hadn't heard the door open or shut, but a small breakfast sat on the room's lone table. Starbride lay under the blankets, her head on one arm. "You always have food for me, but I hardly ever see you eat."

"A servant's footsteps are made of shadows."

"That one never made sense to me. It's too tangled a metaphor."

"Horsestrong knew what he meant when he said it." Dawnmother poured a cup of tea. "And I know as well."

As Starbride ate, Dawnmother got her clothes ready for the day, one of the voluminous dessert dresses. Starbride made a face but didn't argue. Once dressed, she tucked her scroll and pencil in her sleeve and opened the door, staring when Dawnmother followed her out with an embroidery basket over one arm. "Where are you off to?"

"I'm coming with you."

Starbride bit her lip, torn between the concern in Dawnmother's eyes and her own need to rise above the fear of being alone. In the end, she had to admit having Dawnmother along would make both of them feel better.

Dawnmother locked their door and slipped the key into one of the pockets of her simple dress. She paused after she tested the handle. "I didn't notice that earlier."

Starbride followed her gaze to the little pyramid wedged above the door. "Crowe mentioned he was going to put a pyramid there."

"Guarded by the king's pyradisté? Well, well. I suppose the princess can't be all bad if she's setting her personal guards to watch over you. But what does it do?"

"He said it was an alarm."

"And he doesn't need to be there to use it?"

"Your guess is as good as mine. He said there are some pyramids that can be set to a task and then placed or used by anyone. He said mind magic had to be directed." She frowned as she thought of the shopkeeper's pyramid. "Mind magic..."

"What about it?"

"The shopkeeper used a pyramid to hypnotize Katya, but when he held it before me, I felt nothing."

"Perhaps it no longer worked. You said it went dark."

"That was after Katya's…friends broke in."

"Perhaps it only works on Farradains."

"That could be." Even with the words, she had her doubts.

When they reached the library, Starbride gathered a stack of books and tried to put all but studying out of her mind. The usual gathering of blue-robed monks roamed the aisles, but few others came and went. Dawnmother took the next seat and began her needlework. The steady sound of the thread gliding through the fabric cast a spell of its own, giving Starbride a feeling of normalcy, and she studied easier.

She'd been reading for about an hour when the sound of Dawnmother's needle stopped. It took Starbride a moment to notice the difference, but the lack of the sound interrupted her concentration as surely as a loud bang. She glanced over to find Dawnmother staring across the room, a pose that recalled Katya's hypnotized face. Starbride's belly froze with fear, but before she could leap to her feet, Dawnmother leaned toward her ear.

"There's a man lurking in the aisles, straight ahead. I've caught him staring at you five times."

Starbride set her pencil down and stretched her neck. While she moved, she scanned the aisles of books but saw only monks. Resting her chin on her fist, she pretended to read again but glanced up every few seconds. Beside her, Dawnmother resumed her needlework.

A slight movement near the back of the library, several aisles away, caught her attention. The figure was half in shadow, and one of the monks obscured him slightly, but he had to be the man Dawnmother had seen. He stood still, his head turned in Starbride's direction. When the monk moved on, the shadow man slid behind a bookshelf.

"I see him," Starbride said.

"Should we leave?"

If he was an enemy, he seemed loath to attempt anything with so many witnesses. And it *was* possible that he was simply curious about her. She bit her lip. It was too soon after the attack to put anything down to coincidence.

"We can't stay in here forever," Dawnmother said. "We should leave now, during daylight, when the halls are filled with people."

"Right." Starbride rolled up her scroll and tucked it inside her sleeve. "Let's go." They stood at the same time, and Starbride shuddered as Dawnmother palmed a pair of scissors. She slid the bulk of them up her sleeve and let the points rest between her forefinger and thumb. They hurried into the hall. Dawnmother kept her body between Starbride and the library doors.

Starbride listened to her pulse in her ears and wished that either Katya or Katya's powerful friends would walk around the corner. Even young Maia would be a comfort. To be a bodyguard, she must have known something about fighting. Starbride walked faster, unable to keep her thoughts from the scissors in Dawnmother's sleeve. Voices drifted down the hall, and she headed for them like an arrow.

"He's behind us," Dawnmother said.

Starbride hurried, resisting the urge to pick up her skirt and run. She turned a corner, and the voices grew louder. She didn't know where this hallway led, but as she and Dawnmother emerged into an alcove peppered with courtiers, she didn't care. A large window with a view of the garden let in a stream of sunshine, and the sill beneath it had been carved into a stone bench. Courtiers sat along it and babbled with others who stood before them. Starbride slowed and turned as she reached the alcove's outskirts. She maneuvered herself and Dawnmother out of the hallway, but stayed far enough away from the courtiers that it wouldn't seem as if she was trying to engage any in conversation.

"Breathe," Dawnmother said. She'd hidden her scissor-wielding hand in her basket.

Starbride nodded and watched the hallway over Dawnmother's shoulder.

"Even the men have those little pillows I was talking about. Yours should be ready soon."

Starbride nearly screamed that she didn't care about little pillows, but that was just her nerves trying to get the better of her. No, another part of her said, that was sense. Who cared about little pillows when she'd nearly had her fingers cut off, when a strange man was following her? And what did *he* have in mind? She had to dig her nails into her palms to force herself to calm down; her injured finger protested.

A young man turned the corner into the alcove, and Starbride held her breath. She hadn't been able to see his face in the library's shadows, but this had to be him. He was younger than she'd imagined, maybe thirteen or fourteen, with what looked like a first beard dotting his upper lip and chin. His light brown curls were tousled in the manner of many Farradain noblemen and courtiers, styled to look as if he'd just leapt from bed. He broke into a smile when his light blue eyes met Starbride's, and he didn't exude the menace she'd attributed to him when he'd stood in shadow. He seemed almost happy to see her, as if they were old friends. Boyish exuberance shone in his face, not the lust for violence she'd feared.

Dawnmother turned, and when the young man glanced at her stern expression, his face fell. He stepped forward, and the sunlight glinted off the crushed velvet creases of his dark green coat. "Oh, did I scare you? I'm sorry. I only wanted to meet you."

Starbride glanced to her right. Some of the courtiers were watching them, a few with appreciative, even lustful, looks at the young man. There was no one within earshot, though, not if they spoke quietly. "You know me?"

"Only that you're Allusian." He made a shallow bow. "Forgive me. Introductions should have come first, but I was afraid I would blurt out something stupid and then ramble on." He cleared his throat. "Kind of like now."

Starbride curtsied, calming in the face of his embarrassment "I'm Starbride."

He bowed again, and Starbride almost laughed at the double greeting. "Lord Hugo Sandy at your service."

"If you're a lord, I don't think you're at any courtier's service."

"My father says to always be at a lady's service, whether she has a title or not."

Starbride chuckled, nearly snorting. The boy's father should have taught him to guard his expressions better. Ah well, she supposed court would teach him that lesson soon enough. She hoped it would also teach him that lurking in shadows and following women was not the way to meet them. "What can I do for you, Lord Hugo?"

"Well." He rubbed the back of his neck. "I…I wanted to meet an Allusian. You see, my family just bought a villa in Newhope."

"Ah, and what did someone so young do to be banished to the most provincial of provinces?"

"No, no, I want to go! I've been studying your culture, and it's fascinating."

Starbride nearly rolled her eyes. No one said anything like that unless they wanted something. "Why not introduce yourself in the library?"

"Well, that would have been the logical thing to do. And, um, now that I've said the bit about Allusian culture out loud, I realize it sounds a lot stupider than it did in my head. I *am* sorry I scared you."

"Not a bit. My maid is a master of *jashida*. I was never worried."

Lord Hugo gave Dawnmother a worried glance. She gave him a

level stare, her scissors still hidden. "Ah," he said. "Yes. Well. Perhaps we might...speak a bit? One day when you're not busy? Or if you have the time now?"

A rise in the courtiers' noise level caught Starbride's attention before she could answer. Letting Dawnmother watch Lord Hugo, she turned just at Katya entered the hall. The courtiers rose from their seats to flutter around her, but Katya glanced at Starbride, her expression one of concern mixed with relief.

"Oh, there's the princess," Lord Hugo said.

Even with her bored mask on, even while fielding inane courtier comments, Katya had an undeniable grace, her movements sure and fluid. Her eyes darted toward Starbride, and her hand rested near her rapier as she edged closer. "I don't recognize you," she said to Lord Hugo in a drawl. "Are you new?"

Lord Hugo bowed, his lips pinched as if fighting to keep the boyish grin from his face. "Lord Hugo Sandy, Highness. I'm just out in society. First time at court."

"Oh." Katya's expression stayed languid, but Starbride could feel the tension in her body and knew she was ready to spring at this man if he so much as sneered in Starbride's direction.

Starbride's heart beat faster for a reason other than fear, and she kept herself from taking Katya's hand by clasping her own together.

"Where have you been hiding yourself?" a sultry voice asked from beside them.

Starbride groaned as Lady Hilda slinked forward. The courtiers fell back, fading to the buzz of irritated insects. Katya's expression went from bored to amused, and then back to bored in a second, and Starbride wondered what she was up to.

"Lady Hilda." Katya nodded as Lady Hilda curtsied. Starbride sneaked a glance at Lord Hugo to find him staring so widely at Lady Hilda's cleavage she feared his eyes might come loose from their sockets. "There's someone I'd like you to meet."

Lady Hilda's gaze snapped to Starbride, and her eyes held such acid that Starbride nearly flinched. Lady Hilda's expression changed to curious, however, when Katya gestured to Lord Hugo. "Lady Hilda Montenegro, meet Lord Hugo Sandy, new to court."

Lord Hugo bowed, and Lady Hilda curtsied, though not as deeply as for Katya. "Charmed," Lord Hugo said. "Rumors of your great beauty do not do you justice, Lady Hilda."

"Thank you, Lord Hugo. You'll go far in society, I'm sure." She turned her attention back to Katya, but before she could speak, Katya interrupted.

"I was just feeling sorry for Lord Hugo having to learn the palace on his own when up you popped like a jack-in-the-box. You always know where to be."

Lady Hilda's brow knit in obvious confusion. "Highness?"

"Show him around!" Katya spread her arms wide as if she'd come up with the perfect plan. Lady Hilda frowned as if she might protest, but Katya waved her away. "I insist upon it. A personal favor."

Lady Hilda had no choice but to curtsy again, and Starbride bit the insides of her cheeks. "Of course," Lady Hilda said. "If you'll come this way, Lord Hugo."

Equally confused, Lord Hugo couldn't argue any more than Lady Hilda. "I'd be delighted."

They moved off together, and before the courtiers could buzz back in, Katya gave Starbride a quick wink and whispered, "Hanna's Retreat."

Starbride nodded and waited until Katya was mobbed again to make a quick exit. As they turned the next corner, Dawnmother asked, "What was all that about?"

"I have no idea what Lord Hugo wanted, but Katya wants me to meet her on that balcony I told you about."

"This place becomes more complicated all the time."

Starbride and Dawnmother kept climbing stairways until they *had* to be near the secret passageway, or so Starbride thought. One dead end held the wrong tapestry, just as the one before had. As they began to retrace their steps, Katya crested a nearby staircase. "I thought you'd beat me there for sure."

"I get lost easily."

"You're on the right path, anyway." Katya led them to the right tapestry in a few short turns. They'd missed it by one.

Dawnmother gave Starbride a knowing look and stopped at a small bench just down the hallway. "I'll wait here."

"Thank you. We shouldn't be long."

"Take your time."

Shaking her head at Dawnmother's softly wicked smile, Starbride followed Katya through the passageway and up the stairs, her heart a little heavier than the last time. Katya seemed to feel the same weight; she didn't sport her infectious grin.

When they reached the top and Farraday spread out below them, Katya asked, "What did young Lord Hugo want?"

Starbride thought to tease Katya about jealousy, but she couldn't do that just yet. She told all that had happened.

"And what is *jashida*?"

"A spicy duck pie. And Dawnmother *is* a master of it."

"I'm sorry he scared you. If you want, I can get you another alarm pyramid from Crowe, and you can carry it with you."

"But it will only alert him, right? Not you?"

"They're attuned to the pyradisté that made them. I'm not sure what their range is, probably close." She touched her coat, and Starbride knew she was thinking of the pyramid necklace, the one that kept the Aspect at bay.

"Are all pyradistés pyramid users?"

"Yes, but not all pyramid users are pyradistés, though they're supposed to be."

"So, the man in the shop was a rogue?"

Katya's eyes shut tight for a moment, and Starbride saw her shiver. "Trained by someone else, or he joined the Pyradisté Academy, got his training, and then abandoned that path, something that should have been spotted."

Starbride put an arm around her back. "What happened is not your fault."

"It is." Starbride started to shake her head, but Katya caught her by the chin and held it gently between thumb and forefinger. "You will be safe. It's my only wish."

Starbride held her breath, caught by Katya's eyes, her warmth. "If Lord Hugo had attacked me…"

"I would have killed him a thousand times, even with everyone present, in spite of everything else."

They stared at one another in the quiet, and a cool breeze drifted over Starbride's skin as the moment lingered, but it wasn't the air that gave her gooseflesh. Katya leaned forward as slowly as when she'd pulled the clip from Starbride's hair.

As Katya's lips brushed hers, Starbride's eyes drifted shut, and her pounding heart and tightening belly told her what to do. Her lips parted, and she offered a hint of pressure that Katya returned, but not too much, not pushing. As the kiss went on, Katya's other hand slipped under Starbride's elbow and pulled her an inch closer, and Starbride half wished Katya *would* push her. Rumors painted Katya as a great lover, and the blood pounding through Starbride's veins wanted to know if it was true.

Katya broke away first, but she didn't wear the same cocky smile that had followed their first kiss. This was full of tenderness and, Starbride dared to think, gratitude. "I wanted to make sure you were all right."

Starbride sighed and irritation wound through her affection like a sour note. "That sounds a lot like the beginning of a good-bye."

Katya hung her head. "It is."

"I know you're busy." But she wanted to say, "Why must you kiss and run?"

"It's more than that. Crowe is investigating the people from that shop, and I want to hear what he has to say."

"But...shouldn't he report to the king?"

"Daughters can eavesdrop."

"Will you let me know what you find out?"

"Star, you shouldn't be involved."

Starbride crossed her arms and hoped her incredulous expression said it all.

Katya rubbed the bridge of her nose, and Starbride knew she got the message. "You're *already* involved."

"And so?"

"All right, all right. If it's not a state secret, I'll let you know what Crowe uncovers."

"Thank you."

"Think you'll be fine with just your maid to escort you?"

"Don't worry. She's armed with scissors."

"And there's always *jashida*."

Starbride couldn't help but laugh, and as they started down the stairs, her heart felt lighter. Katya would help her watch for danger; Katya would share the results of Crowe's investigation, and together, she and Katya would figure out what had happened and how to prevent it from happening again. Dawnmother didn't lose her suspicious look. Starbride supposed it was just as well that one of them kept a level head. It gave her permission to lose hers when she needed to, whenever Katya entered the room.

CHAPTER ELEVEN: KATYA

As Katya bid Starbride and Dawnmother farewell, she carried the memory of Starbride's lovely face and soft lips and promised herself that she had until Crowe's office to linger on those thoughts.

A full day hadn't passed since the attack, but Starbride seemed to need some physical contact—Katya damned sure needed it—and she *hadn't* pulled away, had even responded with a kiss of her own, flushing when Katya touched her, her breath coming quicker. Katya whistled as she walked.

Katya wouldn't push—she couldn't—and not just because of what had nearly happened at the shop. She wanted their relationship to unfold as slowly as it needed to, as Starbride needed it to. It was the perfect course of action, unless Starbride insisted on looking so beautiful all the time, and then Katya didn't know how to keep from kissing her at every opportunity.

When she reached her apartment, she forced herself to switch focus to the task ahead and took the secret passageway to Crowe's office. She paused to listen outside the hidden door.

"Of course it's not going to hurt, Williams. Trust me," Crowe said. "I just place it on your forehead so…" He fell silent, and Katya scratched on the door. It was opened a moment later by Pennynail, and Katya stepped out from behind a bookcase.

Crowe's study smelled of paper, ink, and old leather. The scent made her grimace at first, but she grew used to it in seconds, rather like Crowe's personality. Books and scrolls sat neatly assembled on his mahogany desk and the shelves of his many bookcases as well as the nooks of his leather sofa and chairs.

In the middle of the floor, on a giant Allusian rug, one of the grooms knelt with a pyramid pressed to his forehead. Crowe stood over him, eyes closed. Pennynail tapped Katya's shoulder and pointed to the large clock on the mantelpiece.

"I know," she said, "I had something to do." Starbride's lips warmed her thoughts again until she shook her head. "What have I missed?"

Pennynail put a hand to his forehead and shook his head as if in despair.

"Nothing yet, huh?"

Crowe's wrinkled face seemed even more creased, the strain evident in his lined forehead and in the puckered skin around his eyes and mouth. With a gasp, he stood back, separating the pyramid from the groom. "What in the spirits' names?" he asked. The groom collapsed to the rug.

"What is it?" Katya asked.

Crowe whirled around and stumbled. Katya and Pennynail reached to steady him. "Oh, Katya, I didn't know you'd arrived."

"You were in deep."

"I've never felt anything like it. This man supplied information to the traitors who attacked you, but it seems that he thought he was safe, that…that his memories would be erased. It's likely he doesn't even remember what he's done or why he did it." He grabbed hold of Katya's shoulders; awe and desperation fought on his features. "Katya, I've never seen such skill."

Katya kept hold of his arms, not wanting to risk him falling over. "I don't understand. They swayed him to their cause, got their information, and then blanked his mind?"

"No, no, they buried the memories so deep that I almost couldn't find them." He swallowed and stood up straighter, dropping his arms. "Extraordinary skill."

Katya let him go as he steadied. "So, even though we have him, not only can he not remember what he did, he can't remember why?"

"That's right."

"Can you make him remember?"

Crowe shook his head angrily. "I don't have the skill! Who does?"

The enemy pyradisté did, though she couldn't say that. "Well, what else is buried from him but not you?"

"He fed his information to the man posing as the shopkeeper, though I don't think they met in that shop."

"That's it?" Katya held her arms to the sides, forcing down the urge to lash out. "Is he the last one?"

Crowe nodded wearily.

Katya took a deep breath. They'd hit another dead end, and now she had to question whether or not they could punish a man who was unaware of what he'd done. "The Shadow said they had a highly placed agent. A groom is not highly placed."

"No." Crowe sagged onto the arm of his sofa. "But where do we look?"

Anger pounded at Katya's temples, making her necklace burn against her chest. Crowe eyed her with a wary stare. "Get everything from this groom," she said before he could tell her to calm down. "Try to make him remember. Find out who his friends are and see if any of them remember any *new* friends he made. Maybe we'll find the original people who talked him into being a traitor."

Crowe's mouth set in a line. "More pyramid interrogations will attract too much unwanted attention as well as fan the fires of anti-monarchy sentiment."

"Then *ask* them. Tell Brutal and Maia to help you. In the meantime, we need to find out if the shopkeeper was our master pyradisté or if it's someone else. Let's dig into the Pyradisté Academy and find everyone of this skill level. There can't be that many."

"You're right."

She clapped him on the shoulder, glad to turn her passion to planning. "Whoever he is, I know he won't measure up against you in the end. If you weren't the most powerful, my father never would have chosen you as his pyradisté."

"Thank you. That's good to hear now and again."

"No sarcasm, Crowe. We're on the right track. Don't burn out now."

"I'll get what I can." He opened one of the drawers and lifted a pyramid necklace. "Here, I stayed up making this last night."

"What about the one I'm wearing?"

"Supposed to be temporary. I'd like to see you break through that!"

Katya traded one necklace for the other. "I was happy to break it, you know."

"Yes. She's a beautiful girl."

The thought of Starbride almost drove Katya's anger away, but she set her jaw, needing to hold on to the feeling for the time being. "I'll keep her safe." Certain they'd carry out the tasks she'd given them, Katya stepped back into the secret passageway and headed for her parents' rooms, determined to keep them informed.

But what to tell Starbride? She had the sinking suspicion that Starbride wouldn't forget the promise of information. The next time they met, she'd want answers, and Katya was quickly learning that all the romantic gestures in the world couldn't stand between her and a secret. Once the Order had figured out the puzzle, Katya could pick and choose what would steer Starbride away from the Order itself. It was a perilous dance, and all she could hope for was that she wouldn't have to lie *too* much.

"Enter!" her father called when she knocked. He bustled around the sitting room with a leather folio. "Ah, Katya, you haven't seen the wheat crop report, have you?"

"It's not my day to watch it."

Da simply blinked at her. "Why would it be?"

"It's a joke, Da. Where did you last see your report?" She glanced at the various papers lying about the room.

"How the deuce should I know? My new clerk's a menace. 'Where's the wheat crop report?' I ask him, and do you know what he says?"

Katya shook her head, but Da didn't seem to expect her to keep up an end of the conversation.

"'In your office, Majesty?' Just like that, with a question mark at the end, as if *unsure*. Can you believe the man? As if I would keep such an important document that I *must* read in my office, for spirits' sake!"

"No, of course not. Anyone who knows you should know that you hate to sit and read."

"What are clerks for if not to keep up with these mountains of paper always flocking around me? If I set a piece of paper down, they're supposed to pick the damn thing up and keep it until I need it again!" He tossed a pillow aside.

Katya watched the pillow bounce across the floor. "Where is he now?"

"I sent him to the kitchens, told him to count all the spoons, and report back. That'll teach him a lesson!"

"And now you don't have a clerk."

"Bloody useless." Da stomped over to a small serving table and glared at it. A moment later, he glanced up at Katya with a confused look on his face. "Something you wanted to say to me, was there, my girl?"

"We caught a crooked groom who doesn't even know he's a traitor."

Da sank into a chair as Katya told him all about it. At the end, he jumped up to pace again. "How the deuce do you hang a man who doesn't know what he's done?"

"You don't."

"Sounds damned odd, pretending to blank a man's mind. From everything my brother used to say, blanking it wholesale would be easier. Of course, he was always a little too heavy-handed with the mind blanking."

Katya wished they had Uncle Roland to help them. She didn't know how his skills had stood up to Crowe's, but two pyradistés would be more useful than one. "I don't know if the traitors wanted us to find this groom, but if they did, maybe they wanted to keep our focus on him."

"A scapegoat, eh? But where else can you focus?"

"The Pyradisté Academy. I'm tired of following these people. I want to get ahead of them."

"Crowe's your access there."

Katya thought of Crowe's haggard face. "He may be doing too much, Da. His skill is the same as always, but he doesn't have as much energy as he used to."

"He is getting on in years, my girl. Time will soon come when you'll have to choose another, and Crowe can stay on as my advisor and pyradisté."

"That would kill him, Da." Katya squirmed at the thought of Crowe's betrayed expression.

"Then get him some help."

"He would mercilessly bully any sort of help from within a jealous funk."

"Ha! Once this current investigation passes, start looking into the Academy yourself, and find someone younger for the Order."

Katya nodded, still reluctant, but she couldn't argue with her father once he'd made up his mind. She joined his search and found what he was looking for under a flower arrangement on a side table.

"Right where I left it!" Da winked as he took the report. "Well, I'll read this on my way to a meeting with the artists and artisans guild. They want funding for a statue or some such."

"How do you keep all this stuff straight in your head? Crop reports before statues?"

"Simple. I don't pay attention to most of it and let those involved argue it out; I step in if there's a stalemate. Otherwise, it would be too oppressive. Plus, by keeping my mouth shut and looking wise, everyone feels they have a say in how things are run *and* thinks I knew the outcome from the beginning."

Katya frowned. "But if you don't speak up, *don't* they have a say?"

"Of course, but they've still got to convince everyone else that their way is the right way. And most of them are satisfied with small decisions, and they leave the big ones to me." Katya continued to frown, and Da clapped her on the shoulder. "Don't worry about it unless you have to, my girl, and right now, you don't have to."

"That's so. Where's Ma?"

"The deuce if I know. Probably hip-deep in plans for Reinholt's arrival."

Katya suppressed a scowl. The days were ticking away until her brother's visit, before which she hoped to have this newest business sorted. She prayed that Crowe got some new information soon.

As if summoned by her prayers, Crowe burst through the door. "Not Longside!"

Katya and her father stared at Crowe as he glanced between their two faces. "Majesty," he said to her father and bowed.

"Crowe, what are you babbling about, man?"

"Not Longside?" Katya asked.

Crowe beamed and rubbed his hands together as if he couldn't contain his excitement. "Not *in* Longside, *near* Longside, on the way to it. With two minds to plunder, I could put it in order. The Shadow gave me Longside, but the groom's memories of the man posing as the shopkeeper were in an old manor house."

Katya still stared. "I'm not quite—"

"The old manor house is on the way to Longside, don't you see? The images I got from the Shadow featured the journey to Longside and the tavern in Longside, which he frequented, but he concealed the manor house from me. One bit of forest looks like another, you see, but the groom could hide nothing because he didn't even know he was hiding it! It was buried behind the other memory blocks. The people who erased bits of his memories might have missed this!"

Da glanced at Katya. "So," he said, "the traitors are meeting at a manor house on the road to Longside? Is that what you're trying to say by way of long, unneeded explanation?"

Crowe seemed as if he might bristle. Instead, he bowed.

"Well, my girl," Da said, "you're on your way to a manor house near Longside."

"The other traitors might not even know we've found the groom yet," Katya said, her mind racing.

"We kept that quiet," Crowe added. He bounced on the balls of his feet.

Da clapped once, a loud, cracking sound. "Aha! Catch them with their trousers down! How I wish I could come with you."

Katya bit the insides of her cheeks to keep from asking her father how often he wished to catch people with their trousers down. "If we start now, we won't be there until after dark."

"We can't ride into the unknown in the dark," Crowe said.

"Right. We set out in the morning, but we won't go rushing in. We'll get close and then scout. We'll do this right and won't get caught with *our* trousers down."

Crowe's mouth twisted in a wry smile. "That would be unfortunate."

"You're damned right," Da said. "Go, make ready. The excitement is killing me! Damned if I know how I'll be able to focus on crop reports and statues now."

Katya hugged her father good-bye and hustled from the room with Crowe. "Good work," she said once they were out in the hallway. "Excellent work."

"After so long, it's nice to catch a break!" He spoke in a loud whisper, and she knew what he was feeling, swallowing the urge to make a triumphant yell herself.

"I'll tell Averie. Will you inform the others?"

"Absolutely. We're one step ahead at last."

They parted at the next hallway, and Katya continued to her rooms. If the traitors didn't expect their hideout to be revealed, who knew what the Order might find? On the other hand, if the traitors wanted Katya to find the manor house, they would set a trap. Well, she'd be careful not to fall into it. The Order would walk with caution, scout, and scan the area with Crowe's pyramid magic, and the traitors would find any trap turned back on them. They'd tell no one, and she'd saddle their horses herself if she had to.

In Katya's personal sitting room, Averie's eyes lit up as Katya told her of the plan. "Excellent, at last."

"I want you to come with us all the way to the manor house, Averie. No hunting this time. We'll need your tracking skills."

"Well, the court can't expect you to make a kill every time you go out."

"Oh, we'll make one. It just won't be animals." She tried to sit, but she had to get up and pace.

"Is Starbride invited to dinner?" Averie asked.

Katya stopped in the middle of the rug. It would be nice, very much so, to see Starbride again so soon, but she didn't think she could contain her excitement about the next morning's journey. Starbride would want to know the reason. Katya could almost hear the conversation in her head. "Why must you go and not the king's Guard?" Starbride would ask.

And Katya couldn't tell her about the Order. She could make up an excuse that she was the best one to go because the Umbriels tried to keep the Aspect a secret, and the fewer who knew the better, but Starbride would still want to know why Katya had to go *personally*. Spirits knew she'd want to tag along, saying that if it was safe enough for Katya, it was safe enough for anyone.

Katya would have to stare into those warm eyes and say no, offering no explanation, and she couldn't stand the thought of those eyes turning hard and resentful. "No, I won't invite her. I don't want to have to explain my mood."

"You could tell her it's the excitement of seeing her again."

"I, um, sort of promised that I'd keep her informed of the investigation into what happened at the shop."

"I know you're in charge, but is that wise?"

"Wise or not, it's what happened."

"Are you going to tell her about the Order of Vestra?"

Katya paused again. If their relationship continued, if Katya eventually took Starbride to be her consort, she'd find out about the Order sooner or later, but now wasn't the time, not with the future so uncertain; she couldn't drop another secret on Starbride so soon. "Not right now. I'll find a way to dance around it."

"A difficult dance, to say the least."

"But necessary."

Averie nodded. "I'll lay our hunting leather out for tomorrow. Will you roam the halls for the rest of today?"

"No, I don't want to chance giving anything away to the court, and I don't want to risk running into Starbride again."

"Again?"

Katya sank into one of the plush chairs. "We had an…encounter, on the Retreat."

"Aha! Double the reason for a good mood."

Katya draped her leg over one of the chair's arms as she thought back to the kiss. For a moment, it drove thoughts of the next day from her mind, but when she coupled the thoughts together, it added up to an excitement she couldn't quench, and she had to stand and pace again.

CHAPTER TWELVE: STARBRIDE

Starbride made an early start. Lurking young lords or not, she would spend the new day in study. Dawnmother stopped her at the door. "I can come with you again."

"I have to get used to going out alone. I can't live in fear. If there's any trouble, I'll seek out another room full of people." Dawnmother frowned, her eyes worried. Starbride faked all the confidence she didn't feel. "Check on me as often as you'd like."

Near the stables, she spotted Katya striding through an intersection, her friends behind her, all except the masked man and Crowe. Starbride prepared to call out, but then she paused. Katya couldn't be going hunting, not with traitors hiding around every corner. But if not hunting, what? A break from court that left Starbride behind?

Starbride bit her lip. True, one kiss did not mean their lives were irrevocably tied or that they had to spend every free moment together. But Katya was always so busy. Free moments were all they had, and Katya had given the impression she wanted to spend them with Starbride. Then where was she going? Starbride's feet followed Katya as her mind worked. She was almost to the stables when she had it. Katya was investigating the incident at the shop *without* her father's pyradisté and with just a few friends to guard her!

More importantly, though, Katya was heading off to investigate without *Starbride*. After Katya had looked her in the eye and promised to keep her informed, Katya was striking out alone. Crowe must have told her something of note, and wherever she was going couldn't be all that dangerous if she chose to go herself.

Why couldn't Starbride go as well? Anger hurried her footsteps. Katya was leaving early, no doubt hoping to elude her, to be back later in the day in time for a quick cuddle and a dose of misinformation. As she rounded the next corner, she saw that Katya had stopped. Starbride leapt back the way she'd come. Katya's friends loitered, their backs discreetly turned from where Katya stood with a young blond woman, a courtier Starbride had seen before. It wasn't Lady Hilda, but as the blond courtier giggled at something Katya said and smiled coquettishly, who she *wasn't* brought little comfort. Their words just reached Starbride down the hallway.

"Where have you been hiding yourself, Highness?" The blond courtier lowered her eyes and looked up through her lashes. "Not that I have the right to ask, but I have missed you."

"We all have," another voice said. Several courtiers, men and women, approached Katya from an intersecting hallway. So, Starbride wasn't the only one up early, but of course, she hadn't gotten up to catch a princess.

Katya leered before she raised the blond courtier's hand and kissed it. Starbride bit her lip so hard it pained her. The kiss was slow and languid, exactly as it had once been on Starbride's own hand. "I promise, Miss Greyson, that when I come back from the hunt, your company will be the first I seek out." Katya bid them all farewell, and then she was gone down the hallway. The courtiers clustered around Miss Greyson and led her away in a gabbling horde.

Starbride stood still for a moment, her legs paralyzed. A kiss, a promise to return? It all sounded terribly familiar. Was Starbride the same as everyone else, then? Or was Katya only paying her special attention out of guilt? If Miss Greyson had been tied to that shop table, would she have earned a trip to Hanna's Retreat?

Starbride clenched her fists and told herself it couldn't be true. It was an act, like when Katya had to follow Lady Hilda into the Courtiers Ball and leave Starbride on the balcony. Katya's face with the courtiers was a mask, but Starbride had seen her real face.

Hadn't she? She hurried after Katya again, telling herself that Katya didn't want her out of the way in order to go whoring. No, it couldn't be true, it couldn't! Katya was being *protective*. She was *worried*.

However, a promise was a promise, and there Katya went, breaking it and being a flirtatious ass on the way. If Katya wanted Starbride in her life, she would have to learn she couldn't just *choose* to shut Starbride out, especially to act like an idiot. It seemed there was only one way to teach her.

The stable yard stood empty of grooms. Without calling for help, Katya's group saddled four horses and rode out. Starbride waited in the doorway, wondering at the lack of grooms, before she decided to take advantage of the situation. She slipped into the closest occupied paddock, and when her eyes adjusted to the gloom, she spied the horse she'd ridden before and moved toward it. She took a saddle blanket from a pile in the corner. The horse turned one large eye toward her, and Starbride mumbled to it as she eased the blanket over its back and tied the strings underneath.

After glancing at the saddles, Starbride shook her head. Under her ridiculous gown, a saddle would chafe horribly. She bridled the animal and led it out of the stable. The grooms still hadn't emerged.

Before anyone could notice, or at least before they could stop her, Starbride guided her horse out of the yard. She walked it after Katya's party, keeping her eyes on the large man and his equally large horse. Any crowd parted before him like wheat in a high wind. They moved quickly, and Starbride tried her best to keep pace without mounting. She was saving that embarrassment until the very last minute.

Katya and her friends arrived at a side gate packed with produce-laden wagons and a flock of sheep. Starbride waited on a corner and craned her neck to see, until Katya passed out of sight. She then walked her horse closer and paused again, letting the sheep pass by and allowing Katya to get well ahead on the road.

She glanced at her patient horse and around the crowded street until she spied an empty crate on the side of the road, near the gate itself, and led the horse to it. Once atop the crate, she hoped she hadn't forgotten everything about riding bareback, bounced on her toes several times, and then jumped, pushing on the horse's back to help her up. Her legs tangled in her wide skirt, but her push and jump were enough to lie across the horse. It shied, whickering, and she muttered to it, ignoring the farmers' laughter as she swung one leg around the back and pulled toward the front of the horse until she could sit astride it. She pushed as much of her dress underneath her as she could, but she knew she looked silly sitting on the horse with her skirt just above her knees.

The gate guards whistled when they saw her. She heard a few mutters about strange Allusian customs, and one of the farmers called, "Forgot your saddle and your trousers, miss!" Starbride set her jaw even as she blushed, not giving them the pleasure of any other reaction.

Katya had nearly reached the forest when Starbride set off down the road. She couldn't get too close, but she didn't want Katya to get too far ahead. It would be safer to stay in shouting range. She hoped to tail Katya's party for about an hour before she caught up, far enough away from Marienne that Katya couldn't just send her back.

Just outside the gate, someone said, "Starbride!" and Lord Hugo Sandy rode out of the gate, waving his arm, and grinning like a fool.

"Damn." Starbride kept going, pretending she hadn't heard, but he caught up to her a little way down the road.

He doffed his cap and stared at her legs. "Um." With a swallow, he tore his gaze from her legs, focused on her face, and put on his cap again. "You, um, don't have a saddle."

"This is how we ride in Allusia."

He accepted the lie without question. "Right, and where you're from, everyone usually wears trousers, correct?"

Starbride straightened with surprise. He *had* been studying. "Yes."

"Did they not have a sidesaddle in the barn?"

"A what?"

"A saddle that allows a lady to wear a dress and still ride, um, comfortably."

"There's a...?" Starbride clenched a fist. Damn, she'd never heard of such a thing! "I...was in a hurry."

"I see." He stared ahead for a moment. "Will you allow me to ride with you?"

Starbride cast a glance ahead. Katya disappeared as the road wound into the woods, and Starbride kicked her horse into a canter. "It'll be very boring. I'm not going far."

"More entertaining than a tour with Lady Hilda! It was like an inquisition. She grilled me about you and the princess the entire time. She certainly loves gossip."

"Does she?" Starbride tried to think of some way to leave him behind. She couldn't even fake an interest in what he'd said to Lady Hilda.

"She wanted to meet again today. I think she thinks I'm keeping something from her, but I sent her a note saying I'll be out all day, so I have to make up lots of things to do. I'd be happy to spend a few hours with you if you're amenable."

"Actually, Lord Hugo. I've got a lot of thinking to do...about how my time would best be spent in Marienne." It sounded feeble, even to her ears. "I might go into the woods to, um, meditate."

"Ah," he said, and she thought that might be an end of it. "I can be very quiet. I can meditate, too."

"But, Lord Hugo, as I said—"

"I'm sorry, Miss Starbride, but I can't let you go into the forest alone."

Starbride stared at him; he'd followed her from the library, and now they were outside of Marienne, with only a handful of people on the road, and those not within earshot. Lord Hugo was armed with a rapier and a belt knife, and Starbride didn't even have Dawnmother's scissors to protect her. She stopped her horse and called herself a fool. "Why not, Lord Hugo?"

He didn't meet her eyes for a moment but finally nodded, seeming resolved as he looked up. "Because you are a young lady, Miss Starbride. Who knows what ruffians await you out there?" He took his cap off again and pressed it to his breast. "Forgive me. I didn't say this at first because I didn't want to scare you, but the reason I caught up when I saw you riding alone is because the world outside the city can be a dangerous place. It is my duty to act as your escort."

Starbride forced down the urge to laugh at his earnest face. His sentiment was sweet, very old-fashioned, and a wee bit self-important, but he also had a good point, even if he was unaware that the world *inside* the city was also a dangerous place. But if she got into trouble outside, she could call for Katya, *if* Katya didn't get away while she was wasting time with Lord Hugo.

Starbride rode for the forest again, harder this time. She didn't know Lord Hugo, but she supposed Katya could protect her from him, too, if it came to that. "You don't need to come with me, Lord Hugo. I take responsibility for my own safety; no blame shall fall on you."

He slid his cap back on as he kept pace with her. "Forgive me again, Miss Starbride, but that just won't do. My conscience would never recover, and my honor will not let me turn back."

Starbride looked away from him and rolled her eyes.

"Isn't this the very track the princess just took?"

Starbride slowly turned her head and stared at him.

A flush crept from his collar to his ears. "Are you...meeting Princess Katyarianna, and that's why you don't want me along? I don't mean to pry," he said hurriedly. "After yesterday, all of Lady Hilda's questions and everything, I assumed you and the princess might be..." His face turned a deeper crimson, and he cleared his throat again. "Well, none of my business. Just...just let me escort you to wherever it is you're meeting. I'm sure she wouldn't want anything to happen to you, and you'd probably be safe enough since she knows you're following her, but still...I'd...I really would feel awful if anything, well..."

Starbride didn't know what to say. Lord Hugo had the right road, but the wrong end, as Horsestrong once said. "Let's just hope Lady Hilda isn't following you following me following her, or we really will be in the middle of a farce, Lord Hugo."

"I'm surprised at Princess Katyarianna for not giving you an escort."

"Actually, I'm going to surprise *her*...on a hunting trip. It was a last-minute decision."

"I heard that she likes to hunt. So, a surprise, eh? No wonder you didn't stop for trousers or a sidesaddle." He glanced at her legs, went crimson again, and stared ahead.

He clearly expected them to catch up with Katya right away and reveal themselves, and Katya would wonder what they were up to. Starbride would have to talk very quickly and dismiss Lord Hugo before he had a chance to speak or to see and hear anything he wasn't supposed to.

Inside the forest, Katya was lost from sight, but the dust from her passage floated above the road. Starbride didn't want to run her horse, even along the packed dirt. She couldn't risk unseating herself. Part of her brain told her to just pack it in, to go back to the library, and study. If he was serious about protecting her, Lord Hugo would turn around with her. But then she thought of Katya leaving her behind and flirting with courtiers, and anger spurred her onward. She wouldn't just be a convenience, even to a princess. And she wouldn't let Katya go back on a promise. She remembered the kiss on Miss Greyson's hand and leaned forward.

An hour passed, and Starbride made small talk with Lord Hugo about the court, about the weather, about Allusia. Well into their second hour, her answers became monosyllabic as worry tightened her insides. Katya's dust cloud had disappeared.

"What's wrong, Miss Starbride?" Lord Hugo asked.

"There's no more dust."

"Beg pardon?"

"The dust cloud is gone. Katya...Princess Katyarianna has either left us too far behind or she's left the road."

Lord Hugo took a long look around and frowned. "So, you decided at the last minute to surprise her, but you didn't know her destination?"

Starbride shook her head, feeling more foolish with each passing second. Katya had left the road at some point, and Starbride hadn't noticed where. And she didn't know Lord Hugo, not really. She sidled her horse away from him.

"I know I'm always asking for forgiveness," Lord Hugo said, "and I'm going to do it again now. Let's return to Marienne. Perhaps you can think of another surprise?"

Starbride pressed her lips together. Oh, she'd have a surprise for Katya all right: scathing recrimination. Could she yell at Katya for leaving her in the woods if Katya didn't know she was there?

They turned back toward Marienne, and Starbride stared at her horse's neck and wondered what in Darkstrong's name she'd been thinking. She *hadn't* been thinking, that was the problem. She'd just reacted, and that wasn't like her, not at all. Another trouble to lay at Katya's feet. Starbride tried to tell herself to stop being unfair, but everything that had happened built up in her: meeting Katya and getting to know her, finding a friend and possibly more, and then being attacked and afterward being left out and feeling cheated. Her head felt like a jumble, never mind her heart.

"Don't take it so badly, Miss Starbride," Lord Hugo said. "Sometimes things don't work out, that's all"

"I'll be all right, Lord Hugo."

"Tell you what! Let's watch the bushes and underbrush. Maybe we'll be able to tell where she cut through." His forced cheerfulness grated, but Starbride had to agree. There was no choice when someone was trying so hard to cheer her up.

"Ah," he said a few minutes later, "I think I see something." He dismounted and hurried to the ditch on the side of the road. "This bush has been flattened recently!" With one more step, he pitched headlong into the bush with a cry.

"Lord Hugo!" Starbride called. "Did you fall?" She slipped down from her horse and hurried over.

A dark-haired man stepped from the cover of the undergrowth. Older than Lord Hugo, around twenty, he was dressed in leather, a woodsman's or a hunter's outfit. He eyed Starbride with a grin. "Well, two for the price of one."

Starbride stepped back toward her horse.

The young man held up an arm. "Whoa there, miss, stand fast unless you want your lord to suffer."

Another man stepped from the underbrush, mid-twenties and large, his coloring and features similar to the younger man. Both had swords and knives at their belts, and the large man held Lord Hugo close, one hand over his mouth. Lord Hugo struggled, and the young man relieved him of his rapier and knife before the larger shoved him toward Starbride.

"Thieves!" Lord Hugo moved in front of Starbride. "You'll not get away with this."

Starbride jabbed him in the back, wishing he'd keep his tongue. She began to edge toward the horses. They'd shied away from the noise. She pulled on Lord Hugo's coat and hoped he would take the hint. They needed to ride away at all speed. The shop flitted to the front of her memory, and she pushed it away.

The two robbers glanced at one another. "And how will you stop us, young lord?" the younger man said.

Starbride continued to back away, trying to drag Lord Hugo, but his chin inched up by degrees. She didn't want to abandon him, but what could she do to help besides encourage him to run?

She could call for Katya. Starbride gathered breath for a scream, but someone grabbed her shoulder. Her breath left her in a rush, and she spun to face another man, this one in his thirties, his clothes a little better than the other two: a leather vest on top of a clean white shirt and cloth trousers. His hard blue eyes bored into her. "Cooperate," he said, "and you won't be hurt."

"Let her go!" Lord Hugo cried. There was the crunch of feet on gravel, and someone tugged Starbride's arm once before letting go. She tried to turn, but the bearded man grabbed her shoulders.

He frowned. "I've seen you before, or maybe I've just heard about you."

Starbride tried to keep calm and think. Behind her, she heard a sharp cry and the sounds of a struggle. "What…do you want with me?"

"It's not what I want, but it is fortuitous. We were hoping to catch one of her friends in our net, but now here *you* are." He turned her around but kept hold of her shoulders. Lord Hugo was struggling to his feet. He grasped his stomach and faced the other two men who stood between him and Starbride. "But what should we do with your young friend?"

"Fight me like men!" Lord Hugo said. "One at a time!"

The younger man glanced over his shoulder and then gestured to the larger man. "Fight him, Cassius. He might even be an adequate swordsman."

Cassius drew his short blade, and the younger man threw Lord Hugo's rapier to the ground. Lord Hugo scooped it up and took a stance that seemed clumsy even to Starbride's untrained eye. His whole body shook, and his wrist didn't seem adequate to the task.

Cassius lumbered in with a quick jab. Lord Hugo darted out of the way like a bolt of lightning and stabbed Cassius in the shoulder. Cassius leapt back with a yelp.

Lord Hugo saluted with his rapier. "I am an *exceptional* swordsman." He took a different stance, compact and protected, and then launched an attack. Better prepared, Cassius blocked, but Starbride saw blood dribble out of his leather sleeve, and he sought to keep his wounded arm behind him. Lord Hugo zipped and stabbed, and soon Cassius had more shallow cuts, more limbs to favor. Starbride began to hope they might get out of this, that whatever these men had planned would go up in smoke.

After a moment, though, the bearded man said, "Enough. Darren, stop this."

The young man looked over his shoulder again. "Are you sure, my lord?"

"We've no more time to waste."

As Darren lifted Lord Hugo's knife, Starbride opened her mouth to shout, but the bearded man grabbed her throat, cutting off her voice and her air. Darren threw the knife into Lord Hugo's back. With a cry, Lord Hugo pitched forward, and Cassius struck him across the face with the pommel of the short blade. The rapier fell from Lord Hugo's grip as he collapsed into the dirt and lay still.

The bearded man released Starbride's throat as stars danced before her eyes. With a harsh inhale, she coughed, and the bearded man's breath whispered against her ear. "Scream and you join him."

Starbride's teeth came together. She tried to cross to Lord Hugo, but the bearded man wouldn't let her go, and she could only watch his still form and fight despair. She rounded on the bearded man. "Is he dead? Did you kill him?"

"His pain is done. Your princess's is just beginning."

Starbride shrank back and snarled. "I will never help you, whatever you have planned."

"All you need to do is be present."

Starbride thought of the short table and the knife between her fingers. She gripped her bandage and tried to fight her panic.

The bearded man shook his head as if reading her mind. "No, no. We are not those ruffians."

"We're much…friendlier," Darren said from behind her. His touch grazed her shoulder.

Starbride took a step away from Darren, her hatred for him growing every second. The bearded man gave him a level look over her head. "That's enough, Darren. Did you help Cassius patch himself up?"

"Yes." Darren moved closer. Starbride shifted away.

"You're in for a short trip." The bearded man reached in his trouser pocket and pulled out a pyramid. "And you don't even need to remember it." He held the pyramid in front of Starbride's face, and just as in the shop, she felt nothing.

His eyes widened. "That's…unexpected."

"What is it, my lord?" Darren asked.

"I hadn't heard that you're a pyradisté," the bearded man said.

"I'm…"

"Ah, you didn't know? No training, then. I guess we'll have to do this the old-fashioned way." He shook the pyramid slightly. "Look deep into this, and all your questions will be answered."

Starbride couldn't help it. She looked, barely registering the footstep behind her and the pain that detonated inside her skull as something collided with it. Her legs wouldn't hold her all of a sudden, and her mind couldn't stay awake.

It was cold, the chill of a strong wind and not enough clothing to protect her from it. Starbride was lying on something equally cold, bare stone by the feel against her shoulder, and she'd been lying there much too long. Her feet were numb, and she smelled mustiness, the scent of old cloth.

As recent memories returned, Starbride lay still and pretended to sleep. She listened hard and heard nothing but the wind. She risked cracking one eye open and saw only a dark swath of cloth covering her face. A flex of her hands revealed that they were bound in front of her. She moved her feet and found them unbound. Starbride paused, waiting to hear if her slight movement induced anyone else to move. When she heard nothing, she felt along the bag covering her head and then tugged it off. A long expanse of stone bricks led to a wall in disrepair, half of it gone around what remained of a window. A tattered tapestry trailed from the wall, gone to threads. Starbride saw the tops of trees beyond the wall and knew she must be on a second or third story.

She lifted her head, her every thought tuned to escape. Pain throbbed in the back of her skull, her bound wrists, and a spot on her side. Her room had no roof, and wisps of cloud scudded across the blue sky. Through a doorway behind her, a staircase led downward. The only other exit was blocked by fallen stone.

With a slight groan, Starbride sat up. Pain reached a crescendo in her brain; she breathed deep and waited for it to still. Her side ached, but she couldn't reach to touch it. She'd been lying on several small stones, one of them with a fresh red stain where it had dug into her. But she still had all of her limbs. She thanked Horsestrong and turned her attention to unbinding her wrists. These men couldn't do anything to her or to Katya if she escaped.

Starbride tried to gnaw on the cord, but it felt like leather wrapped over wire. She sought the ends but couldn't spot them in the figure eight looped around her wrists. Trying to stretch the cord made it bite into her skin, so she gave up on it for the moment and stood. Her only comfort was that her dress was dirty and tattered, torn in several places, and there had to be a bloodstain on the side. Completely unsalvageable.

She choked back a laugh, afraid of hysteria. The men had taken her shoes. Did they think that would prevent her from going anywhere? The floor was strewn with broken brick and bits of masonry, but she could step around them. The stones were bitterly cold in the shade of the collapsed wall. Maybe they thought it would be too chilly for her pampered little toes.

Starbride approached the gap in the wall from the side, keeping herself hidden in the hope of remaining unseen by anyone standing below. When she reached the window, she peeked around at a small clearing being taken over by the forest, a garden overrun by weeds and a flagstone path that had been knocked askew by roots reclaiming the ground.

Creeping to the head of the stairs, she listened, ignoring her numb feet. She took one step down and listened again. Light flickered up the circular stairway, but to descend, she'd have to cross a patch of complete darkness. Starbride felt with her foot first, her toes passing over loose stones as she tried to find a clear place to stand. When she heard voices, she froze.

"...be out at least another few hours," one said. Darren.

"How do you know?" another asked. Cassius.

"You cracked her a good one, and she's just a little courtier after all."

Starbride hurried across the floor and resumed her original position, on her side facing away from the staircase. She slipped the bag over her head again before footsteps crested the stairs. She fought not to hold her breath, to keep it deep and even, and tried not to think of what they intended to do with her. She didn't trust the bearded man's promise and begged Katya to show up soon and rip them apart.

The sound of booted feet paused behind her. "See?" Darren said.

"Yeah, but—"

"Relax. She'll stay put until the princess comes."

Starbride's heart pounded, but she didn't let her body respond.

"The lord said not to touch her," Cassius said. Starbride bit her lip harder and forced herself not to roll away. She couldn't help but wonder what part of her Darren had been close to touching. Bile gathered in her throat, and she swallowed it.

"Come on," Cassius said. "Out of temptation's path." Darren chuckled as their footsteps receded down the stairs.

Starbride counted to sixty, took a deep breath, sat up, and pulled the bag off her head. She made herself take a rational look at the circumstances—anything was better than dwelling on Darren's odious hands. They planned to use her against Katya somehow. A lure? A trap? Probably both.

Starbride crossed to the window again. The trees were too far away to use, and she didn't think she could climb down the wall with bound wrists; she'd never been a good climber. She also couldn't sneak down the stairs with the two men around. Resting her forehead against the cold stone, she willed herself to think of something better. Cassius and Darren had to return to find their bird flown. Starbride leaned out the window and glanced along the sides of the building. What if she flew to another part of the nest?

The structure looked like some old manor house, big enough to keep them chasing her for a long time. The broken wall was large enough to step through, and the ledge that ran to the next room was intact. Before her good sense had the chance to speak, Starbride stepped out onto the ledge. It held her, and she inched toward the next gap, her face to the wall. She blocked out the thought of the ground below her and hung on to whatever she could find.

CHAPTER THIRTEEN: KATYA

Katya gritted her teeth and fought the impatience that told her to just pick a direction and ride. Ahead of her, Averie studied the forest floor. She straightened after only a moment and jogged back to where the rest of the Order waited on horseback. "The tracks have turned," Averie said. "These lead back to the road."

Katya rubbed the back of her neck, trying to stop the ache that was creeping up from her shoulders. "A false trail?"

"Perhaps."

"Crowe, are we even close to the manor house?"

"I know this is the right area. The memories I saw in the pyramid correspond with what I'm seeing now. It just…rings true. I don't know how else to explain it."

Katya gestured at the forest. "And yet, no manor house. And these tracks don't lead anywhere."

"Oh, they lead somewhere," Brutal said. "Round the garden path."

"Back to the road?" Maia suggested. "Maybe Crowe can get a better bearing." She shifted when Crowe gave her a sullen glance. "Another bearing, I meant another. Nothing wrong with this one…"

"Back to the road," Katya said, her excited mood gone. "Let's follow this double-backing trail."

Averie took point again, and Katya bent close to Crowe. "Why are you always giving Maia dirty looks or heaps of sarcasm?"

Crowe stared at his pyramid and didn't look at her. "I don't know what you mean."

"Why are you always so *mean* to the girl?"

"Can we please focus on the mission before we wander into a great big trap?"

"Certainly," Katya said, but she promised herself she'd have an answer later. The trail led to the road as they'd guessed, but just before they reached it, Averie rushed back to them.

"There's someone lying in the road," she said.

"Dead or alive?"

"I can't tell."

"The trap we're expecting?" Brutal asked.

Katya clutched her pommel. "If we suspect traps from every angle, we'll never get anywhere. Pennynail, drag this person to the gap just ahead. Averie, stay by the road, and once you've checked our mystery guest out, signal us either to come forward or stay back."

The two sped away. "Spread out," Katya said. She almost wished for a little ambush to release the tension. Ahead, Pennynail dragged someone into sight, and Averie bent over the person before waving the Order forward.

"Who is it?" Katya dismounted. Close up, she saw it was a man, face-down, with a knife sticking out of his back.

"The wound's not that deep." Averie lifted the fabric of his coat and peeked under it. "His clothing shielded him a little. He's got a coat, a shirt, and what looks like an undershirt…two undershirts."

"Two?" Katya asked.

Averie turned the downed man's face to the side. His nose was a mess, bloodied, bruised, and swollen, undoubtedly broken. "He's pretty young. I'd guess he was bulking up to impress everybody."

Katya sucked in a breath as she recognized him. "Lord Hugo."

"Will you cut these clothes down the back, Pennynail?" Averie asked. "Carefully. This knife would have fallen out by now if he'd been lying on his side."

Using one of his thin stilettos, Pennynail sliced the fabric in half with a soft rip. Katya bent closer. The knife had penetrated Lord Hugo's back an inch or so. Luckily, it was small; the weight of it hadn't torn it from his flesh.

"This needs Brutal," Averie said.

Katya waved him forward. "Bring the patch-up kit, Brutal."

He eyed Lord Hugo's wound. "Not so bad."

"What do you think?" Averie asked. "A quick pull and then bandages?"

"Nah." Brutal rooted around in the medical satchel and pulled out a handful of soft bandages. "Had a brother fall against a table last year during a duel. Got a knife stuck in his leg, and one of the chapterhouse heads wrapped a bandage around the knife, on the wound, and then pulled it out. Then they could put pressure on it right away, see?"

"Good thinking."

Katya watched them work. They could fix up Lord Hugo, but then she intended to wake him and find out why he was there. As soon as the knife left him, however, he came awake with a grunt and tried to push off the ground. Brutal shoved him down, pushing on the wound. Lord Hugo cried out, and Katya knelt by his head. His eyes rolled, panicked.

"Easy, Lord Hugo," she said. "We're trying to help you."

He focused on her face. "Highness?"

"That's right. Can you sit up so we can wind a bandage around you?"

As he did, his clothes slipped down his arms, exposing his rather skinny chest. He made a grab for one of his shirts, but Katya made him sit still. As Averie wound the bandages around his bare torso, he squirmed and wouldn't meet anyone's gaze.

Katya had the grace to look away until Averie finished. Lord Hugo clutched the remains of his coat around his thin body. "Is Miss Starbride all right?" he asked, his voice distorted by his broken nose.

Katya paused, trying to tell herself she'd misheard. "Who?"

"Miss Starbride." He glanced around. "Isn't she here?"

Katya gripped him by the shoulders and pulled him close. "Tell me everything that happened to you this day, Lord Hugo. Tell it clear and in order."

He swallowed hard, but he followed instructions. Blood raced through Katya's temples as he spoke. She didn't believe for one second that Starbride thought she'd gone hunting, or that Starbride had planned a good-natured surprise. She had acted exactly as Katya imagined she would. Only instead of confronting her, Starbride had followed her, the damned little ferreter of secrets!

Lord Hugo winced as Averie wiped the blood from his face. "The robbers said they wanted 'one of her friends.' That must be you, Highness."

"Did you recognize them?"

He started to shake his head, and then stopped, grimaced, and reached for his face.

"Describe them."

He did, adding the name he'd caught: Cassius. Katya paced and bit her index finger. She didn't recognize the name or the descriptions. "They wanted one of us and got her instead."

"No doubt for ransom," Lord Hugo said.

"And how do you know that, Lord Hugo?"

He shifted. "Well, if you two are romantically involved…"

Katya knelt in front of him so quickly he shrank back. Brutal laid a large hand on his shoulder. "And how do you know we are…romantically involved, Lord Hugo?"

He blinked, and Katya could almost see the fear ooze across his features. "I...assumed, Highness, after she said she wanted to surprise you, and after Lady Hilda seemed so interested in your relationship..."

Katya's fingers rested on the grip of her rapier. "And who else have you and Lady Hilda been talking to, eh?"

Lord Hugo glanced at her rapier and then her eyes. "No...no one, Highness."

"As I recall, this is twice you've been caught following Starbride."

"I wanted to protect her this time. The first time was a mistake."

"Where did they go?" He shook his head slowly. Katya stood and slid her rapier from its sheath with a slow rasp. "Where did they go?"

His unblinking eyes grew wide as saucers. "I don't know, Highness. I was incapacitated."

"Convenient, that," Brutal rumbled.

"Where?" Katya pointed the rapier under Lord Hugo's neck, forcing his chin up.

"I swear on my honor and on the ten spirits, I do not know."

Katya turned from him, sheathed her rapier, and marched to Crowe. "Can you pyramid him?"

Crowe's mouth turned down as if he'd bitten into something sour. "The king's pyradisté pyramiding a nobleman without a trial will have them all in a tizzy. The traitors would suddenly find themselves overburdened with allies."

Katya clenched her fist. "What if you erased his memory?"

Crowe gave her an angry look. "I'd have to take out the entire thread of this incident, maybe of Starbride, maybe of you, and it would look damned funny if he suddenly forgot who *you* are. Someone would catch on, and then they'd take him to the Pyradisté Academy, and holes in his memory would be discovered."

Katya nearly told him to do it and be damned, but he leaned forward, cutting off her thoughts. "You can't kick the anthill like this, Katya, not for one of us or for Starbride. We have to find another way. Your threatening him was bad enough."

Katya strode back to Lord Hugo as Brutal and Averie helped him to his feet. "If you're lying to me..."

"I swear I'm not!"

Katya leaned close to Averie. "Get me a path to follow." With a nod, Averie hurried away. Katya stared at Lord Hugo again. She couldn't let him loose to go blabbing at court, but she couldn't share why they were out in the middle of nowhere. "Lord Hugo, you have a chance to redeem yourself."

His chin lifted again, his eyes glittered, and she knew he blamed himself for losing Starbride. Tickle his pride, give him a way out of guilt, and he'd do anything.

"You will help me rescue her."

Lord Hugo nodded before wincing and touching his face. Katya just kept from rolling her eyes. He hadn't even asked why they weren't summoning the king's Guard, as if he'd already assumed they'd storm the heights and rescue Starbride themselves. That was what all the great heroes from the storybooks did, wasn't it? No self-respecting hero sent for the Guard. When they led him to the horses, he stopped and stared at Maia with his mouth open.

Maia frowned and glanced down as if worried she'd spilled something on the front of her coat. "What is it?"

"I beg your pardon," Lord Hugo said. "It was...nothing."

Brutal gave him a nudge. "Keep moving, my lord."

Katya filed his reaction away for later and mounted up. Brutal lent him a cloak and hoisted him onto Averie's horse. Lord Hugo's eyes bulged at being handled as easily as a babe in swaddling, and he stared at Brutal with naked awe.

Averie waved them on. "Two horses led off the road by three people; the last set of footprints is much deeper than the other two. He was carrying...something." Her mouth a tight line, she looked away.

Katya's jaw clenched. The "something" had to be Starbride. With a start, she realized that as angry as she'd gotten, her pyramid necklace hadn't tingled once. "Lead on." She rode near Crowe again. "Is my necklace working?"

"I haven't sensed anything wrong."

"I've been close to rage, and it hasn't tingled or burned."

Crowe smiled, seemingly pleased with himself. "I told you I made it extra strong. Your anger isn't even affecting it. It should keep the Aspect contained despite your feelings."

Katya resisted the urge to touch her chest and remind herself that the necklace was still there.

Crowe cleared his throat. "You know this is a trap."

"Of course."

"She might already be dead."

Katya turned her head slowly, her stomach roiling at the thought. "We will act as if she's still alive, Crowe."

"Katya, I don't wish to hurt you, but—"

"She's alive."

Up ahead, Averie signaled them to halt. "There's a large clearing ahead," she said when she returned. "This path is a very old one, not used for a long time and then used heavily recently."

"Crowe?" Katya asked.

He nodded. "I can find out if anyone is using a pyramid nearby, but if the traitor pyradisté is watching for us, he could be doing the same thing."

"It's a risk we have to take if we're going to use pyramids at all," Katya said. "Do it."

Crowe pulled a pyramid from his satchel and went silent a moment. "Nothing, as far as I can tell."

"Search instead for active pyramids." She could *not* force the pace; she had to remain calm. If only her necklace would burn as a reminder. "Averie, you and Pennynail creep toward the clearing. If you see any kind of structure, stay at the edge of cover and send Pennynail to scout while you watch." They started off. "Wait. Maia, go with Pennynail. Cover him and watch for archers. Step in his footsteps, though," she cautioned her. "Keep a keen eye for traps."

"I don't sense any active pyramids in the immediate woods," Crowe said.

"Good, then you're going to tail Maia tailing Pennynail. I want to know what exactly is ahead of us."

Lord Hugo sat swathed in the dark red fabric of Brutal's cloak, pale and nervous, his bruised face darkening by the second, and his mouth open to breathe. "What shall we do, Highness?"

"We wait."

If these traitors thought that kidnapping Starbride would make Katya careless, well, they were right. If she'd been alone, she would have been careless, but she had the Order to think about—and Lord Hugo, providing he was innocent. She couldn't throw away their lives in a fit of passion.

Maia, Averie, and Pennynail returned in a clump. "It's the remains of a manor house," Averie reported.

"No active pyramids in the woods," Crowe said. He stooped, out of breath, and then straightened with a grimace. "I'm no longer built for sneaking."

"No traps," Maia said, "at least, none that we saw. No visible people, either."

Katya tapped her chin. "Brutal and I go in first. Maia and Crowe, come in just after us and get ready to cover us. Pennynail, search for

Starbride. Averie, you and Lord Hugo will watch for anyone escaping. If anyone does, you'll have to follow him, Lord Hugo, especially if he looks like he's carrying someone."

Lord Hugo nodded, and Averie nodded with him. She cast a quick glance at him before looking to Katya. Masking the gesture as she passed a hand through her hair, Katya nodded, too, signaling that Averie would also be watching Lord Hugo.

They tethered their horses and crept toward the clearing. Katya tried to tell herself that the kidnappers wouldn't harm Starbride. To set a trap, they needed live bait. This, of course, assumed Lord Hugo was telling the truth. If he wasn't, he was dead, sure as the sunset.

The manor house was more dilapidated than Katya had imagined. Most of the woodwork had fallen off, leaving sad, sagging stone. The eight windows on their side stood as still and empty as a skull's eyes but had the good fortune to be close to the forest. They snuck one by one through bushes, weeds, and overgrown shrubs until they stood against the wall near a window.

Crowe clenched his pyramid and closed his eyes. He leaned to Katya's ear. "There is a pyramid protecting this window and the next. We must assume every gap on the first floor is so protected. I sense nothing on the windows above."

"Can you cancel this pyramid?"

"Yes, but if the owner missed us before, he'll know about us now."

"There's nothing for it." She pulled Pennynail close to whisper in his mask's ear. "Can you scale this wall and go in via the second story?"

He nodded. Katya let him go and signaled the others to get ready.

Maia put her bow under one arm, and Brutal took his spiked mace from his belt. Crowe lifted his pyramid, his forehead creased, and then he nodded.

Brutal grabbed the lip of the window and heaved his body inside. Once he was clear, Katya followed and drew her rapier once inside the old stone room. She and Brutal took positions beside the doorway as Crowe and Maia followed them inside.

Crowe lifted his pyramid and then shook his head. Brutal and Katya stepped out of the room to a short hallway that led to an adjacent room and then around a corner. In the other direction, the short hallway led to a longer hallway with daylight leaking down it. Katya chose the long hallway and sneaked through the still air in eerie quiet. Brutal followed her. Maia took the other path, and Crowe stayed behind Katya. Motes of dust drifted through the light, and from somewhere ahead came the rasping sound of booted feet on dusty stone. Katya and Brutal froze.

"Come out, come out, Princess," someone called from deeper in the house. "We have a very short time in which to play."

Katya glanced at Brutal; he led the way, Katya a step behind. In the crumbled remains of a main hall—a dining room or ballroom—four men waited. One matched the description of Lord Hugo's stabber, and one of the others, a larger man, seemed a good fit for Cassius, but the other two were also twenty-something, and neither had a beard.

The lanky, young stabber smiled from where he stood atop of a pile of rubble. His brown hair curled across his forehead, and his brown eyes held amused contempt. Katya hung back in the hallway. A balcony ringed the large room, and the walls above it were decorated with the remains of old paintings, nice camouflage for archers.

"Well, I'm here," Katya said, not stepping out into the open. "Who are you, and what do you want?"

The young stabber grinned. "Darren is my name, and I've taken great pains to get to this moment."

"You're about to experience great pain," Brutal said.

Darren chuckled and crossed his arms. "We'll see."

"I don't recognize your name or your face," Katya said. "If you wanted to meet me, you could have introduced yourself at the Courtiers Ball, unless of course, you weren't invited."

"What a delightful attempt to try to get information from me! Or were you meaning to prick my pride?"

"Whatever I could get." Katya hoped to stall him until her team could get in position and prayed that Pennynail would find Starbride before the fighting began.

CHAPTER FOURTEEN: STARBRIDE

Starbride heard Katya's voice and paused. Her climb along the ledge had taken moments, but it had seemed like hours of inching along, trying to make her numb hands get a grip on smooth stone while she fought to maintain her balance. After she'd climbed into the house through another window, she'd started down this hallway, searching for a staircase. Darren's voice had made her pause. She didn't want to run into him, but Katya got her feet moving again. The thought of freedom quickened her steps nearly as much as the desire to keep Katya from walking into an ambush.

Sunlight streamed through a gap in the wall, and Starbride peeked through at a balcony surrounding a large room. Katya's voice drifted upward, but Starbride couldn't see the floor or any of the room's occupants. "I don't recognize your name or your face," Katya said. "If you wanted to meet me, you could have introduced yourself at the Courtiers Ball, unless of course, you weren't invited."

Starbride failed to hear his response as a man moved past the gap, cutting off her view. He crouched, facing away from her, a crossbow at the ready. As he sidled along the balcony, his head bobbed to and fro as if searching the floor below for a clear shot.

Starbride glanced up and down the hallway and bit her lip. She couldn't let Katya be shot by this assassin, but what to do? If she called out, she would give away the fact that she was free, and any lurking enemies could collect her and use her as a hostage. Maybe she could lead the crossbowman away? She hurried down the hallway as she thought about it and tried to ignore her throbbing head and aching side.

At the next corner, a narrow stairway stood across the hall, and a doorway onto the balcony opened just to her left around the corner. She paused, torn between running for it and trying to stop the crossbowman. If she got to Katya, she could do both. She started to move and pulled up short as the crossbowman backed from the balcony doorway, between her and the stairway. She paused in the shadows, and he didn't seem to spot her. He was too busy staring at the balcony doorway and then looking in the other direction down the hall. He rubbed his chin as if trying to calculate the best place to position himself.

He took a step toward the stairway. Starbride had to act. Katya's life was in her bound hands. Her bare feet made little sound as she sprinted. The crossbowman didn't turn. She hit him full force and knocked the breath from her lungs. She hoped to push him down the stairs, but he grabbed her as he started to fall, and his crossbow thumped to the ground. She shoved as hard as she could, but he made a grab for the wall, and their legs tangled together. They fell at the top of the stairs.

The crossbowman cursed, rolled Starbride off him, and got to his knees. He grabbed her bound wrists while reaching back a fist. Starbride tried to push him away with her feet and fought the urge to scream. Agony spiked through her wrists and shoulders, and she would've sworn her hands were about to come off. The crossbowman slapped at her legs and drew back again to hit her, but a leather-clad arm tangled with his before he could launch the fist at her head. The crossbowman turned, and Katya's masked man stuck a knife in his throat.

Starbride stared as blood welled around the blade and dripped on the front of her dress. She swallowed and strained away. The masked man pulled the dead man off her and laid him to the side. Starbride opened her mouth to ask about Katya, but the masked man laid a finger across the lips of his mask and then untied her wrists with long, quick fingers.

"They don't know I'm loose," she whispered.

He nodded, stepped back, and pulled her to her feet to eye her up and down.

"What?" For a moment, she thought he was going to remark on the hideousness of her dress. Instead, he bent and removed the dead man's clothing quickly, as if he was used to undressing dead men. He gave her the pilfered clothes and then pointed at her dress.

She glanced from her dress to the clothes and tried to forget they belonged to a corpse. "You're right. They're better than what I'm wearing." This man was on Katya's side—Starbride supposed she had to trust him. "I'll need help with my laces." He nodded, and she turned. She shuddered as he unlaced her, though the mask made her more comfortable than if his face had been bare. No matter what he was feeling, she couldn't see it, and if he wouldn't speak, she couldn't hear it. Gooseflesh ran over her entire body, and she fought the urge to wrap her arms around herself.

When the masked man finished with the laces, he turned his back, and she hauled the dress over her head, threw it to the floor, and shivered in her meager undergarments. She donned the dead man's clothes as best she could, stuffing the long legs of the trousers into the large boots. The shirt hung to her knees. She tapped the masked man on the shoulder, and to her surprise, he picked up the dress and held it against his lean frame.

Starbride choked off a laugh. "Do you think it suits you?"

He draped the dress over one arm, laced his fingers together, and put the backs of his hands under his chin, tilting his head. Starbride chuckled but then paused. "They don't know I'm loose," she whispered again. An idea formed in her head.

He tapped the side of the mask's nose and pointed at her, and she knew they had the same idea. "Come on," she said. "I'll show you where they kept me. I had a bag over my head, but you'll have to give me your boots and gloves."

CHAPTER FIFTEEN: KATYA

K atya once again had to clamp her teeth on her impatience as she waited for Darren to make his move. He had to have a trick in mind. No one who talked as much as he did operated without a card up his sleeve. She'd started to tune him out when he finally said, "Enough talk. I've got a surprise for you, Princess."

"Finally," Katya whispered. "Ready flash bomb."

"Bring her!" Darren said. One of his men went up a stairway at the back, and Katya tightened her grip on her rapier. When they brought Starbride in, she planned to hit them hard. She cleared her throat, and Brutal cleared his, signaling that he understood.

In a matter of moments, they led Starbride down the stairway. She had a bag over her head that also covered her shoulders, but there was no mistaking the dress. Blood spotted the front of it, and Katya's temples began to pound with her pulse. Her leading foot moved, but then she paused, hearing Brutal pause beside her. Unless Katya was much mistaken, Starbride had gotten taller.

"Who's that?" Crowe said.

Darren frowned before he hauled Starbride toward him. Her wrists were bound in front of her, and her feet were bare, but both hands and feet seemed larger and paler than they should have been. "A simple trade," Darren said. "You for this girl."

Katya almost said, "And what girl would this be?" but she kept herself to, "And what will you do with me once you've got me?"

Darren pulled a knife from his belt and waved it near the false-Starbride's bagged head.

Behind Katya, Crowe gasped. "That knife."

Katya didn't have time to ask. "Ready flash bomb."

"Time's up," Darren said. He pulled the hood up over a Laughing Jack mask and stared as the binding fell from Pennynail's wrists. With one quick motion, Pennynail stabbed Darren in the shoulder with a hidden knife.

"Now," Katya said.

"Temperance!" Crowe yelled, and something flew over Katya's head. She averted her eyes, hoping Pennynail heard the signal. Too many enemies closed their eyes when someone said, "Flash bomb!" The residue of the bright flash lit the inside of her closed eyelids, and one person cried out in pain.

Katya and Brutal ran toward where Pennynail wrestled with Darren. One of the other men held his face and shook his head, but the other two, Cassius and one of the unnamed fellows, leapt forward, their faces clear of confusion and pain.

In the corner, a crossbowman stood from behind a pile of rubble, his weapon raised. He fell backward with a yelp as a green-fletched arrow appeared in his chest as if by magic. Maia had reached the balcony. Katya heard another cry from the rubble pile behind her.

Katya reached her opponent just as he drew his sword. She launched an attack, but he countered and dropped into a defensive stance. She lunged; he blocked again and shifted position amongst the rubble, trying to get higher. Katya stepped lightly onto a pile of bricks, and he pressed his attack while she was off balance. She blocked his sword and then kicked his knee, making him stagger. He recovered quickly and slashed, slicing her calf in a quick arc of pain. She climbed farther up the rubble, and he jumped after her.

He hacked, using the strength in his taller body, but she didn't play his game. She left off blocking and stayed ahead of his swings, turning his lunges into stumbles. Nearby, Katya heard Brutal roar, and one of his opponents went flying behind hers, the man's chest a ruin. Her opponent tripped, and Katya ducked under his halfhearted slash. She stuck one leg out behind her as she stabbed forward and sank her rapier into his heart. His eyes rolled as he slumped, and she slid her sword from his chest.

Pennynail had Darren on his knees with both arms behind his back. Katya gestured at the gown over his usual leather. "Tell me you found more than just the dress."

He nodded and jerked Darren's arms higher. Darren twisted, his face creased with pain and anger. "Let go of me, peasant!"

"That's always a dead giveaway," Brutal said. Not even breathing hard, he held Cassius in a chokehold. Cassius's face went from red to purple, and he tugged on Brutal's arms to no avail.

"Are you planning to kill him, Brutal?" Katya asked.

"Just waiting for a bit of the fight to go out of him. You want him alive, yeah?"

"Please." She turned back to Pennynail. "Where—?"

Crowe grabbed Darren's dropped knife and waved it. "Where did you get this?"

"Crowe?" Katya asked.

He ignored her and pressed the knife close to Darren's smug mouth. "Where did you get this?"

"From his body, old man, before we gave it to the dogs."

Crowe punched Darren across the face. Darren's head twisted to the side, and he half slumped before Pennynail hauled him upright again.

Katya grabbed Crowe's arm. "*What* are you doing?"

He shook the knife at her. "Do you know who this belonged to?"

A small emerald glittered in the knife's guard. Memory stirred, but Katya couldn't place it. "Save it. We've got to clear the rest of this place."

Crowe tucked the knife into his satchel, and Katya turned to the others. Cassius had stopped kicking, and Brutal let him slide to the ground. "Tie these two up. One of you stays with them while the other goes with Crowe. Where's Starbride?"

Pennynail pointed at the staircase. "Safe?" Katya asked. He nodded. "Maia?" she called.

Maia stood from behind the balcony railing. "Here."

"Crowe and either Brutal or Pennynail is coming to join you."

"Gotcha."

Katya started up the stairs. Minimal traps, a pushover of a villain, it was all too easy. There had to be something else to all this. A single room waited at the top of the staircase; the only other exit was blocked by rubble. "Star?"

Starbride peeked through a gap in the wall, and Katya realized she'd been hiding outside the building. It was brilliant and perfect. She stepped inside wearing too-large clothing, and she was the cutest thing Katya had ever seen, in spite of the danger, in spite of everything. Katya sheathed her blade, crossed the room in a few strides, and threw her arms around Starbride, her anger forgotten as she buried her face in Starbride's hair.

"I'm all right," Starbride mumbled into her shoulder.

"And you're better dressed."

Starbride tilted her head, her eyes tired. "It's been a long week."

"Want a ride home?"

"You left me in the palace while you went investigating."

"Yes." She knew this conversation had to happen but hoped to postpone it.

"And I saw you kiss that courtier."

Katya nearly stepped back. "It seems I've met the most observant woman alive." After a long sigh, she stroked Starbride's cheek. "It's a part I have to play, and I hate it." Tears threatened the corners of her eyes. "You see everything. You saw *me*, the thing inside me, and you didn't run away. You saw everything, and you still came running after me. Star, I'm so sorry I hurt you."

"I was going to yell at you like you'd never been yelled at before."

"Let's skip that and go right to I'm sorry, and I love you."

Starbride's eyes widened before she wrapped her arms around Katya's neck and pressed their lips together. Katya didn't waste the moment. She clasped Starbride's waist and drew their bodies closer.

From the doorway, someone cleared her throat. Katya almost expected to see Averie, but Maia stood there, grinning from ear to ear. "I came to get Pennynail's boots and gloves. And Brutal's calling for us downstairs."

Katya glared at her. "We're coming."

"The boots and gloves are in the corner," Starbride said.

Maia retrieved them, winked, and hurried away. Katya helped Starbride clonk down the stairs in her too-large boots. "I can carry you part of the way, if you'd like," Katya said.

Starbride snorted. "Part of the way, no doubt. And after that, you'd stagger and fall, and we'd break our necks." She gave Katya a serious look. "I still plan to yell at you, love or not."

Once outside, Starbride and Lord Hugo clasped hands, each exclaiming relief at seeing the other alive. Crowe sat on the ground near the horses and held a bloody cloth over his left knee. He glared at the injury with an affronted expression.

Brutal and Pennynail loaded Cassius and Darren, both bound and gagged, on top of the horses. After helping to tie them in the saddles, Averie knelt by Crowe and replaced his bloody cloth with a clean one. Katya crouched beside them. "What happened, Crowe?"

He nodded at the house. "I found and canceled every active pyramid and then stumbled over a broken brick."

"How bad are you?"

"I'm fine."

Katya nodded at his knee. "Do you want me to poke that to show you how hurt you are?"

He gave her a sullen look but didn't argue. Katya took one of the bandages and tied it around her calf. The damage was minimal, but it seeped a bit, and she didn't want to leak all the way home.

When she stood, she stared at the manor house. These criminals were cunning and adept. Lord Hugo mentioned that they'd meant to take one of Katya's friends. When presented with Starbride instead, they'd adapted. They were too smart to be hiding out with minimal protection and a few thugs. The only wounds they'd managed to inflict had been a slice to Katya's calf, an accidental gouge to Crowe's knee, Lord Hugo's injuries, and some minor scrapes.

"What now?" Brutal asked from beside her.

"Were you hurt, Brutal?"

He shrugged. "A few bruises."

"This is too easy. The only one we didn't catch was the thirty-something bearded man. The rest went down like warm milk."

"We've already searched the place. Nothing interesting. Let's take our new friends back to the palace and have a chat."

"What if that's what they wanted all along?"

"To be taken inside the palace? Well, we could pyramid them out here."

"No!" Crowe said from their feet. He struggled to stand. "We wait until the palace to interrogate them!" he said in a strangled whisper.

Katya stared. "What is going on with you?"

He swallowed and turned his gaze to the ground. "I'm sorry, Highness. Please, I'd like to wait until the palace."

Everyone stared at them. Even Darren and Cassius watched, and Darren still had some of his smug look, even with a reddened, bruising cheek and his bandaged shoulder. "Crowe, come and speak with me," Katya said. He limped forward, and she led him a short distance from the others. "Tell me."

"I can't."

"The knife?"

"It's caught up with me."

Katya blinked. "What has?"

"Time!" He spat the word. "The thing no man can outrun: time!"

"Crowe…" She'd never considered his hold on sanity fragile, but he sounded too much the madman.

"Please, Katya." He looked deep in her eyes, and she was shocked to see unshed tears in his. "I'll use the pyramid on them in the palace, but not out here, not in front of others. Please. This was all too easy. You must have felt it."

"Yes."

"Not…not if their aim was to split us up." He caressed his satchel and stared at nothing. "I pray they haven't succeeded." Quick as a snake, he focused on her again. "Please, let's go back."

"Well, we can't do it in front of Lord Hugo, anyway. Here, let me carry the satchel."

The unshed tears nearly fell, and she could see that her words wounded him. For everything he said about suspecting everyone, distrust cut him to the core.

"Because it seems to pain you and because your obsession with it amuses one of our guests." She nodded at Darren, and Crowe gave her the satchel, but his hurt expression didn't change.

"Mount up," Katya said. Pennynail offered Starbride the dress again, but she refused after a little laugh. Katya stepped close to her. "If I didn't know better, I'd say you were enjoying yourself just a little."

"This is my second adventure in a very short time, and it's turning out much better than the first, despite the fact that I was scared out of my mind for most of it."

Katya kissed Starbride's temple, but she couldn't relax and enjoy the moment. The situation didn't smell right no matter how she moved it around in her mind. The entire house should have been trapped. There should have been twice as many guards. They never should have left Starbride alone. What had been the point of it all? Was there a trap they didn't spring? Maybe it was a trick to get her *out* of the palace.

"Let's move." She guided her horse to Lord Hugo's. "I don't wish this adventure bandied about court, Lord Hugo."

"But, Princess, you saved your lady from a band of ruffians. All should praise you!"

"Honor lives in one's own heart, don't you think? It doesn't need court gossip to puff it up. That leads to ego and too much pride."

He nodded slowly, and she knew she had him. "Admirable thought, truly admirable."

"Thank you. And as for your nose..."

"I'll tell everyone I was involved in a fight, but due to a matter of honor, I cannot elaborate. Your man Brutal was kind enough to recover my rapier from these rogues, so I needn't admit I was robbed."

"Excellent. And if this adventure does get around court..." She leaned forward, a sinister smile in place. "I'll know who started the rumor."

Lord Hugo's answering look carried a twinge of worry. "Indeed, Highness. You've nothing to fear from me."

"Good man." She clapped him lightly on the shoulder. As she rode back to Starbride, she rolled her eyes to the heavens.

CHAPTER SIXTEEN: STARBRIDE

Starbride rode next to Lord Hugo for most of the trip, with Katya coming to her side now and again before circulating among their companions. At the head of the group, the two men Maia had named Brutal and Pennynail rode on either side of the captives.

In her head, Starbride tried to make a list of everything she would say to Katya once they were alone. If these men were the ones Katya had been seeking, or if she'd been on the trail of someone else, why hadn't she involved the king's Guard? How did Crowe and Pennynail become part of the expedition when Starbride hadn't seen them leave Marienne with Katya? There were secrets here, and she couldn't leave them alone when they involved her. Well, she couldn't leave secrets alone at the best of times, she admitted that, but this wasn't the best of times. Secrets now could get her killed.

And she'd have to discuss with someone the fact that she'd been called a pyradisté. She thought Crowe would be badgering her for information already, but he seemed distracted, staring ahead with a morose look on his face and talking to no one. Starbride decided to tell Katya when they were alone, *after* she'd been given some answers.

She glanced at Lord Hugo and wondered what all he'd been told. He smiled when he caught her looking, his mouth slightly open so he could breathe; the middle of his face was one large bruise, and he hunched slightly because of the knife wound in his back. Through most of the trip, he'd been sneaking glances at Maia. "She's very pretty."

Lord Hugo blinked. "Who?"

Starbride gave him a level look. "I have eyes."

"Oh." Lord Hugo hung his head; he didn't wear the blush she expected. "No, it's not that. I mean, she is very pretty, but I just…We've never met, but I feel like we've always known one another."

Crowe's previous words came back in a rush. *Memory erasure works in threads.* "Lord Hugo, have you ever had a pyramid used on you?"

"No, why would I?"

"No reason." But with his strange reaction, she had to ask. She reminded herself not to jump to conclusions. Maybe he and Maia were kindred souls, and his recognized hers even though their bodies had never been introduced. There were too many maybes, one more thing to discuss with Katya. Their future conversation was getting longer and longer; she'd have to tell Katya to block off an entire day.

Up ahead, Katya took Brutal's place beside the prisoners, and he rode to the back of the column. "How are you two doing?"

"Achy but tolerable," Starbride said.

"No sharp pains when you move? Dizzy spells? Headache?"

"I've got the headache but not the other two."

"Let me know if you get either. We have too many injuries in my chapterhouse not to know the signs of a serious one."

"Thank you," Starbride said. He had a tender way for such a large man. She'd heard of the fighting monks, but she'd never seen one in combat. Brother Brutal *had* managed to hold down Katya after she'd turned into a Fiend, though; he had to be amazingly strong.

"Once the swelling goes down," he said, "I can fix your nose, Lord Hugo."

Lord Hugo frowned. "Fix it?"

"Set it. So it won't be crooked," He grinned. "Unless you want it that way? Some women love a crooked nose."

Lord Hugo blushed slightly. He cast a quick glance toward Maia, probably before he knew what he was doing. Starbride looked to Brutal; his easy smile was gone. In its place was an intense, nearly unreadable expression, but it said enough. Brutal didn't want Lord Hugo interested in Maia, which meant he was either family or interested in her himself. And why would family object to her having a lord as a suitor?

She cleared her throat. "Have you and Princess Katyarianna been friends long, Brother Brutal?"

His face slid back into an easy chuckle. "Six years. I was already on the path to enlightenment at thirteen, and I ran into her in the city, literally. I wasn't watching where I was going. I didn't know she was the princess, and like every cocky youth on the path, I challenged everyone I met to a fight."

"You fought her?"

"And she beat me."

Starbride gaped, picturing a scrawny young Katya fighting a shorter, less-muscled Brutal, but she couldn't divest him of all his bulk, even in her mind. "How?"

"Well, as I found out later, she'd trained in combat since she could toddle. I used the strength that Best and Berth gave me, but I never bothered to tax my brain, and I wasn't fast. She had brains, and deft Jack and Jan were with her in spirit; she stayed a step ahead of me. Even without her blade, she struck and moved. I couldn't catch her. Soon enough, she had me winded, and after that, she had me down. I expected her to taunt me, but she invited me for tea. She didn't have many friends, see, and well, we've been close ever since."

"Did you ever ask for a rematch?"

"We spar. Sometimes, she accuses me of going easy on her because she's the princess."

"And do you?" Lord Hugo asked.

"If we see the other is distracted. If we ever gave it all we had, who knows?"

Starbride gave him a critical look. "If you ever got a hold of her, you could tear her apart."

He winked. "I'd have to catch her first."

Starbride smiled, but the comment about Katya not having many friends tugged at her. She didn't have many friends, either, so she kept those she made. "If you're her childhood friend, what's the story with the masked man?"

"Pennynail never takes off that mask, and he never speaks. Crowe trusts him, though, and that's a rare thing."

"Pennynail sounds Allusian, though I don't know what a parent would be hoping for with the 'nail' part."

"So, your parents were hoping for a 'bride,' eh?"

"That would be my mother. Sometimes, I think she just loves a grand ceremony." She didn't mention how her mother also hoped she'd bag an influential spouse. Luckily, she didn't have to think of anything else to say. Katya beckoned Brutal forward and then took his place at Starbride's side. She kept them all changing positions, and it began to look more like a military unit than a group of friends.

Even though she burned with questions, Starbride kept them inside. She didn't know who among the group was entitled to what information, but she was certain Lord Hugo wasn't allowed any of it. Just before they emerged into the fields surrounding Marienne, Katya dismounted and waved for Starbride to follow her. "I know you want answers," she said.

"Yes, and I can hear the 'but' coming."

Katya took a deep breath, and Starbride reminded herself that it'd been a long week for all of them. "I have to do this a certain way, Star. I have to send the prisoners and Crowe one way, and I'll have to send you another and take a third for myself."

"Embarrassed to be seen with me in these clothes?" Starbride plucked at the too-large garments, but only part of the question was frivolous. It hurt to ask if Katya was embarrassed to be seen with her, no matter her clothing.

"Nothing in the world would make me embarrassed of you, Star. You are...sublime."

Heat rushed to Starbride's cheeks, embarrassing her, which made them burn more. How did Katya make Starbride's anger melt with a few well-chosen words? "And your tongue is made of silver."

"You'll find out."

Starbride met Katya's eyes and saw desire there, the kind that echoed within her, making her flush for another reason. Her anger had fled, and now need hummed in her. Her emotions were harp strings, and Katya was a master player. Starbride laughed and heard the breathlessness there. "No one has ever made me feel like you do. It has to be love."

With a bright, beaming smile, Katya lifted Starbride's hand and kissed it, a soft touch against her knuckles. "I'm going to send you with Brutal, Lord Hugo, and Maia; Brutal's going to escort you all the way to your room. Please, stay there until I send for you, and then I promise, there will be answers."

"All right, but I will hold you to that promise if I have to write it out and pin it to your coat."

Katya winked, and they returned to the party to split up again. Crowe, Pennynail, and the prisoners went off into the trees. Starbride and her party went down the road; Averie and Katya would follow later. Starbride cast a glance over her shoulder, and Katya waved her on.

Inside the city gates, Lord Hugo doffed his cap, returned Brutal's cloak, and clutched his ruined coat round him. "My path doesn't take me to the royal stables, I'm afraid." He sniffled. "Good-bye, Miss Starbride. I'm overjoyed that you're safe, though I'm afraid I wasn't much help."

Starbride touched his shoulder gently. "You did fine, Lord Hugo. Thank you. Without you, the princess would never have found me."

"And that honor will live in my heart, as the princess says. Good-bye, Brother Brutal."

"Lord Hugo." Brutal bowed from the saddle. "Come and find me at the chapterhouse when you're ready to fix that nose."

"Thank you. Farewell to you, too, Miss Maia." He didn't look at Maia as he spoke, only turned his horse and rode down the lane.

"You know what to do?" Brutal asked.

Maia nodded. "I'll keep a discreet eye on him."

"Watch your back," Brutal said.

Starbride didn't ask. She'd already guessed that these people were more than friends. Brutal lent her the enormous cloak and accompanied her back to her room without a word. Wrapped in the cloak, she got only a few odd looks instead of nothing *but* odd looks, and when they arrived at her room, he left her. She almost wished he'd reminded her to stay put so she could let a little of her anger out. It would've been good practice.

Just inside the door, Dawnmother fell to her knees and threw her arms around Starbride's legs. "Dawn?" Starbride asked. She leaned against the door to avoid toppling over.

"When I couldn't find you, I was so worried! I searched the entire palace, top to bottom!" She tugged at the dead man's clothes. "Star, what has *happened* to you?"

"I have a long story to tell." They didn't bother to move to chairs but sat by the door and held one another.

Dawnmother's face ran a gamut of emotions before settling on anger by the end of the tale. "I should have been with you. I should have insisted."

"You would have talked me out of such a foolhardy course."

"Even if I had to lock my arms around your legs and hold on!"

"I want to get out of these clothes, and then I hope you'll burn them."

"Oh, of course, of course. Where is my head?" She helped Starbride into a dressing gown and then ducked into the hallway to send a servant for hot water.

"How do you get them to do what you want?"

"I've earned some favors; I won't bore you with details. Now, let me look at the wound on your side."

"Wound?" With a start, she remembered the bloody stone that had dug into her. "I don't think it's more than a scratch." She disrobed enough to investigate her side.

"It's a cut under one of your ribs, not too deep but deep enough. Now that I've touched it, it's started bleeding again. When the hot water arrives, we'll wash and bandage it." She turned Starbride's hands over. "You'll have some bruises from the bindings, but the cut on your finger hasn't reopened." A knock sounded on the door, and Dawnmother let in the water-bearing servants.

Starbride had forgotten how good it could feel to wash after a long dirty day. It'd been a long time since she'd acquired so much filth. It wasn't a full bath, but two buckets of hot water and some soap did the trick.

When she was clean, dressed, and safe in a soft chair, her thoughts drifted to Katya. She tried to drum up her anger, but her thoughts kept wandering to their more tender moments. When Katya kissed her, it was like a swallow of strong wine. Her head spun, her cheeks burned, even her toes tingled. She worried about the state of her balance. How could their relationship be fair if Katya kept spinning her around? Of course, there was no denying that she spun Katya as well. She glanced up to find Dawnmother watching her.

"You're smiling and blushing just a little. Thinking of the princess?"

"There isn't much to tell."

"Do you think there will be? Soon?"

"Dawn." She and Katya had only kissed, and she'd tell Dawnmother more after they'd... She chuckled softly at the thought. Was it a foregone conclusion that they'd be lovers in every way? The idea brought heat to more than just her cheeks.

When Starbride glanced up again, though, Dawnmother's face wasn't inquisitive or impish, but stone-like. "I'll order you some food."

Starbride crossed her arms. "Out with it, and don't just say your life for me and also the truth."

Dawnmother's expression didn't soften. "Even if it's so?"

"Tell me, even if you know I don't want to hear it."

"This woman is too dangerous for you, Star."

"What would you have us do? Return home?"

"No, your mother would only send you back. Does the princess have some hold on your heart?"

Starbride's mind whirled, remembering Katya's proclamation of love, remembering her own. *It has to be love.* "I..."

"Are you not sure?" Dawnmother knelt in front of the chair, her face earnest, even angry. "Then tell her to leave you alone, Star. She cannot pursue you without your permission. And if she tries to, we'll leave in the middle of the night, and your mother's servant will have to *kill* me to send you back."

Starbride breathed out in a rush before she wrapped Dawnmother in a hug. "Thank you, Dawn, for always taking such good care of me."

"My life for you, but this hug tells me you won't do what I'm suggesting."

"I don't know how to explain it. It's like I've come too far." It was true, in many ways. She had undeniable feelings on many levels, not the least of which was a strange protectiveness for Katya. The people after Katya wanted to harm her and her family because they were different, something Starbride could identify with. But no one had ever tried to kill

Starbride because she was Allusian. Katya was a stranger hiding among her own people; she couldn't completely be one of them, even though she and her family had to protect them from the wrath of Yanchasa. And with the populace willing to kill her if they found out about the Fiend, Katya was besieged on all sides.

Averie arrived at Starbride's room a moment later. Dressed in Katya's livery, she offered Starbride a curtsy and Dawnmother a nod. "The princess is in council with the king and queen. I came to assure you that she hasn't forgotten about you. She'd rather be here, believe me." Her expression was light, jovial, as if she was happy that Katya had found someone to care for.

"Can you tell me why the king and queen rely on their daughter and her friends to investigate these matters?"

Averie's face went still. "Well, Katya does things on her own sometimes. That's why her parents are probably a hair's breadth from giving her a hiding, no matter her age and position."

Starbride kept her face composed. It was an elusive answer to say the least, and she didn't know how much to believe. She wished for a little more from Katya at that moment, like a note, something more personal. One more thing to discuss, if her turn with Katya ever came. "Thank you for coming."

"She *will* join you as soon as she's able." At a short knock on the door, she said, "Ah, right on time." She admitted a page boy with a large stack of books. "The princess ordered these for you." The boy set the books on the table, and Averie dismissed him.

"She outthinks us, your princess," Dawnmother said. "I was just about to suggest we fetch some books from the library." She gave Averie a look of deep respect. Katya was winning over Dawnmother without even being in the room.

"She's a smart woman," Averie said. "She knows the right path when she sees it." After a second curtsy, she departed.

When Starbride investigated the law books, she found the note she'd been hoping for. *Dine with me tonight*, it said, *if it pleases you. Otherwise, I'll throw myself from Hanna's Retreat. I'll come as soon as I can. K.*

Dawnmother read over her shoulder and snorted. "Throw herself to her death, indeed."

"It's sweet."

"Sending her servants to appease you is sweet?"

"She's more than a servant. I think their relationship is more like ours, like friends."

"Are you as sure of your position as before, Star? If things progress and she sends a 'friend' to make her apologies on your birthday, will you be so calm?"

"Why not a scenario where we're already married and she sends her apologies via a potboy while I'm giving birth to our first child?"

"You cannot have children together."

"In this imaginary setting, Katya has arranged for a surrogate father, but she and I will raise the child together."

"And who is the father?"

"A handsomely paid man unaware of the identities of those he aided."

"She'd save time and have *him* deliver her apologies *and* help raise the child."

"You've created a monster in your head. This *is* what my mother had in mind for me, remember? And you wanted me to go along with Mother's wishes and snag a wealthy, powerful individual that could help our people."

"But you won't allow her to help. You won't even ask her to help."

Starbride shook her head, too tired to argue. "I want to think of other things. I'm too tired to sleep, if that makes any sense."

"Forgive me. I speak out of worry for you."

"There's nothing to forgive." She put her arms over her head and stretched. "Well, if I can't sleep, I can read."

"I will be as quiet as dust." Sitting on her low stool, Dawnmother took out her needlework, and Starbride leaned back in her comfortable chair and opened the first book.

CHAPTER SEVENTEEN: KATYA

Katya paused in the secret passageway to the summer apartments and took a few deep breaths. In her own apartment, she'd taken a moment to change, order some books for Starbride, and give Averie instructions. Now, as she stepped through the door and watched Crowe turn the mysterious knife over and over while staring at the blade, Katya wished she'd gone to see Starbride instead. Crowe had such a pall of misery hanging on him that Katya didn't know if she wanted to hear what he had to say. She thought he would pyramid the captives before he summoned the Order, but he'd done just the opposite.

"Whose knife is that, Crowe?" Katya asked.

"It was your father's, Maia," he said, not looking at anyone.

Across the table, Maia frowned. "That can't…How did it wind up at that house? You said Father was killed by an assassin. He threw himself in the path of an arrow intended for King Einrich."

Katya slapped the table, making Maia jump. "You told her and not me, Crowe? Did you think the leader of the Order didn't deserve to know?"

"Katya, he was *my* father," Maia protested.

"I don't care if—"

"Enough," Crowe barked. He glared at both of them before his eyes grew sad again. "Peace." He set the knife on the table and licked his lips. Pennynail laid a hand on his arm, and Crowe patted it absently. It seemed to center him. "I lied to you, Maia, because I hoped it would give you some peace. I asked you to keep it secret because I did not want to speak so blatant a lie to Katya."

Maia continued to frown. An angry flush climbed above her collar. "Then how did he die?" Katya asked.

Crowe took a steadying breath, eyes unfocused as if looking into the past. "Seven years ago, a woman arrived in Marienne as a courtier. She caused a bit of commotion because she was older than average, and she'd never been to court. She'd made some money as a lawyer and bought her way in. She claimed to be the daughter of King Bastian, his eldest child, as a matter of fact."

"Grandfather's illegitimate daughter?" Katya asked.

"From what I heard," Brutal said, "Bastian had a roving eye."

Crowe snorted. "Correct, but his pyradisté made sure it was only his eye that roved."

"Pyradisté Vanielle," Katya said. "I remember her. I was five when she retired after Grandfather died, but I remember her."

"Well, what most people don't know is that she was also Queen Meredin's cousin," Crowe said, "and she took care of both your grandparents' roving eyes."

Brutal whistled. "The queen liked the young men, did she?"

"Pyradisté Vanielle used to shove Bastian and Meredin in a room together when their impulses to stray became too strong," Crowe said. "She let them fight it out, eventually to make up in the classic fashion."

"The old devils!" Katya said. "I'm going to ask Grandmother about that the next time we visit her on the coast."

"At your peril," Crowe said.

They all chuckled, except for Maia, who said, "Get to the part where my father died." The words cut through their mirth like a knife.

Crowe blanched. "The courtier's name was Carmen Van Sleeting. She was a widow who claimed to be the daughter of Bastian and a serving girl. The common people lapped it up. One of their own and the King of Farraday? They were ready to believe, and they had a share of nobles on their side that would put this woman on the throne just to chuck her off later.

"Carmen claimed to have letters written by Bastian to her mother, love letters marked with the royal seal. We had to get them to prove they were forgeries. There was some talk of simply disposing of Carmen."

"That would never have worked," Katya said. "If she disappeared without being disproven, it would fan the flames of her claim. She had children?"

"Three, tucked away somewhere secret."

"Then her death or disappearance would have bolstered *their* claims to the throne, especially if the people didn't take the Waltz and Yanchasa into account."

"Correct." Crowe glanced at Maia and cleared his throat. "Carmen must not have felt safe at Marienne, or she didn't feel her letters were safe. She claimed she'd made copies, but who cares about copies? People wanted to see the real thing. She used her money to rent a house on the

Lavine River, an old building downriver from Dockland, dating from the Tide Wars, and it was built like a fortress."

He rubbed his wrinkled cheeks and looked every bit his sixty-odd years. Katya was ashamed to find she couldn't recall his exact age. Sixty-six? Sixty-seven?

"Roland was determined to go with just the Order. He said a small force had a greater chance of success. Einrich was against it—he always thought Roland too reckless—but Catirin and I outvoted him. Roland was the leader of the Order, and the mission seemed a simple one."

Crowe tapped the knife lightly as he spoke. "It was dark when we got to the house. We waited until midnight or so. It was Roland, myself, two brothers—Roland's friends—Arvid and Alistair, and Layra, our archer. Layra covered us as we went into the house, picking off guards from a distance. Arvid and Alistair provided a distraction inside while Roland and I went for the letters. I already knew these so-called *love letters* couldn't be real. Bastian was a good man but not a great writer. He dictated, just like your father, Katya, and also like Einrich, Bastian's handwriting was awful. If he had to send a personal letter, Queen Meredin wrote it for him."

Crowe moved from the knife to tracing the wood grain of the table. "So, we needed to compare handwriting, and we needed the letters to do so." He closed his eyes, and Katya knew he was stalling. Her ears rang in the silence. Maia's jaw clenched, and the angry flush made her cheeks bright; her eyes seemed to flicker with standing tears.

"We got over the wall," Crowe said, "with Layra dropping guards right and left. The brothers went one way; Roland and I headed for the top of the house. I wish you could have seen your father then, Maia. He was a brilliant pyramid-user, a wonderful pyradisté. His skill allowed us to reach the upper levels of the house far faster than mine."

Maia's face softened but didn't lose its intensity. Staring at nothing, Crowe continued, "We had to use weapons at times—thankfully, not often—but we eventually found Carmen's chamber. Roland held the door while I rifled the room and found the forged letters. More than that, I found that Carmen had been writing to various nobles, encouraging dissent, buying support where she could. She was plotting a civil war.

"Carmen's guards fought like Fiends, but we managed to reach the dock with all the evidence. Arvid and Alistair didn't emerge, and we couldn't wait for them. They'd gotten out of tight spots before. Layra picked off several of our pursuers, and Roland and I jumped into a little skiff and launched it. Carmen's guards pursued us in other boats.

"We were sailing into pitch, dead night," he said, almost a whisper, "and the current was fierce. We couldn't see the bank. We hoped to get as far away as we could and then make our way back to Marienne after dawn, but something struck the side of the skiff and jarred us. It didn't pierce the hull, but we had to light a lantern. If we hit something like a floating tree dead-on, we'd be doomed, thrown in the water with no idea how far it was to shore, at the mercy of the current." He shook his head, his face showing some of the desperation he must have felt back then. "The following boats had lights hanging from their bows, so we lit ours. We could see a little way in front of us, enough to avoid large obstacles. Our pursuers fired arrows, a few coming too close for comfort. Roland braced himself in the back of the skiff and tried to attack with a pyramid."

He paused and took several deep breaths. "They had a bigger ship that we...that we hadn't seen. It must have come from upriver. It was a sloop...a small sailing ship with one...one mast." He took another breath. "It had a weapon mounted at the bow, a large crossbow. The, uh, the bolts are bigger than normal." His voice faded, and his eyes slipped shut. "Their first bolt skipped off the side and hit Roland in the leg. In the dim light, it seemed like it nearly...took his leg off. There was so much blood..." He swallowed several times. Katya bit her lip until it hurt. Maia stared at the table, her fingers white where they gripped the wood.

"He staggered and tumbled into the water," Crowe said, "but the strap of his satchel caught on one of the boat pegs, and the skiff dragged him, keeping his head just above water. I...I tried to pull him in, but I wasn't strong enough. I tried to get him to help me. I pleaded with him to help me pull him on board, but he was facing away from the boat, and he seemed out of his mind with pain and shock." Crowe wiped at the tears dribbling down his cheeks and shook his head as if denying the memory.

"His dragging weight slowed us down. The sloop was catching up. I had the evidence in my satchel, the letters that would prove Carmen Van Sleeting a liar and a traitor." He spoke slowly, as if in a trance. "He looked at me, and even though I could barely see his face, I knew he understood. I couldn't pull him into the boat. I couldn't let him hang from the side and die slowly or be battered to death by river flotsam until Carmen's men caught us. I couldn't cut the satchel loose and let him float. If he was recovered by the enemy, he would make too valuable a hostage.

"I took his face," he whispered, "and I held it under the water. I thumped his back to drive the air from his lungs. He went still, and I kept holding him. When I was sure, I cut the strap to his satchel."

Maia launched herself across the table. "Murderer!" she screamed.

Pennynail grabbed her. She struggled and screamed in his grasp, reaching for Crowe. "Murdering son-of-a-whore! I'll kill you! I'll kill you!"

Crowe didn't move, only covered his eyes and wept. "There would have been civil war."

"I don't care!" Maia shouted. "You wanted to save your own skin! Bastard, murdering bastard!"

Katya started for Maia, but Brutal got there first. He lifted Maia and wrapped her wholly in his large embrace. "Kill you!" she screamed again. "I wish my Fiend could come out! I wish it could so it could tear you apart!" Her voice broke on the last word, and her head sank over Brutal's clasped arms as she sobbed loud and long. He turned her until her head could rest on his shoulder.

Katya caught Brutal's eye and gestured at the door. He nodded and carried Maia from the room.

Crowe wiped his cheeks. "At dawn, I returned to Marienne and found out that Carmen Van Sleeting had fled to her homeland in the north. The Guard pursued her, but her kin got to her first. To get the king off their backs, they sent us her head. The nobles who'd colluded with her were taken care of silently, mostly with threats. The problem seemed to be solved, just at a terrible cost." He touched the knife. "Carmen and her guards must have found…Roland's body…before they fled. I wouldn't be surprised to find that our two captives are her children and that the mysterious bearded man is as well."

"Seeking revenge," Katya said.

"We robbed them of a mother and a throne."

Without warning, Katya's mind conjured a clear memory of a picnic when she was ten. Da, Roland, and Crowe stood under an oak tree, laughing together, enjoying a rare family moment in the royal garden. Grandmother had come from the coast, and she and Ma relaxed on cushions and sipped white wine under a bright red awning. Grandma and Grandda, her mother's parents, played croquet with Katya, Maia, and Reinholt. It was two days before Da's thirty-fourth birthday, and the family celebrated privately before the city's public celebration. There would be a ball Katya wouldn't be allowed to go to.

She'd been pouting, she smiled to remember, and Grandma and Grandda played with her to try to lift her spirits. But as she watched the three men, Crowe and Roland in their black pyradisté cassocks and Da in blue and deep purple, she was happy. Uncle Roland winked at her, and her father called her over and lifted her up. "Here's my fearless girl!" he'd said, and she was the luckiest little girl in the world as the three men she worshiped grinned at her.

Two years later, one had died by another's hand. And now, seven years after that, the killer finally admitted it to her. Katya's eyes swam as she stared at Crowe, and he met her stare with his own-tear filled gaze. "I loved him like family," he said. "More than I love your father, Katya. Roland was like a son. I couldn't…I couldn't just watch…" He mashed his lips together and tucked his chin into his chest. Pennynail laid an arm across his shoulders.

Katya tried hard to be angry, tried it for Maia's sake, but the damnable thing was that she understood. It was a hard choice, but the Order of Vestra was made of hard choices. He'd made one that she might have to make herself one day. Katya stepped toward them, and both Crowe and Pennynail looked up at her. The Laughing Jack mask was the same as always, but Crowe's face was white and anxious, as if he feared she would plunge her rapier into his chest. Even then, he didn't move, and Katya knew part of him wanted her to do it, as if death would somehow absolve him.

Instead, she opened her arms, offering consolation but not forcing it on him. His lips trembled, and he heaved himself from his seat and embraced her. As he trembled and wept, he seemed so fragile. Pennynail helped support him from the side, and for a time, all of them did nothing but grieve.

"So, that's why you're always so mean to Maia?" Katya asked at last.

Crowe wiped his face. "I couldn't be kind to her. I couldn't have her *like* me. I don't deserve her friendship or her love. It's also why Queen Catirin is more than brusque with me, at times. She loved Roland like a blood brother instead of one by marriage. She blames both herself and me for his death, since we all agreed he should go."

"It was his decision."

"Say that over and over, and it won't make us feel any better. Roland was always putting himself in danger, always attacking straight on. He thought Einrich was too soft. They had some terrible arguments. Roland wanted to experiment on traitors to see if he could…retrain them into being loyal using mind magic."

Katya's mouth twisted at the thought. "That's a little darker than I recall."

"When it came to protecting his family, he could get very dark indeed. He and Catirin shared that a little, I think." He stared at the wall. "She was always trying to find him another wife after Maia's mother died. She threw countless dinner parties and fetes, all to find him a good bride."

"I didn't know that."

"She thought he was lonely. Well, she didn't know about Layra."

"Uncle Roland was having an affair with someone in his Order?"

"It started when Maia was about three. He never found a way to break the news to Catirin. Layra wasn't a noblewoman, and she didn't have the cash or connections to be a courtier, but she was Roland's friend, had been for years, and they just sort of…found each other. She wouldn't have married him anyway, even if they'd gotten approval. She couldn't stand the restrictions of court life." Crowe shrugged. "Everyone in the Order knew. We just kept it from your mother and father."

Katya leaned against the table in wonder. It was so hard to imagine the uncle in her memory having a romance with anyone. Roland had always been so…solitary. "What happened to Layra and the brothers?"

"The poor brothers never made it out of the house. Layra escaped, but when she heard Roland had died, it broke her heart. She wanted nothing more to do with the Order. I told Einrich about their relationship, and he paid for Layra to move far out into the country, which was her wish, to a little farm. We used to exchange letters, but we fell out of practice as the years went on."

Katya began to pace, her mind done with grieving and leaping to the puzzle in front of them. "Did you use 'temperance' as the code for a flash bomb back when Roland was alive?"

"Um, I can't recall. I think so. Why?"

"Because some of our traitors seemed to know it. They weren't caught by the flash."

"You think it's Layra that's been feeding the traitors information? But…why would she work with the children of the woman responsible for Roland's death?"

"We don't know that Darren or Cassius are Carmen's children. And even if they are, revenge makes people do funny things. Use the pyramid on our captives, and then I want you to get in touch with Layra. Find out if she's still where she's supposed to be."

His face was still pale and his eyes fever bright, but he nodded. "As you will."

"Right. I'm going to check on Maia."

When she reached Maia's door, she found Brutal outside rather than inside where she expected him to be. "She sent me out," he said. From inside the room, Katya heard a distinct *thunk*. "I figured that when it went quiet, I'd try again."

"Breaking things, is she?"

He shrugged. "Try your luck."

"Thank you, Brutal, for seeing to her." Brutal nodded, but his baby face stayed pinched and worried. Katya knocked on the door.

"Go away!" Maia said from inside. There was another *thunk*.

Katya cracked the door open. "I'm coming in."

"I don't want company!"

Katya stuck her head inside. Several green-fletched arrows jutted from the wardrobe in the corner. Katya stepped in and shut the door behind her. All the wooden surfaces in the room had a few arrows sprouting from them. Maia stood on the center rug, her face red and puffy. Her bowstring hummed as she pulled back for another shot.

Thunk. An arrow lodged in the dresser. "I said I don't want company." She glared at Katya and then pulled another arrow from the quiver on the bed. "Unless you want to send that murdering bastard in here." She sank an arrow into her headboard.

Katya leaned against the bare stone wall, out of the line of fire. "You're running out of ammunition." She glanced at the wall opposite. The portraits of Maia's parents and of Roland with the infant Maia had been spared the deluge of arrows, though one had been shot in the frame.

"I've got other weapons." Maia fired another arrow in the headboard and hit it dead center before she flipped open the lid of the trunk at the foot of her bed. "Throwing daggers." She tossed a brace of knives onto the bed. "I've even got this." She held up a carved wooden case. "It's a blowgun like the ancient Uanai used to use. I had a historian make it for me. I thought it might come in useful someday. Fires teeny-tiny poison needles." She chucked it back in the trunk and then threw her bow in, too.

Katya didn't know what to say. She had no idea that Maia researched new throwing weapons, especially poisoned ones. Maia's aim was unparalleled, and Katya needed that, but she didn't want Maia thinking of death all the time. "Maia."

Maia ignored her and slipped one of the stilettos free of its sheath. Jerking her arm to the side in a blur, she launched the knife at a table mirror and shattered it into a dozen pieces.

"That's enough, Maia," Katya snapped.

Maia turned, her body vibrating as if she were a bowstring, her face swinging between sorrow and defiance. "He…he…" Her lip quivered, and strands of hair floated around her head, much like the baby in the portrait behind her. Katya stepped forward and wrapped her in an embrace. Maia stiffened, and Katya thought she might push away, but then, with a sob, she melted in Katya's arms. "He killed Da."

"I know, coz." Katya tightened her grip, feeling her own tears. She stared at Roland's portrait and mourned the fact that she'd never get to speak with her uncle as one adult to another, that they would never lead the Order of Vestra together.

Pity made her tears flow harder. Maia had no father and could have no surrogate father in either churlish Crowe or Katya's often-absent father. No wonder she'd fallen for strong, capable, kind-hearted Brutal. "I'm so sorry, coz."

"I want to kill him."

"No, you don't."

"I do!" Maia flopped at the foot of the bed and wrapped her arms under her knees. "I want to shoot him! And drown him! I want to kill him a thousand times!"

"No, you want your father back. I do, too."

"You have a father."

"Roland was a far better father than mine."

"What?"

"Well, I love my father, but he's a bit...absent sometimes, even when he's in the room. He's loving, no doubt, but he's, well, the king. I don't think being king leaves much room for tenderness in a person's life. Roland was very tender. His love was like a great big blanket, and it was all for you, coz. Da's love is kind of..."

"Loud?"

Katya gave her a sideways hug. "Boisterous. He couldn't read a bedtime story without getting bored in the middle and finishing early." She cleared her throat and deepened her voice. "And then, some prince or another did something heroic, and they all went home for tea. I say, my girl, this is rather a bore, isn't it?"

Maia laughed a little. "Look here, I know you're six, but these books don't have enough murders."

"How the deuce is a man supposed to make it through a book without murders?"

"You can finish it yourself, can't you, my girl? If you can't figure out the words, just look at the pictures!" Even as they chuckled, Maia's eyes filled with tears again. She scooted up the bed and leaned against the headboard between two arrows. "Da read to me every night, and he always finished. I miss him, Katya."

"I know."

Maia yanked one of the arrows out of the wood, the head groaning as it came loose. "Would you kill me? If you had to? Would you hold my face under the water?"

Spirits forbid she would ever have to make that choice, but Katya answered with what Maia needed to hear, not daring to question whether or not it was the truth. "No, you and I would have gone to the bottom of the river together, taking the evidence with us."

"If Crowe had killed himself with Da, Da would still be dead."

"Yes."

"Was there no other way?"

"No, not when the kingdom is at stake."

Maia snapped the arrow in two. "Then I'll spread my hatred to Carmen Van Sleeting and her children."

"But you won't remove it from Crowe?"

Maia rubbed her face again. "I can't forgive him just like that, Katya. I can't just *understand*."

"All right. Do I have your word you won't kill him?" With all their talk of death, it was a serious question.

"Yes, not if you still need him."

Katya reminded herself never to let Crowe retire. "Brutal's still outside. Do you want me to send him in?"

Maia shook her head. "I look a mess."

All that had gone on, and that was what she was worried about? "He won't mind."

Maia glared at her.

"All right. I'll tell him to clear off."

"Are you seeing Starbride tonight?"

"Absolutely."

"Will I get details?"

"Absolutely not."

"You're no fun at all."

Katya kissed her forehead. "If it gets too hard on your own, send for me."

"I'd rather you be having fun."

Katya slipped out the door. Brutal glanced at her, his eyes hopeful. "Sorry, Brutal. She doesn't want you to see her when she's a mess."

"I don't care about that."

"I know, but a sixteen-year-old girl won't be budged when she thinks she looks terrible."

Brutal leaned against the wall. "I'll hang around in case she changes her mind. Maybe she'll talk to me through the door."

"Maybe. Thanks, Brutal." Katya strode away, wanting to be with Starbride more than anything, wanting to live in Starbride's arms forever. But, she reminded herself, there was another dreaded conversation that had to happen first. Perhaps a little dinner would smooth things over. She tapped her chin as she thought about it. There were so many instances in life she didn't know how to handle; arranging dinner for two was not one of them. And she couldn't force the Order to heal. She'd stopped the bleeding, but only time would close the wound.

CHAPTER EIGHTEEN: STARBRIDE

Starbride changed into the outfit Katya had given her; she'd earned a break from the frothy dresses.

"Are you sure the dress you wore this morning couldn't be salvaged?" Dawnmother asked. "Did you even *try* to save it?"

"It was completely ruined."

"I'm sure you wept."

"One down."

Dawnmother stood back and surveyed the red outfit. "Hair half-down again, I think. Jewelry?"

"Something simple."

Dawnmother whisked a small ruby pendant and matching stud earrings from the jewelry box, and Starbride stood still for the fastening and styling. When Dawnmother held the mirror in front of her, she nodded. The top half of her hair had been pulled behind her head in a simple twist, showing off her earrings, while the rest hung free.

"Very elegant," Dawnmother said.

"Maybe we can sell some of the frothy dresses and have more Allusian outfits made."

Dawnmother snorted. "And then what will you have to ruin when you go gallivanting into the woods looking for danger?"

"We'll keep one dress around, then."

"After a few forays, you'll be as ragged as a beggar." Dawnmother picked imaginary lint from Starbride's shoulder.

"Stop fussing, Dawn. I'm fine. I swear that I will not be leaving the palace tonight."

"I'm becoming a worrier."

"Becoming?" Even as she teased, guilt pricked her. She'd been angry that Katya left her behind, but she'd done the same to Dawnmother, without even a clue as to where she'd gone. "I'm sorry, Dawn. I've always been more trouble than I'm worth."

Dawnmother waved the apology away and straightened Starbride's clothing again. Standing still seemed a small price to pay to put her at ease.

After night had fallen, Katya arrived as promised, her face a little haggard but her attire impeccable. She wore a dark coat slightly less embellished than the one she wore at the Courtiers Ball, and Starbride noted with a chuckle that her trousers were just as tight.

"You look tired," Starbride said. "Has something happened?"

"I found something out. I don't know if I was ready to hear it. To tell the truth, I'm not ready to repeat it."

"Don't speak of it. Do you still want to have dinner?"

"It's the only thing today I've looked forward to." Katya offered an arm, and Starbride slipped hers through as they ventured into the corridor. "Averie's arranged everything on Hanna's Retreat. Let's take a more direct route than last time."

Starbride resisted the urge to snuggle close until they were out of the halls. "Direct route?"

"Well, since my enemies already know about you, I want the courtiers to know we're seeing one another, but tonight, I want to avoid enough of them not to get stopped."

"Why do you want them to know we're seeing one another?"

"To show you off, of course. That, and the more eyes on you, the more you'll be protected."

Starbride squeezed Katya's arm and chuckled. "I'm not a prize pony."

"One look at you and the courtiers will be envious of me as a suitor, rather than as the princess."

Starbride shook her head even as she blushed. There was that Katya charm again. The recriminations she'd been guarding all afternoon were slipping away. She lined them up in a neat row in her head and built a wall around them.

Katya led her near gangs of whispering courtiers but not among them, and the surge of muted conversation at their appearance was like a disturbed beehive. Starbride had to wonder how many people would be following her through the hallways from then on. She ignored the stares and the whispers, though she clutched Katya's arm a little tighter, and she was more than happy to leave them behind and reach Hanna's Retreat.

As she mounted the steps, Starbride saw that a candlelit table had been laid under the starry sky. "Romantic."

Katya's teeth shone in the trickle of light. "You asked me once if I was going to seduce you."

"And?"

"I wanted you to see what it's like when I really try."

Starbride took her seat, and Katya lifted the silver covers from the food. Starbride leaned over her plate, inhaling the heady aroma. In the dim light, the dinner was hard to see but delicious all the same. Perfectly cooked roast beef and creamy potatoes melted in her mouth. The mousse was like chocolate velvet, and she couldn't help thinking it must be nice to be royalty once in a while if that was their standard fare.

She waited until dessert was almost over before she opened the gate to her wall and let her feelings out. "I don't want to pick at your bad news, but you did say there would be an explanation of today."

"I know." Katya tapped the rim of her wineglass with one finger. "I don't know quite how to reveal this—I never got a chance to ask anyone how to handle it—so I'm just going to blurt it out. When it comes to protecting my family, I am the first line of defense."

"I don't understand."

"I protect them."

"Like a guard?"

"Exactly."

"But...what...? And why...?" It was obviously a secret, but why would the princess be a secret guard? Frowning hard, Starbride got her tangled thoughts together. "Do your parents approve of this?"

"My parents insist. The second child of the King or Queen of Farraday has always led a secret order—the Order of Vestra—tasked to protect the royal family and the crown. That's why I tackle problems on my own instead of calling the Guard. Conspiracies are easier sought out in secret, especially if they touch on affairs that the king wants hidden from the public."

"But..." Starbride paused, and pieces of the puzzle fell into place in her head. "Ah, the mystery of the princess who loves and hates hunting becomes clearer."

Katya raised her glass in salute.

"This Order seems a good idea in itself, for the very reasons you stated, but must it be you who leads it? Isn't it terribly dangerous? If something happened to you and then to your brother..."

"The throne would go to my brother's daughter—his eldest—after my father's death, and Maia would lead the Order until my nephew was old enough or until she...died."

Starbride heard the pause and knew there was more behind it than just the thought of a cousin's death. "Has someone died?"

"Yes."

Starbride placed her hand over Katya's cool fingers. "I'm sorry."

"It was a long time ago, but I just found out the details tonight."

"I'm sorry anyway."

"Thank you."

"So, you went out alone today to fulfill your duties as leader of this Order."

"Yes, and that's why you must never follow me again."

Starbride heard the admonishment in the statement and tossed her hair over one shoulder. "*And* why you mustn't keep secrets unless you want me to act impulsively."

Katya placed a hand on her chest in mock indignation. "Oh, so your following me today is my fault?"

"Yes."

"I must remember that one. When in doubt, pass the blame."

"A tactic that has worked for my mother for years." Starbride toyed with her wine for a moment. "And the men you found, they had something to do with this long-ago death?"

"We're still trying to determine that, Star. Things aren't always simple enough for an easy explanation."

Starbride held up a hand, forestalling the aggravated lecture. "Based on what the bearded man said, I think he was connected to the men who accosted us in the scarf shop. He seemed to know what had…almost been done there." She cringed to think about the table and the knife and shook her head to banish the memory.

"Really? Tell me."

Starbride told her everything the three men had said and done, keeping back one fact for last. "The bearded man called me a pyradisté when his pyramid wouldn't work on me."

"Well, well, well." Katya tapped her chin. "Now that I think about it, the shopkeeper held his pyramid in front of you, and nothing happened. I didn't put two and two together at the time, but now…You *are* a sleeper, aren't you?"

"Is that another Farradain saying that doesn't make any sense?"

"It means that you have unexpected talents."

"But everyone knows how to sleep."

"I don't know the origin of the expression, but it's wonderful to watch you try to work it out. I could watch you do almost anything."

"What do you *think* of my being a pyradisté?"

"I think it's wonderful. We'll talk to Crowe in the morning. After everything that's happened today, I ordered him to bed."

Starbride pulled her soft napkin through her fingers, pausing at the embroidered royal crest. "My people have no pyradistés. Those who use the pyramids are called *adsnazi*, and their pyramids look crude compared to those I've seen in Farraday."

"Here, everyone is tested at thirteen to see if they could be a pyradisté. It's not the same in Allusia?"

"It's not really an honor there. And the *adsnazi* can't accomplish the wonders I've seen in Farraday. They live in the hills north of Newhope. They rarely came into town, but they always had a pack of children following them by midday when they did."

"Did they give out sweets?"

"No, strings of red amber beads. They wore multicolored shirts and cut their hair very short, except for one long lock at the back of their heads. Whenever we elected a new governor, they'd gather in the square and make lights dance in the sky."

"You won't have to cut your hair, will you?"

Starbride curled one of her locks around her finger. "Not if I'm a pyradisté instead of an *adsnazi*." She didn't even know if she wanted to be one, but she saved that worry for later.

"Good. I'll buy you all the multicolored shirts and amber beads you like. Just leave your hair alone."

"Speaking of people in need of shirts, what will happen to Lord Hugo?"

"He'll be watched until I'm sure he has no connection to these traitors."

"He won me over when he got stabbed." She rested her head on one fist. "He feels that he and Maia are kindred spirits."

"I noticed his shock when he first saw her."

"Could it be that he saw her sometime or met her, and his memory was erased but not completely? Do such things happen?"

"Something else to discuss with Crowe, but good thought."

Starbride tossed her hair again. "See? You should have let me in from the start."

"So I see."

Starbride folded her napkin beside her plate. She paused before she spoke again, thinking of Katya kissing Miss Greyson's hand. "I always thought your personality was…different with me than with the other courtiers, especially a certain lady. Is your court face all an act, something to throw people off the scent of the Order?"

"Most of the time. I couldn't live the lie with you, though. Rather, I didn't want to."

Starbride tried not to let suspicion get the best of her. Still, she had to speak one of her worries. "It's a little disconcerting to know that you're such an exceptional liar."

Katya sputtered a laugh, but Starbride heard sadness in the sound. "The court face, as you call it, is second nature now. Sometimes, I worry that it'll become reality, and I'll lose my real self one day."

Sadness tightened Starbride's throat. Katya had three faces, not two as Starbride had originally thought. She pretended to be fully human; she acted the pampered princess; she had the dangerous job of guarding not only her family, but the crown of Farraday. It was no wonder she felt she was losing herself. "Let's move away from the candle and look at the stars."

"No more questions?"

Starbride shook her head, but her mind didn't stop poring over the answers she'd been given. A family of Fiends guarding each other made an odd sort of sense, though she didn't want to say that aloud, not wanting to spoil the evening by bringing up Katya's heritage. She'd have to put it together in her mind later and make sure she got any new pieces of the puzzle. Hopefully, she'd proven the worth of her insight.

They moved their chairs in front of the table, their backs to the candlelight, and sat side by side, gazing up at the twinkling sky. "I'm surprised you don't have a string quartet hidden somewhere," Starbride said.

"I'm keeping them in reserve. They're hanging off the ledge in front of us."

"Their fingers will be too tired to play."

"They're in a harness; they'll be fine."

Starbride laid her head on Katya's shoulder and breathed deeply of the chill night air. "Can we stay here?"

"For how long?"

"Forever."

"I'd love to. You have to explain to my mother why I'm shirking my court duties, though."

"Done." Starbride picked her head up and looked into Katya's eyes. "I'll just say, 'it's love,' and the world will smile upon us."

Katya's mouth slipped open, her expression one of wonder. She leaned forward with a suddenness she hadn't shown before, and Starbride almost drew back in surprise. As their lips touched, though, the passion behind the kiss washed over Starbride, and she pressed forward.

Their mouths opened together, tongues meeting. Katya stood and pulled them together with such force it was a wonder they didn't wind up on opposite sides of one another. Starbride gave herself to the sudden heat that hammered in her and pleaded with the spirits of both their peoples that no one would interrupt them with the clearing of a throat.

Katya's hands wandered, leaving Starbride gasping and arching, and her kisses left trails of fire along Starbride's neck and shoulders. When Katya stepped back, Starbride nearly growled in protest.

Katya's breath came hard. "This is not the venue I imagined for this."

"You started it." She tried to keep from gasping. "And you're the one that spoke of seduction."

"I was joking, well, half-joking. But I didn't want us to be together for the first time on top of cold stone."

"Be together? What were you thinking? One dinner and I'm yours, Highness? I was just about to stop you."

Katya leaned to the right, and Starbride held her breath as soft lips trailed along her jaw. "Shall we test your willpower?" Her breath tickled Starbride's ear and sent sweeps of desire down her spine.

"I was just testing yours."

After a kiss or two, Katya pulled away again. "My willpower's in tatters when I'm around you, but I still object to the bare stone."

Starbride caressed Katya's face, and her next words tumbled from her lips before she could think too hard about them. "I've never been... intimate with anyone."

"Never?"

"Before you, I kissed exactly one person who was not a relation."

"And?"

"He ran and told his parents. We were six."

Katya gave her a sweet look, full of affection. "Then you absolutely cannot have your first time here. You must have a bed the size of a galleon, or at the very least, a large soft rug."

"And rose petals?"

"A must."

"And the string quartet?"

"Will be discreetly blindfolded."

Starbride buried her head in the hollow between Katya's neck and shoulder. After a second's hesitation, she let her hands do a little experimental wandering across the dark coat.

"Are you testing my willpower again?" Katya asked.

"Perhaps I want to see how quickly you can arrange a bed the size of a galleon covered in rose petals with a blind string quartet."

"I can amaze when I put my mind to it." She lifted Starbride's hands and kissed them, backs then palms. Her eyes offered pleasure, offered her heart.

Starbride kissed along Katya's soft cheek. "Then amaze me, dear Princess. I want you to. I hope I can amaze you, too."

Katya kissed her again, another of those fervent explosions that left her weak-kneed, and then led her down the stairs and through the secret passageways, pausing often to hold her close and kiss and caress her until Starbride thought she would melt like warmed butter. They emerged at last into Katya's bedroom, and Starbride stopped to gawk at the moon and stars painted on the ceiling, at the general size of the room, so much larger than hers.

Katya released her to lock the doors. "To keep the throat clearers at bay."

Starbride held out her arms, and Katya was there in an instant, leading her to a bed that wasn't the size of a galleon, with not a rose petal or a blindfolded string quartet in sight, but the promise was the same. Her heart pounded, and her mind tried to intervene, to speak hidden fears or anxieties. What should she do? What should she say?

Katya didn't leave her time to wonder. Her touch, her lips, her tongue, her flesh, they drove all thought away. Every time Starbride thought she might surface, passion found her and wrapped her in its tight embrace. The sensations that coursed through her left no room for embarrassment.

Starbride learned, hoping to give a fraction of what she received; she let Katya's moans be her guide, and Katya writhed, pulling the sheets from the mattress. Starbride took that to mean she'd learned well until Katya rolled her over and taught her all over again, driving the lessons from her conscious thoughts. She had time for one fleeting notion, and it was that Katya's reputation as a lover was well deserved.

When they were still, both of them sweating and breathing hard, Starbride said, "I'm spoiled, spoiled forever."

Katya laughed breathlessly and moved over the wadded blue sheets, her skin shining against them. "I certainly hope so."

Starbride kissed every inch of flesh she could reach. Her entire body hummed, and she'd never felt so tired or alive. Still, even with the bliss, her mind wouldn't be silent, not now that it wasn't distracted. "Was it… was I…?"

Katya kissed her urgently. Even as Starbride tried to return the intensity, she wondered where Katya summoned the energy from. "After you, I'm spoiled, too."

Starbride had just enough energy to pull the sheet across them both before she fell asleep; she let Katya's words soothe her mind. Her body had already been well taken care of.

CHAPTER NINETEEN: KATYA

Katya awoke just before dawn. She'd been getting up at the same time for so long that she no longer needed calling. In any case, Averie would be thwarted by the locked door, as she'd been before. Katya could almost see her knowing smile.

Nestled close, Starbride slept like a log, jewelry her only clothing. Rubies winked from both ears and a golden chain around her throat. As much as Katya wanted to wrap her arms around the soft curves and inhale the warm scent of Starbride's skin, she restrained herself.

It was hard not to be proud, and for the moment, her ego swelled to the point where she stretched like a cat in satisfaction. Last night, after the third or fourth time—Katya had lost track—Starbride's sweat-slicked body had gone boneless. She'd kissed Katya with a last jolt of passion before lying back and smiling, her face glowing. What she lacked in experience, she made up for in enthusiasm. That combined with the joy of giving Starbride pleasure had granted Katya everything she'd needed.

She played with an errant strand of Starbride's hair. Starbride muttered in her sleep, and Katya had to stop or risk waking her. She used as much stealth as she could and slipped out from under the sheets, fumbling in the turned-down light of the wall lantern until she found her robe draped over the chair next to her vanity. With a glance in the mirror, she slipped the robe on and grinned at her reflection. Half her hair had come undone. She looked like she'd been doing exactly what she'd been doing all night.

In front of the mirror, Katya took the rest of the pins out and let her hair fall before she brushed it and pinned it up again in its usual loose bun. She noted the slight love bite on the side of her neck. In one passionate upheaval, Starbride had kissed her a little too hard; there'd even been a few teeth. Ah well, it would add to her persona, but if it bothered Starbride, Katya had a few high collars.

Once she was finished with her hair, she tiptoed to the door and unlocked it, moving with aching slowness, and casting glance after glance back at the bed. She opened the door just enough to slip through and then shut it behind her as noiselessly as she could. In the private sitting room, Averie was already setting breakfast on the table. She cast pointed glances at Katya's bedroom door.

"No comment," Katya said.

Averie banged the lid shut on a platter of eggs, put her fists on her hips, and stared.

"You've become too accustomed to privileged information."

Turning up her nose, Averie filled Katya's plate.

"And I've become too accustomed to food without spit in it; is that what you're implying?"

Averie shrugged, still not speaking.

"She's in there."

Averie dropped into the chair opposite, her eyes aglow. "I'm very glad for you."

Katya pushed the toast rack across the table. "Eat with me."

Without looking at it, Averie took a slice of bread and set it on a plate. "And?"

"Would you like some eggs, too?"

"It must have been nice if you're avoiding talking about it this much."

"One of the best nights I've ever had."

Leaning back in her chair, Averie pressed a hand to her heart. "Ah!"

"You live vicariously through me too often."

"I'm just happy for you."

As she stared at Averie's joyous expression, Katya realized just how much truth lay in her own words. Averie didn't have a life of her own and probably never would, even if she wanted one. Being the lady-in-waiting of the Princess of Farraday and a member of the Order of Vestra, Averie didn't have time for anything else. Living vicariously was all she could do.

"Do you ever want to be elsewhere, Averie?"

"Like where?"

"Well, it's not that I don't love you. I do, and I wouldn't trade your service for anyone's, but if you're ever unhappy—"

"Stop right there. I will die as your servant. There is no place I'd rather be than with you, Highness."

"A husband? Children?"

"I can have those and still be your lady-in-waiting."

"And when would you see them? Between when you put me to bed late at night and serve me breakfast at the crack of dawn?"

"They could learn to be nocturnal."

"So, they'd see you while you're asleep?"

Averie slathered jam on her toast. "Well then, they could see me during the day while you're out, unless I was supposed to be out with you."

"Not good enough."

"I know many ladies-in-waiting, enough to know that I'm unique. Others are not so fortunate. They stand in the corner at attention, waiting for the first dropped hanky. Some ladies are treated worse than illegitimate stepchildren; some ladies are treated horribly *by* the illegitimate stepchildren. The Duchess of Blenbraddyn would have apoplexy if her lady sat down to have toast with her, and the young Countess Fanchion, though only nine years old, slaps her lady-in-waiting at least ten times a day."

"Why doesn't the lady quit?"

"Pride. It's a good position, nice pay, hand-me-down clothes, and full care by the countess's physician for the lady's family. She was the former countess's lady-in-waiting, too. Perhaps she thinks she can endure."

"Well, there's one person who keeps a family on the side."

"You see? And you don't even slap me."

Katya sputtered on her coffee. "Well, I'm certain that Countess Fanchion's lady-in-waiting is not in the Order of Vestra."

"I can find a balance. Now, is Starbride a good kisser?"

"It's rude to kiss and tell. You know that."

"I know nothing of the kind. Was she very passionate? I've heard Allusians can be passionate."

"Who have you been talking to about Allusians?"

"This person and that. Is it true?"

Katya gave her a dark look. "It's never too late to start slapping you, I suppose."

"I knew it." Averie sat back and crossed her arms, a self-satisfied look on her face.

"I'll have to get used to people discussing our relationship, I suppose." Spirits knew it would be better with Averie than with the courtiers with their prying eyes and probing questions. Either the princess's Allusian lover would be embraced with false sentiment, or she'd be ridiculed. Probably both. Luckily, the embracers would somewhat shield Starbride from the ridiculers. Katya sighed. They were problems for later. "Can you send a message to Dawnmother? I wouldn't want her to worry."

"I sent one last night."

"How did you know I came back?"

"A good servant knows all her mistress's comings and goings."

"Then why did you ask me if she was in there?"

"Ah, I meant, is she *still* in there? Eat your breakfast before it gets cold."

Katya dug in until she heard a small thump from the bedroom, followed by what sounded like a curse. "I think someone's stubbed a toe."

"I'll make myself scarce."

"If you don't think you can control your lustful thoughts, do so."

Inside the bedroom, Starbride sat on the floor, wrapped in a sheet and rubbing her foot. Katya knelt next to her. "It's the bed legs. They stick out too far."

"You need some kind of a sign."

Katya raised the injured foot to her lips and kissed the top. "Thank you for thinking I have enough people in here to warrant a sign."

Starbride wrapped her arms around Katya's waist, and Katya drew her in with her acre of sheet and kissed the top of her head. Starbride tugged at her bun. "I know your hair wasn't this tidy last night."

"I fixed it. I can't stand having it down."

"Among my people, those who've taken up the sword often shave their heads."

"I'll threaten my mother with that the next time she tries to make me wear a more fashionable style."

"You're fashionable enough."

Katya kissed her gently, then more deeply. The sheet was easy to unwind.

Starbride stopped her quickly. "Haven't we been in here for a week already?"

"Only three days."

"Liar. I need to go back to my room and change." She played with the top of the sheet for a moment. "I talk to Dawnmother about everything. She can be trusted."

"Not with all of it, not yet, please. Don't mention the Fiend or the Order."

"Is that a royal command?"

"You *know* it's a request. If I was throwing around orders, I'd order you back into bed."

Starbride chuckled and threw her hair over one shoulder. "I'll keep your secrets."

"Thank you." Katya kissed her again and helped her hunt down her clothes before leaving Starbride to dress alone. She couldn't promise to keep her hands to herself. "Breakfast?"

"Dawnmother will have something for me."

The thought of sending her away made Katya's chest ache, but she couldn't ignore her responsibilities forever. "Will Dawnmother forgive me if I send you back to your room with an escort that isn't me?"

"She'll have to. Besides, I don't want to wait on my breakfast until you're dressed, and you can't go through the hallway in your robe."

"You'd better go, then. If I get ahold of you again…" Katya started forward, and Starbride darted for the door, laughing over her shoulder.

"When will we see one another?"

"As soon as I can manage it, I swear."

"And you'll tell me any new developments?"

"*Yes*, I will. And I'll talk to Crowe about you. And you will know all."

"You know what?" Starbride's bright eyes filled with mischief.

"What?"

"I love you."

Katya's breath caught, and she took a step forward. "Ah, Star, I love you, too."

"Back, back, before I stay another three days! My escort, please."

"Averie! Escort this rascal back to her room before I order her imprisonment in our royal apartment."

Averie curtsied as she entered, her cheeks taut with a contained grin. Starbride gave one wink over her shoulder, and then they were gone. Katya sat and ate and reveled in recent memory, smiling again and again until it hurt. When she finished, she pushed away her plate, closed her eyes, and prayed to Matter and Marla for wisdom. "It is love, oh spirits, it must be. I've seen it now, and I've felt it. She's seen the Fiend and the trouble in my life, and she hasn't run away. I was ready to play the rake forever, but now I want one person. Spirits, I've used the gifts you've given me, and all I see is love. Put my doubts to rest."

Her heart lighter, only a single great hurdle remained, and Katya doubted that even the spirits could help her with her mother. She'd put that off as long as possible.

Once Averie returned, Katya forced herself to look ahead to the unpleasant task of dealing with the traitors. Averie helped her dress in midnight blue and black. Setting her face to stone and her mind to the forthcoming task, Katya strode through the secret passageways until she reached the anteroom to the dungeons. Crowe leaned against the wall, facing the door as if waiting for her. His wrinkled face seemed more haggard in the shadowy light.

"Crowe? I thought you'd be in there by now."

"I was."

Katya frowned. "I expected to catch at least *some* of the interrogation."

"Both Darren's and Cassius's minds are closed. They're either pyradistés, or they've both been warded by a pyramid user of incredible skill. I might have known."

Katya's stomach went cold. "By the bearded man?"

"What makes you think so?"

Katya told him about the bearded man trying to hypnotize Starbride, about him calling her a pyradisté.

Crowe ran his fingers through his hair, making it stick out at the sides. "It might be him, I suppose. Starbride's a pyradisté, eh? Ha. Well, now I know it was useless to offer to erase her memories when she found out about the Fiend."

"I...I didn't know you offered. You can't break through these wards?"

Crowe rubbed the dark circles under his eyes. Katya wondered if he'd slept at all. "I don't know. Given time? I still don't know."

Katya watched him stare into space and frowned again. She wanted to be kind, but they had a job to do. If he'd become incapable, she needed a way to either motivate him or replace him. "Pennynail taking care of you?"

"I don't need taking care of."

She resisted the urge to glare. Her father would've barked at him, but that wasn't the way she wanted to play it. He'd do his duty, but she didn't want his mind clouded by resentment. A way out of an impending argument leapt to mind. Starbride was again to be her salvation. "My father wants you to begin training your inevitable replacement."

"What?" The pallor of his face gave way as two spots of red bloomed in his cheeks. "He said what?"

"He said—"

"I heard you! Of all the...I will do this, Katya! I can figure it out." His eyes blazed, and he looked more alive than she'd seen in days.

"I know you can. That's why I'm not going to make you do it."

"I don't understand. If your father commanded it, you have to do it."

"Whose side are you on?"

"No, no. I will do it. I mean, I don't want to be replaced, but if that...
if your father wants me to be replaced, don't anger him on my account."

"I've thought of a way to keep you working and keep him happy."

Crowe's brows turned down before they shot up. "You clever thing,
you. You want me to train Starbride."

"It'll keep her out of the Pyradisté Academy—so I can see her
more often—it'll get her an education, and you'll be training your
replacement."

"Do you really want her in the Order?"

"Well...she wants to be involved, and I love her, Crowe. I really
do."

His face softened. "Yes, I can tell. And I'm happy for you, but you
have to make sure she wants to go on dangerous missions when called.
And you can't keep her a secret from the king and queen."

"I know. One thing at a time. Will you do it? The training, I mean."

"If she agrees, of course."

Katya gripped his shoulder once before letting go. "Have you
written to Layra?"

"No, I was waiting to tell you about the captives before I did."

"Start writing, then. And I want the best pyramids you can make
guarding our *guests.*"

"Done."

"Maybe," Katya said idly, "Pennynail can get some of his friends
to help you look into the Pyradisté Academy and see if they can find this
bearded man."

Crowe stared at her, his expression flat. "Nice try."

"What?"

"Discover the identity of Pennynail's friends and you discover his,
is that it?"

"Guilty."

He snorted. "I'll go up and get to that letter now."

"Good. I want a word with one of our guests, and then I'm off to
check on Maia again."

"Darren's second on the left. Cassius is last on the right."

"What happened to the Shadow?"

"I got everything I could from him, Katya."

With a shiver, Katya nodded. "Gallows or headsman's axe?"

"Never mind that. How was Maia last night?"

"Angry. She promised not to kill you, though."

"I wouldn't mind if she did."

"She'll forgive you one of these days, Crowe."

He didn't respond, and as Katya stepped to the dungeon door, she thought she heard him whisper, "I hope not."

The door to the dungeon proper had no locks, no door handle, no opening of any kind. Instead, she pushed her palm to a pyramid set in the wood, and it tingled under her palm as it recognized the Fiend. The only people who could get past it were those who carried the Umbriel Fiend and those Crowe had tuned the pyramids to recognize, like himself and Pennynail. She supposed Crowe brought the prisoners food himself.

She held her lamp high in the dark space beyond the door. Wan light shone from pyramids set in the walls, but darker pyramids glinted in the flickering light. Those would do more than just cast illumination. Some were alarms, some weapons. They sparkled like dozens of little eyes. With a shiver, Katya moved on to the cells guarding Darren. The door swung open with a creak as the pyramid recognized her, and Katya let her eyes adjust to the dim light penetrating the darkness of his cell before she stepped inside.

Darren sat on the stone floor against the far wall; his manacled wrists lay in his lap, and his chains coiled on either side of him before leading back to the wall he sat against. "To what do I owe the pleasure?" His eyes were still as smug as they had been at the manor house, and his smile was as certain.

"You knew the mind pyramid wouldn't work on you."

He shrugged, making his chains jingle.

"And yet, here you are. Your secrets might be out of reach of our pyramids, for now, but your body is still in a cage."

"But my imagination is free to roam. I've been picturing a golden-haired princess entwined with a dark-skinned Allusian, and it's kept me, oh, very entertained. It would be better if you described *exactly* what it's like to fuck her. Do you use something special or just your fist?"

Katya raised an eyebrow, all the rise he would get from her if his ammunition was so weak. "How long will your confidence last? Until you crack here in the dark, or until we string you up in the courtyard?"

"Let's find out."

"How about your brother? Will he be as haughty after a few days?"

Darren tsked. "She tries and tries to get me to admit things, and yet she never succeeds."

"I don't need you to admit it. I know you're Darren and Cassius Sleeting."

He stroked chin. "Sleeting, Sleeting...Ah! Now I remember. The woman who should have been queen. If that had been our mother, wouldn't we be Darren and Cassius Nar Umbriel?"

Katya felt her face twitch and hoped he wouldn't see it in the dim light. "You're right. It wouldn't be Sleeting. It would be Darren and Cassius Whoreson." Darren's face went cold. "Aha, a hit at last. You are Carmen Van Sleeting's children."

"Any man would object to his mother being called a whore."

"Except the sons of whores. Or should I say the grandsons of whores? I wonder if this servant girl, your grandmother, actually worked in the palace. And if she did, if she tried to get into my grandfather's bed, failed at that, and had to bed the dog boy or the privy man instead. Did you know her? Was she very ugly?"

Darren's arms flexed, and the chains jingled again. Katya set her footing in case he rushed at her, though she didn't think he could reach her with the chains. "Perhaps you'd like to talk about your father," she said. "I heard he died before his time. Was it syphilis? I've heard that can be a very painful death."

"You'll find out what it's like to die painfully."

"I'm not the one in chains."

He leaned forward. "You will be."

Katya knew it was nonsense, but something about the sureness of his tone sent a shiver down her spine. "We'll talk more later."

"I look forward to it."

As the door swung shut, she called, "Good day, Whoreson or Grandwhoreson."

She heard him mutter "Bitch," and knew she'd left him with some nasty thoughts. She'd let him remember them, over and over again, in the dark.

CHAPTER TWENTY: STARBRIDE

Dawnmother had both breakfast and a knowing smile waiting when Starbride returned. "I don't need to ask how it went, do I?"

"Dawn, I'm so happy."

"So I see."

"Are you still suspicious?"

"Always." Dawnmother laid out a pot of tea and a few slices of bread with fruit.

Sitting with a cup of tea, Starbride told Dawnmother everything about the night before, shivers running up and down her spine as she recalled the finer points. Dawnmother listened with rapt attention and asked the occasional question, but there was so much Starbride didn't even have words for.

"Ah, Star, it sounds perfect."

"Like one of your many hayloft trips?"

"It reminds me of Shinehorseman. With him, it was perfect."

"I remember. Well, I remember what you would tell me about him. Why didn't the two of you stay together?"

"He moved to one of the smaller Farradain cities between Marienne and Newhope. It wouldn't have worked anyway. Only servant caste can really understand the servant's pledge." She brought her gaze back to the present. "Did the princess provide some of the promised answers?"

"Yes, but, I can't share them, even with you."

Dawnmother raised her hands to the ceiling and then dropped them. "These people and their secrets! Our lives are one, can't they see?"

"I know, I know." She thought of Crowe, a secret half-Allusian trying to operate in Farradain society with an Allusian servant's mind. "I don't know if I could explain the bond, but a promise is a promise. Katya will relax that promise—soon, I hope—and I'll tell you everything. Someday, the truth for you."

Someone knocked on the door. Dawnmother cracked it open and

peeked out. Starbride strained to hear a muted conversation before Dawnmother turned with an envelope. "It's an invitation to tea with a party of courtiers and also Baroness Jacintha Veronda."

Starbride blinked. "A baroness?"

"Quite a coup."

"It must be for all the courtiers." There was another knock, and Dawnmother collected another invitation, this one to a riding party the following day with a host of courtiers and also Countess Nadia Van Hale and Viscount Lenvis Neversfall.

Starbride frowned. "Is that one for all the courtiers, too?"

Dawnmother turned the invitation over. "It's addressed to you personally."

"What's going on?"

"You're the princess's lover."

"More eyes on me, she said."

"And she was right."

Another knock came and then another; invitations poured in, some with small gifts of ribbons or sweets. Letter after letter came from courtiers who gushed about how sorry they were that they hadn't invited Starbride to come and see them earlier. Things had been so busy, no doubt she understood.

Starbride put her head in her hands. "This is just what I need. I'll never finish my work now."

"You have to go to some of these, you know, those hosted or attended by nobles."

"I know, I know. It's one thing if they ignore me, but quite another if I ignore them."

"Time to dress. This tea party starts in an hour."

Starbride wore an ugly dress; everyone at the party did. She carried the little pillow Dawnmother had made for her, gratified to see that *they* all carried them, too. The ladies gathered around her like a flock of curious magpies covered in pastel froth. She wore her mint, and they clucked over its design and color. Compliments poured from them as they shepherded her to a small settee, and she put her tiny pillow under her and sat. She faced the one woman who hadn't risen at her entrance.

The other courtiers introduced her to Baroness Jacintha, a slight, dark-haired woman in her late twenties, and then they began to chatter at such a pace that it was difficult to keep up. They'd fall silent when Baroness Jacintha spoke, and after she'd finished, they'd all talk at once as if they were clockwork toys powered by her voice. Starbride sipped from her delicate teacup and let the scene wash over her.

"Allusians are so *interesting*," Baroness Jacintha said, momentarily quieting the courtier horde. They all inhaled to speak, but Baroness Jacintha opened her mouth again, and Starbride could almost hear the courtiers holding their breath. How many would pass out and die if she didn't speak soon? "I acquired an *exquisite* fan last summer that the seller *assured* me was Allusian." The courtiers breathed out and in again. "I simply *adore* your hair."

"Thank you."

The courtiers paused, waiting for Baroness Jacintha to speak again, but when she lifted her teacup to her lips, they talked over one another, talking *at* Starbride but rarely to her.

One of them called her Star, making her cringe. She gritted her teeth and bore it, fighting not to think of Katya breathing the familiar name into her ear. Baroness Jacintha made a little cry of protest, and everyone froze. She waved a finger at the offending courtier. "No, no, ladies, none of that. The shortening of an Allusian name is reserved for *intimates*." She put on a fantastic smile. The rest of the horde tittered.

Starbride inclined her head. "Thank you, Baroness Jacintha." She saw to the heart of the calculated slip-up. It shouted, "Speaking of *intimates*..." Well, she wouldn't rise to the bait. Let them name Katya if they wanted to speak of her. She did wonder which of them had researched Allusia for the baroness, but in the end, it didn't matter. She sipped her tea and listened. They talked about fashion; they talked about riding and tea and croquet. They talked about gifts they'd received from lovers they were considering. When she couldn't stand talking of nothing anymore, Starbride asked Baroness Jacintha about herself.

"Me?" Baroness Jacintha placed a hand on the flounces of her bosom.

"The highland lakes are your home, correct? I hear it's very beautiful." They weren't the only ones who could do a bit of research. Dawnmother had run to the library on feet made of wings.

For a moment, Baroness Jacintha's expression turned wistful. "Yes, autumn is the best time, when the leaves begin to turn..." She shook her head at the glittering crowd around her. "Of course, one prefers court to trees." The throng giggled and nodded. Starbride fought a frown. They hung on Baroness Jacintha's every word, emulated her every gesture. What could a baroness be worried about? Their opinions? Hers seemed to matter so much more.

"How long have you been at court?" Starbride asked.

"Five years." She lifted her chin and then leaned in close as if they were alone. "And with nearly as many lovers."

The crowd erupted in giggles and girlish squeals. They covered their mouths like children. Starbride put on her best smile. According to the gossip Dawnmother had uncovered, Baroness Jacintha's lovers numbered twice that many.

Maybe she could steer the subject to something she could at least stand. "Who are the best jewelers in town?"

They spent the next fifteen minutes or more informing her of various artists. This craftsman did his best, but his creations were simply *yesterday*, though one handsome lord with interesting prospects favored his creations. Some jewelers were old and established; others up and coming. It was an absolute *pity* that a few promising newcomers didn't have much money and had a hard time keeping their businesses running, but one could always commission them if one needed a gift.

Starbride nodded until the very end, when one of them asked, "Do you need a gift for someone?"

The question hung heavy in the air. Baroness Jacintha put her teacup down to listen, and they all leaned in a little farther. Starbride almost laughed, a loud guffaw that would make them jump back. "No, I'm just curious."

They sat back, disappointment radiating from their expressions. Baroness Jacintha seemed a little vexed, and Starbride wondered if she'd be invited for tea again. She didn't think it likely. Ah well, that left more time for the library.

And more time for Katya, it seemed. After the tea party, Katya surprised Starbride an hour into her studies, proving she wasn't above a rendezvous amidst stacks of old books. Starbride pulled away from her embrace after a long moment. "Just how many women have you kissed in this library?"

"You're the first."

"Well." Starbride ran her fingers over Katya's coat buttons, "now that you know your way around, maybe you'll try reading the books, too."

"Hmm. How about I leave the studying to you and just drop in from time to time." Someone cleared his throat from the other side of the shelf just as Katya leaned in for another kiss.

"I should stick my signet ring around the corner," Katya grumbled.

"Don't be a bully, dear Princess."

Katya kissed her gently. "I obey your every command, Miss Meringue. Unfortunately, I have to dash."

Disappointment made her chest ache, but Starbride reminded herself that she also had work to do. "I'll see you tomorrow after riding?"

"I'll send you a note when I'm free, I promise."

A riding party sounded so much better than tea. Starbride wore her Allusian outfit, and the courtiers exclaimed over it. She wondered if her clothing would start a new trend at court and fervently hoped so. Her mother couldn't object then.

Viscount Lenvis had tanned skin, reminding Starbride a little of her people. His features were all Farradain, though, lacking the rounder face and higher cheekbones of an Allusian. He talked about his homeland with a relaxed air, so different from the baroness. "I live in Lucienne-by-the-Sea," he said, "but don't get me started about her. I could talk someone to death about the ocean, the sky, the bracing salt air…"

"Viscount Lenvis has one love," Countess Nadia said, "and she is big and wet and miles away. He has no time for us poor human women."

"Not true, Countess Nadia! How could I ignore such beauty as rides with me today?" He gestured toward them. The other courtiers were spread out, riding slowly over the rolling fields.

Countess Nadia inclined her head at the compliment and cast a glance at Starbride, quick and appraising. She then threw a calculating glance at the viscount that carried more than a little lust.

Starbride had a revelation. The countess was trying to charm the viscount out of his trousers—even though she had to be twenty years his senior—and she clearly wanted to see if Starbride had the same intention. Well, here was one woman who wasn't taking rumors of Starbride and Katya for granted.

Still, Starbride would have to put Countess Nadia's suspicions to bed somehow; she couldn't risk making an enemy. After a quick glance at the countess's jewelry, Starbride decided that the best way to reassure her was to make a stab at friendship.

When Viscount Lenvis rode forward to speak with another knot of people, Starbride grabbed the opportunity, gesturing to a ruby the size of a pinky nail that blazed on Countess Nadia's finger. "I couldn't help noticing your beautiful ring, Countess. My father taught me much about jewelry, but I'm afraid I don't recognize the maker."

"Thank you, child. Métrande himself made it."

Starbride's mouth went dry. "Spirits above! He made one of the queen's crowns!"

The countess nodded, her eyes sparkling.

"The craftsmanship is amazing."

"I was thinking the same thing about your necklace. Your father's creation?"

Starbride touched the diamonds she had worn to the Courtiers Ball. Dawnmother had said that a countess deserved to see the best. "Yes. He always said he was lucky to have a daughter who loves jewelry as much as he does."

Countess Nadia laughed, and Starbride knew she'd scored a point. They shared a passion. Countess Nadia lifted the large diamond resting on its chain just above her cleavage. "I do love my baubles. I've many more, if you'd like to see them sometime. Not by Métrande, of course, but I've a few pieces from his contemporaries and quite a few more from craftsmen of only slightly less caliber." She leaned closer. "Including a string of Lanaster pearls."

"I'd love to see your collection." That was a social gathering she could get behind. "My father used to speak longingly of Lanaster pearls. If you don't mind my asking, Countess, how did you come by an entire strand?"

She winked. "A naughty story for another time." Viscount Lenvis rejoined them then, and Countess Nadia turned her attention fully on him.

Starbride couldn't help but like her. Countess Nadia didn't dig for details on Katya; her invitation seemed unmotivated by anything but mutual interest, and she'd even alluded to naughty stories. With an impish surety, Starbride knew just how to cement their friendship. The countess loved pretty baubles, and the viscount was the prettiest around.

"What have you two been talking about?" he asked.

"Countess Nadia's exquisite jewelry," Starbride replied, "especially the diamond around her neck."

Viscount Lenvis was obligated to bend forward and investigate the necklace, giving Countess Nadia the opportunity to lean forward and present her cleavage from the best angle.

His eyes lit up as his glance wandered to the diamond and then below. "Very…very nice."

"Thank you, Viscount," Countess Nadia said. When he sat back in his saddle, she gave Starbride another wink.

"How did it go?" Dawnmother asked after Starbride returned to their room.

"Much better than yesterday. What else do I have today?"

Dawnmother scanned a list beside her. "That's it. The rest of these are just courtier parties."

"Ha! You've changed your tune. I thought you'd have me going to all of them."

"After you've been out with nobles, you can't settle for courtier functions."

"Library, then."

"Well, there is one invitation, but it's for tonight." She handed over a note.

An early evening? it said. *If I go any longer without seeing you, I'll lose my mind. K.*

Starbride grinned and bit her lip. "Well, that still leaves time for a bit of study and a quick note to my friend in Newhope. I've got some interesting new laws for him."

"And a letter for your mother?"

"Oh, I don't think there's that much time."

"Star, you have to tell her."

"You could write to her maid instead."

"Oh yes, one always wants such news as 'your daughter has become the princess's lover' to come from one's maid."

"Later, later." Starbride grabbed her scroll and pencil. "I'm off to the library."

"I'd better come with you. Once you start studying, you forget to keep one eye on the candle. I wouldn't want you to miss your...early evening."

Much later that night, as Starbride rested in Katya's arms, she spoke about her day, and Katya succumbed to a fit of laughter when Starbride recounted the tale of Countess Nadia's necklace. "If the viscount's not in her bed right now, he's dreaming of her breasts."

"I hope so."

"So, you made some friends?"

"One, I think."

"Besides me, of course."

Starbride tilted her head up to snatch a kiss. "Two, then, and no, I didn't mention you. I know you're dying of curiosity."

"Just a little."

"You're none of their business."

"Quite."

"Did you learn anything from the captives?"

Katya paused before she said, "Crowe says their minds are blocked.

They're either pyradistés, or they've been heavily warded by a very good one."

"What can you do?"

"I don't know."

Starbride focused on Katya's face in the near darkness. "I didn't mean to upset you."

Katya bent slightly and kissed her. "It's not you. I've just been thinking that, well, if you know everything that's going on with the Order, I can't...pretend that it doesn't exist when I'm with you."

"The people you have to pretend with are those who don't know you at all, the courtiers and all the rest who only want what you can give them." She propped herself up on her elbows. "If you have someone else to share your problems with, they'll be easier to bear."

"Are you sure you're not Marla, paragon of wisdom?"

"I'll never tell."

Katya kissed her for a long moment, long enough for Starbride to hope the conversation might be over, but then Katya pulled back. "Do you want to be in the Order of Vestra? If you're going to be so close to... everything going on, I think it's best you learn how to defend yourself. You can train to be a pyradisté."

Starbride blinked, left without words while she tried to think. "Me? In the Order?" The shop and the table sprang to mind, but there was also her second adventure, the manor house, when exhilaration had overcome her terror. If she had the tools to protect herself, she could put her fear to rest.

Aiding her people through the study of the law *and* protecting the crown of Farraday, protecting Katya and her family? Doors opened inside her mind, and Dawnmother's sensible voice seemed to whisper in her ear, "Opened doors for your people as well."

"What do you think?" Katya asked, and Starbride heard the fear there. She wanted Starbride to accept, perhaps so badly she didn't know how to best express it.

"My poor princess. Everything in the world for the asking, but not much you can *actually* ask for."

"Rascal, torture me no longer."

"I'll be a pyradisté and join your Order, both to help you and for the ability to take over courtiers' minds and make them walk into the pond."

Katya grabbed her and rolled them both over until Starbride couldn't stop laughing. "I wouldn't say that last part to Crowe if I were you."

"I'm sure he's thought of it."

"Yes, but he can be a stickler for the rules at times."

"Well, maybe I'll just pry information from their heads, then. I have a croquet match tomorrow, and I have no idea how to play."

"None?"

"Whatsoever."

"Want some backup?"

"You hate courtiers! And probably croquet!"

"I wouldn't be going for the courtiers or the croquet. I'd be going because I love you."

Starbride's heart thudded as her stomach warmed. She took Katya's face and kissed her and didn't think about sleep for quite some time.

CHAPTER TWENTY-ONE: KATYA

Y our brother arrives in under a week," Ma said. Her tone was quiet, and that spoke more to her fear than if she'd trembled.

Katya nodded and fought her frustration. "I know."

Da paced about the sitting room. "Crowe can get nothing from these swine?"

"Their minds are completely warded."

"We should move them," Ma said. "Get them out of the palace for Brom and Reinholt's safety."

"Move them where?" Katya asked.

Ma's eyes flashed. "If we can't move them, kill them."

Da moved behind the settee and rubbed her shoulders. Katya closed her mouth on her reply. Crowe had told them both about Maia's learning the truth of Roland's death and how Darren and Cassius might've been involved. Now that Katya knew how much her mother had loved Roland, she wasn't surprised at her mother's reaction.

"We shouldn't kill them," Katya said, "until we know what they were up to at that manor house."

"But you think they wanted to be captured?" Ma asked.

"I can't see another reason for how easily we captured them, but what good does it do them to be locked in a cell?"

"Deuce if I know, my girl," Da said. He moved around the settee and took Ma's hand.

Smiling at the two of them, Katya thought of Starbride. In the light of day, she'd begun to regret inviting Starbride into the Order. No, it was too late for such thoughts. Her mother's stare was far away, but her father grinned at her.

"Thinking of your Allusian friend?" he asked. Ma's eyes refocused on Katya with lightning quickness.

"I was, actually."

"Starbride, yes?"

"You do have your sources, Da."

"She's become the guest to have at various court dos."

"And all before she's met your parents," Ma said.

"I didn't want to present her to you at court, Ma. How about I bring her to the family dinner after Reinholt arrives?"

Ma blinked. "To the—?"

Da interrupted her with a clap. "Sounds perfect!"

Ma glared at him, but he gave her a level stare, and she eventually nodded. Katya avoiding gaping and wondered how many vetoes her father got after all their years together. She closed her mouth on the news that she was bringing Starbride into the Order. She'd save that for later.

"How is Maia?" Da asked, his change of subject as tactful as a hammer.

"Angry. Last time I visited, she'd dampened to a simmer, but the anger's still there. We can't keep her and Crowe apart forever."

"Take them out together. Didn't you say you needed to investigate the Pyradisté Academy? You could distract the heads and the master while Crowe and Maia do a little snooping."

"I don't think they should be left alone together."

"Then have them *snoop* in different directions," Ma said, "but your father's right. They have to be able to get along if they're going to remain in the Order."

"Well." Katya's stomach sank at the thought of taking Crowe and Maia out together. "That's going to be lots of fun."

Crowe and Maia agreed to go only reluctantly, but Katya didn't give them a chance to argue. She made her desires into commands that even her family couldn't ignore. They could all be surly together.

The Pyradisté Academy was a ten-minute walk from the palace, but Katya saw it long before she reached it. The three-story stone pyramid at its center was a sight to rival the palace's towers. The morning sun glinted off the pyramid's crystal capstone and threw rays of light onto the nearby buildings.

Katya and her party entered the large courtyard that divided the academy from the Halls of Law, the lawyer's and magistrate's college. The open space bustled with activity as men and women hurried through the campuses. The Pyradisté Academy boasted three other buildings, but Katya strode past them, uninterested in classrooms and dormitories.

Near the door to the massive pyramid, two cassocked young men stood talking, occasionally sipping from mugs, and leaning against the pyramid's side. As one, they glanced up, and Katya didn't know if it was the sight of her or of Crowe in his black cassock with purple piping, but one thrust his mug at the other and then dashed through the doors. The other glanced back and forth between his two mugs and gave Crowe a worried, sickly smile. His cassock had no special piping. Not a head, then, probably a teacher, and the other had undoubtedly gone to inform the master. It saved them the bother of looking for him.

Inside the pyramid, Katya fell into step with Maia. Rooms lined the pyramid walls, but the middle had been left hollow in a shaft that ran from the capstone to the floor. Light filtering down the shaft caught the sides of other pyramids as it descended, sending light blazing throughout the entire first floor. It made her recall festival times when the master and heads lit the capstone itself, making it a beacon in the sky.

Katya glanced at Maia. The muscles of her jaw stuck out like bands, and her eyes were dry but hard. She stared at a point over Crowe's head. Katya nudged her and then pointed ahead to the middle of the first floor beneath the shaft, to a columned area alive with an indoor garden. A water-filled basin sat in the center, and a crystal pyramid as large as Katya rotated above it. The pyramid sparkled and shone in the light from above, almost too brilliantly to look at. Maia blinked, and some of the anger left her face as she stared.

Two staircases descended on either side of the small pool, and as their party approached, a group of men and women hustled from the floor above, most with the white piping of a head of the academy and one with the red piping of the master.

"Crowe!" Master Bernard called as if they'd just met on the street. "How good of you to visit!" He bowed, and those around him did the same half a second later.

Master Bernard was a big man, nearly as large as Brutal, with a shock of wild red hair and an almost equally wild red beard. The skin of his nose and cheeks was rosy, as if he'd spent far too much time in the sun. Katya had to wonder if the light of the capstone had burned him at some point. "Highness," he said, "please, forgive this, ahem, lukewarm reception. We had no idea you were coming."

Katya put on her best royal leniency smile. "Not at all, Master Bernard. Pyradisté Crowe told me he had business here, and as I take every chance to come inside this magnificent structure, I decided to accompany him."

"Welcome, welcome. Please, let me introduce my staff." He went over the heads behind him.

"Well, you all know Pyradisté Crowe," Katya said. She waved toward him as they chuckled and nodded. "This is my cousin Maia." Another round of bows. Maia's nod was gracious if a little stiff.

"I just need to speak with someone upstairs, Highness, if you'll excuse me?" Crowe said.

Master Bernard opened his mouth as if he might protest, no doubt because he wanted to keep an eye on all of his esteemed guests at once, but Katya waved Crowe away before Master Bernard could utter a word. She turned to Maia. "Explore, coz, do. I'll be perfectly happy here with the master and his staff."

Maia wandered away, and no one could argue. Nor could they leave. She'd all but ordered them to entertain her, and they did their best. They led her on a tour around the base of the pyramid and then across the grounds. She made certain it was as slow as could be. She asked many questions and kept track of all her hosts by speaking to each one personally so that they knew they'd be missed if they tried to wander away.

With their education in pyramids came lessons in logic and science. These weren't stupid people. The looks they cast at the central pyramid said they wanted to know what Crowe was up to, but even if she let them go, all they could have done was trail in Crowe's wake. As the king's pyradisté, he trumped even the master, but it would have been awkward for him to force his way into one of their offices with them watching.

Crowe found them soon enough. "All done, Crowe?" Katya asked.

"Just a trifle, after all, Highness. More of a social call."

"Splendid. Well, thank you, Master, ladies and gentlemen, for a lovely tour."

They bowed, some pleased, some confused, one or two with slightly put-out faces for having wasted an entire morning. As she and Crowe started back through the main pyramid, she said, "Anything?"

"Several graduates from the past twenty years with the skill we're attributing to the bearded man. I discounted all the women, but we can't be sure of any of the men."

"How many?"

"Ten."

Katya ground her teeth. It was better than nothing, she supposed, but she'd been hoping for one name. "Nice work."

Maia loitered near the gates. When she turned to look at Crowe, intensity flared in her eyes, as if the time between when he'd disappeared and that moment had fanned her anger into fire again. "There's no buzz about anyone powerful leaving the academy suddenly. At least, none that the students or teachers let me hear."

"What's got you so—?"

"They couldn't stop talking about him once they found out who I am."

Katya didn't have to ask who she meant, but Crowe foolishly asked, "Roland?"

"Don't say his name!" Maia said. Crowe took a step back.

"Maia," Katya said.

Maia spat, "Stay out of this, coz," just as Crowe said, "Let her speak if she needs to."

Katya glared at both of them. "This is not the time or the place." She hustled them through the courtyard and into an abandoned side street, hoping to sneak them back to the palace quickly.

Maia didn't stop staring at Crowe as she walked. "If not now, when?"

"Later." Katya glanced at Crowe and expected to see a sullen, ashamed silence, but his brow darkened.

He pulled up short, and Katya knew by his face that he was either tired of feeling guilty—she couldn't imagine that—or he needed an outlet for his frustration and decided the best way was to get beaten by a young girl. "Come on then, if that's the way you want it."

Katya gaped at him just as Maia did.

"What?" Crowe asked. "I can't function with this nonsense. Say what you have to say, little girl."

Maia leapt on him. She led with a bestial snarl that didn't fade as his arm smacked against her head. She tackled him to the street, kicking and punching, her teeth snapping like some feral thing.

Katya grabbed her around the middle and heaved upward, but Maia turned and pushed with unexpected strength, and Katya stumbled backward. She skidded in something slick, and her feet shot out from under her. Her shoulder slammed into the corner of a wall, and the rest of her body tried to fall into an alleyway without it. A sudden pop filled her head just as a sickening wave of pain flooded her shoulder socket. Coughing, she tried to draw breath to scream just as she crashed to the ground, and the shock of hitting the pavement forced a cry from her lips. Someone had filled her shoulder with molten lead. When she opened her eyes, someone was touching her, and Maia's and Crowe's anxious faces hovered in front of her.

"Oh, Katya, I'm so sorry," Maia said.

"No, no, I'm sorry," Crowe said, "I don't know what I was thinking, I—"

Katya pointed at her wounded shoulder with her good hand. "Shut up and help me!"

Crowe probed she shoulder. Katya snarled at him. "Her shoulder is dislocated," Crowe said.

"What do we do?" Maia asked.

"Get ready to push here." Crowe positioned Maia's hands, and Katya closed her eyes until she heard Crowe say, "One, two, three," and then her world was reduced to pain again, and nausea clenched her teeth.

When the sickness passed and only the ache remained, Katya opened her eyes to two guilty faces. "Not another word," she said. They nodded as one and helped her to her feet. No one else seemed to have noticed them, and if they had been noticed, no one seemed to know who they were. Katya only hoped her accident would keep Maia and Crowe from more fighting. That might be worth the pain of a bone that felt loose in its socket.

At the palace, Katya stared at them until they squirmed. "I'm going to have a nice long soak, and then we're going to have a chat." She trudged to her apartment without waiting for an answer.

When she arrived, Averie came out of her room to stare. "What are you doing here?"

"I live here," Katya said, and she knew it sounded sulky. She didn't care. "I need a good long bath. My shoulder got dislocated."

"How?"

"Long story. How about that bath?"

"Um, don't you have a croquet match to go to? I thought you'd be there by now."

Katya froze. "Oh, spirits. I forgot!"

"If you hurry, you can make it. Do you need a sling?"

"No, I can't start any rumors. I'll just have to be careful."

"Let me change your coat, at least."

Once she'd donned a fresh coat, Katya jammed her hand in her pocket and hurried from her room, willing the croquet match not to have started, willing Starbride to forgive her if it had. She'd lost track of time at the Pyradisté Academy, but surely the injury would make her worthy of forgiveness, even though she couldn't tell that tale until later. She pictured Starbride's insistence upon explanation, and willed her feet to go faster.

CHAPTER TWENTY-TWO: STARBRIDE

Starbride rested her croquet mallet on the ground and tried to pretend she knew what she was doing. The attending courtiers and nobles watched with frosty, appraising eyes. No one had offered to teach her the rules of the game; no one even offered a kind word. She should have been in the library. The wasted time rankled more than the judging eyes.

Katya hadn't come, and Dawnmother's earlier words echoed through Starbride's head. How many no-shows and apologies could she take? It was hard to forgive a broken promise, no matter who made it, no matter how busy the promise breaker was.

When her turn came, Starbride approached the little ball with her chin held high. The other attendees smiled with all the affection of a pack of jackals. She tried to ignore their whispers and tried to recall how they'd hit the ball. One of the watchers giggled, and Starbride wanted to throw the mallet at them, tell them to jump from a cliff, and then stomp away in a fit of temper. She froze when a pair of arms wrapped around her and shifted her grip on the mallet.

Starbride tensed, but the signet ring on the left forefinger stopped her from throwing the arms away. "Like this," Katya breathed in her ear. "Let's do it together."

Starbride suppressed the tears that wanted to spring to her eyes. They made the shot together, and Katya grunted as if injured, but Starbride didn't have time to ask as the crowd applauded. No more titters or giggles—not with Katya present—only envious looks from some and calculating glances from others.

Katya glanced at her gown. "Lemon custard?"

Starbride plucked at the skirt of her pale yellow dress. "I should have worn what you gave me. If I make my people's clothing all the rage, I won't have to look like dessert anymore." Ignoring the crowd, she dropped her mallet to the grass, threaded her arm through Katya's, and strolled across the lawn.

Courtiers bowed to Katya and asked after her family. Now they nodded at Starbride and smiled, asking a few polite questions, and all because Katya had arrived. Opportunistic vipers. Did any of them know a true expression anymore? Katya navigated their clutches expertly, her face as false as theirs, and unease tingled on the edge of Starbride's consciousness. Why all this deception, this fakery? Why would no one just say what they wanted? She gritted her teeth and asked herself again why she was even there.

Status could help her people. That's what her mother would say. But Starbride knew what else could help them: law, a wealth of books waiting to be studied. As she kept from sneering at the poisonous smiles around her, she could almost hear Dawnmother's voice saying that Katya could help the people of Newhope with a wave of the royal arm. But too many dangers lay along the path, too many opportunities to turn into just another grasping courtier.

Lord Hugo emerged from the crowd like a rescue ship. "Are you bored by croquet, Highness?"

Starbride's stomach unknotted. "Lord Hugo! A pleasure to see you again. Don't tell me you've been here the entire time?"

He bowed. "Highness. Miss Starbride. No, I just arrived."

"Croquet is decidedly boring," Katya drawled, "but one does appreciate fresh air from time to time."

"Fresh air can be found on the hunt." Lord Hugo put on what he probably thought was a sly smile. He winked, and Starbride wondered if he could get any more obvious.

"Ah, but hunting takes place in decidedly rougher company." Katya raised Starbride's hand to her lips and kissed it. Could she even *stop* herself from playing along anymore?

"Well said!" one of the courtiers said as if he were in on the joke. Others agreed and fell over themselves to repeat Katya's words and then say things like, "I must remember that one."

With clenched teeth, Starbride made small talk, held on to Katya as if to a buoy, and floated through the next hour secure and safe, even as she counted the moments until they could leave. Lord Hugo shored up her other side and filled in conversations meant for Katya and not for her. She squeezed his hand once when they parted, and she and Katya were paroled back to the royal apartments.

Once alone, Starbride turned an appraising eye on Katya. "Your face is very pale, and you gasped whenever someone bumped your left arm. Has something happened to you?"

"I dislocated my shoulder."

"What? How? Shouldn't you be in bed?"

Katya gave her a good-natured leer, but it seemed a little tired. "A promise is a promise."

Starbride felt a stab of guilt, turning her mood blacker. "All the bowing and scraping, all the innuendo and mock concern. If you hadn't been there to hold me up, I would have lain down on the lawn and laughed until I was sick. They talked about nothing and meant even less!"

Katya sat and brought Starbride with her onto a divan, half on a cushion, half on her lap. "They don't think of it as nothing."

"Shouldn't you have someone look at your shoulder?"

"I'm fine. Only time will heal it. Let's relax and not speak of it."

"Why did that one courtier want you to wear his brother's boots?"

"The brother is a boot-maker trying to drum up business. If I wore boots from his shop, they'd be buried in orders."

Starbride pressed her palms to Katya's face. "Princess Steppingstone."

"It can be tedious. I told you. Everyone wants something."

Starbride thought fleetingly of Newhope's problems. "And what do you want?"

"I want to take you to a little country cottage for a week or four."

"Your duties stop you?"

"Always."

"Preparations for your brother's arrival? Can't others handle that?"

Katya stared into the distance. "No, the Order does it."

"Ah, what do you have to do?"

"I don't want to talk about it right now, Star."

How many topics would be forbidden that day? How many the next? "You invited me in."

"I know."

"If you want me to be a part of the Order…"

"I'm starting to rethink it."

"Fine." She scooted out of Katya's lap. "You need rest, and I have work to do anyway." She heard the childishness in her voice but couldn't stop it.

Katya sighed, a sound that said, "Great, now I have *this* to deal with." She massaged her injured shoulder and grimaced.

Pity moved Starbride a fraction closer. "How *did* that happen?"

Katya sat back again and gave Starbride a tired look.

"Ah, right, you don't want to talk about it."

"Star, I've…just had a long day. I have a lot to deal with right now."

"As I said, fine. I have a lot to deal with, too." Katya snorted. Starbride crossed her arms. "What do you know about how busy I am?"

Katya started to shrug and then winced. It gave Starbride a certain amount of satisfaction that she regretted immediately. She smoothed her skirts and stood. "I'm going."

"Don't," Katya said, but her expression didn't echo the words. If anything, she seemed even more tired.

"Is that a command?"

"Is that what you're waiting for, me to start ordering you around?"

"You're in charge. If you say we don't talk about something, then we don't talk about it. If you tell me not to leave, I guess I'm staying. There are guards wandering the hallway who could keep me here since you're incapacitated."

"You know damn well that those guards are for everyone's protection."

"Right." Because she was angry, because it had been an emotional afternoon, an emotional time in her life, her next words simply tumbled from her mouth. "Everyone needs protection with you around."

Katya's face went as still as stone, but Starbride saw the tightening mouth, the guilt that still traveled on her back for the shop and the knife, for the Fiend. "You're right," Katya said. "You should go."

It hurt more than expected, but Starbride kept her mouth closed, her tears inside. She didn't want their usefulness. Her mother would have called her a fool. She just wanted to be somewhere else. "Don't bother with an escort."

When she reached her room, Dawnmother wasn't there. Starbride resisted taking her tantrum to the point of hurling herself onto the bed and weeping. Instead, she sat at her table and pretended to read a law book. She slammed it shut after just a moment and pushed her scroll away.

Damn Katya's arrogance, thinking she was the only one who ever had a difficult time! *But*, a little voice whispered inside, *she can't know of your troubles unless you tell her.* Starbride crossed her arms and put her head down. She couldn't share her problems, not yet, but she wanted Katya to see all that she was doing to help Allusia, not just to prove herself capable, but to show that she wasn't idle in Katya's absence.

She tried to reverse their positions. If Starbride was the princess and Katya's family needed something, would Starbride use her influence to help them? Of course she would. Would she feel resentful for being asked? No, she would feel needed and happy. And just a bit smug, if she was honest.

But Katya was already swimming in pleas. Starbride sat up and rubbed her forehead. She shouldn't have made that crack about the Fiend. Maybe she shouldn't have been in such a complicated relationship at all. The choice was probably out of her hands now. She tried to tell herself that Katya wouldn't be so petty as to cast her aside after one fight, but they were still getting to know one another, and Katya didn't have time for an argumentative child. "Damn!" she said just as the door opened.

Dawnmother stopped in the doorway, her arms full of parcels. "What is it?"

"It's…nothing. What have you got there?"

"A few items from the city, some soap. I had the gifts from your admirers delivered to one of the stewards. We were running out of room in here. This," she gestured to a few of the smaller boxes, "is the pick of the litter. I left all the flowers. We'd be drowning in blossoms." She sat on the bed. "Star, what's wrong?"

"I…got angry and said some stupid things."

"To the princess? Did you have a fight?"

"A stupid one."

"Most are."

"She's probably wondering who replaced me with a sulky child."

"What set you off?"

Starbride thought a moment. "Troubles," she settled on.

"Ah. Hers or yours?"

"Yes."

"Ah. This had to happen, Star. She is the princess, and you are a courtier, much as you don't want to play those roles with each other. Add to that the fact that you're both strong-willed women in love, and fights are inevitable."

"We could share our troubles."

"You don't want her help."

"I don't want her to feel she *has* to help."

"Then tell her why you came to Marienne, the exact reasons, and forbid her from helping."

"This from you," Starbride said, "the woman who wanted me to ask for her help in the first place."

"I want you to be happy. If you have to be foolish to be happy, well…"

Starbride poked her in the side. "Thanks."

"My pleasure."

"And her troubles?"

"When and if she shares them will be up to her. You can't force her to tell you everything, Star. Didn't you say she'd been keeping her secrets for a long time? That she even wants them kept from me? Talking about them casually can't be easy for her."

Starbride felt the tears threatening. She used all her mother's lessons to keep them down. "She asked me in and now shuts me out."

"Give her time. You know that she loves you?"

"Yes." Her vision swam. "She gave me her intimate name when we first met."

"The Farradains say nickname. They use it with all those familiar to them."

"She was familiar then, or she wanted me to be."

Dawnmother took Starbride's chin in hand. "Go and see her."

"Without being invited?"

"I'll come with you. We'll bull our way in."

Starbride stared down for a moment. She'd lost her temper; they both had. Pride told her to wait, to let Katya make the first move. Something in her expression caused Dawnmother's fingers to tighten, forcing her eyes up.

"Pride is a comfortable shackle," Dawnmother said.

"I'm lucky Horsestrong had a saying for every occasion."

"We all are. Let's go."

"Right now?"

"Yes, before your thoughts have time to turn against your good sense again."

"What if she won't see me?" One tear dribbled down her face, and she dashed it away.

Dawnmother clucked her tongue and pulled Starbride to her feet. "Then she's a fool who doesn't deserve you, and I'll tell her that myself."

"You'll get strung up in the courtyard."

"Then I'll go to my grave knowing I was right. Come."

Starbride nodded and allowed herself to be led from the room before she straightened her spine and took the lead down the hallway.

CHAPTER TWENTY-THREE: KATYA

A verie helped Katya bind her shoulder in place, and Katya welcomed the pain. Averie didn't ask questions, and Katya was, as ever, grateful for her silence. It gave her the opportunity to try to puzzle out how Starbride had gone from sitting in her lap to slamming out the door after Katya told her to leave. Katya rubbed her pounding temples and wished she'd kept the Order a secret. Everything it touched turned to disaster.

Starbride kept hinting at the work she did, but she wouldn't say what it was. The fact that she mentioned it at all, after their agreement not to speak of it, had to mean she wanted Katya to ask, but Katya simply didn't have the energy. Starbride was proud. It had to cost her something just to *look* like she needed help. "You should have asked," she said after Averie left her alone. "Fool, you should have been asking all along."

A knock sounded from the other room, and Katya listened to muted voices. "It's Starbride and Dawnmother," Averie said through the sitting room door.

Icy fear seized Katya's chest. Had Starbride come to say she was leaving? Was it some formal declaration that had to be witnessed by Dawnmother? "Show them in."

When the door opened, Starbride slipped inside alone. Katya drew breath to speak, but Starbride beat her to it. "I'm sorry." Tears hovered in her eyes.

"Me, too." Katya's anxiety left her in a rush as she stepped forward.

"Please, I need you to listen."

Katya's nerves jangled again, but she sat down and gestured for Starbride to take the divan across from her.

"I'm going to take a page from your book and just blurt it out. Farradain traders are taking advantage of the law in Newhope to unfairly tax individuals who want to trade up and down the river. Since they've got more money coming in, they're underbidding other trading businesses and forming a monopoly."

Katya had never thought of herself as stupid, but Starbride's words sounded almost like another language.

"That's why I'm here." Starbride gestured around her as if she meant not just the room but the kingdom. "Our problem is ignorance. We don't know the laws well enough, so we've just been *mimicking* the Farradains. Lately, there have been some, well, antiquated laws popping up, that hinder Allusian traders only." She gripped the edge of the divan and seemed more tired than Katya had ever seen her. "When we complain to the magistrate, the Farradains hide behind these old laws. My family is financially secure. We trade overland, but other families haven't been so lucky. People look to us for answers. I've come to find some."

She paused, but Katya sensed she wasn't finished,

"My mother wanted me to marry someone with influence, not only for my own status and hers, but for what a person with influence could do for our people. She puts personal status first, of course, but I know she cares about the families of Newhope. Our local magistrate is a good man, but he has to be impartial. He can't counsel us on what to do, but I've learned a lot about tariffs and taxes and trade laws. Some of what the Farradains are doing is illegal, and I'm sending my research home."

Starbride clasped her hands in her lap and stared at them. "Meeting you was more than my mother hoped for. She'd ride high on the status alone, but I can picture her marching to the Farradain families' doors and telling them that the princess is going to make them play nice."

Katya cleared her throat. "You shouldn't have kept this from me. People breaking the law is every inch my business."

"I know, I know. It was pride, but also, we have to learn to defend ourselves. Every time a Farradain tries to take advantage of us, we can't go running to another Farradain to make it better. We have to learn the law."

"I understand." Katya moved next to her. "And you're right. I shouldn't just ride in and stop it, even if I learned all the law. It would change nothing in the future, and it would make your people feel that they can't defend themselves. What I *can* do is bring over some scholars, picked by the people of Newhope, to study in the Halls of Law to become lawyers."

"You can…what?"

"If they can't afford it, the royal family offers scholarships to the different colleges all the time. Why shouldn't they extend to Newhope? I'm allowed several patronages based on my position; I almost never use them." Starbride only stared. Katya grinned. "Send your letters. See what you can do about the immediate problem, but send other letters as well, and get some of your people to the Halls. They could start at the winter term."

Starbride held her arms out slowly, and Katya drew her in. "Thank you," Starbride said. "That was so different from anything I hoped for or even dreaded."

Katya took a deep breath. It was her turn to tell a secret, fair being fair. "Do you remember the death I mentioned on Hanna's Retreat? Well, that was the death of Maia's father seven years ago. We think the children of the woman who caused his death are the ringleaders of our current troubles: Darren, Cassius, and the bearded man." She rubbed her aching shoulder. "Today, we went to the Pyradisté Academy to see if we could find the most powerful pyradistés to graduate in the past twenty years or so. Crowe found ten names."

Starbride's brow furrowed. "Do you have locations for these men?"

"Not yet."

"I'm sorry about your uncle. And poor Maia."

"She's been a little ball of anger ever since she found out the circumstances of her father's death. She picked a fight with someone in an alley, and I dislocated my shoulder pulling them apart."

Starbride pressed her warm lips to Katya's cheek. "Poor Princess."

Katya hugged Starbride closer with one arm. "Better now." The divan was comfortable; Starbride smelled amazing. Even with her injured shoulder, Katya lay back and pulled Starbride with her.

Starbride laid a finger across Katya's lips. "You're injured, and Dawnmother is probably wondering what happened to me."

"Dawnmother doesn't think I'd hurt you, does she?"

"She never rules anything out."

"Would she run in here and stab me?"

"She would impose her body between us. Her life for mine, that's the servant's code."

"Our servants are made; yours are born."

Starbride shrugged, but Katya didn't expect an explanation. Like many cultural customs, it was what it was. It didn't matter if she could understand it. "I wonder how late it is."

"You've more to do today?"

"Always."

"Want some company?"

"The thought of exposing you to danger terrifies me, Star."

"You'll have to get used to it."

Katya had to laugh. It wasn't the response she expected. "You're right. Let's go see what Crowe's up to. Will you tell Dawnmother that you're safe and in one good hand?"

Starbride went out, passing Averie on her way.

"All better?" Averie asked. Katya put on her best enigmatic face. "We knew you'd work it out."

"You and Dawnmother discussed our troubles?"

"No, we had tea in relative silence, but we both knew anyway."

"The psychic powers of ladies-in-waiting."

Averie winked just as Starbride came in. "Dawnmother said she knew we'd find common ground."

Katya kissed Starbride once more and ushered her into the secret passageway that led to Crowe's study.

"How did you ever learn to find your way in these cramped spaces?" Starbride said softly. The dark tunnels seemed to require whispering.

"There are symbols at the junctions that tell you where you are."

"I remember." She felt a tug as Starbride paused. "Circle, circle, square."

"To my parents' rooms."

"And this side says X, grid, square."

"That eventually leads to the stable but also goes other places."

"I trust you."

Katya smiled again, her heart wide open. "Would you like to come to my brother's welcoming dinner?"

"Your brother's...? The crown prince's dinner? It's...a banquet?"

Katya cleared her throat, amazed at the nervous fluttering in her belly. "No, after he's formally greeted by the court, we have a small family dinner in my parents' dining room."

She heard Starbride's sharp intake of breath but didn't turn around. "Should I?" Starbride asked. "I mean, if it's just for family..."

"I've already approved it with my parents, but if you don't want to go..."

"No! It's not that, it's just, well, wouldn't I be an intruder?"

Katya did turn then, her lantern revealing Starbride's anxious face. "I've never brought anyone before."

"That makes it worse!"

"No, it means that you're already such an essential part of my life you can't possibly intrude." Starbride leaned forward, and Katya obliged her with a quick kiss. "You'll come?"

"Of course! But if the air does turn thick, promise that you'll let me leave early. Oh! I'll have a new outfit made. You've given me inspiration."

"An Allusian outfit? I'll buy that for you."

"If you buy it for me, how can it be a surprise? Besides, it gives me the opportunity to sell one of these awful dresses for some ready cash."

"I can't get in the way of such deviousness." As she resumed walking, she thought of one way Starbride would never feel like an outsider, if she *became* family. Of course, no one became part of the royal family overnight. Consortship came before marriage. The butterflies within her took wing again as Katya really considered that for the first time: Starbride as princess consort.

At Crowe's study, she knocked lightly. "Come in," he called. When they emerged from behind the bookcase, Crowe blinked once before he bowed. Katya waved him down and took one of the couches, Starbride beside her.

"How's your shoulder?" he asked.

"Better, but that's not why we're here."

"Maia and I both went to your apartment, but Averie told us you'd gone out."

"I had a prior engagement."

"So I see. Time to begin the training?"

"Now?" Starbride asked. "Don't I have to...go somewhere special?"

"If Crowe is teaching you, you don't have to go to the academy."

"Your doing?"

"Being royalty has its perks."

Crowe snorted. "As much as I love witty banter, I do have preparations for Crown Prince Reinholt's visit, so if we're not going to begin today—"

"That's why we're here." At Starbride's further look of alarm, Katya hurried on. "Aren't there preliminary tests you can do? Assessment of ability? A pyradisté obstacle course?"

"This isn't show-jumping, Katya." Crowe waved Starbride over to a small table in the corner. "We can test your general aptitude. Sit there." He took the seat opposite, and Katya stayed put, watching them.

"Now," he said, "we'll see how easily you fall into a pyramid. No one can hypnotize you, as you've already discovered, but a pyradisté must be able to hypnotize himself, to merge with the pyramid he's using and thus access its powers." He grabbed a small pyramid off the shelf behind him. "Some pyramids can only be accessed by the maker, and some can be used by anyone. This produces light, so you don't need to worry about anything dire. Now, take hold and look into it. Feel it, the smoothness of the sides and the sharpness of the points, how the entire shape focuses at the top, all of its power channeled into the tiny capstone."

Starbride's brow furrowed as she stared at the pyramid. After a moment, she glanced up at Crowe. "You're trying too hard," he said. "Don't think at it, just think *about* it."

Starbride gave Katya an annoyed look and tried again. Tiny lines of frustration stood on her forehead, but they quickly smoothed away in the quiet room. She ran one thumb across the pyramid's edges, and blinked once, twice, and then not again.

"Now," Crowe said, "think of light."

Light blazed from Starbride's pyramid, and she yelped, tossing it into the air. Crowe reached across the table and caught it as it faded back to normal. Starbride pointed at it, all traces of concentration gone. "It... it..."

"It did as it was supposed to."

Katya applauded, and Starbride's confused expression melted into one of joy. "I did it!"

"I knew you would," Katya said.

"Your happiness is well deserved, no doubt, but we have a long road ahead of us, one which we'll have to explore later." As Crowe came around the other side of the table, Starbride embraced him and whispered something. He grinned and gave Katya a glimpse of a much younger man. "You're quite welcome, child."

Katya frowned. No one hugged Crowe. Most were afraid of him. But if Starbride could win him over, she could win anyone. "Well, you two can work out your own schedule, then. We'll leave you to your preparations, Crowe. No word yet from Layra?"

"I don't expect it for another few days."

"And nothing new on our guests?"

He shook his head. "They're better guarded than the crown jewels, though."

Good and bad news always came at the same time, it seemed. Crowe waved them farewell, and Katya led the way back toward her apartment. "I've got to speak with my parents and tell them you're coming to the welcome dinner. My mother requires knowledge of her guests' likes and dislikes so she can make appropriate conversation."

"Oh *dear*," Starbride said. "Well, that'll make things easier. I won't speak unless she does, and we'll be guaranteed not to stray into unknown territory."

"Wise." They walked in silence for a moment. "What did you whisper to Crowe?"

"Aha! Good to know I'm not the only one with the curiosity bug. I just said thank you."

"He grinned like a schoolboy."

"Maybe no one ever thanks him."

"I thank him all the time."

Starbride said no more about it, and Katya didn't press. Whatever endeared her to Crowe was a step in the right direction, just as long as Crowe didn't share Pennynail's identity with her. Well, not unless she then shared it with Katya.

When they entered her apartment again, they faced one another. "You don't mind going back to your room without me, do you?" Katya asked. "It's a skip to my parents from here."

"I'll forgive it this time, on account of the injured shoulder."

"Oh, thank you ever so much, Miss Meringue. What would I do without your consideration?"

Starbride's smile made the day seem bright again until Katya's throbbing shoulder reminded her that fortune was a two-sided coin.

CHAPTER TWENTY-FOUR: STARBRIDE

Handwritten on creamy white paper with a matching envelope, the invitation awaiting Starbride in her room was simple in its elegance. "My, my." She turned the card over and over. "It's from Lady Hilda."

"No perfume, no crests, no monogram. Just a little note," Dawnmother said.

Starbride read it aloud. "'I'd be honored if you'd have dinner with me. Lady Hilda Montenegro.'"

"She left off the crest because she doesn't want to be traced. She's planning to kill you."

"If she wanted to kill me, she wouldn't have signed it."

"Humph. She'll claim she *didn't* sign it. When she bashes your skull in near her rooms, she'll point to this note and say, 'If I'd sent it, it would've been on my private stationary,' and she'll deny all knowledge. Mark my words."

"They'll find my body in a ditch?"

"They won't find it at all."

A chill traveled down Starbride's spine. "You're coming with me, right?"

"You're accepting?"

"I *have* to see what she wants, Dawn."

"If you must. Well, she'll have to bash both our skulls in."

"Yours is far too hard."

"True. I'll throw my head in the path of the stick."

Starbride put her nose in the air. "*Lady Hilda* would never use something so common as a stick."

"I'll throw my head in the path of the bejeweled scepter."

"Speaking of jewels, I wonder if it would be gauche to bring a guest."

"Countess Nadia Van Hale?"

"I'll write her a note. I believe she'd be amused by my situation."

"Lady Hilda is sure to behave herself in that august company. Ask her to show up late. It'll be a nasty little surprise. While you write the countess, I'll write Averie and tell her where we'll be."

"Why?"

"Just in case."

With a chuckle, Starbride set to work.

Lady Hilda had two rooms to herself, a small sitting room and probably a bedroom, but the door stood shut. Her two maids set out a small dinner before withdrawing. Dawnmother sat on her little stool in one corner with a stubborn air and pulled an embroidery hoop from her basket. Lady Hilda raised a perfectly arched eyebrow at her presence. Starbride shrugged. She couldn't have moved Dawnmother with a team of horses.

"Allusian custom," Starbride said.

"Of course." Lady Hilda offered a smile that was false to the hilt. "Will you try the walnut salad?"

"It looks lovely." Starbride held up the cloth-wrapped bundle she'd brought. "Do have one of these rolls my maid baked in the kitchen."

Lady Hilda stared before taking one. Starbride spooned a bit of walnut salad onto her plate. As one, they took a bite. "I'm so glad you could make it with your busy social calendar," Lady Hilda said.

Starbride ate slowly and didn't put anything on her plate unless Lady Hilda had it also. She knew the rolls weren't poisoned, but she couldn't be sure about the rest. "I was honored by your invitation and happy to fit you in."

Lady Hilda offered a polite smile, but Starbride could tell she wasn't used to being *fit in*. "The princess must keep you busy."

Ah, there it was. Her bluntness was rather refreshing after the hordes of courtiers waiting for news of Katya. "Indeed. We've much in common."

"Let's cut to it, shall we? Your maid's presence won't keep me from speaking my mind."

"Allusian maids respect privacy."

"Custom?"

"Yes."

"I want what you have."

Starbride wondered just how nasty she could be, how much scorn she could get away with. "What do you expect me to do about it?"

"Leave." Lady Hilda took a folded bit of paper from the flounces of her dress—a concealed pocket—and pushed it across the table.

Starbride envied the pocket for a moment, picked up the paper, and glanced at it, an offer for two hundred thousand gold crowns. Not a king's ransom. Not quite a princess's either, but a fortune nonetheless.

"You have this much?"

Lady Hilda's look said, "Backwoods peasant." Starbride had no idea that any of the titled people had that much ready cash, but it wasn't impossible. "You want proof?"

Starbride shrugged.

"Not enough?"

"She's not a commodity. And neither am I."

"She'll tire of you. She has favorites, but she always leaves them with nothing in the end. You'll have the money."

"What makes you think she'll let me go?"

Lady Hilda toyed with the neckline of her dress. "I'll distract her."

"You couldn't manage it before I showed up."

Lady Hilda's face turned to stone, her eyes hardening to jade, a real expression at last. "I won't discuss my relationship with the princess with the likes of you."

"I was just about to say the same thing. Keep your money."

"And how many Allusian troubles can this buy away? Your people can hire proper lawyers; you can break the Farradain monopoly in Newhope and get some of your own people in charge."

Starbride marveled at Lady Hilda's spy network, a system that was good, but wasn't good enough. "I've already taken care of that."

Lady Hilda blinked, and Starbride could almost see the wheels spinning in her mind. "How?"

Starbride shrugged again.

"If you don't take this offer, you're a fool."

"If we're down to name-calling, it's time to go."

"We're not finished talking."

Dawnmother's stool scraped against the stone as she rose. Lady Hilda sneered and dropped a fork on the floor. As it clattered against the stone, her bedroom door and the door to the hallway opened, and her two maids stepped inside. Starbride kept her face composed as she heard her mother's appalled voice in her mind. Lady Hilda couldn't be preparing to attack, to *brawl* with her. Surely not!

But Lady Hilda was always trying to impress Katya, and Katya was good with weapons. What if Lady Hilda thought the best way to impress was to share in her would-be lover's interests? What if she demanded the same of her staff?

The whole room crawled with tension for half a second before someone asked, "Am I late to the party?" Exhaling, Starbride turned to where Countess Nadia stood in the doorway.

"Countess Nadia," Lady Hilda said. "I'm…It's a pleasure to see you. What, uh, what brings you by?" Her two maids faded to the back of the room.

Countess Nadia gave everyone a curious look and then cast a pointed glance at the dinner table. "I was curious as to what you were up to. I don't suppose there's room for one more? I do miss your conversation, Lady Hilda."

Lady Hilda bowed, her courtly composure returned. "Please, join us." They sat around the table again, and Dawnmother resumed her little stool. The other maids withdrew after a curt gesture from their mistress.

Lady Hilda didn't seem nervous over Countess Nadia eating the food, convincing Starbride that it wasn't poisoned. Poisoning was probably for peasants. That left direct attack, though Starbride couldn't be sure of what they had intended to do. For all she knew, they were going to make fun of her until she acquiesced. With her wedding cake of a dress, they would've had plenty of ammunition.

Dinner went on for another half hour, filled with empty pleasantries, idle gossip, and the occasional jibe from Countess Nadia to Lady Hilda about this or that. All Lady Hilda could do was laugh in her brittle-glass way. When Countess Nadia seemed tired of it, she took Starbride's arm. "Walk me to my room, child."

Starbride held in a smirk. Lady Hilda couldn't argue; she could only bow and remark on how pleasant it all had been. Starbride kept her chuckle inside until they were a good deal down the hallway.

Countess Nadia tsked. "You play with a viper, child."

"You made her toothless."

"I won't help you in these games. It amused me this once, but I will not be available at your every call."

"No, of course not. Please, excuse me, Countess. I involved you because I thought it would entertain you."

"That's the end of that, then. Now, what was going on as I came in? You looked like tavern brawlers."

"You've seen a tavern brawl?"

"I've seen things that would turn your hair white." The truth shone in those pale eyes.

"I don't doubt that. She was warning me away from the princess. She tried to bribe me."

"I see. A considerable sum?"

"Considerable."

"And your answer was undoubtedly no. Hmm, I wonder if she was going to kill you or beat you into submission."

"I had a plan in case the evening turned violent. Lady Hilda's letter and a letter stating my whereabouts are with the princess's lady-in-waiting."

"Smart."

"Thank you, Countess Nadia."

"And you indicated a time at which you would report to the princess or the lady-in-waiting, and if you did not make this report, they would know that something had happened to you?"

"Yes, Countess."

"And you would still be dead or injured?"

"Well, yes, but—"

Countess Nadia didn't let her finish. "And so these precautions helped you how?"

"Um, I was just about to inform Lady Hilda of them."

"As she was beating you to death?"

"It would have stopped her," Starbride said, but she realized how lame it sounded.

"Ah, I see. You put yourself in danger and then inform your attacker that your whereabouts are known to a particular lady-in-waiting, therefore giving your attacker her next target."

"She…she couldn't have gotten into the royal apartments!"

Countess Nadia snorted. "Do not underestimate a determined member of the nobility, my dear, especially that one. You walked into a bear's den with a paper spear, as my grandmother used to say."

"What would you have done?"

She tilted her head. "Declined her invitation but made one of my own. Invented some excuse to maneuver her to a time and place of *my* choosing. I would have informed the princess *and* had her present. Not in the room, of course, since you wanted to know Lady Hilda's intentions, but close by, eavesdropping. I would've had at least one other person nearby, besides your maid, someone familiar with weapons."

"But surely Lady Hilda wouldn't…" She trailed away. Now that she thought about it, she had no real idea what Lady Hilda would or wouldn't do.

Countess Nadia stopped and looked her in the eyes. "Child, you should not have gone; you should not have eaten that food. She chose not to poison you this time, trying to see if the money would work, but you have no idea what she had up her sleeve. There are poisons in this world that can kill you in a *snap* and those that can put you to sleep in an instant.

You thought of violence, but you weren't prepared for it. More likely, she would've drugged you and stuck you in a stranger's bed."

Starbride shook her head rapidly. "The princess would never believe I went willingly, not with the letters in her possession, not to mention the fact that she knows me."

"How much would that matter if you became pregnant by an unknown father?"

Starbride's mouth dropped open as horror crept through her belly.

"What would that do to your family? The princess couldn't keep a pregnant lover, and you would be gone from court in a twinkling, just as Lady Hilda wanted you gone."

"But Lady Hilda would be punished!"

"What would her punishment mean to you if you were already neck-deep in trouble? You *must* use your head. Protect yourself. If she wanted to, Lady Hilda could escape even the princess's rage."

Starbride thought of Katya's Fiend and doubted it, but Countess Nadia's words sank into her chest. "Thank you. I will follow your advice to the letter."

Countess Nadia chucked her under the chin. "There, now. Didn't I say you were smart?"

Even though it was still early when she reached her room again, Starbride felt like crawling into bed. "Well." Dawnmother set her stool and basket down. "What do you make of all that?"

"It was foolish to go. The countess saved us both."

"I agree, but we didn't know all that we were getting into, Star. Learn from this, but don't be too hard on yourself."

"My stalwart supporter."

"Always. Now, I'll send Averie the note saying that we're both in one piece. Did you get enough to eat with Lady Viper?"

"Ugh, my stomach's still turned."

Dawnmother bent to pick up an envelope near the door. "Another invitation while we were gone."

"Unless it's from Katya or the king and queen, let's ignore it!"

"Are you sure? Pyradisté Crowe says that if you're not busy, he has some free time this evening, and would you like to really begin your training?"

Starbride leapt from her seat, remembering the way the pyramid lit up, the tingling that ran through her body. "Really?"

"That put the spring back in your step."

"I'll go now!"

"Will it be dangerous?"

"It wasn't the last time, but come along if you like. As far as I know, it will drain me to the point of exhaustion, and I'll need your help limping home."

"Now my curiosity is piqued. If we see Lady Viper again, I'll scream that I've got Countess Nadia in my basket. That ought to stop her long enough for us to run away."

"Maybe I should hire a bodyguard."

"Not a bad idea, but ask the princess for a free one. She has plenty, I'm sure."

Starbride thought of being tailed through the halls by Pennynail. People would be so busy staring at him that they wouldn't notice her.

She and Dawnmother didn't know their way into or through the secret passageways, so they hurried to the royal section and sent their intentions to Crowe and the note to Averie by messenger. Once they were in his office, Crowe greeted them with a friendly smile. He bowed to Starbride and then clasped his hands in front of him and pressed them to his heart when he faced Dawnmother, one servant greeting another.

Dawnmother returned the greeting. "Our lives for them," she said in Allusian.

"And also the truth," he replied. His accent sounded more than a little rusty.

"Until death," they said together.

"Well, well," Dawnmother said, "I am continually amazed by the events around me."

Crowe leaned on the arm of a couch. "We all have secrets on top of secrets."

"So I begin to see. Is it all right if I stay for the training?"

"Of course. An untrusted servant is a jar with no bottom."

Starbride laughed. "No matter how far we are from home, Horsestrong lives in us still."

Crowe waved her over to the same table she'd sat at that afternoon. "I've had enough gloomy business for today and decided to do something I take joy in."

"Teaching others?"

"I don't often get to. I think the last person whose education I had a hand in was…um, Prince Roland."

Starbride reached across the table and took his cold hand. "I'm sorry."

"Katya told you about Roland?"

"Only that he died long ago, but the subject has resurfaced lately."

Crowe glanced at Dawnmother, but she'd withdrawn to a corner of the room, out of earshot of their low conversation. "Let's begin, shall we?" Crowe said. "Let's begin, shall we?"

He pulled a length of velvet from the table, revealing a cluster of pyramids set into four rows. "Destruction, mind magic, utility." He touched the first three rows as he spoke and paused on the last. "Fiend magic."

Her breath caught as she burned with questions, but she only nodded for him to continue.

Crowe moved back to the first row and touched the three pyramids that sat in it. "Flash bomb, fire, disintegration." All three had very sharp points and steep angles. The fire pyramid was red near the points, and the disintegration pyramid had caps with filigree like the shopkeeper's pyramid, but these were oily black. "I don't currently have them made, but there are also death and detonation pyramids. When broken into someone, a death pyramid can shock them to death." His mouth twisted into a grimace. "I don't like to make detonation pyramids. The risks of them blowing up before you mean them to are far too great. Destruction has always been my strongest area, and each of the pyramids within that area can be made to different strengths."

"Does everyone have a strongest area?"

He nodded. "At the academy, you're ranked based on your strength in pyramid use and how skilled you are at crafting pyramids, both for your own use, and for the use of another pyradisté." He tapped the three destruction pyramids again. "Destructive pyramids are the only kind that can be used by non-pyradistés because they simply have to be broken. The death pyramid, despite its ominous name, is relatively easy to use, but it takes skill to make one that can actually cause death and not just serious injury. Most destruction pyramids are difficult to craft."

She leaned forward, almost touching the pyramids, but she didn't dare. "And the guardian pyramids that you put in the walls?"

"A mix of destruction and mind. They can be tuned to attack or ignore certain people or even certain states of mind. They are the very hardest to craft."

"All the glittering pyramids in the hall...They must have taken forever, generations of pyradistés."

"Retuned by each monarch's pyradisté. I've tuned them to recognize you." He touched the row of mind pyramids. "Mind magic is not the hardest pyramid to craft, but is the hardest to master. Simple pyramids can be used to hypnotize; more complicated are used to control."

"And they don't work on pyradistés."

"Exactly. Utility you're well familiar with. That's our light pyramid, your new best friend, as well as pyramids for detecting other pyramids in use. Utility and mind magic were both…Roland's specialty." He shook his head after a moment of silence. "When he left us, he was working on a new pyramid that could hide an active one from prying eyes."

"You can create new *kinds* of pyramids?"

"Oh yes. I'm good, my dear, but he was better."

Starbride blinked. "As king's pyradisté, aren't you the best?"

"I was when I graduated. I haven't tested myself against any of the academy graduates in years, though. The king can't replace me on a whim, you know. The Order *is* supposed to be secret. Now, the last category, something they don't teach at the academy. Fiend magic."

He tapped the pyramids in the last row. "Far to the north, the Fiends lived in glaciers made from ice and pure crystal." He held a pyramid up to catch the light. "Pyramid crystal. As such, they are both susceptible to pyramid magic and attracted to it. It's almost part of them. That's why a pyramid is the only thing that can suppress them once they've emerged from inside the Umbriels. It's also the magic that keeps Yanchasa prisoner, though the Umbriels have to use their Fiends in conjunction with the magic in order to pacify him."

Starbride touched one of the pyramid's smooth sides. "So, if there were ever a Fiendish pyradisté…?"

He blinked. "That would be… Maybe that was why Roland was so good at the craft. Well, that's enough history for the moment. Let's try some practice."

He had her stare at the light pyramid again, his soft, even voice leading her into the crystalline sides, the sharp points. The five sides contained the entire world and nothing, all at the same time. When she fell into its depths, she lost track of where the pyramid was, in her palm or in her mind.

They practiced over and over. Fall into it, light it, bring herself awake, fall into it, light it, bring herself awake… Again and again it went, until he said, "Look at me." She glanced up. "Light it."

The pyramid blazed with light. Starbride gasped and nearly tossed it into the air as she had the first time. "But I didn't fall into it!"

"You did. You just weren't thinking about it." He took the pyramid, and it went dark as it left her hands but brightened in his. "After you've been using them for a time, you won't have to focus so hard. You can fall into them without thinking, without trying, and without losing your awareness of the outside world. When you hold them, you feel them here." He tapped his temple. "Try again."

Starbride tried to feel it without looking at it, but it stayed dark. Crowe shook his head. "From the beginning. Stare at it. Fall into it…"

They practiced for hours until Starbride could set the pyramid on the table, reach for it, and light it as soon as her fingers touched it. She lost track of the number of times she did it and paused at last to yawn.

"I think that's enough for today," Crowe said. "Master this and the rest of your education will go much easier. Self-hypnosis is the basis for all pyramid use. We'll train your mind to sense all pyramids, but it's something you have to practice. Even then, you'll have to be close to them, they'll have to be active, and you won't know what kind of pyramid it is until it goes off. To sense types from a distance, you'll need a detection pyramid." He handed her the light pyramid. "Keep it and practice just before we meet again. That way, we won't have to do this warm-up."

"When will we meet again?"

"That's the difficult part. How about this? Practice every day, and then when I send you a note during some of my precious free time, you'll be ready."

Starbride stepped forward and embraced him like she had the first time. "Thank you, Cinnamoncrow. You carry the honor of your caste." It was the highest compliment she could give to a servant not her own, and it caused him to beam again as it had the first time.

"You're quite welcome." He led them to the door, and Dawnmother secured the little pyramid in her basket for the trip back to their room.

"I'm going to fall into bed and sleep for days," Starbride said.

"No princess?"

"I said fall into bed and *sleep*."

"You must at least send her a note."

"You're a romantic."

"I want to avoid another fight. You'll be happy, Star, if I have anything to say about it."

CHAPTER TWENTY-FIVE: KATYA

Katya slumped on a settee in her parents' private sitting room. She helped her mother sort through a mound of papers, some with swatches of material neatly pinned to them. It was all in aid of decorating for Reinholt's welcoming ball. Katya rubbed her injured shoulder. The only bright spot of the days following her fight with Starbride had been her shoulder having a chance to heal.

During the past three days, she could count her time with Starbride in glancing moments, a few hurried kisses, or conversations. Starbride had thrown herself into training with Crowe, and Katya had been too busy wandering the halls or poring over reports from the Order. Now, instead of stealing a few precious snips of time with her beloved or hunting traitors, she was studying fabric.

"Let's just make it all blue." She laid aside an unneeded treatise on why pink pastel curtains would reflect the light through the hall better than green pastel curtains.

"A little variety is in order. Besides, I know which blue you would choose, and it would be too dark."

"Let's just turn it over to one of the decorators." She wondered what Starbride was doing at that moment. Anything was better than wading through bunting.

"Picking one decorator would show too much favoritism." Ma set another swatch aside, "One decorator would try too hard. The entire ball would look as if it's taking place inside a brothel."

"A well-funded brothel," Katya muttered.

A loud voice from the hall heralded her father, and he swung open the door mid-sentence, a clerk on his heels. "With our fondest wishes for your continued prosperity, King Einrich Nar Umbriel of Farraday, etc. etc." He turned, and the rapidly writing clerk nearly ran into him. "Write up two copies. There's a good man." After shutting the door in the clerk's face, he rubbed his hands together. "Well, my love, still at it, I see. I thought you decided on gold last night."

"Gold and bright blue would look nice," Katya said.

"Too heavy," Ma said. "I want something light and airy, something unreflective of our current situation."

"What color will you wear?" Katya asked.

"Coral."

"Well, that's out." Da dropped into an armchair. "Can't have my wife matching the bunting."

"Thank you, Einrich, very helpful."

Katya smiled as she watched them. "Very light blue?"

"I've a mind to send you away with all your blues."

"*Can* I go?"

"You won't be paroled that easy, my girl," Da said. "Might as well move along the old color wheel."

Katya thought of Starbride and her frothy dresses, trying to remember their various colors. "Mint?"

"Mint." Ma stared into space for a moment. "Mint and…white. Or cream? I knew you'd get a taste for this, Katya."

Da snorted. "A taste for mint. Ha!"

Ma shifted the piles of paper and fabric off her lap. "I'll have to talk to the decorators, but mint…"

A knock sounded on the door, and Katya groaned. She'd hoped she would be let go for the morning, but if something else about decorations had come up…

"Come," Da called.

Crowe slipped inside. It couldn't be good news if his pinched expression was any indication. "The courier I sent to Layra has returned."

"And?" Da sat forward. "What news?"

"Layra is not at her farmhouse. According to her neighbors, she left a few years ago…with her son."

"Son?" Ma asked. "She married after she left the Order?"

Crowe cast a glance at Katya and then at her father. Katya looked at Da, and she saw that he knew what she did, that Layra and Roland had been involved. "Da…"

"Catirin," Da said slowly, "there is a possibility the child might be Roland's."

She blinked for a moment, silent. "Layra and Roland?" Color bloomed in her cheeks, and her eyes flashed as she stood. "And you knew about it? All that matchmaking I went through for him and you knew that he was…And with a commoner!"

Katya rolled her eyes. "That attitude would be why he didn't tell you, Ma."

Ma rounded on her. "You knew as well? You were a *child*, and you knew?"

"No, no." Crowe stepped forward. "She found out recently."

"He told *you*, Crowe?" Ma asked. "Who else?"

"Roland and I were in the Order together." Crowe frowned. "I was his confidant in many things, commoner though I may be."

Her face softened. "Crowe, I'm sorry. I didn't mean to imply…"

Crowe bowed. "No need for apologies, Majesty."

"Yes, yes, yes, very well," Da said. "Back to the point, please. So, these neighbors claim Layra had a son. She could've had a child with someone after Roland died. It needn't be his. And you can't be thinking such a child could have anything to do with our current troubles. Why, even if he is Roland's, he has to be a boy younger than Maia."

"Too young to be any of our guests in the cells." Katya tapped her chin. "If Layra is involved, why would she side *with* Carmen Van Sleeting's children?"

"Banding together against those responsible for the deaths of people they loved," Ma said. Tears glittered in her eyes, but she didn't shed them. "Oh, poor Roland. And that poor boy, too."

Katya patted her mother gently on the back. "Crowe, pass Layra's description along to the Guard. We'll watch for her at Reinholt's reception and then at the ball."

Crowe bowed. "It will be done."

"Ma," Katya said, "I think you've got to parole me now. I need to speak to the Order."

"Go, go. You've given me mint. Your part is done. See that your own clothes are in order, though."

"I won't match the bunting, rest assured." She rose and followed Crowe from the room, her mind racing. "Spirits, Crowe, what if Roland has a son that's involved in all this? Maia's brother! Spirits above!"

He stopped and caught Katya's good arm. "We should not mention this to Maia."

"Crowe, if you lie to her again—"

"I know, I know, but this may turn out to be nothing. We have no proof."

"We can't wound my poor cousin like this again."

"We must. She'll need her head in the days to come. We mention

Layra and the son, but not their connection to Roland. Not until it's all over, Katya. You must see the sense in this."

Katya rubbed her temples as a headache began to grow. "What if the son appears and dies in a fight, killed by his own sister, maybe? We take him alive, Crowe, if we see him. No matter what."

"Agreed."

"And after it's over, we tell her everything. If she wants to walk away, leave the Order, we let her."

His mouth set into a thin line, but he nodded. "There's something else."

"*More* bad news?"

"I found the locations of seven of our suspects for the bearded man."

A shiver of excitement passed along Katya's spine. "Wonderful!"

"Five within the city and two just outside. Inside, most work for organizations, but two are hooked to prominent households. One outside works for a dowager duchess, and the other is attached to a chapterhouse seeking enlightenment through beauty."

"Do those prominent households belong to nobles?"

"Yes, and they both keep rooms in the palace as well as houses in Marienne." He put on a wry smile. "One is Lady Hilda Montenegro."

"I always thought of her as an opportunist but never a true villain."

"What better disguise for a villain than as a lesser villain?"

Katya thought back to the flirtations, the cleavage, the obviousness that made up Lady Hilda. "Now that I think about it, such wantonness was too good to be true."

"Too good?"

"Ha! We need to divide up the Order and check these places out."

"Of course. And Starbride?"

"What about her?"

"She needs to be on one of the teams, Katya. She's the only one of us who's seen this man in the flesh. The rest of us can go on a rough description, but she'll need to see any true candidates."

There was no way to rationalize the choice. If Katya agreed, she would be deliberately putting Starbride in danger. But as Starbride said, Katya had invited her in. It was too late to start closing doors. "I'll go and ask her now."

"I'll gather the Order."

It went as Katya knew and feared it would; Starbride was not only ready but eager to help. She wore a heavy cloak over the Allusian outfit Katya had given her as the Order set out into the city, and her face shone with anticipation. "How did you get Dawnmother to agree to let you go alone with us?" Katya asked.

"I didn't tell her about the Order, if that's what you're asking. I said you needed my help finding one of the kidnappers. Averie convinced her that the two of them would be more useful sifting through servant gossip in the palace."

"Our ladies and their secret lives." Katya pointed ahead. "Crowe and Pennynail have the horses around that corner."

"Do we need them?"

"Some of us more than others. We're splitting. One party is taking the candidates outside of the city, and the other is taking those inside."

"Which will I be in?"

"Mine, of course."

"Is that wise? Won't we be thinking of one another the entire time and not of what we're supposed to be doing?"

Katya's mouth opened and closed as she tried to think of a protest. She needed Starbride with *her* to be sure she was protected, but what did that say about her trust in her Order?

"Katya," Crowe said when they reached him. "A word." He walked her several steps from the others. "I don't think you and Starbride should be on the same team. You'll distract one another."

"She just said that."

"Don't get your feelings hurt, just see the sense."

After a moment, Katya nodded. "I suppose I must."

"Good."

By the spirits, though, she'd give Starbride the safer mission. "Starbride, Maia, and Pennynail," she said as she returned, "take the locations in the city. Crowe, Brutal, and I will explore outside of the city." She gave the first three a long stare. "If you find him, don't engage him."

"We'll ride straight for the palace," Maia said. "Don't worry. If it looks clear, Pennynail or I can stick around to spy."

Katya gave Starbride one last pointed look. "No unnecessary risks."

Starbride bowed. "As commanded."

"Don't enjoy yourself too much. I'm counting on you." She trusted Pennynail and Maia to do their jobs, and she had to trust them to keep Starbride safe, though she ached to go with them, and as they parted, Katya found again that absence did not equal lack of thought. Her gut clenched as her party rode through the city gates and into the forest.

Many times, she came within a heartbeat of turning around. Her world snapped back into focus when the first crossbow bolt flew at them from the surrounding trees.

"Ambush!" Brutal cried.

Katya pulled her feet from the stirrups, slid to the ground, and dove into the bushes. Crowe tripped, and Brutal put one large arm around him and half helped, half threw him into cover. The horses clattered off down the road. As another bolt sailed over Katya's head, she knew they'd made the right choice to dismount. Staying on the horses might have carried them away from combat, but they'd be sitting targets on the way.

Ignoring her throbbing shoulder, Katya drew her rapier as the forest went quiet. Brutal and Crowe settled beside her. A quick glance revealed no one behind them, but the undergrowth was thick in the shallow ditch. Katya held her breath and listened for movement. Crowe pulled a pyramid from his satchel, and Brutal took the spiked mace from his belt.

"We'll take your purses, make you lighter for the walk home," someone called from the other side of the road. "Your money or your lives. It's an easy choice."

Katya glanced at Brutal and Crowe. "Robbers?" she whispered.

Crowe shrugged. Brutal rubbed his chin, a hopeful gleam in his eye. Well, here was a chance to vent their frustrations at last. "Come and claim them," she said loudly. She bent close to Crowe. "Flash bomb."

He nodded, and Katya heard what she was waiting for, a footstep on the gravel road. Katya and Brutal shielded their eyes as Crowe lobbed a pyramid over the bushes. The clunk of a crossbow sounded just before the flash went off, and as the light died, Katya and Brutal sprang from the bushes. The crossbowman knelt in the middle of the road, his weapon at his feet and his hands over his eyes. Four swordsmen leapt from cover behind him. They rubbed their eyes and squinted, but the bushes had shielded them from some of the flash.

Brutal punched the crossbowman in the side of the head, almost casually, and the man fell in a heap.

"It's a thrice-bedamned pyradisté!" one of the swordsmen said. All four stood dressed in dirty homespun and leather, with several days' worth of whiskers on their smudged faces. The one who'd spoken brushed the sandy-blond hair out of his eyes. "That's not…fair!"

"Life is hard for a band of thieves." Katya waved the tip of her rapier at them. "Come on if you're coming."

Sandy glanced at the others and licked his lips. The eldest of them nodded at the bushes behind Katya. "Your pyradisté didn't come out with you. Maybe he only has one trick up his sleeve."

"One way to find out," Brutal rumbled. "I've always wondered what makes a man a thief. Come and teach me, brothers."

Sandy licked his lips again and then ran away. The two who hadn't spoken shifted their feet. "Coward!" Eldest said, but he didn't take his eyes off Katya and Brutal.

"Enough of this." Brutal stepped forward. Eldest moved to intercept him with more skill than Katya would have credited. The other two, one with a mangy fur mantle and the other with a bright green cloak, rushed her.

Katya brushed aside Mangy's initial thrust and skipped to the side, not wanting to let Greencloak flank her. Greencloak didn't try for any such subtlety, however. He came on like a whirlwind, hacking and chopping as if he wielded an iron bar instead of a sword. He made mewling noises as he struck, and his eyes were bloodshot and terrified.

Katya didn't block his attacks as much as divert them. His blade was heavier, and his ferocity could have knocked her rapier from her hands or snapped the thinner blade. She angled his swings wide of her body, and her shoulder sang with the effort. For all his lack of grace, Greencloak kept her attention away from Mangy, and Katya knew she had to take the first opportunity.

Greencloak lifted his sword far to the left, leaving an opening straight to his chest. Katya leaned away from his swing and then twisted her rapier, coming in under his arms. She stabbed him in the heart and then leapt past his falling body, bringing her sword up as she sought Mangy.

As she'd guessed, he'd been coming up behind her and had to spring out of the path of Greencloak's falling body. He came on more cautiously. Katya kept her injured arm turned away and hoped this one wasn't as big a swinger as the last. Mangy took one step forward before something as long as Katya's arm crashed into his side. He staggered once and fell, grasping his ribs. Brutal's spiked mace fell to the ground beside him.

Katya prodded the heavy mace with one foot. "You're throwing this thing, now?"

As he dragged Eldest's body into the road, Brutal shrugged. "You shouldn't have this much activity with that shoulder."

"You're always so considerate, Brutal." At her feet, Mangy coughed blood onto the pale gravel of the road.

"Punctured lung," Brutal said.

"Fatal?"

"Eventually." He bent and picked up his mace. "Go in peace, brother. Nothing is served by your suffering."

Katya turned away as Brutal put Mangy out of his misery. She checked the pulses of Eldest and Greencloak. Both were dead. To be on the safe side, she also checked them for pyramids or insignia. Nothing. The crossbowman lived, but he was as empty of clues as the other two.

"Crowe's not in the ditch," Brutal said.

"Where could he have gotten to?" Katya froze as hoofbeats sounded down the road. "Brutal, quick!" They dove into the bushes.

Crowe rode down the road a moment later, the other two horses in tow.

"Glad to know you were covering us," Katya said.

"You can handle a few ruffians. I looked for the man who ran away, but tracking has never been my specialty."

"Leave him. Without the rest, he's nothing. We've got a friend for you here."

Crowe dismounted and knelt by the crossbowman. "Sleeping minds are harder to sort through."

"I doubt you'll find anything."

With a shrug, he pressed a pyramid to the crossbowman's forehead, and after a moment, he opened his eyes and stood. "As you thought. He had an elder brother who enticed him into thievery with romantic tales of a bandit's life only to find that life full of starvation and fleas."

"We don't have time to take him in right now. Brutal, tie him to one of these trees, and we'll collect him when we head back this way."

After it was done, Katya rode on with a renewed sense of purpose. A problem she could put her sword to had lightened her mind. It made her think Starbride's day would be less eventful. After all, it wouldn't do for both of them to find trouble at the same time. It was a foolish, hopeful thought, but she had to cling to it.

They found one of their pyradistés in a small wooded glade, a gathering spot for those who sought enlightenment through Ellias and Elody, twins of love and beauty; in this case, the beauty of nature. Men and women sat cross-legged on cushions under silken canopies or strolled through the long grass or swam in the small creek that trickled by, all of them without a stitch of clothing.

From her hiding place among the bushes, Katya bit her hand to keep from laughing. "Which one is he?"

"I can't tell. I think one of those?" Crowe pointed to two men talking under an elm tree. "Their hair is the right color, and they have the right build."

"Nowhere to hide a pyramid," Brutal said.

Katya pressed her lips together hard but couldn't suppress a small snigger.

"Let's away," Crowe said, "before I qualify to be a dirty old man."

They slipped away, and Katya let out a laugh once they'd ridden far enough down the road. "I can't imagine our ruthless bearded man as a beauty-worshiping nudist."

"It would be a good disguise," Brutal said. "Or rather, it wouldn't be any disguise at all."

"Revealing nothing by revealing everything?"

Crowe shook his head. "I think we can count this one out. Our man is supposed to be smart. No one who sits near a patch of poison oak with his dangler out is that smart."

That did it. Katya laughed until she felt weak. Brutal muttered, "Dangler," once or twice. Each time, Katya doubled over in her saddle again.

When at last she wiped her eyes and paid attention to her surroundings, she saw that even Crowe had a bright smile on his face. "Yes, yes." He waved their mirth back down. "One more to go."

Their second quarry worked at the country estate of the dowager Duchess Julietta Van Umberholme. Katya played Lady Marchessa Gant, with the others as her servants. The dowager duchess seemed happy to receive her, the old lady not getting much company in the middle of nowhere. Katya didn't tell her about the nudists who were frolicking practically on her doorstep. With the duchess's poor eyesight, she wouldn't even have been able to sneak a surreptitious peek.

Amidst talk of court, Katya casually mentioned that she had a cousin who was just admitted to the Pyradisté Academy. Duchess Julietta was only too happy to produce her resident pyradisté, a portly man, talented but lazy, who was content to live in the country, collect wages from the duchess for the minimal work she assigned him, and pursue his one true passion: fishing.

Katya's spirits dampened as she and the others began the ride back to Marienne. If the bearded man wasn't in the country, he might be in the city. Starbride could be headed toward him at that very moment. They picked up the pace and collected the crossbowman on their way.

CHAPTER TWENTY-SIX: STARBRIDE

Starbride had pictured alleyways and dens of ill repute. When Dawnmother had lent her a heavy cloak with a hood, it seemed perfect for skulking. She'd never skulked in her life, but she'd been looking forward to it with a palpable thrill. Her disappointment proved keen, then, when she began her journey through Farraday's pristine streets mounted and with her hood down, doing her best to keep up the spirits of a moody young girl.

"It's a nice day. Not too chilly." She gave Maia what she hoped was a warm smile.

Maia mumbled and continued staring ahead or glancing at the buildings around them. Her forehead bore the same pinched expression she'd had from the start.

Starbride cursed the fact that she wasn't with Pennynail. He'd left them to spy on their target houses, leaving the businesses to them. *He* was probably skulking to his heart's content. "So, where are we going again?"

"I already told you." She sighed, an over-exaggerated sound. "The King's Street counting house, the largest chapterhouse of knowledge, and the Daishun trading company."

Starbride gritted her teeth. She felt sorry for Maia's reopened wounds about Roland's death, but as Katya always said, they had a job to do. Dawnmother never let her sulk for long, but Maia had no bond servant. "Well." She kicked her horse forward. "I won't keep you, since you obviously have other things to do. If you'll just give me directions…"

"What?"

"Directions. Since you're eager to be off? I'm sure I can handle a little spying."

"You can't do this without me."

"Why not? If I see the bearded man, I'll return to the palace. Isn't that the plan?"

"Well, yes, but—"

"Then you have to be here why?"

Redness spread over Maia's cheeks. "Look, I've been doing this a lot longer than you."

"True."

"Then you should listen to what I'm saying!"

"All right. What *are* you saying?"

"I'm...very good at my job!"

"We just crossed King's Street. Didn't you want to turn there?"

Maia started in her saddle. "You were distracting me!"

"You were distracting yourself." Maia glared down at her pommel, her jaw tight. Starbride reached out to her shoulder. "Maia, I don't want to make you feel worse, and I won't claim to know what's going on in your head, but we do have an assignment. And I do *not* want to mess it up. It's my first, after all. You're the veteran here. Please, say you'll help me."

Maia nodded. "I'm sorry I wasn't paying attention."

"It's all right. Look, after this is over, why don't we spend some time together? Apart from Katya and Dawnmother, I don't have any real friends here, no one I can just talk to. Dawnmother can secure a bottle of wine."

Maia smiled brighter than Starbride had seen for the entire trip. "I'd like that. I don't have many friends, either. This job is...It's a lot."

"Then it's settled. Let's find our bearded man so we can have some fun." As they turned up King's Street, Starbride leaned close. "Who owns the houses Pennynail's going to look at?"

"Chelius and Montenegro."

"Lady Hilda!"

"The lady of cleavage herself."

Starbride thought back to the disastrous dinner, the one that could have ended with her in some strange man's bed. Spying on such a person's household would be like getting her back, at least a little. She summed up the story for Maia's benefit.

"Wow. Lucky you having Countess Nadia on your side. If Lady Hilda's harboring the bearded man, her goose is cooked."

"I'm guessing that means she's done as a noble?"

"Definitely."

"Strange. A cooked goose is usually a good thing."

"Unless you're the goose."

"Ah, now I understand." Horsestrong's many sayings were metaphorical in nature, but they didn't seem as hard to puzzle out as these Farradain idioms.

"Your story makes me want to check out the Montenegro house ourselves, but we're almost to the counting house," Maia said. "Now I hope the bearded man *is* at Lady Hilda's. Then we could just get rid of her!"

Starbride chuckled, glad to have another ally. At the King's Street counting house, Maia pretended to be a rich lady, new to Marienne, and traveling with her Allusian friend. Starbride hung back and pretended to look around the enormous, columned lobby, all marble and granite. She peeked into the barred hallways where the actual counting and storing of coin took place. Did Lady Hilda's two hundred thousand gold crowns rest in there somewhere?

Maia pretended to be overly worried over security and what "Mumsy" would say if anything should happen to "poor Da's" money.

The counting house attendant placated and reassured, but Maia wouldn't be satisfied until she met this extraordinary pyradisté he kept talking about. The attendant happily produced him. Starbride watched from near a pillar, as deep in the shadows as she could get and breathed a sigh of relief when the, "highly trained, powerful pyradisté," was a small, clean-shaven, weasel of a man with lank brown hair and a complexion so pale it was almost gray, definitely not the large strong man who'd attempted to pyramid her in the woods.

Maia assured them that she would bring the money in the next few days. As they left, Starbride put a hand to her chest. "I didn't realize how my heart was pounding until now."

"Getting a taste for this?"

"I'm going to have to get better at schooling myself. If that pyradisté had been our man, I think I'd have leapt from behind the pillar and shouted, 'Aha!'"

"If you get too tense, pinch your leg. That's what I do. After a bit, you'll be so annoyed with the pinching you'll forget about fear."

Starbride tried it at the large library at the front of the knowledge chapterhouse. She needed pinching to keep her from the acres of books. Larger even than the palace library, the chapterhouse contained scrolls in display cases and rare volumes in bookshelves fronted with glass. Two grand staircases led up behind a large oval reception desk, and rooms lining the balcony above hinted at locked-away treasures.

"Like books, do you?" Maia said with a mischievous grin. "You're drooling."

"Where has this place been all my life?"

"Under lock and key. The brothers and sisters of Matter and Marla only let other knowledge monks and those with appointments study here.

And they have back rooms that only the monks can enter. I've heard that you have to wear gloves just to touch the books." She pulled on Starbride's arm before they reached the desk. "Why don't you play this one?"

"What do you mean?"

"Tell them you've a rare book you want to donate, and you want to make sure it's kept safe. Say you want to see their security measures, and when they refuse, say you'll need to at least meet the person who put those measures in place."

"But…but if our man is here and he sees me…"

"From what I've heard, he knows what we all look like, Starbride. We took a chance in the counting house because I didn't know how else to play it, but if you'd like, we'll stand off to the side while they fetch their pyradisté. If he's our man, we'll run for it or try to hide."

Starbride glanced around. There were quite a few places to duck out of the way. She nodded before her brain could argue. "Let's do it."

"Right." Maia took her arm and walked to the reception desk. She stopped in front of a blue-robed clerk who glanced up as they approached.

"Can I help you?" He tapped a book on his desk as if reminding them he had other things to do.

"Good day," Starbride said after Maia squeezed her arm. "My name is…Jewelnoble, and I've come to donate a book."

He brightened moderately. "A donation?"

Starbride rushed ahead with another quick idea. "It's an early copy of Skystalwart's journal."

The clerk stood slowly, his young face paling. "You have an early copy of the journal of the most infamous Allusian in history?"

Part of her expected him not to know what she was talking about, but she supposed that monks who sought enlightenment through books would know even the classics of Allusia. "Copied from his original journal months after his death and handed from family to family until it found its way into mine."

"Its condition?"

"A little battered," she said. He winced. "A tad weathered." He put a hand to his mouth. Starbride put on a remorseful look. "We don't wish its condition to worsen."

"Of course, of course." He shuffled some papers on his desk. "Do you have it with you now, or…?"

Starbride leaned on the desk, warming to the game. "I have to impress upon you, sir, the importance of this book to my family. We want it kept here in Farraday, in this chapterhouse, so far from our country, for its own safety."

"Oh, if more people thought like you, we could save so many texts, but people hoard them, you see, afraid for the books' safety, but we can care for them so much better than the average person!"

Starbride almost took his hand, but that might be going too far. "I need some assurances."

"I've told her that your security is the best," Maia said in a drawl that echoed Katya. "But she *would* come and see for herself."

"What measures have you taken to safeguard your treasures?" Starbride asked.

"The best. We don't rely on our guards and glass cases. We protect the building with pyramids fashioned by the best pyradisté of his class."

"What sorts of pyramids?"

The clerk waggled a finger at her. "Are you testing me? If I gave that away to anyone who asked, people could find a way around our precautions."

Starbride stiffened and tried to look as affronted as possible. "That is not good enough." She half turned as if she might storm away.

The clerk babbled. Maia caught Starbride's arm. "Spirits above, Jewelnoble, you are *forever* reactionary. Look here, good monk, if you won't tell us about the pyramids, can we at least meet the man who made them? Would that suffice, Jewelnoble?"

Starbride tilted her head back and forth. "I suppose."

"I can arrange that. Let me go see if he's available." He hurried up the stairs.

Starbride towed Maia across the room. "We're lucky it's so dark in here."

"I suppose it's good for the books."

Starbride peeked at the scrolls inside the cases and wished she had time to study them. If she did come back, she'd have to do it in disguise and go to one of the other clerks for help. One other monk manned the desk, but he appeared engrossed in his work. He hadn't even glanced up during their entire exchange.

"Someone's coming," Maia said. "Get ready to duck."

Starbride gripped her arm as the clerk marched back down the staircase with another man behind him. Tall and powerfully built but gray-haired and wrinkled, this pyradisté was far older than their bearded man. Maia and Starbride moved forward to finish their ruse. They found out that this pyradisté had proudly come to work for the knowledge chapterhouse as he had a love for books himself.

In good time, they made their excuses and promised to return in a few days, just as they had at the counting house. As they rode toward the trading company, Maia asked, "Who was Skystalwart, anyway?"

"An Allusian who twisted the servants' code. He saw his master heading down the path of corruption, and instead of following, he decided to save his master, his master's family, and all the servants from themselves. He killed seven people in all, four of them children, two his own." She shivered in the bright sun. "The last entry in his journal admitted why he did it, and he gave himself up right after he wrote it."

"What happened to him?"

"They tied each of his limbs to a different horse, and—"

"That's enough. I don't need to know the rest."

"Old copies of his journals are rare. At one point, several servant caste families revolted and treated him like a hero, even though he always said his actions were for the good of the family he served. For a time, his journal was banned, and old copies were destroyed. Now he's a cautionary tale."

"Quite the bait for our hook."

"Indeed. You take the next one. My knees are still shaking."

They had no more luck at the trading company, and they played much the same routine as at the counting house. Traveling nobles, lots of cash, worried for the safety of their valuables, etc. etc. Starbride was happier standing back in the noisy, dirty warehouse and letting Maia take the lead, but she could see how a person could get accustomed to such playacting. Lying was easier than she thought it would be. She had to admit it was also more fun, but she wouldn't want to do it all the time. Easy to see, then, why Katya wanted to get away from it once in a while, to just be herself and not act the part of the languid princess.

The thought that she was one of the few people who really knew what being the Princess of Farraday entailed pleased Starbride to the bone. In a world of sycophantic copies, she was almost unique. She shook her head to bring her back to task as Maia was introduced to the trading company's pyradisté. Once again, no luck.

In a stable yard at the back of a high-priced inn, they met Pennynail. He sat on a barrel and rolled a knife over his gloved fingers. He pointed to the sky when he saw them.

"I know we're late," Maia said. "We had three places to do, and you only had two."

"You've already spied on the noble houses?" Starbride asked. He nodded.

"We've had no luck," Maia said. "How about you?"

He held up one finger and then pointed at Starbride and the eyeholes of the mask.

"One person you want me to see?" Starbride asked. "Which house?" In her head, she dared him to pantomime Chelius or Montenegro.

Pennynail sheathed his small knife, put both hands palm up at chest level, and cupped them as if he were holding two large balls. Starbride burst out laughing. "That woman is defined by her figure!"

Pennynail saluted. "So," Maia said, "the Montenegro pyradisté might be our man. What a surprise. You peeked in windows until you spied him?" Pennynail nodded. Maia tapped her chin with one finger, reminding Starbride of Katya again. "How do we get Starbride in to see him, then? Without him seeing her, I mean."

"Skulking!" Starbride clenched her hands. They both turned to stare at her, and she blushed. "I've, um, always wanted to…sneak. You know, surreptitious spying just seems…"

Pennynail put a hand to his mask's mouth and turned away as if embarrassed for her.

"Well," Starbride said, "it's the best way, isn't it?"

Lying belly-down in Lady Hilda's back garden, Starbride rethought her position on skulking. It was dirty and hot and took hours of patient waiting while not speaking or moving much, not that her companion would have spoken anyway. Pennynail lay beside her, his stare not wandering from the large picture window in front of them. He wasn't able to tell her, but she guessed this must be where he'd spotted the pyradisté. The room stood empty, and they could see inside because it sat in the shade, and even though the sun was high, the room had been lit with several lamps sitting along a table piled high with books.

Starbride wished she had a book. Anything would be better than the empty-handed waiting. Pennynail had insisted she keep her cloak on. He'd pointed to her red outfit and then put a hand to his eyes as if the color blinded him. It was cooler under the bushes than it would have been in the sun, but out of the breeze, the heavy cloak began to stifle. It had already hampered her climb over the wall. Pennynail practically had to hoist her up and then toss her over.

Starbride told herself to stop complaining. She wasn't in immediate danger, and now she was qualified to write a treatise on how odious skulking was. Stretching as much as she could, she rested her chin on her arms and glanced at Pennynail. He turned her head back to the window again.

She wanted to yell, "But there's no one there!" Maybe he didn't like people staring at him. But how could someone who wore a mask not like people staring at him? The mask's rosy cheeks, empty eyeholes, and ear-to-ear grin invited stares, even more so with the dirt he'd smeared on it to help him hide. Encased in leather, his identity remained a mystery. Such a person was *invented* to be stared at.

Maybe there was a flaw in his costume. Maybe if she looked hard, she could figure out who he was. If she knew him without the mask, she could pick out a detail that would reveal his identity. She tried to look without turning her head. He poked her in the shoulder, and she snapped her gaze back to the window.

Lady Hilda glided into the room in front of them. Starbride held her breath. She didn't expect Lady Hilda to be in the house at all, but why keep the house if she never used it? A tall man in a pyradisté's cassock followed her inside, and Starbride squinted, straining to see him in the dim light. Lady Hilda gestured as she spoke, but they couldn't hear her, and he stayed toward the back of the room. Starbride pushed forward a little, and Pennynail grabbed her arm. She froze. Moving would attract too much attention, and Lady Hilda wouldn't have the trouble seeing them as they did seeing her or her pyradisté.

Starbride willed the pyradisté to step closer to the window, and he did at last. Her heartbeat pounded in her ears as she saw his face, and for a moment, she was certain he was the same man from the woods. She shut her eyes hard and then opened them again, and this man became similar to the one she'd seen, but there were differences now that she stared.

Her memory wanted this man to fit her mental picture, but if she was honest with herself, he didn't. The hair was a different tint, the face and nose a different shape. He stared out the window, and she looked at his eyes. Yes, his were definitely a darker shade. She glanced at Pennynail's masked face and shook her head very slightly.

He nodded just as softly, and all they had to do was wait until the room was unoccupied again. Pennynail backed out of the bushes and then pulled her after him, making her wait until he seemed certain they should proceed. On their way to the wall, he had her stop and crouch in the bushes half a dozen times. She saw and heard nothing, and when they reached the wall again, she wondered if he was doing it just to annoy her or teach her once and for all that sneaking through others' lives wasn't all she'd made it to be in her imagination.

After he hoisted her up the wall and tossed her over again, she was certain of it. "I get it. I shouldn't be so eager."

He saluted her, and she couldn't guess at all of the gesture's meaning.

She hoped Katya was having better luck. Maybe she'd already caught and killed their rogue pyradisté. Sneaking and playacting, flirting with danger, it still thrilled and terrified her. She just hadn't known it would be so draining. She reminded herself to ask Katya and Maia what they did to keep their energy up. She could nap for years.

CHAPTER TWENTY-SEVEN: KATYA

After their day of hunting the bearded man and not finding him, Katya awoke to good news. Crowe tactfully waited until she and Starbride were dressed to tell them about it. When they both emerged into the private sitting room, he coughed into his fist, but Katya had pulled that trick too many times to miss his smile.

"Good, well, you're both here," he said. "I have located our remaining three pyradistés."

"We won't have to skulk, will we?" Starbride said.

"Didn't enjoy your time with Pennynail, eh?" Katya asked.

"Once was enough."

"Well," Crowe said, "I don't know about skulking, but one should be very easy to find. He's dead."

"How long?" Katya asked.

"A month, by all accounts. Accidental death. Trampled by a runaway horse."

"Poor man," Starbride said.

Katya nearly kissed her but resisted in front of Crowe. "And the other two?"

"One is working for a noble, doing some delicate work in the north. I had a long talk with the noble in question, and I believe the tale is legitimate."

"Which noble?" Katya asked.

Crowe gave her a sardonic look. "I promised not to tell."

"Crowe…"

He held up a hand. "Nothing that affects the security of the kingdom or the crown."

Starbride scooted to the edge of her seat. "It must be some vulgar intrigue if this noble doesn't want people to know."

"Dying of curiosity?" Katya asked.

"I bet I could find out if I asked—"

"Don't even think it!" Crowe said. "Or you'll swiftly find yourself without a teacher." Starbride pressed her lips together as if swallowing a laugh.

"All right, Crowe. Who's our third candidate? He has to be our man."

"He's a free agent, a pyradisté for hire, so to speak, and from what Pennynail and I have been able to gather, he's not too picky about who he associates with as long as they can pay."

"Sounds ideal."

"But we always thought of the bearded man as the leader," Starbride said. "Darren and Cassius both deferred to him. The man you're describing sounds more like a follower."

"Maybe there's someone above him." Katya stroked her chin. "There could be another person in charge of the bearded man, and he's just over Darren and Cassius."

"And who might this ultimate leader be?" Crowe cast a glance at Starbride.

Katya waved the glance away. "Layra. I told Starbride all about it last night."

"How do we find him?" Starbride asked.

"Pennynail found out how he meets his clients. We can arrange a meeting this afternoon."

"How did Pennynail discover that?" Katya asked.

Crowe simply stared at her.

"You know," Katya said, "sometimes I get really tired of secrets."

Starbride prodded her calf with one bare foot. "How's it feel?"

Katya smelled Dockland long before they entered; the miasma of fish, wet wood, and general dampness threatened to overpower her as they drew closer to the trading town on the Lavine River. She pulled at the hood that obscured her hair and wished she could pull it all the way down over her nose.

She'd thought at first to dress as plainly as she could, but they needed a reason to "hire" the renegade pyradisté, so she went as a noble in disguise: shirt and trousers and leather vest not only well-made but tooled. Her rapier was a step above her regular weapon, but below the jeweled piece she wore at court functions. And like any noble that feared recognition, she wore a black domino mask, using it as she hoped a conceited noblewoman would to conceal her identity.

Brutal had forsaken his red robes for leather and homespun. Maia had washed her hair with ash water, darkening it, and the heavy mantle resting across her shoulders pooled under her chin so she could hide the lower half of her face. Crowe wore a cap, and Katya thought he'd darkened his face with something, but she didn't have time to ask as they entered the muddy, unpaved streets of Dockland proper.

Katya resisted the urge to glance around and try to spot Pennynail shadowing them with Starbride in tow. She couldn't help but wonder if she was enjoying skulking any more than she had the first time.

"Way," Brutal called as he moved to the side of the street. Maia, Crowe, and Katya moved with him. A guarded wagon covered with a canvas tarp rolled past, some merchant and his goods straight off the river. Crossbowmen perched along the sides. As the cart rattled by, Katya saw slight movement under its tarp and guessed that more guards awaited any thief intent on a pounce.

There were plenty of covetous, sideways glances at the cart from pedestrians, but Katya paid them no mind. The merchants could take care of themselves.

"You can see the greed on people's faces," Maia said. "King Einrich needs to send in the Guard again."

Katya tsked. "I was just thinking that the inhabitants of Marienne are happy to have all the gangs an hour away and in one place."

From behind them, Crowe snorted. "No matter how many times they're cleared out for the sake of propriety, Dockland's inhabitants come scurrying back like cockroaches."

They found their particular cockroach in a tavern near the docks, at the sign of a goblet next to a long pipe, signifying both cheap wine and opium within. Two women with the over-painted faces and billowing blouses of whores leaned near the door. They dipped in mock curtsy to Brutal and licked their lips. Katya saw a flash of metal from the waist of one and amended her assessment. Not whores, but tricks. Take one or both into an alley, and all a customer would get would be freedom from his purse.

Brutal brushed past them without a word. Katya and the others followed suit, and one of the tricks called, "Too good for a roll, my *lord*?"

The inside of the tavern was as dingy and hazy as a bog. Crowe took the lead, and Katya grabbed Maia's arm and stayed on his heels, not wanting to risk losing him in the gloom. "Short breaths, coz."

Maia pressed her face into her mantle to block out the poisonous atmosphere. Crowe pushed through a curtain at the back of the tavern, and the air behind it didn't hang so heavy. A middle-aged man with a greasy, stubble-dotted face sat on a stool at the small room's single table, a window thrown open behind him. He glanced up as they entered and then gave them a watery stare before he turned back to the bowl of stew in front of him.

"I don't hire women guards," he said around a mouthful. "Too much trouble."

"We're not looking for work," Crowe said.

Greasy looked them over again. "Nah, should have reckoned as much. No one wants to hire old duffers like you, either."

With a slow, easy movement, Crowe eased a gold coin out of his belt and sat it noiselessly on the table. Greasy wiped his mouth on his sleeve and stood. "Apologies, my lords, ladies. I see you're people of principle."

"Indeed," Crowe said. "I need guards for a very special shipment."

"How special?"

"Five thousand crowns of special."

Greasy nodded slowly. "That *is* special, my lord."

"And before you get any ideas, my man, I don't have the money with me now."

"Nah, nah, my lord," Greasy said. "Wasn't thinking that, nah. Incoming or outgoing?"

"Outgoing."

"When?"

"Soon."

"Hard to find good men for a 'soon' job, my lord. Type of cargo?"

Crowe stared, but Greasy didn't squirm. He wasn't afraid, and Katya knew they were being watched. "Living," Crowe said.

With another slow nod and a glance at Katya's masked face, Greasy rubbed his chin. "How many?"

"Just one."

"Just one that's worth five thousand?"

Crowe only smiled. Greasy gave no outward appearance of wonder, but Katya could almost smell the anticipation rolling off him. A single person that needed to be guarded by criminals had to be kidnapped, and no one besides nobility could generate such a price. Greasy glanced at all of them again, no doubt wondering if, when the time came, his guards could kill them and take this valuable hostage for himself.

"We need the best," Crowe said.

Greasy shrugged, his eyes half-lidded. "I don't use lowlifes."

"It would be better if our guest were made...pliable."

"Could light a censor of opium in your guest's, uh, accommodations."

"Humph, if that's the best you can do."

"I'm talking premium quality."

"Addictive premium quality."

Greasy leaned against the wall and crossed his arms over his skinny chest. "Got something else I could do, but it's costly. He'll eat up most of your cash."

"Another dealer?"

"Nah, don't you worry, you'll be happy. This man doesn't leave a mark, no damage."

"Ah," Crowe said. "Pyradisté."

"Sharp, my lord, very sharp."

"Can we meet him? Perhaps a demonstration?" His hand rested very near the gold crown, fingers twitching as if to whisk it back into his pocket.

Greasy cast a quick glance at the hand and then shrugged. "Yeah, why not. I warn you, though, no tricks. He won't be the only one there."

"Not a problem."

"The warehouse just shy of dock fifteen. One hour."

Crowe flicked the coin across the table. "For your trouble."

Katya's fingers itched as she opened the door to the warehouse. Dark and dingy, it smelled of rotten fish and garbage. The sounds of dockworkers loading and unloading the ships outside rose and fell over the scrabbling of rats in the shadows. It seemed the perfect place for dark deeds, reminding her of the pyramid meant to kill her father. Stacks of boxes and coils of rope lay around the interior. Light flooded as far as it could through the small doors on either end and through the many holes in the ceiling, peppering the ground with dots of sunlight. Katya peered into the gloom but saw no one. A rickety staircase led up to a catwalk, and Katya nudged Maia in that direction. Maia drew her bow and tiptoed up the stairs. The rest of them clung to the wall, not wanting to call out or be seen until they had a chance to look.

"Well," someone said, "are we going to deal or just hide in the shadows all day?"

Katya glanced at Crowe and nodded. "We're here," he said. "Where are you?"

A cloaked and hooded form moved into one of the rays of light near the center of the room. "Here."

Crowe moved forward with Katya, Brutal a step behind. "You know of our problem?" Crowe asked.

"Tricky. Living cargo rarely sits still."

"Know something about it, do you?" Crowe asked.

A low laugh issued from the hood. "I don't come cheap."

"We don't pay cheap."

"Let me see the money."

"We aren't fools."

The hooded man spread his arms. "Well, then, how can I be sure you're not poor, either?"

"Here is the deposit slip." Katya brushed past Crowe into a ray of light. "My counting house holds the five thousand crowns. Note the mark, made by the house pyradisté himself." She put her thumb over the name on the slip, letting only the *Lady* show of her alias, Lady Marchessa Gant.

"Ah." The hooded man stepped forward, out of the light. "The money speaks at last. And whom would I be transporting...Lady?"

"It's Miss, actually. I...work for the interested party, and I can see no reason why you need to know the identities of anyone involved."

"I'm a curious person."

Mashing her lips together, Katya pretended to think it over.

The hooded man waved her pause away. "Well, I have plenty of work, so if you don't want to share..."

"Let us just say that some people have sisters, and those sisters stand to inherit greater titles simply because they are *older*. All right?"

"Ah, such a sister might be simply disposed of, were she to exist."

"If we were barbarians." Katya tilted her nose high. "Many things can spoil an inheritance. An unapproved marriage, for instance."

"Oh yes, so much less barbaric than murder."

"If you're not interested, fine."

"Wait, wait, miss," the hooded man said. "I'm interested."

"Well, let's shake on it. I do believe that is the expression."

He stepped into the light. "Call me Kenrick." Tall and powerfully built, he seemed a good candidate for their man, down to the low beard on his chin. They moved closer just as a *twang* came from above them, and a green-fletched arrow punched into his shoulder.

Kenrick spun around with a cry, and his unseen partners leapt from their hiding places. Katya lunged for him, but one of his comrades swung at her with a short sword as another dragged him away. Katya ducked and drew her rapier; she backed up until she felt the solidness of Crowe and Brutal. They kept their backs together as much as they could, and Katya lost track of the assailants flitting through the dark.

CHAPTER TWENTY-EIGHT: STARBRIDE

Starbride stepped carefully across the roof of a warehouse, reminding herself with every movement that a mistake could send her tumbling two stories to the ground. Pennynail guided her toward the window of the warehouse Katya had entered, but he grabbed her arm as shouts and the ring of steel against steel drifted through the window. He pointed at her and at the roof they stood on, signaling her to stay put. "Right," she said.

He ducked inside, and the seconds ticked by. Starbride rubbed the elbows of her borrowed shirt and wondered how long she was supposed to wait. Active skulking hadn't been any better than passive skulking. Scuttling along rooftops and through windows was all fingers and toes work, and her limbs were aching.

She counted to sixty, then a hundred. When she reached a hundred and thirty, she peeked in the window until her eyes adjusted. A walkway clung to two of the walls, but not the one beneath her. A stack of crates loomed near the window—Pennynail's way down, she supposed. She searched the shadowy forms darting in and out of small rays of light, but couldn't distinguish friend from foe.

Starbride patted her leather vest, making sure her lone pyramid rested in the pocket. Perhaps the light pyramid would make it easier for Katya and the others to see, or maybe it would illuminate the enemy pyradisté and allow her to see his face. One way to find out. Hesitantly, she stepped out onto the tower of crates. As they shifted, she clambered onto the next closest stack, just inches from hers. Sick in the pit of her stomach, she clamped her teeth as the crates tilted, but couldn't stifle a cry as the rough wood slid out from under her and she toppled. She had a moment's thought to try to curl into a ball as she landed on a coil of rope. She kept her arms over her head, but when nothing fell on her, she stood and rubbed her aching side and hip.

The fighting seemed to be contained to the middle of the floor. One dark figure took a swing at Katya, but she blocked. Her face was fixed in an intense, concentrated stare as she moved into a beam of light before dancing out of it again. Brutal had three still forms at his feet, and as Starbride watched, he planted a foot in the chest of another and kicked his opponent back to stumble and lie prone. Before the opponent could rise again, a green-fletched arrow lodged in his chest.

Crowe ducked behind Brutal and chucked a pyramid at two enemies who moved to accost Katya. It shattered in a large sphere of blackness so profound it engulfed the two men whole. It faded in a blink of deep sound that made Starbride's ears ache, taking the men with it, and leaving a perfect bowl-shaped divot in the dirt floor.

Starbride gaped. It had to be the disintegration pyramid. Would she learn that? Did she even want to? A step rasped in the dirt behind her, and she turned, holding her pyramid aloft. A burly woman with a short sword paused, eyes on the pyramid. Starbride did the only thing she could think of. She let her mind fall into the pyramid and watched the following glow reflected in the woman's dark eyes.

The burly woman put an arm up as if to shield herself. Starbride backpedaled away, and when nothing else happened, the burly woman dropped the arm. An arrow plunked into her chest, and she toppled.

Starbride let the light fade as she realized why Maia wasn't shooting more of the attackers. As they came into the little shafts of light, she could get them, but she couldn't see them otherwise. Smiling so she wouldn't acknowledge how insane her idea was, Starbride moved through the crates and ropes and flotsam. She worked her way behind the enemies that accosted Katya. As she lit the pyramid again, one enemy turned, and Maia got him in the back. Another focused on Katya before Maia took him in the neck. Katya frowned as the light faded, her face harsh behind her domino mask as she pulled Starbride close. "Stay behind me."

Starbride wedged herself with Crowe between the two fighters, and when one of them moved to engage, she lit her little pyramid and gave Maia a chance to fire. The enemy fighters backed off, one after another, and a small glittering object sailed toward Starbride's group over a stack of crates.

"Scatter!" Crowe yelled.

Katya hauled Starbride to the side. She stumbled and struggled to keep up. Katya shoved her down as flame exploded in a roar of heat and light where they'd been standing.

"Star, are you hurt?"

"No. You?"

Katya shook her head. "Bastards." She scrambled to her feet, and

Starbride followed, seeing two men hurrying a third through the door at the rear of the building.

"Look!" Starbride said.

"I see them. Crowe? Brutal?"

Cries of "Fine" and "Here" reached them at the same time, and Starbride turned at the sound of running feet. Katya pressed Starbride behind her and brought her rapier on guard, but it was only Maia running for the door, chasing the fleeing men.

"Maia!" Katya yelled, but she was already past. Starbride started after her even as Katya did. They cleared the doors as Pennynail sprang from cover to join them.

The three men were slow-going; the healthier two helped the third between them. The third threw something over his shoulder, and Katya pushed Starbride to the side again. Katya yelled, "Scatter," this time, but as they hit the dirt, the pyramid struck the ground and shattered, doing nothing.

"A trick," Starbride said, but it had stopped every pursuit except Maia's. On a long pier, Maia slid to a stop on one knee and fired once, twice, taking both helpers. The wounded man they'd been supporting tottered and clutched his shoulder.

"Turn, turn," Starbride said. All she needed to do was see the pyradisté's face. He hustled toward the gangplank of a small ship and half turned, his hood concealing all but his chin. Starbride put a hand up to block the sun's glare.

Maia's first arrow took him in the side. Her second bit into his back as he spun. Katya sprinted toward him as he tried to stagger along. When at last he came to a halt, still on his feet, Maia nailed him in the back of the head, and he fell almost lazily into the river.

Katya reached the end of the pier mere seconds later. Starbride ran after her and skidded to a stop on the wet planks. The dark, muddy waters of the Lavine had swallowed the pyradisté as completely as if he'd never existed, leaving only a few spots of blood where he'd stood.

The rest of their party reached them a heartbeat later. Maia spat into the river, her face red and dirty but for the tear tracks on her cheeks.

"Did you get a look, Star?" Katya stared at the water, her jaw so tight the muscles stood out like cords.

"No."

Katya turned her hard gaze on Maia. "We had him."

"He killed my father," Maia said.

Katya gestured at the swift current. "We'll never know if that was him."

"It was the last one. He matched the description. It was him."

"Maia—" Katya started, but Crowe laid a hand on her shoulder.

"I would have done the same," he said. With a shaky, hesitant start, he patted Maia's shoulder, too. "You thought of it just before I did."

Maia's eyes slipped shut, her face unreadable. She squeezed Crowe's hand—hard if his flinch was any indication—and then dropped her arm to her side.

The bearded man was dead. Starbride knew they all should have been relieved, but no one looked it. Katya grumbled the entire way home. Crowe seemed thoughtful and Maia downcast. The side of Brutal's face was red and raw-looking, singed by the fire pyramid, but other than that and a few scrapes and bruises, they'd gotten away unscathed. Starbride only wished she could have glimpsed the pyradisté's face and given them all a sense of surety.

At the royal stable, Starbride touched Katya's arm gently. "I'll see you later?"

"It'll have to be. I have to tell my parents what happened. Back to the library with you?"

"I think I'll have my promised drink with Maia first."

Katya's lips brushed her cheek. "Go carefully."

Starbride draped her arm across Maia's shoulders. Maia blinked at her in surprise. "Glass of wine?"

Maia sagged against her. "I thought you'd never ask."

Back in Starbride's room, Dawnmother found them a bottle and then retreated to her embroidery. She perched on her low stool in the corner and listened while pretending not to, the servant's illusion.

Maia stared into her glass. "I'm sorry. I guess I'm not a fascinating conversationalist at the moment."

Starbride didn't want to ask about the bearded man. Things were heavy enough in the room. "How are things with Brutal?"

"Brutal? He's fine, I guess. Why?"

Starbride winked.

"Oh. He, well, we're not...together. I, um, I don't know how he thinks of me, not really. I mean, he's, well, he's gorgeous."

"He speaks to you fondly, smiles at you. He cares for you. That's easy to see."

"Yes, I know, but I wonder sometimes if he sees me as a woman or more like a little sister."

Dawnmother didn't look up from her work as she said, "There's one way to know for sure."

Maia craned her neck to look over the chair. "How?"

"Grab his head and kiss him."

Maia gawped, and her face turned a deeper shade. "I can't do that!"

Dawnmother tsked. "If he won't kiss you, kiss him. Then you'll know for certain."

"But, I…but…"

Starbride chuckled. "If you're a sister to him, he'll break apart from you, stammering excuses. If you're a lover…" She left the thought hanging.

Maia made a strangled noise and downed her wine in one gulp.

"Liquid courage?" Starbride filled the glass again.

"I'm not doing that today," Maia said. "I'd kiss him once and then pass out."

"It's been a long day."

"I loved my father very much."

Starbride forced herself to relax. Here was the weight from Maia's shoulders at last.

"I feel like I've done something to avenge him, even though the man in the warehouse wasn't even there when he died."

With a nod, Starbride picked up her glass and remained silent. She hoped there would be many more talks between them, plenty of time for all the words to be spoken. "Let's think on more pleasant things."

"Like Brutal."

"Grab his head and kiss him," Dawnmother said again.

Maia laughed until she snorted. "Is that what always happens in romantic Allusian stories?"

"Ah," Starbride said, "if it's romantic Allusian stories you're looking for, you've come to the right place. Dawnmother and I know them all."

Dawnmother scooted her stool forward, and they spent the next few hours talking, Maia's jaw dropping at the stories' juicier bits. When finally she left them, she had a very thoughtful look on her face.

"The princess will be happy you could turn her mind to other things," Dawnmother said.

"Not if she repeats the tale of the farmer's son and the midwife."

"It's only a saucy story."

"Another thing they try to shield her from," Starbride said. "Let's hope Katya is only happy I helped. And I hope for Maia's sake that she's not a little sister to Brutal. Though I'd love to have her as my younger sister."

Dawnmother kissed the top of her head. "Star, you have a heart made of gold."

"Easily bent?"

"And all the better for it."

CHAPTER TWENTY-NINE: KATYA

Katya stood in front of her long mirror and fastened the last buttons on her coat. Dark blue adorned with silver braid, it befitted the greeting of a dignitary…or a royal brother. The breast bore her personal hawk and rose. She had a rapier at her side, the pommel and guard dotted with jewels. It was a showy piece, but the blade was as sharp as any of her others.

In the mirror, hands curved up around her shoulders and fingered the braids at the sleeve. "Very stylish." Starbride's face appeared over Katya's shoulder. "Beautiful."

"I clean up nice when I want to." She fastened opal studs in her ears. Averie had already set her silver diadem at her forehead and hidden the ends in her hair. "How's the hair in the back?"

Soft hands patted here and there. "Flawless. I like the small braids. They make your usual style a bit more…dramatic."

"I learned it from you."

Holding her petal-layered dress out to the sides, Starbride made a face. "I don't see what you can learn from this besides what two tons of napkins should look like."

"I meant your natural style." She tugged Starbride forward, her shoulder protesting a bit after the tumbles she'd taken the previous day, but she forgot the pain in favor of the soft lips.

After too few kisses, Starbride pulled back. "Averie will be here any moment to clear her throat and take you away."

"You'll see me again soon enough."

"At the family dinner."

"Nervous?"

"Aren't you? I'm meeting your entire family tonight. Your brother's reception will be the perfect place for Layra to strike."

Katya nodded, her stomach clenching at the words. "I'm hoping the sheer number of people and the fact that she's lost her pyradisté will dissuade her. I'm only sorry you'll be at the back of the crowd with the other courtiers."

"I'll keep my eyes open."

"I know. We all will."

"I'm sorry I mentioned it. I just wanted someone to be as nervous as I am."

"You have nothing to worry about as far as the dinner is concerned. They'll love you."

"At least I know that you and Maia will be my allies."

"She's much happier with you around. You're invaluable, do you know that?"

"Of course!"

Katya bent in for another kiss just as Averie opened the door and said, "It's time."

Arm in arm, Katya and Starbride strode to the great hall just inside the main doors of the palace. There, Katya kissed Starbride's hand and had to leave her amidst the courtiers at the rear of the hall. They crowded around her like feasting crabs.

The crowd of nobles gathered on the steps parted for Katya's passage and opened a route to the lowest steps of the entryway where her family waited. The sea of people yielded no one suspicious to her eye, but she didn't have much time to look. She knew her Order was hidden in the crowd, and Crowe was in the gallery above, watching. In the city beyond, cheers marked the passage of Reinholt's carriage through the streets.

Ma lifted an eyebrow as Katya arrived, radiating maternal disapproval. Katya tossed her head, conveying childish rebelliousness. The crowd behind them would eat it up, never guessing that the night before, Katya and her mother had timed her entrance to just before Reinholt's carriage rolled into sight.

Reinholt looked splendidly happy as he alighted and held a hand out to his wife. Brom beamed up at the royal family, though she quickly brought her non-aristocratic smile under control. She'd been learning in her years away from court. Katya settled for a fond look. She wished that their children could be beside them, but all members of the royal family were only supposed to occupy the same place at the same time once a year, during the king's birthday celebration.

Reinholt flashed a grin that sent sighs sweeping through the nobles and those courtiers who had a view. He was a handsome devil; even Katya had to admit it. Darkly blond, his eyes were a light blue like their mother's instead of cobalt like Katya's and their father's. Not a gray hair touched his head, a sign that he didn't have enough to do. Brom didn't bother with flounces on her gown. She favored an empire waist that hugged her ample bosom before falling to the floor. Katya almost expected to hear a joyous cry from Starbride. If the crown prince's wife could thumb her nose at current fashion, Starbride could do it, too.

Reinholt kissed their father's signet ring. Da restrained himself to a clap on the shoulder, though Katya saw his shoulders twitching with the desire to embrace his son.

"Majesty, I, Reinholt Nar Umbriel, Duke of Lanaster, Lord of the Western March, Crown Prince of Farraday, seek entrance to the palace at Marienne," Reinholt said. The sound boomed through the entryway and sounded so much like their father that Katya nearly sputtered in surprise.

"I, Einrich Nar Umbriel, Lord of Marienne, foe of Yanchasa the Mighty, King of all Farraday, bid you enter and welcome."

Brom bowed over Da's ring next, and he gripped both her hands in his and murmured a welcome that Katya couldn't hear. Reinholt bowed to their mother and Katya, kissing each of their hands in turn.

As he straightened before Katya, Reinholt whispered, "Still not wearing dresses, eh?"

"I was just about to ask you the same thing."

He snorted, and she noticed with glee that he barely held in a bellow. He'd been gone from court a long time, too.

Da turned to the gathered crowd, every inch a king. "Lords and Ladies, ladies and gentlemen, the crown prince and princess!" Cheers and applause rolled over them like a tidal wave as every single resident tried to outdo the others. Katya spotted servants watching and cheering from the palace windows but didn't see anyone suspicious. The common people's worship of Reinholt for his looks seemed more genuine than the nobles' and courtiers' favor currying.

They hurried Reinholt and Brom through the receiving line of nobles as quickly as they could, setting a new best time of three hours. At the forefront of the courtiers, Starbride offered a wink, and even though Katya couldn't return the gesture, she appreciated it.

Once the family stood alone in their parents' sitting room, they dissolved into kisses and hugs. "I had a safe, boring trip," Reinholt said as he let Katya go. "Do I have you to thank for that, little K? I bet you've flushed out all enemies of the crown by now."

Katya shrugged and fought a blush. Growing up, she'd idolized her older brother almost as one of the spirits; it was still hard not to be knocked flat by his praise. "All in a day."

"Nonsense." Brom added another hug to Katya's already full repertoire. "You've done a wonderful job, I'm sure."

It was a compliment fit for the decorators, but Katya understood that her sister-in-law was proud of her. That was all she needed to know.

"How goes it in the Order of Vestra?" Reinholt asked.

Katya glanced at Brom's wide brown eyes and wished Reinholt hadn't brought up one of the most dangerous parts of her life. Now was not the time for worry. "Same as always. Enemies pop up, and we deal with them."

Brom's grip tightened on Katya's arm. "What sorts of enemies?"

"Now, don't you worry." Da took Brom's elbow and led her to a seat. "You're perfectly safe."

"I was just thinking of the children at home."

Maia shook her head. "Didn't you leave Lord Vincent with them?"

"Definitely," Reinholt said. "The trouble hasn't been invented that could knock down the Champion of Farraday."

Brom laughed, but the sound had a bit of force in it. "You're right, I know you are." She grasped Maia's chin. "You look more lovely every time I see you, Maia, and more like your—"

"How *are* Bastian and Vierdrin?" Katya asked quickly. She didn't know if Brom had been about to compare Maia to a dead parent or a living relative, but she didn't want to take chances. "Does Bastian have his own horse yet? Did Vierdrin get the little sword I sent her?"

Brom fell to talking about her children with the same happy intensity as any mother. Reinholt chimed in, tidbits of this and that, though his contact with the children sounded more limited than Brom's. His duties kept him too busy, or so he claimed. Katya chuckled at the thought. Reinholt sounded more like their father all the time.

"Still," Brom said, "there are days when they come bursting into our bedroom at the crack of dawn, and we wish they were with their grandmother and grandfather."

"Ah, anytime!" Ma said. "I miss the voices of children."

Reinholt chuckled. "We can fix that for you, Mother. One month with ours and you'll be full up for another few years."

"Never, dear, never."

"Distance gives one the opportunity to seem like the perfect grandparent," Da said. Ma gave him a cold stare while the rest of them laughed. Soon enough, Ma smiled with them, looking more relaxed than Katya had seen in a long time.

❖

They separated to rest, and when they gathered again for their private dinner, Reinholt pulled Katya aside. "So, now will you tell me of your adventures?"

"No, Rein. One of my jobs is to keep the rest of the family from worrying too much."

"You won't tell me? This close to the Waltz? If there's anything wrong—"

"I'm on it. My team is on it," Katya said. Reinholt rubbed his chin, his eyes half-hooded as if disappointed. Katya squeezed his shoulder. "Let me worry about protecting you. It's my duty *and* my honor."

He smiled the soft Reinholt grin he reserved for friends and family. "I won't step on your toes, little K, but I do want to be prepared."

"Crowe will prepare you as much as you need to be."

"So, I understand we'll be entertaining a special guest at our private table this evening."

Katya couldn't contain a grin. "I remember the first night you brought Brom. Mother made looking her over into an art form."

"Ma's good. Brom never suspected a thing. Has she checked out your girl yet? This is the first time you've brought someone to dinner. Unless you've been doing it since I've been gone."

Katya thought back on all her past conquests and winced. "She's the first. There was one other I considered—I thought I was in love—but Mother stared at me for a good five minutes before she said no."

"Oh, that stare. It's like she can tell if it's real before she even meets the person." He shuddered, his expression one of mock horror. "She always knew when we were sneaking sweets, too."

Katya snorted. "She agreed to dine with Starbride after only a little stare."

"Starbride?"

Katya could picture Starbride's impatient look upon the repetition of her name. She nodded.

"Allusian?" Reinholt gave her a long look, a half leer hovering around his mouth. "You blushed, and now you're grinning like a loon. Is consortship soon to follow our little dinner date?"

Katya's stomach tilted to the side. "Mother wouldn't be happy if I asked her to be my consort this early in our relationship, though we're already known as a couple."

"But you'd ask her if you could?"

"Yes." Katya couldn't keep all her feelings inside. That was the spell Starbride cast on her.

To her surprise, Reinholt gripped her shoulders and beamed. "I'm so happy for you, little K."

She was surprised to find tears at the corners of her eyes. "Thank you, Rein. She makes me very happy."

"Then I like her already. But if she's good-looking enough to have caught your eye, I can't promise not to have a look myself."

"Eyes are fine. No hands."

Starbride arrived right on time dressed in a dark blue outfit similar to the shirt, trousers, and bodice Katya had bought her, except for the silver cord that outlined the bodice and then subtly coiled across the front, making spirals and small patterns. They might have been Allusian characters for all Katya knew. She wore a necklace of sapphires, simple and elegantly done. Her hair had been pulled behind her head, the front of it leading back in two braids to join the rest gathered at the back in gold wire. Katya had to fight not to beam. In the candlelight, her skin seemed to glow, and the flames made gold highlights in her hair. Her radiance put the light to shame.

She bowed deeply. Da took her arm and led her to a seat across from Katya before he took the head of the table. Behind Starbride's back, Reinholt bit his fist as if he couldn't control his desire before he took a seat beside her. Katya nearly threw her napkin at him. From Katya's right, Brom nudged her in the ribs.

Katya tried not to roll her eyes. Starbride's glance darted up and down the table, and Katya didn't want her to worry over anyone's wayward expressions. Most everyone approved. Ma's face betrayed nothing, and Da nodded to himself, though he was smart enough not to express more in front of Ma.

Throughout the dinner, Starbride made polite conversation, but she seemed more subdued than usual. Katya tried to put her at ease, but Starbride's quiet attitude would impress Ma more than her beauty ever could. Starbride didn't fawn or laugh too loudly or bring up her own agenda every five minutes. *And* she didn't flirt with everyone, a mistake some of the other courtiers might have made, thinking to move from the princess to bigger game.

After dinner, they were free to move about the room. Ma settled next to Starbride and asked about her jewelry. Katya blessed her mother's name. Starbride warmed to the topic and exclaimed over Ma's equally elegant pieces, a mix of fire opals and pearls.

"I like how your coat and her outfit match," Reinholt said in Katya's ear.

"If you're going to make fun, go away."

"Yes." Brom moved up on the other side of Reinholt. "Stop teasing, and go rescue poor Maia from your father's rant about clerks."

Reinholt moved away with a chuckle. Brom sat next to Katya at the divan near the fireplace. "She's very lovely, almost exotic."

Katya ducked her head. She knew that Brom meant no harm by it, but she understood Starbride's exasperation at being a curiosity. "She's a wonderful person, very caring."

"Catirin's taken a shine to her."

"She took a shine to you when you first met."

Brom laughed her high, bell-like laugh. "She had me petrified, even as kind as she was. I felt like I was being weighed and measured, no matter what she said." Her eyes went far away for a moment. "Sometimes, I feel it even now."

"I know."

"You can't. You're her daughter; you've never been on the receiving end of her true measurement. She's got a way of looking at people…"

"No need to dwell. You passed. You're here."

"I'm sorry. I get lost in the past sometimes."

"Should I rescue her?"

"At your peril."

"Well, I know my mother won't have me killed. Being her child guarantees that."

"How about flogged? Whipped?"

Katya tilted her head back and forth. "Could be."

"Is Starbride worth a whipping or two?"

"Absolutely." Katya perched on the ottoman in front of Ma and Starbride, and her mother gave her a look that Katya knew was just for occupying a footstool. "What are we talking about?"

Starbride smiled "Horses."

Another topic Starbride was familiar with. Katya almost winked at her mother; Ma seemed to sense that very desire. She sipped her brandy and stood. "I'd better keep your father away from the cakes."

Katya chuckled and took her mother's place. "I thought you might need a rescue."

"Your mother is very nice. She's just so…"

"Intense."

"That's a perfect word."

"Having a good time?"

"Yes, actually, for being so nervous earlier. They're all nice, and it's wonderful to be at a family gathering where my mother isn't tutting over my hair the entire time."

"Your hair is perfect, but I could tut over it if you want."

"It wouldn't be the same. Your fixes would turn into caresses."

"Do you think it would be too scandalous if I kissed you?"

"You'd better not. Your family has the same talent for watching while not-watching that mine has."

"I've already decided that you're worth a whipping or two if they want to punish me."

"They'd whip you, but I'd be on the executioner's block."

"Oh no," Katya said, using her court drawl, "they're not that hard. You'd be married to some old landowner on the outskirts of the kingdom, far from where you could trouble me."

"My mother wouldn't stand for that. She'd ride in, carry me off, and marry me to someone else."

"Spirits help us if our mothers ever butt heads." Katya was silent for a moment, taking in the atmosphere and listening to the muted conversations around them. "Would you like to be my consort?" She couldn't help herself, not with the candles and the feeling of being surrounded by family, not with the warm smile and skin perfumed with spice.

Starbride stared into her drink. Katya thought she might be holding her breath.

"It's not marriage." The fear of being rejected roared in Katya, something she hadn't experienced in a long time. "It comes before marriage, when you're...us. It's like, official companion, more than just bedmate. It's..." She bit her lip. "If you don't want to, it's all right. My mother would've had a fit if I'd asked before she met you, but I've wanted to ask, and I know we still don't know each other *that* well, and that's another reason I waited." She was babbling, something else she hadn't done for ages. Her grip tightened on her glass as she tried to think of something else to say.

"If..." Starbride said, "if my mother tries to take advantage of you, please forgive her."

"What?"

"Once she hears that I'm your consort, she'll start asking for things, and you'll have to let me tell her no and promise to forgive her."

Katya's heart thudded for a few more seconds before she realized she'd been holding her breath, too. It was all she could do not to take Starbride's face and kiss the soft lips. In another half second, she decided it was worth it. They'd barely begun when Ma cleared her throat.

"People are always clearing their throats around us," Katya said.

Starbride hid her laugh behind a cough. "Will I...see you later?" Her eyes were hidden behind her downturned lashes.

Heat billowed through Katya's insides, making her hyperaware of Starbride's smooth skin. The thought led her to images of that skin unclothed, and her breath caught as she said, "Oh yes."

Starbride bade them all good night shortly afterward, her eyes on Katya holding a promise of the evening to come. Katya used all her determination to stay rooted to the spot. Once Starbride departed, Katya's family turned to her, their expression carrying curiosity mixed with a multitude of feelings.

"You asked her after all, didn't you?" Reinholt asked. "Sly one."

Maia looked back and forth between them. "Asked her what?"

"To be her consort!" Reinholt said.

"Brilliant!" Maia said.

Ma stiffened, and Katya gave her brother a dark look. Her mother didn't like surprises, much less surprises delivered amongst a group. "She's seen the Fiend. She knows my secrets, Ma, even the Order. All I was waiting for was your approval." The last part was half-true, and it seemed to mollify her mother a bit, but Ma's expression warned that there would be words between them later.

"Well done, my girl!" Da kissed her temple and gave her a wink and a nudge as if they were two old dogs. The rest of them grilled her on Starbride, and she put them off as best she could. When she was more than ready to go, she hugged them all again, leaving her mother for last.

Katya kissed her mother's cheek. "Thank you, Ma."

"Go on, rascal."

Katya nearly whooped as she left them. She'd send Starbride a note inviting her to come over, and then she'd light some candles, scented ones, maybe... Deep in plans, she opened the door to her apartment and stopped as Averie and Dawnmother rose from the table. "What's this?"

Averie pointed toward the bedroom door. Well, if Dawnmother was in the sitting room... It was better than any plan Katya could have made. She strode past the maids without another word.

In the bedroom, candles shone from every surface, making it seem as if the stars from the ceiling mural had descended to hover about the room. Starbride lay on her stomach, her head propped on one hand, the other toying with a strand of her loose hair.

"What kept you?" The light played over her bare curves as she moved her legs up and back, her ankles crossed.

Katya willed her feet to overcome her awe. She moved forward, unbuttoning her coat as she walked. "I don't know. Right now, I can't remember anything outside of this room."

Starbride chuckled, another throaty sound that traveled along Katya's body like a caress. When she reached the bed, Starbride sat up, taking Katya's breath away again. She gasped as Starbride grabbed her shoulders and pulled her down, pouncing on her. Katya closed her eyes as their lips met and gave in to passionate intensity. The Order and all her responsibilities dissolved. Time itself became lost, and Katya had never been happier to cast it aside.

CHAPTER THIRTY: STARBRIDE

Starbride studied the bracelet on her wrist. Made of twisted silver, it resembled strands of ivy, the junctions of the strands set with tiny emeralds. It seemed almost too delicate to be worn.

Averie had delivered it that morning in an antique box, saying, "Crown Princess Brom wore this, and Queen Catirin, and all the men and women who've been consorts to the Umbriels." Starbride had lifted it with reverence and thought all the while that she was lucky the last two wearers had been women. It didn't need resizing.

Just over four inches long, it clasped about her wrist like a cuff, and the illusion of a manacle wasn't lost on her. Better a beautiful manacle than a plain one, though. She turned it in the light and watched the tiny emeralds sparkle. The accompanying note had simply said, *My consort, I love you. K.*

Dawnmother slipped into their room, her spine so stiff with pride it was a wonder she didn't lift from the ground. "News of your consortship has flown on the wings of gossip."

"The princess consort looks no different from Starbride the courtier."

"Yet the difference is huge. I've ordered more Allusian-style outfits, and the tailors have been quicker to answer. Also, the section housekeeper has arranged for a better apartment, so we'd better get hopping. I'll pack our things."

"So soon?"

"Well, it's only fitting. Hurry now, the servants will be coming for the luggage."

Starbride had to smirk as Dawnmother shepherded servants to and fro and took possession of the keys to Starbride's quarters with a stately air. Bigger than Lady Hilda's, the new apartment boasted three rooms, a bedroom and a sitting room, plus a small room for Dawnmother. It was also a skip from Katya's apartment, Starbride noted. After the servants had departed, she spent an hour knocking on the walls and had nearly given up on secret passageways when she heard a knock from the other side.

"Who is it?"

"It's me," Katya's voice said.

"Come in." Dawnmother retreated to her room as a small section of wall swung out, and Katya stepped through. "Let me guess," Starbride said, "that leads to your apartment?"

"More or less. Take the wrong turn and you'll end up in my parents' bedroom."

"Kiss me hello, and later you can show me the way."

"Ah, but it's *my* job to visit you in the middle of the night, to sweep in unannounced and catch you in your nightie."

"I don't have a nightie, and you can't sweep in unannounced if you knock."

"I'm a considerate seducer."

Starbride pointed to the table where her newest mound of invitations and gifts lay. "And I'm going to be busy for the next five years."

"Ignore most of them, send a polite decline to others, and only accept those from people who interest you or can aid you."

"Aid me?"

"It's not always a bad thing. Everyone comes to court in order to make connections. If you meet someone who can aid you in some way, and you can aid them in turn, then make that connection. The people you have to be wary of are those who want something from you but have nothing to offer."

"No wonder you get surly sometimes. They all want something from *you*, but what can they offer?"

"Not much." Her lips brushed Starbride's cheek. "Remember, a hand that claims to be extended in friendship and yet grabs for everything it can reach is not a friendly hand."

Starbride caressed Katya's chin with her thumb, and the bracelet glinted on her wrist. "My hands are friendly."

"And I'm eternally grateful for that, Miss Meringue."

"That's Princess Consort Meringue to you."

"Are you ready for tonight?"

"I think so. It'll certainly be different from my first ball." She tried not to let all the recent changes overtake her thoughts. "My first official function by your side."

"Don't worry. I won't leave you alone for Lady Hilda to poison."

Starbride flashed back on Countess Nadia's words and repressed a shiver. "I should eat before I go. Then I won't be tempted by anything anyone gives me."

Katya shook her head, her expression as serious as Starbride had ever seen. "Don't take anything that isn't given to you by Dawnmother, Averie, me, or my family's personal servants."

"Why?"

"The royal party is only served by our trusted servants. It's always been that way."

Starbride's fingers curled around the bracelet. She thought her world was dangerous before, but now she could take her food and drink from only a handful of people? "I didn't know Dawnmother could come."

"Definitely. She'll hover in the background with Averie."

Relief trickled over the wall of ice in Starbride's belly. "She'll like that. Good. I won't have to worry, then. Dawnmother will probably taste everything if she's not in the kitchen cooking it herself." She put on a brighter smile. "Will you be wearing your blue coat?"

"Not if you're wearing blue. I don't want everyone cooing over how we match all night. I'll wear the black."

Starbride snuggled into Katya's shoulder. "I like the black."

Dressmakers had been working for two days on Starbride's ball gown, a blend of Allusian and Farradain style. The cobalt-blue fabric was embroidered with silver thread and tiny crystal beads. It had a scoop-necked, fitted, Allusian bodice, with the same flared sleeves attached at the shoulders. Instead of a long shirt over pants, though, a sleek flaring skirt began under the bodice's hem and hung to the floor, held out by a petticoat with not a flounce in sight.

The ball was a hidden pocket of sound in the next room. Starbride clutched Katya's arm. Katya's fitted coat flared at the waist and then continued to the knee over tight white trousers. Bright gold buttons ran down the middle, and the same braid as on her welcoming coat adorned her shoulders. Her diadem glittered at her brow, and the butterfly pin she'd made from Starbride's old hairclip rested on her breast, near her heart. She was a gorgeous painting brought to life.

It was stuffy in the small waiting room, and Starbride was glad she'd worn her hair piled on her head in one of Dawnmother's artful creations. She resisted the urge to fidget with her diamond necklace.

In front of her stood Brom and Reinholt and in front of them Queen Catirin and King Einrich. She heard Maia whisper, "Hurry up, hurry up," behind her and grinned over her shoulder.

Maia smiled back, her hair glowing against her turquoise gown. Starbride had been thrilled to find Brother Brutal acting as her escort. She didn't know how many bolts of fabric it took, but his coat seemed tight around his shoulders, and he pulled at the high collar as if it choked him. The side of his face was still a little singed from the fire pyramid at the dock warehouse. Whenever he looked down at Maia, though, his frown lifted into a smile. Starbride wondered if Maia's courage in asking him to the ball had extended to grabbing his head and kissing him, but she thought not.

At some unseen signal, they stepped onto the grand ballroom's dais to thunderous applause. Starbride gripped Katya's arm and tried to let the attention of the glittering sea of people wash over her. She'd hated being stared at when she'd first arrived. She thought it would be different being stared at from a position of power, but her tightened muscles wouldn't loosen. Katya patted her arm as they descended the dais into the ballroom.

As the crowd pushed forward to speak with them, Starbride couldn't help but compare this party to the Courtiers Ball. At that one, she'd been afforded the same respect one gave to a potted plant. At Reinholt's ball, she could've whipped off her dress and still would've been surrounded by sycophants complimenting her undergarments.

Baroness Jacintha pushed by a group of courtiers. "You *must* tell me the name of your jeweler. I never got to ask during our tea." She said the last part loudly, turning her head for maximum volume.

"My father's creations," Starbride replied. "His name is Sunjoyful."

"They're lovely."

"Just what I was going to say, Baroness Jacintha." Countess Nadia emerged from the crowd to stand beside them, her arm twined through Viscount Lenvis's. He seemed extremely pleased with himself and maybe a tiny bit nervous. No doubt Countess Nadia had landed him, or nearly had, and he was thinking about what to make of such an opportunity.

Baroness Jacintha blinked as she turned. "Ah, Countess Nadia. Everyone knows you have fine taste."

"Indeed. I believe you're wanted by the buffet, Baroness."

Baroness Jacintha started but covered it by a low curtsy before leaving.

Starbride smiled slyly. "Thank you, Countess. Good evening, Viscount."

Viscount Lenvis inclined his head. "Princess Consort." He gazed down at Countess Nadia. "Not a fan of Baroness Jacintha's, my dear?"

"That woman is as annoying as a talking bird. I can land you a bigger fish, Princess Consort."

"Landing yourself one as well?"

Countess Nadia winked. "A fine idea."

"Starbride will meet all the nobles in good time," Katya drawled. "The crown won't forget your kindness to the princess consort, Countess. With Starbride as your friend, I'm sure you'll rise to great heights. Duchess Skelda Van Nispin's sewing circle, perhaps?"

Countess Nadia shrugged. Starbride leaned closer to her. "Do you really want to be part of a sewing circle, Countess?"

"No, but I would love to have Duchess Skelda and all her friends thinking they should invite me to everything and wondering to what extent I have your ear. I can filter gossip for you while extending my network of intelligence."

Starbride had to blink to keep her eyes from bulging. Was everyone so calculating? She supposed she'd have to get used to it. "I like the idea of mutual aid, Countess."

"Call me Nadia."

She curtsied, and the viscount bowed as they moved away. Starbride just heard Viscount Lenvis say, "I never knew you were so well connected, Nadia! A friend of the crown."

Katya snorted. "Good luck, Lenvis."

"He's baited and hooked," Starbride said.

"Let's hope he can survive it."

"Good evening, Princess. Princess Consort," someone beside them said.

Starbride nearly dropped her drink when she focused on him. "Lord Hugo! Another friendly face. You always know just when to pop up!"

"I wouldn't want to lose my ability to surprise you. I was worried that I'd never top myself after foolishly spying on you in the library."

Lord Hugo bowed, but Starbride saw the wariness in Katya's stance. Lord Hugo had kept the affair in the woods a secret, as far as they'd been able to tell, but that wouldn't set Katya at ease.

Starbride's shoulders relaxed at the sight of him, though. Lord Hugo simply rang true to her; she sensed honor in his very nature. "So nice to see you. If I had my way, I'd keep my few friends around me at all times."

With a slight blush to his cheeks, he said, "Thank you, Miss, uh, Princess Consort." He gestured toward the bracelet on her wrist.

"You can call me Starbride. I think you've earned it."

Katya snorted softly and turned to speak with someone else.

Lord Hugo bowed again. "Then I must insist that you call me Hugo."

Starbride tapped her chin and made a show of thinking that over. "No, no, I don't think I could ever say Hugo without the Lord. I picture you being called Lord Hugo even as a babe in arms."

"Actually..." His eyes lost focus. Blinking rapidly, he put one hand to his forehead and staggered as if overcome.

Starbride reached to steady him. "Are you all right?"

"I..." He stared at her, frowning, as if he couldn't figure out who she was. "I..."

"Is it the heat? The crowd?" She waved Dawnmother over. "Water," she mouthed. Around them, people nodded at Lord Hugo and whispered amongst themselves. One woman sniggered, and Starbride wanted to slap her. Instead, she patted Lord Hugo's back as he shook his head, his eyes near frantic. "Maybe you should go into the hall and catch your—"

"I'm fine." His face relaxed as he took a few deep breaths. "I'm sorry I frightened you." With a trembling hand, he reached out, and his fingers just brushed her cheek. "I'm sorry." He turned and fled through the crowd.

Dawnmother arrived with a glass of water. "What was that about?"

"I don't know." The alarm crawling inside her didn't subside. "I think something's wrong." She staggered as a shudder rocked the room, and the din of conversation turned into piercing screams as half the room's occupants fell to the floor.

"What in Darkstrong's name?" Starbride said. Katya hurried to her side.

Another quake shook the building. The domed ceiling cracked, and pieces of plaster fell like snowflakes among the screaming crowd. Starbride gaped as several people toppled from the balcony into the night outside. Katya's arm went around her waist as people surged against them, running for the exits, and Starbride sucked in a deep breath as Katya held her tight with one arm and grasped Dawnmother with the other. She guided both of them toward the dais.

The crowd became a mob, fierce as any river, which battered them as they struggled to push through. Dawnmother escaped Katya's grip and grabbed Starbride's free arm. Katya elbowed people aside. They didn't even seem to see her. She had Starbride's arm in a grip of steel that wouldn't let go no matter how many bumps and bruises, how many collisions they suffered. Dawnmother clutched Starbride's other arm with both hands. Starbride held on to both her saviors, knowing the crowd could sweep any one of them away.

When they reached the dais, the royal family helped them up and into the doorway of the waiting room. Starbride turned to watch the fleeing crowd in horror. "What is it?" she said as another tremor shook the building. She held on to everyone around her and noticed two of them missing. "Where are Maia and Brutal?"

"It can't be him," Katya said to King Einrich as if she hadn't heard.

"Can you think of something else?" he asked.

"Is the palace under siege?" Reinholt said.

Queen Catirin shook her head. "A siege party couldn't sneak through the city to get to us."

Starbride scanned the crowd. "Maia!" she shouted, but she had no hope of being heard over the screams.

"It's all right," Averie said from beside her. "She was near the doors. She knows what to do in a crisis. Stay close to us."

"It has to be Yanchasa!" Queen Catirin said, catching Starbride's attention.

"Rein." Brom pulled on Reinholt's arm. Her eyes were wide, terrified. Starbride laid a hand on her shoulder, and Brom covered it with her own but stared into her husband's face.

"It'll be all right, love," Reinholt said. "It doesn't hurt. Afterward, you won't even remember."

Brutal lifted Maia onto the dais and then vaulted up after her. "Crowe's got the Guard working to keep the crowd in order," Maia said. "He said he'll get Pennynail and meet us in the pyramid chamber."

"The Waltz," Starbride said. Brom's horror made sudden sense. After the Waltz, she'd have to wear a pyramid necklace to keep her Fiend under control.

But there was no time for sympathy. Starbride and Dawnmother stayed with the royals as they hurried into the corridor behind the entry room and then into a secret passageway. They grabbed a lantern there and wound deeper into the palace, past bedrock, deeper and deeper, through tunnels of rough-hewn stone. The marks on the hallway junctions disappeared. If a person didn't already know their way through these tunnels, they could be lost forever. Starbride supposed that was the idea. The depths to which the Farradains would go to preserve their secrets never ceased to amaze.

Crowe met them at one junction. He held a brightly lit pyramid and had Pennynail beside him. "It's not an attack. It's Yanchasa."

"He's early," King Einrich said. "He's never been this early before."

Another quake shook the passageway, making tiny cracks in the stone. The party broke into a run until they reached a dead end. King Einrich pressed his hand to a large pyramid set in the wall, and it opened like a door into a cavernous chamber that still felt airless for all its size.

Starbride turned full circle as she walked and stared at the natural cavern that the palace sat atop. Stalagmites littered the floor, and their companion stalactites clung to the ceiling. What caught her attention, though, was the enormous glowing pyramid in the middle of the chamber. She thought at first that it rested on the bare rock, but the stone of the floor clung to it, hiding the very bottom, and she realized it was the top of an even larger pyramid that lay buried underground. She recognized Allusian crystal, but what touched the floor was a darker, green-flecked stone. "Horsestrong preserve us. If that's just the capstone, the rest of the pyramid must be…" She couldn't picture its true size. "Is he…under there?" she whispered, not willing to risk an echo. "Yanchasa?"

"Yes," Crowe answered from beside her, "he's contained in the pyramid."

Katya gave her one quick kiss and moved closer to the pyramid. "Stay by the wall with Averie and Dawnmother. The rest of us are going to watch over the Waltz."

With an actual Fiend right under her feet, Starbride wanted to retreat down the tunnel, but she couldn't leave. She loved Katya too much to leave her in what might become a dangerous situation. Well, that and she *had* to see what happened next.

"What is happening?" Dawnmother whispered.

Starbride bit her lip. All the royal secrets were about to be revealed. One by one, they'd been alarming. She didn't envy Dawnmother getting all of them at once. "Don't be afraid, but prepare yourself. The Umbriels are more than they appear to be."

CHAPTER THIRTY-ONE: KATYA

K atya stood well back from the pyramid as Crowe chained her
family's feet to the floor. She'd Waltzed once, before Reinholt had
married. She remembered the cold shackles around her ankles, and even
that feeling had been dwarfed by the coldness building within her as the
Fiend, Yanchasa's Aspect, fought to get out.

Crowe took her family's necklaces one by one. He shackled their
ankles. Their human faces fell away as they leaned forward to rest their
hands on the capstone. Lit by the light of the glowing pyramid, her father,
then her mother, then her brother changed. Her father sprouted two horns
that curled back over his head. His eyes turned all blue, and a spike jutted
from his chin.

Ma had no horns on her head or spikes on her face. Instead, the
wings of a crow sprouted from her back in four places, ripping through
the fabric of her dress. Her eyes shone light blue, and fangs pressed down
from her upper jaw against her lower lip.

Reinholt's horns came from his temples and traced the sides of his
head back, just over his ears. Two wings sprouted from his back, and the
spike on his chin mirrored their father's.

Katya wondered, and not for the first time, what her own Aspect
looked like. She glanced at Starbride, who'd seen it, and wondered if
Starbride was comparing them all. The Fiendish faces were cold and
impassive, yet a tightening of their skin revealed an underlying rage.
With the shackles, however, and with their hands on the pyramid's sides,
they could do nothing but feed their energy downward to quiet Yanchasa.
If they were to get free, Katya had no doubt that they would kill everyone
in the kingdom.

Crowe looked to Brom. She stared at Reinholt with open fear and
shock, her hand pressed to her mouth. "It's time." Crowe knelt and held
up the fourth and final pair of shackles. "If you love your husband and
your kingdom, it's time."

"I love my children more."

Katya stepped forward just as Crowe stood, but something whizzed past Katya's ear and buried itself in Crowe's gut. With a grunt, he sank to his knees, clutching an arrow shaft. Brom darted away, and Crowe banged off the side of the pyramid and slumped to the floor.

Katya spun, drawing her rapier as she turned. In the doorway stood three men: Darren, Cassius, and Lord Hugo. Armed with bow and sword, the first sported smug smirks. Lord Hugo, his rapier held defensively in front of him, seemed more uncertain, apologetic even.

Katya felt movement beside her as Brutal and Maia stepped close. Brutal's bare fists clenched in front of him, and Maia pulled a throwing knife from her skirt.

"When I say—" Katya began.

"Hold," a voice interrupted.

Two people emerged from behind stalagmites on the far right of the cavern. One was a woman, her face gray, her eyes a dead-looking white, though it was the pyramid embedded in her forehead that drew the eye, that and her drawn bow. As Katya turned her attention to the other new arrival, her breath stopped.

It had been seven years since he died, but Roland Nar Umbriel looked exactly the same.

"Father?" Maia whispered.

"Come to me, daughter," Roland said.

Katya grabbed Maia's arm. "It's a trick."

Footsteps sounded from behind them as Brom ran for the doorway. Brutal stuck out a leg and tripped her. He bent, grabbed her ankle, pulled her to him, and then lifted her to stand in front of him like a shield. He stepped between Katya and Maia and the three men in the doorway.

Katya glanced over her shoulder. Starbride, Averie, and Dawnmother sidled along the wall, away from the doorway, watching her. Crowe cried out somewhere behind her, and Katya hoped Pennynail was helping him.

"I did it for my children." Brom sobbed as she dangled in Brutal's arms. "They wanted to make my children into monsters!"

"Shut up and you might live," Brutal snapped.

"Who are you?" Katya pointed her rapier at the false Roland. "What are you? You're not my uncle."

Roland laughed, deep and rich. "You know." He strolled toward the doorway with a casual air. "That was the very thought I had as I sank under the river. What am I? It was my death that made me think of my life, of everything in it. Of my daughter." Maia jerked in Katya's grasp. Katya clamped down harder and ignored the tears cascading down Maia's cheeks.

"And I thought of my lover." Roland gestured at the gray-skinned woman, and Katya realized with a roiling stomach that it was Layra. "The mother of my son." He gestured to Lord Hugo. "I thought of all the things I would miss if I died in the water. I'd stopped breathing already. It was just a matter of waiting for my mind to give in." He tapped his skull and grinned. "But the Fiend wasn't ready to let go."

Katya's mouth dropped open. "You...merged with it?"

Roland smiled, and the features of his Aspect dropped over his face: horns like her father's, fangs like her mother's, and his eyes the deep rich blue of her own. But his expression didn't lose its character, didn't become the Fiend's. He was himself, even with the Aspect. "It showed me what a fool I've been to live life as a normal human." His voice grated along the nerves, deeper, but with an echoing tininess that made her feel like she had a mouth full of blood.

"I wandered the wilderness for years, trying to put my mind back together again, and then all I had to do was wait the five years for the Waltz to come around again."

Another shock wave rocked the cavern, and Roland tilted his horned head back. "Yes, old boy, I hear you."

Katya raised her rapier. "*You're* the bearded man, the one who kidnapped Starbride, the one we couldn't find."

"I'm not here to harm you, little K. I've come to collect you and my daughter. I'll help you put Yanchasa to bed for good. All I ask is a kingdom ruled the right way, my way. A small price to pay, if you really cared about it. I'll let your Fiends out for you." He stepped forward. "You'll discover *unimaginable* heights when we tap Yanchasa for all he has, and the people of Marienne will finally get a ruler they deserve, one who will protect and guide them by any means necessary."

Katya glanced at Brutal. He nodded. She shook her head at Roland. "You've done too much evil, uncle. We're not interested in what you have to offer." Her heart hurt, but she shoved the feelings down.

"Ah well, if you won't cooperate, I'll still have myself, my children, and my niece-in-law to help me draw Yanchasa's power and to make sure the people do as they're told."

"No! No!" Brom screamed. "You promised me. My children and I could go free. We'd never be Fiends! We'd never Waltz!"

Something darted through the air from behind them. With preternatural speed, Roland plucked the throwing knife from its flight. Pennynail was on the move. Roland snapped the thin metal as if it were an old twig. "So be it." He opened his left hand, revealing a pyramid, and then closed it swiftly, shattering the crystal. From her place on the wall, Starbride screamed and fell.

Darren and Layra loosed arrows; Katya and Brutal dove behind stalagmites. Maia stayed rooted to the spot and stared at her father with tear-stained cheeks, a knife clutched in her fist. "Maia, down!" Katya yelled. She paid no heed, and Katya looked for a way to get to Starbride.

Roland appeared in a blur at her side. Katya brought her sword to bear, but he leaned past her thrust as if she moved through water. He reached inside the neck of her coat and jerked her pyramid necklace from her throat.

"I know now what sets you off, little K," he whispered. The cold of his breath burned her cheeks. "I'll kill your brother and your father and save your mother and your consort. Your Fiendish face will smile while I rape and torture them at the same time."

"No!" Katya shrieked, her anger spiking. Roland planted a pyramid in the middle of her chest, and Katya felt a surge of bitter cold before everything went dim around the edges and complete calm overtook her, quieting her conscious mind.

CHAPTER THIRTY-TWO: STARBRIDE

Starbride's pain smothered her, a stake through her side, a sword slicing her in half, a giant wasp stinging its way out of her body. She tore a hole in her gown and tried to dig out the pain, but the skin was too hot to touch. Katya needed her. She had to get up, but her whole world was pushed through the eye of agony. Cool hands touched her face, and she whipped her head toward them, seeking a balm.

Dawnmother's anxious face filled her vision. Someone was holding her on her side, pushing her down. "Hold her still," Averie said.

Dawnmother's face came closer. "Peace, Star. Lie still."

Starbride couldn't speak. She needed to scratch the pain out. Didn't they understand? It grew and grew the more she lay there, agony on top of agonies. It would consume her, leaving nothing behind.

She closed her eyes and centered on the pain. A fire pyramid, a tiny thing, dormant until now, was embedded in her flesh; it sought to burn her up from the inside out. Desperate, she focused and pit her mind against it, but it defied her. With a howl, she drove her thoughts into it and smothered it, cooler and cooler.

"Get it out," she said. She couldn't hold it for long. She pointed to her side, on top of the small scar. "Here."

New pain assaulted her, that of a knife against her skin. The burning became searing, and Averie shouted, "I've got it!" before hissing in pain herself. Glass shattered, and the pain changed, newer and duller than before. Cloth ripped, and Dawnmother tied a strip of it tightly around Starbride's middle.

"I'm going to help Katya," Averie said.

"Averie, wait!" Dawnmother hissed, but Averie had already departed.

Starbride pushed on Dawnmother's arms. "We have to help, too."

"We had to cut a small pyramid out of you, Star. You have a hole in your side."

Starbride shook her head, remembering the manor house and the rock she thought had cut her. She hadn't felt it since it wasn't active; that must have been why Crowe missed it, too. "I think he meant to kill me. Bind me tighter. We have to save the family, or we'll all die. Weren't you listening?"

Dawnmother sucked in a breath and helped Starbride to her feet. She felt the cloth bandage around her side, the cooling stickiness of her blood. A little light-headed, she grunted as the movement pulled at the wound. She clutched Dawnmother's arm in the dark and looked out over the room, trying to spot all the players in the light of the central pyramid and the shadows of the stalagmites.

Maia watched her Fiend father, who stood with Katya. "Oh no," Starbride whispered as she saw Katya's Aspect for the second time. "Oh please, no."

Brutal threw Brom to the side and charged Roland. Impossibly fast, Roland lifted an arm, caught Brutal's fist, and tossed him across the room to slam into stone. Brutal tried to rise, shaking his head.

Averie took the opportunity to go for Katya, but Katya was frozen in her Aspect, eyes locked with Roland. Her rapier had fallen into the dirt at her side. "No!" Dawnmother whispered. "The princess will kill her. She's a monster! They all are!"

Cassius sprinted from the doorway to intercept Averie, and Starbride's stomach went cold. Which would be better, caught by him or by the Fiend? Averie faced off with Cassius, his sword to her knife. She ran and led him on a chase through the stalagmites.

"Clever Averie," Starbride whispered. "What can we do?" Two men, one of whom she'd thought a friend, still guarded the entrance. She couldn't spot Pennynail and Crowe. The gray-skinned woman moved closer to the central pyramid, her back to the empty set of shackles. Starbride pulled on Dawnmother's arm. "If we get Brom into those shackles, maybe that will put Yanchasa back to sleep, and Roland will have missed his chance to do whatever it is he wants to do. He had to be waiting for this time for a reason."

"Will that free the rest of them?" Dawnmother helped Starbride shuffle along. If they were quiet, they could get to Brom and drag her with them. All eyes were on the drama between Katya and Roland.

"I don't know." The pain in her side spiked, and she stumbled. "I'm too slow, Dawn. You get Brom. I'll distract everyone else."

"I don't even know what's going on, Star, but my life for yours. I'll distract these…Fiends. You get Brom."

Starbride hissed through her teeth. "If you ever loved me, if Birdfaithful ever loved Horsestrong, *get Brom.*"

Dawnmother stared for a half a heartbeat before she hastened to do as she was told. Starbride limped toward Katya and Roland. Over Katya's shoulder, Roland's eyes settled on her.

"Katya!" Starbride screamed. Everyone turned toward her *except* Katya. Roland chuckled.

Something sparkled in the dirt near Katya's feet, winking in the dim light: Katya's pyramid necklace. Starbride took a step toward it just as someone hit her from the side and knocked her over. Curling around her wound, she stared up into Darren's smirking face. "Well, well," he said, "I suppose you're not off-limits now, eh?" He'd dropped the bow and now swung the tip of his sword up and down her body. "Tell me what you'll do for me to keep me from cutting you."

"I'd rather die a thousand deaths."

"I wonder if you could take a thousand cuts before you die. Shall we start counting?" He laid the cold steel point against her breastbone, dimpling the skin. "Ready?"

Another blade knocked his out of the way, and Lord Hugo stepped into view. Darren stumbled away, his brow thunderous. "You little shit! There's plenty of her to go around."

Lord Hugo grabbed Starbride's arm and hauled her to her feet, making her side ache. She pushed away from him.

Darren's eyes narrowed as Lord Hugo brought his rapier on guard. "What is this?"

"Run, Miss Starbride," Lord Hugo said. "The doorway is open."

"Fucking traitor!" Darren yelled. "You'd betray your own father?"

"He betrays himself. Under his sway, I believed him, but let loose from it, I find that I'm an honorable man."

Darren lunged, and the two fell to fighting, their swords ringing together. Starbride glanced at the doorway and then back at Katya. Roland stared at the two fighting men with his head cocked, as if he couldn't figure out what they were doing.

Brutal hit him from behind. He staggered, but Starbride knew he would dispatch Brutal soon enough. Now was the time to act. She stooped, grabbed the pyramid necklace, and told herself to ignore the pain in her side. She leapt, striving for speed instead of grace, and slammed into Katya, who didn't even rock under the force.

Dimly, she heard someone shrieking, "No!" Dawnmother slapped Brom repeatedly and dragged her toward the central pyramid. Katya turned and caught Starbride's arms in a grip like stone, her expression passive and calm.

Behind her, Roland smashed a fist into Brutal's face and dropped him to the ground. "Layra," he called, "stop those two at the pyramid." The gray-skinned woman turned, and Dawnmother took Brom with her behind a stalagmite as an arrow whistled past them. Pennynail launched from nearby cover and tackled Layra to the ground. Roland took a step that way when a blur as fast as lightning slammed into him and sent him and his attacker spinning across the room.

Katya's grip increased, her face still calm, but now a tiny smile hovered about her lips. Starbride pressed the pyramid necklace to the skin of Katya's throat. Katya gasped, her all-blue eyes flying open and her blood-colored lips going slack, showing her fangs. As her arms loosened, Starbride kissed her frosted lips and tied the chain around her neck. "If he can think while he's a Fiend, so can you. Come back." She made herself fall into the necklace, using its power, pushing it into Katya.

CHAPTER THIRTY-THREE: KATYA

Starbride was in her arms; that was the first thing Katya noticed. The second was that over Starbride's shoulder, by the capstone of the ancient pyramid, her father's shackles were empty.

Her mother and brother still stood there, locked in their Aspects and in communion with Yanchasa. The rest of the room was a scattered wilderness of shouts and fights, the ring of steel and the harsh cry of wounded people.

Strangely enough, she didn't care. It was so hard to care, even with some of her awareness returned to her. She knew she wore her Aspect plain upon her face, and it didn't faze her. She knew that Starbride was wounded and slumping in her arms. That mattered a little more, but no more than if Starbride had stubbed a toe. Averie ran at a glacial pace near the back of the cavern, pursued by Cassius. Brutal was down. Lord Hugo and Darren fought sword-to-sword, but their movements were sluggish and unnatural, distorted in time. The only things moving like normal were her uncle Roland, still in his Aspect, who wrestled with Da, also a Fiend. She wondered dimly who had let him loose.

Maia moved with aching slowness toward Brutal. Cassius came too near his prone form, and Maia threw a knife. Katya watched it spin slowly, as if through molasses. She could have crossed the room in three quick steps and plucked it from the air. Something important was going on, but none of it mattered. Nothing mattered. The entire world was a pit of meaninglessness occasionally lessened by the promise of bloodshed.

Katya stared into Starbride's pleading face. She touched Starbride's waist and felt the blood there. Roland had done this. He'd set the violence loose. At the moment, Katya felt more kinship with him than she ever could with the woman in her arms. Roland was her kin, her mind argued. Roland was her uncle. But Starbride was her consort. Neither tie mattered. The only thing that mattered was the pull she felt to Roland, to the rest of her family, to the Fiends. She was them, loved them, and wanted to kill them even more than these frail humans. It would be a blood-swollen challenge.

She lowered Starbride to the ground with aching slowness. To do anything else would be to ram her into the rock. Katya lifted her rapier and sheathed it. Then, with a step, she was beside Roland and Da where they rolled on the ground. She put a hand on each of them and tugged. They were as strong as she but the slight motion sent them apart.

Both were torn and leaking. She could smell their blood. Her father didn't recognize her, but he recognized the Fiend, and she knew he wanted to tear into her as much as she wanted to tear into him. They'd need the control of a pyramid or Fiend-merge to do anything other than fight one another. Roland was simply amused.

"You're ready to join me?" The words plumed from Roland's mouth in Fiend speech, a tongue she understood perfectly. Da stepped closer, rime forming on his clothes.

Katya considered. Roland promised bloodshed, and that could be amusing for a time. She could kill everyone in the room except her family, her blood kin, and then they could fall on each other. When she was done, she could take Starbride with her. But, her inner voice said, Starbride wouldn't have anything to do with her if she went on a killing spree. The soft hands would never touch her again.

That wouldn't matter. In her current form, she could make Starbride do anything she wished. Her inner voice rebelled, echoed by something deep inside her. Injuring Starbride was not permitted. Roland meant their death, all of them, even her family, even his blood. And he wouldn't save them for last. He'd kill them all as if they were wholly human.

Da leapt. Roland and Katya's arms shot out as one and knocked Da to the ground, though Katya did it to save him. She stared at her uncle and snarled. "I'm above you."

He looked at her, genuine surprise lighting his eyes. "Join me, and we'll have an entire kingdom to play with. We'll make it perfect."

"Play with someone else's. This is mine."

His handsome face frowned, its icy haughtiness calling to her own. "You forget who your elders are, niece."

"Yanchasa is my elder, same as yours." She hit him then, a quick punch that he barely scraped out of. She whipped her rapier from its sheath.

Roland tried to dance away. He brought up his arm to block and called for aid. Katya snorted. Any human moving against her might as well have been moving in thick soup. Roland's son and lover might have possessed the Aspect, but they'd never Waltzed. Katya felt their caged Fiends, pale shadows of what she had, and laughed at them.

Roland cried out as Katya stabbed him in the leg and brought him to his knees. He grabbed her ankles and yanked her feet out from under her. She twisted as she landed and pushed the pain aside. Roland tried to clamber on top of her, but she pushed off the floor with one shoulder and rammed the guard of her rapier against his face.

The guard dented and crumpled, breaking against Roland's Aspect. He snarled, and she knew she'd hurt him a little. She hit him again and again, and the twisted shards of metal dug tiny holes in his skin.

He grabbed her wrist and squeezed. She felt the bones begin to buckle; their grinding filled her head, and she knew she couldn't defeat him with pure force. She gathered her feet between them and shoved. He flew to his feet to stagger backward. She cast her rapier aside, ran for the pyramid, and threw her hands against it. She didn't need the shackles. With her mind awake to guide the Fiend inside her, she'd beat Roland using his own game.

Light blinded her, and her Fiend recognized the experience, remembered it in a way her human mind never could. Down through the capstone her mind traveled, into the ancient pyramid to where a great mind slumbered.

Katya thought that the earthquakes must have been Roland's doing, but not so. There had been too much time, too much diluting of Yanchasa's Aspect. Time had come back to the Fiend, and with it, an awakening mind. Roland had been right. They should have tried to siphon more off, to take some more of the Fiend into themselves, but that might have meant madness, the same as it meant for one of those who'd originally bound Yanchasa, Vestra's own husband.

Well, was that not duty? It would be a sacrifice that Vestra herself would have made, were she given another chance. Katya opened herself to Yanchasa's presence, giving in fully, the Fiend in her wanting the power and the human part fighting to care about the outcome.

Chapter Thirty-four: Starbride

The world went white. There was no other word for it. One moment, Starbride was in Katya's arms, the next she was lowered quickly to the floor. Then Katya moved to join the fight between Roland and King Einrich. Seconds passed between the three of them, and Starbride lost hope. Without King Einrich in his shackles, the plan to complete the Waltz using Brom couldn't work.

Katya and Roland became a blur together, and when a single blur streaked for the pyramid, Starbride's heart sank further When the streak stopped, and she saw it was Katya, Starbride rejoiced until the world went white.

Beside her in the cold white void, Roland said, "The little fool."

Katya had tried to help, and something had gone wrong. Starbride didn't know whether Katya was a fool for trying or if Roland thought Katya a fool for not helping him. She supposed it didn't matter if the world had become a void.

A ripple shook the room as Starbride's sight faded back to normal. Queen Catirin and Prince Reinholt lay on their backs at the pyramid's base, their Aspects gone, faces slack, though she noted with relief that they still breathed. In front of the pyramid, Katya turned.

The horns arcing over Katya's head had grown by a foot, joined by another pair that started at her temples and continued around the sides of her head. Her pupil-less eyes were enormous in a face that had stretched downward, as if someone had shoved a horseshoe where her chin would be. Her too-wide mouth was filled with sharp teeth, and her ears curved up to points high above hair the color of blood. Ice formed under her feet as she examined her hands; the long, birdlike fingers ended in claws. She grunted, and the back of her coat burst open as four feathered wings unfurled in a splash of blood, spattering the pyramid with drops that froze and rolled down in little red beads.

"So, little K," Roland said from Starbride's side. "With me to guide you, we will be unstoppable. You desire slaughter. I can feel it."

Katya stared at him, her head cocked as if he were an interesting new toy. Starbride's insides shriveled in fear, and she cursed Roland for drawing the monster's attention anywhere near her. She couldn't think of this thing as her lover. Ancient parts deep inside of her knew this creature was the embodiment of fear, and she could no more fight that fear than she could her own heartbeat.

Katya's too-large eyes roamed over Roland before she spat something in a language that grated on Starbride's ears and blasted her with wind so cold it made her ache.

"Even more beneath you?" Roland sneered. "We're kin in more ways than one, both blood, both Fiend. Why fight one another? We should be fighting them!" His finger stabbed at Starbride where she lay on the ground.

The creature said something else.

"Prove it," Roland answered. He stooped with a speed like the wind, picked Starbride up by the back of her gown, and hauled her to her feet. She cried out and tried to pull away; her wounded side cried with her. Roland grabbed her throat. She clutched at his wrist but knew she couldn't move him. He shook her lightly at the monster that used to be Katya. "Kill this one, and I'll believe you."

The Katya-Fiend stepped away from the pyramid, each of its steps making Starbride shiver. It stared into her face with no recognition, not even of one human to another. With one of its icy talons, it traced a line down her cheek, a cold that burned. Starbride gasped, but Roland's pressure around her throat wouldn't let her scream. Terror howled inside her, but she couldn't close her eyes.

Something pricked at her senses, and she turned her gaze to the Fiend's throat. The pyramid necklace still hung there, intact. But how could it be intact with the Aspect full upon Katya, with so much of Yanchasa's essence? Starbride fought to swallow some of her fear. If even a little of Katya remained, there was hope.

Starbride forced herself to look the Fiend in the eye, to fight against the cold. She willed herself to see Katya standing there, but inside, she screamed and screamed. She couldn't do it. How could she possibly? This monster was going to kill her and everyone else in the world! She bit her lip until blood trickled down her chin, a bit of warmth before it froze. She let the numbness seeping into her bones fill her emotions, let her stomach become a black pit.

"Kill her!" Roland said.

The remains of Katya's coat still held the butterfly pin. Katya—lover, friend—was somewhere inside, hiding just behind that pyramid necklace. Starbride spoke to her, not to the monstrous face in front of her. "I love you." She put a finger to the pyramid necklace and fell into it, speaking to the soul inside.

The Fiend drew back, surprise lighting its awful face. The *Fiend* was surprised, but Katya wouldn't be. Inside the necklace, Starbride felt her fight.

"Do it," Roland insisted, shaking Starbride again. The Katya-Fiend turned its murderous gaze on him.

Starbride nearly laughed. "I wouldn't do that."

"No one asked you, peasant." He made as if to fling her to the ground. Katya's hand appeared between Starbride and the floor, quicker even than Roland, and the clawed hands settled her more gently.

Roland backed away, his features twisted by disgust. "All that power and you're still just a human at heart, niece. All that mayhem in you and you waste it being tender. You've learned nothing. You're not capable, and you're not worthy to be my kin."

Katya was in front of him then, no blur, just a rush of cold as if she'd disappeared and reappeared. Roland even blinked before she bashed him, hitting him so hard that he flew against the far wall and left a trail of fast-freezing blood in his wake. He bounced off the stone and landed in a heap but rose again. Darren jogged to Roland's side and held his sword in front of both of them. All other activity in the room had stopped. It was quiet as Roland pressed his hand over the bloody gash in his clothes.

Roland drew himself up as if he might fight, but quicker than Starbride had seen, he grabbed Darren and raced for the doorway. Maia stepped into his path, bringing him up short. Starbride thought Maia wanted to stop him, but she cried, "Father, don't leave me!" and leapt for him, her arms out.

"No!" Starbride reached for them, but Roland gathered Maia in his other arm and dashed through the doorway. "Katya, stop them!"

Katya blinked and knelt. She didn't understand, was fixated on Starbride somehow. She lifted Starbride in ice-cold arms and cuddled her close. Starbride pushed back as the cold burned her, but Katya's arms were like steel. Starbride clutched the back of Katya's neck and fought not to squirm. Pennynail's face loomed over Katya's shoulder, and he pressed something into Starbride's palm.

Starbride gripped the smooth sides of a pyramid as Katya's wings began to flap. The monster wanted to take her somewhere, and Darkstrong knew what would happen when they arrived. They lifted from the ground, and Starbride fell into the pyramid, knowing suddenly what it was for. Crowe had once pressed it to Katya's heart to make the Fiend retreat, but that wouldn't be enough this time. It needed blood. "I'm sorry." She ran her free hand down the icy cheek.

She rammed the pyramid into Katya's back and pushed all her spirit into it. She focused, and saw what the pyramid was meant to do as if it were a gigantic switch. She pulled, but it fought her. The Fiend wanted to stay. Starbride ground her teeth and used her desperation as leverage. She would get Katya back, or they'd both die in the effort.

The switch flipped. The Katya-Fiend screamed, and everything went white again as Starbride crashed to the ground.

This time, as everything faded to normal, Starbride heard shouting. Someone was calling her name. "Here," Starbride said, and Dawnmother struggled through a gray haze to her side. The royal family was still splayed about the room. King Einrich had returned to normal. Brutal, Brom, Cassius, and Layra were unmoving heaps. Averie held her bloody arm, and Pennynail carried a bleeding Crowe over to Katya's sprawled body.

Starbride put a hand over her own bloody side and struggled to turn. Dawnmother helped her, and they crouched close to Katya.

Crowe glanced at them with tears in his eyes and agony on his face. Pennynail pressed both hands to Crowe's free-bleeding stomach. "You had to stop her," Crowe said. "If she'd gotten out of the cavern, who knows how we would have gotten her back?"

Starbride shook her head. She couldn't think about that now. "Will she be all right?"

Dawnmother rolled Katya over once they'd removed the pyramid and covered her wound. Her face had returned to normal, but she slept, haggard lines on her face and silver hairs at her temples. Lines of blood left streaks down her forehead and cheeks.

"I don't know," he whispered.

Starbride clutched the pyramid she'd used. "Is Yanchasa's essence in here?"

He shook his head, his face pained, bewildered, and sad, too many hurts piled on top of one another. "I don't know." He took the pyramid. "Pennynail, put this under Katya's coat. It should keep the Fiend at bay for a time. She can't carry that much of the Aspect in her forever, though. We have to find a way to bleed it out."

"We need to get everyone some help," Dawnmother said, always the practical one. She nodded at Crowe's stomach. "You most of all."

"I'm gut-shot. I don't have long, but I need to instruct Starbride before I die." He grabbed one of Starbride's hands with his blood-slicked ones. "You have to put what she took from Yanchasa back into the capstone."

Starbride blinked. He spoke of death and monumental tasks so casually. "Surely there must be something we can do for you?"

"Nothing."

Dawnmother clucked her tongue. "Don't give up so easily."

"Listen to sense—"

"No." Dawnmother put her fists on her hips, a posture even Starbride didn't argue with. "People like us have a duty to each other much like the duty to those we serve." Crowe's jaw dropped. Dawnmother nodded as if that meant an end to the discussion. "Everyone here is wearing plenty of clothing. Let's start making bandages."

Starbride nodded, and Dawnmother cut her skirt off just above her knees, using the fabric and petticoat to bandage Crowe even as he protested.

"Help me hold him down?" she asked Pennynail. He nodded.

"I have tasks I need to perform!" Crowe shouted.

"Do them as we work," Dawnmother said. "You'll live. You're louder than any dying man has a right to be."

Crowe sputtered until he sighed, his face resigned. "The central capstone is Fiend magic, and it holds Yanchasa in his prison. You'll need to create a conduit between it and the pyramid that we used to suppress the extra Fiendish essence Katya absorbed. Once we've done that, we'll put that extra essence back where it belongs."

"Then she'll be herself again?"

"If we get it in time."

Starbride bent over Katya, tucked the necklace more firmly around her neck, and kissed her, a gentle brush of the lips. With a hand over her own seeping bandage, she helped put everyone to rights.

CHAPTER THIRTY-FIVE: KATYA

Katya was falling. Or was she floating? Difficult to tell; life had become a great haze. Pain arced through her body, making her nerves sing. A lovely face hovered in front of her. "I'm sorry! I'm sorry!" it wailed. That didn't matter. Nothing mattered. She would kill every thrice-bedamned one of them.

Silence. Pain was gone. Rage, gone. A silver sea spread out before her, through her. "Focus," someone said. Someone she knew well? Brutal? No. "Focus." Crowe, it had to be Crowe.

"I'm trying," another answered, soft and feminine. Terrified. "I don't want to hurt her again."

Crowe's voice, calm and steady. "If you can't do this…"

"I'll do it. I love her. I'll do it right." Starbride's will. Starbride's determination. Ah, love. Katya loved her, too, but she couldn't speak, couldn't do anything with the silver sea covering her. When it drained away, the rage would come again. They'd drown in seas of blood. She'd smile as she watched. Maybe she'd taste them. She'd—

White light and then nothing. Nothing and then a sky full of stars. Something was taken from her, and she couldn't even make a grab for it. She was hypnotized by the stars. She had such a little bit left.

"Watch what you're doing," Crowe said.

"I don't know how to stop!"

"Spirits above." Had he been whispering the entire time? Had his voice always been so small? "What have you done?"

"I fixed her. Did I fix her?"

Soft hands held Katya's face. Was she broken? Something was missing. Where had the stars gone?

Katya awoke with the certainty that there was a rock in her back. Without opening her eyes, she maneuvered a hand under herself until she felt the wad of bandages just smaller than a croquet ball.

A flood of memories rolled over her. Her uncle Roland, her transformation, which usually took all memory with it, but this time her awareness had returned, and she remembered Starbride's stricken face and her family's plight. She opened her eyes.

Cots and bandages and bowls of water dotted the room; she wasn't alone in the makeshift infirmary in her apartment. Crowe lay on a cot beside her bed, his bare chest swathed in bandages. Brutal sat up in a cot against the wall, one side of his face purple, with a bandage around his head. Averie sat on a settee next to him, a bandage around her arm and a bruise on one cheek. When Brutal turned in Katya's direction, he nodded slowly.

"Good to see you awake," he said.

Katya eased to a sitting position. "I touched the pyramid. I communed with Yanchasa, but then…" She'd done something, but what? She only hoped she hadn't turned on her friends and forced them to stab her in the back. "What are you all doing in here?"

"We thought it best to keep all the wounded together." Brutal eyed her, a little warily to her eyes. "You yourself again? Sure?"

"Why wouldn't I be?"

"It's fine," Averie said. "Starbride took the Aspect out. She's sure she got it all."

Katya touched her chest but felt no necklace beneath her shirt. There wasn't a pyramid in sight. "You mean the extra essence? That I siphoned off Yanchasa?"

"No," Brutal said. "She didn't know when to stop. She says she got it *all*. She put it back in the capstone."

Tears hovered in Averie's eyes. "You almost died so many times. We…I was so worried."

Katya stared at her. No Aspect. No Fiend. That which her parents had passed to her, that which all Umbriels possessed, gone. What did that make her?

The door cracked open, and Starbride stepped inside. Dawnmother held her elbow. "Slowly, Star. You'll open your stitches."

Katya remembered that, a hidden pyramid under Starbride's skin. Starbride sat down carefully on the bed. "How are you feeling?"

"Did I hurt you?"

"You saved us. Better still, no more Fiend! I don't know how I did it. Crowe's not sure, either, but just think, you don't have to worry about it ever again."

"Yes." No more Fiend, maybe no more Umbriel. How could she

lead the Order of Vestra if she didn't have what the original leader of the Order had possessed?

The rest of Katya's family came through the door, minus Brom. Katya winced. She remembered that part, too. Ma hugged her gently, kissing her on the temple. Da squeezed her hand. "Vestra herself would be proud."

Katya shook her head. She wasn't so sure. Reinholt stared at the wall and said nothing. "How's everyone else?"

"We've done what we can for Crowe." Brutal bent to inspect Crowe's bandages. "But he's going to need the healer again. I'm good for a quick patch-up, but this needs more herbs and such, and he's had a busy few days."

"I'm perfectly fine," Crowe whispered, his eyes closed.

Dawnmother sighed, and she wasn't the only one, but whether they were exasperated by Crowe's stubbornness or his deteriorating condition, Katya didn't know.

"Rein." Katya didn't know what to say but needed to say something. "I'm…"

He glanced at her, his face white and pinched. "She's in the dungeon. She knew what would be asked of her when we got married. Maybe I should have married her a year earlier than I did. She could have Waltzed right away then, instead of four years later."

Da patted Reinholt's shoulder. He looked older, the world heavier on his back. He stooped and touched Crowe with more gentleness than many expected from him. "You'll be up and around in no time, old bird."

"Don't lie to me," Crowe said, his eyes still shut.

"You will live," Brutal said, "but you'll never regain your strength entirely."

Crowe opened his eyes. "That's closer to the truth."

"It *is* the truth," Dawnmother said, "but only if you want it to be. Darkstrong sought death, and so he found it. You must *want* to live. For now, you need rest."

"We all do," Averie echoed.

Katya shook her head. "My back aches, but I don't need to sleep."

"I can sleep on my own," Crowe said. "I don't need more of that healer's foul-smelling draughts."

"You rival Starbride's parents in difficulty," Dawnmother said.

"Who made you the healer, anyway?" Crowe glared at her with one eye.

"The same person who gave me so much sense." She glared back at him. Crowe had met his match when it came to being pushy. And unlike everyone else, Dawnmother seemed to have no interest in tiptoeing around Crowe's feelings.

Ma leaned over to pat Crowe's hand. "The royal physician has agreed with her on everything so far." Dawnmother nodded and crossed her arms.

Crowe shut his other eye and mumbled something unintelligible. Dawnmother shrugged. "Mulestubborn will have his way."

Crowe opened both eyes to glare at her that time.

"How's your wound?" Katya said to Starbride.

"Hurting but healing. Luckily, the pyramid was small and not that deep."

"I'm sorry all of this happened to you."

"It was worth it."

Katya smiled, and she tried to mean it, tried to lose herself in love, but she kept searching for something inside herself, something she'd never been without, something she'd never find again. In the sudden silence, she frowned as she noticed the gaps in the room. "Where's Maia? And where's Pennynail?" They threw nervous glances like bolts. "Where are they?"

Reinholt answered first, maybe not as aware of others' pain while lost in his own. "Maia went with Roland. She chose him over us, just like...her."

"Oh, my poor cousin. What are we doing to look? Where—?"

"She's not in the city," Brutal said. "That's where Pennynail is. He's looked everywhere. It's like they vanished."

"He left us a parting gift, though," Reinholt said, and the smile on his face was anything but friendly.

Starbride gave him a nervous, agitated glance before she looked back to Katya's face. "He saved me, Katya. He's done everything he could to help."

"You don't need to appeal to her," Da said. "We're not holding the boy at fault."

"What in the world are you talking about?" Katya glanced from one of them to the other.

"Lord H...just Hugo," Starbride said. "Free of his father's influence, he's decided he wants nothing to do with Roland's schemes."

"Because he's half in love with you." Reinholt sneered. Starbride's cheeks turned red.

Ma gave him a sharp glance. "That's enough, Reinholt." He turned away and walked across the room.

Katya touched Starbride's cheek. "He's still here?"

"Under guard for his own safety," Da said. "Until we're sure, Katya, but Starbride has used a pyramid on him under Crowe's instruction. They found nothing."

"He's a good boy," Crowe said.

Brutal nodded. "He almost broke Roland's control when he saw his own sister. He said he'd had his memory hidden and a new one put in. Left to his own devices, out of his father's control, he made his own decisions. And I thought he had a thing for Maia, but it was half-remembered recognition."

"Family spots family," Dawnmother said.

Across the room, Reinholt snorted. Ma glanced over her shoulder at him. "We've sent for the grandchildren," she said, "to make sure…"

"To make sure they're out of their mother's clutches or those of her sycophants," Reinholt said, not turning.

Katya nodded, guessing the rule about the entire family being in the same place at the same time had to be broken occasionally. Reinholt's little children had hidden Fiends, more Umbriel than her. Clenching her fist, Katya told herself to stop being such a child. They were all alive. Gone as she was, Maia was alive, too, and they'd find her. "Is Hugo the only one we caught?"

Starbride's brows turned down at that, but Katya couldn't take anything for granted at the moment.

"Cassius is dead. And we, um, we found Layra," Brutal said.

"The gray-skinned woman."

"Hid her pregnancy from everyone, from what Hugo told us," Da said. "When she was away on Order business, young Hugo stayed with her relatives in the country."

Crowe snorted. "The year Hugo was born, she told me she had a sick relative to take care of, and I believed her. I should have known better. Now I know why she was gone for so long initially and why she had to make so many 'family visits in the countryside.' I assumed she and Roland were just sneaking away to tryst."

"She's dead?" Katya asked, trying to sort out the conversation.

"She's been dead a long time," Crowe said. "Roland used a pyramid on her somehow, to…preserve her? Control her? I've no idea how he did it. He's gone beyond anyone I've ever heard of. He's a mad genius." He shook his head slowly. "If I had to wager a guess, I'd say she was an experiment. We'll need to keep our eyes open."

"A walking corpse?" Katya asked. "Well, I imagine that didn't make Hugo too charitable toward his father."

"It's a damn lot to sort out, my girl," Da said.

"No time like the present." Katya swung her legs over the side of the bed. A jumble of voices assailed her as everyone protested at once. "I'm tired of lying here. I'm going to see Brom."

"Why?" Reinholt asked.

Katya didn't back down from his gaze. "I need to see how far she was involved with Roland, Rein."

"I'll come with you," Starbride said.

"You'll need someone with a Fiend or that I've specifically tuned the pyramids to recognize," Crowe said.

Hurt and loss whispered through Katya's mind. Ma said, "I'll come, too."

"No, I'll go," Reinholt said.

Katya shook her head. He turned away, his face thunderous. Da put a gentle hand on his shoulder and murmured something in his ear. Ma and Starbride helped Katya dress before they descended into the palace depths once more.

In the dungeon, Katya paused in front of the door to the cells. "I want to see her alone."

Starbride squeezed Katya's hand. "I'll wait here for you."

Katya felt her sense of absence lighten slightly. Ma pressed her hand to the door pyramid, and Katya let the sobs that echoed down the hallway guide her. When Ma opened the door to the first cell on the right, Brom leapt up, manacle chains jangling. Ma retreated without a word, and Katya stepped inside with a single lamp.

"Katya! Let me out of here. I don't belong here!"

Katya swallowed, surprised at the sorrow that came from seeing her buoyant sister-in-law in chains. "You betrayed us."

"I had to save my children!"

"You knew!" Her anger pushed Brom back a step. "You knew about the Aspect when you married Reinholt."

Katya expected Brom to shrink, but Brom surged forward to the end of her chains. "I didn't know how bad it was! I never saw the Fiend, not until Roland showed me!" Spittle flew from her lips, and she backed up until she could wipe her tear-stained face. "He told me how the Fiend thinks, how it becomes a part of you! My children will not be monsters."

"You refused because you're a coward." Katya thought for a moment. "No, Roland was clever when he was alive, but as a Fiend, he's grown devious. He wouldn't let you live just for refusing to Waltz. What did you do for him?"

Brom shook her head.

Katya's mind raced. "Hugo couldn't come into the royal quarters, couldn't take the secret passages from there to the dungeons...but you could."

"I didn't want anyone to get hurt."

Katya stepped forward. "You set Darren and Cassius free. Your dormant Fiendish essence let you open the doors. Did you escort them down there before we arrived? Did you sneak Roland into the palace?"

Brom snarled, the white of her teeth shining against her reddened lips. "I did it for them."

"What did he promise you? What did he give you that you'd risk the lives of everyone in Farraday?"

"One monster or another, what's the difference?"

Katya clenched her fist, but she kept her control. She'd been keeping it too long to lose it now. Besides, there were other ways to hurt a person. "Your children are on their way here now."

What little color remained in Brom's face drained away. "No."

"We need four to Waltz. Unless you want to take their place?"

"What are you talking about? You'd make my children Waltz so you don't have to? Monster! Evil, murdering monster!" She jumped forward again, and the chains took her feet from under her, sending her to the ground where she curled around herself and sobbed. "Leave them alone. They won't be like him. You can't, you can't!"

Katya didn't bother to explain. She had what she needed, anyway. Brom was not opportunistic. She'd colluded with Roland, had met him before she'd come to Marienne. Katya turned and closed the door as Brom cried out her name. Daughter of a noble or not, they'd use a pyramid on her now. Maybe Roland was right about a few things. Maybe Crowe should make her loyal against her will; it was what she deserved.

Katya shook the thought away. She couldn't become like him in order to fight him.

Starbride alone greeted her at the entrance.

"Where's Ma?"

"A discreet withdrawal, I think."

Katya took Starbride's hands, gathering comfort. The stitches in her back pulled and stung, echoing the pain in her chest, the deep ache of loss. "I'm glad you stayed."

Starbride kissed her softly for half a minute. "I'm here, and I'm not leaving you."

Looking into her eyes, Katya thought for the first time that she had all the strength she needed, Fiend or not. "I love you, Star. Never forget that."

"I won't. Even with all the secrets and plots floating around, I'll believe it. And I love you, too."

Katya kissed her hand and tucked it into the crook of her elbow as they left the dark place behind.

About the Author

Barbara Ann Wright writes fantasy and science fiction novels and short stories when not adding to her enormous book collection or ranting on her blog. Her short fiction has appeared twice in *Crossed Genres* magazine and once made *Tangent Online*'s recommended reading list. She is a member of Broad Universe and the Outer Alliance and helped create Writer's Ink in Houston.

She is married, has an army of pets, and lives in Texas. Her writing career can be boiled down to two points: when her mother bought her a typewriter in the sixth grade and when she took second place in the Isaac Asimov Award for Undergraduate Excellence in Science Fiction and Fantasy Writing in 2004. One gave her the means to write and the other gave her the confidence to keep going. Believing in oneself, in her opinion, is the most important thing a person can do.

Books Available From Bold Strokes Books

Month of Sundays by Yolanda Wallace. Love doesn't always happen overnight; sometimes it takes a month of Sundays. (978-1-60282-739-4)

Jacob's War by C.P. Rowlands. ATF Special Agent Allison Jacob's task force is in the middle of an all-out war, from the streets to the boardrooms of America. Small business owner Katie Blackburn is the latest victim who accidentally breaks it wide open, but she may break AJ's heart at the same time. (978-1-60282-740-0)

The Pyramid Waltz by Barbara Ann Wright. Princess Katya Nar Umbriel wants a perfect romance, but her Fiendish nature and duties to the crown mean she can never tell the truth—until she meets Starbride, a woman who gets to the heart of every secret, even if it will be the death of her. (978-1-60282-741-7)

The Secret of Othello by Sam Cameron. Florida teen detectives Steven and Denny risk their lives to search for a sunken NASA satellite—but under the waves, no one can hear you scream… (978-1-60282-742-4)

Andy Squared by Jennifer Lavoie. Andrew never thought anyone could come between him and his twin sister, Andrea…until Ryder rode into town. (978-1-60282-743-1)

Finding Bluefield by Elan Barnehama. Set in the backdrop of Virginia and New York and spanning the years 1960–1982, *Finding Bluefield* chronicles the lives of Nicky Stewart, Barbara Philips, and their son, Paul, as they struggle to define themselves as a family. (978-1-60282-744-8)

The Jettsetters by David-Matthew Barnes. As rock band the Jetsetters skyrocket from obscurity to superstardom, Justin Holt, a lonely barista, and Diego Delgado, the band's guitarist, fight with everything they have to stay together, despite the chaos and fame. (978-1-60282-745-5)

Strange Bedfellows by Rob Byrnes. Partners in life and crime, Grant Lambert and Chase LaMarca are hired to make a politician's compromising photo disappear, but what should be an easy job quickly spins out of control. (978-1-60282-746-2)

Dreaming of Her by Maggie Morton. Isa has begun to dream of the most amazing woman—a woman named Lilith with a gorgeous face, an amazing body, and the ability to turn Isa on like no other. But Lilith is just a dream...isn't she? (978-1-60282-847-6)

Speed Demons by Gun Brooke. When NASCAR star Evangeline Marshall returns to the race track after a close brush with death, will famous photographer Blythe Pierce document her triumph and reciprocate her love—or will they succumb to their respective demons and fail? (978-1-60282-678-6)

Summoning Shadows: A Rosso Lussuria Vampire Novel by Winter Pennington. The Rosso Lussuria vampires face enemies both old and new, and to prevail they must call on even more strange alliances, unite as a clan, and draw on every weapon within their reach—but with a clan of vampires, that's easier said than done. (978-1-60282-679-3)

Sometime Yesterday by Yvonne Heidt. When Natalie Chambers learns her Victorian house is haunted by a pair of lovers and a Dark Man, can she and her lover Van Easton solve the mystery that will set the ghosts free and banish the evil presence in the house? Or will they have to run to survive as well? (978-1-60282-680-9)

Into the Flames by Mel Bossa. In order to save one of his patients, psychiatrist Jamie Scarborough will have to confront his own monsters—including those he unknowingly helped create. (978-1-60282-681-6)

Coming Attractions: Author's Edition by Bobbi Marolt. For Helen Townsend, chasing turns to caring, and caring turns to loving, but will love take five steps back and turn to leaving? (978-1-60282-732-5)

OMGqueer, edited by Radclyffe and Katherine E. Lynch. Through stories imagined and told by youth across America, this anthology provides a snapshot of queerness at the dawn of the new millennium. (978-1-60282-682-3)

Oath of Honor by Radclyffe. A First Responders novel. First do no harm...First Physician of the United States Wes Masters discovers that being the president's doctor demands more than brains and personal sacrifice—especially when politics is the order of the day. (978-1-60282-671-7)

A Question of Ghosts by Cate Culpepper. Becca Healy hopes Dr. Joanne Call can help her learn if her mother really committed suicide—but she's not sure she can handle her mother's ghost, a decades-old mystery, and lusting after the difficult Dr. Call without some serious chocolate consumption. (978-1-60282-672-4)

The Night Off by Meghan O'Brien. When Emily Parker pays for a taboo role-playing fantasy encounter from the Xtreme Scenarios escort agency, she expects to surrender control—but never imagines losing her heart to dangerous butch Nat Swayne. (978-1-60282-673-1)

Sara by Greg Herren. A mysterious and beautiful new student at Southern Heights High School stirs things up when students start dying. (978-1-60282-674-8)

Fontana by Joshua Martino. Fame, obsession, and vengeance collide in a novel that asks: What if America's greatest hero was gay? (978-1-60282-675-5)

Lemon Reef by Robin Silverman. What would you risk for the memory of your first love? When Jenna Ross learns her high school love Del Soto died on Lemon Reef, she refuses to accept the medical examiner's report of a death from natural causes and risks everything to find the truth. (978-1-60282-676-2)

The Dirty Diner: Gay Erotica on the Menu, edited by Jerry L. Wheeler. Gay erotica set in restaurants, featuring food, sex, and men—could you really ask for anything more? (978-1-60282-677-9)

Sweat: Gay Jock Erotica by Todd Gregory. Sizzling tales of smoking-hot sex with the athletic studs everyone fantasizes about. (978-1-60282-669-4)

The Marrying Kind by Ken O'Neill. Just when successful wedding planner Adam More decides to protest inequality by quitting the business and boycotting marriage entirely, his only sibling announces her engagement. (978-1-60282-670-0)

Missing by P.J. Trebelhorn. FBI agent Olivia Andrews knows exactly what she wants out of life, but then she's forced to rethink everything when she meets fellow agent Sophie Kane while investigating a child abduction. (978-1-60282-668-7)